Desert Queen

By the same author

ROYAL SLAVE
SLAVE LADY
SCARLET WOMAN
SALAMANDER
VENUS RISING
LOVE SONG (as Julia Watson)
FALLEN WOMAN
FIREBIRD
THE PRINCESS AND THE PAGAN
THE JEWELLED SERPENT
TABOO
FLAME OF THE EAST
DAUGHTER OF THE GODS
PASODOBLE
A KISS FROM APHRODITE
CASTLE OF THE ENCHANTRESS

DESERT QUEEN

Julia Fitzgerald

C

CENTURY

LONDON MELBOURNE AUCKLAND JOHANNESBURG

M 63018
F

Copyright © Julia Fitzgerald 1986

First published in Great Britain in 1986 by
Century Hutchinson Ltd,
Brookmount House, 62–65 Chandos Place,
London WC2N 4NW

Century Hutchinson Publishing Group (Australia) Pty Ltd,
16–22 Church Street, Hawthorn, Melbourne, Victoria 3122

Century Hutchinson Group (NZ) Ltd,
32–34 View Road, PO Box 40–086, Glenfield, Auckland 10

Century Hutchinson Group (SA) Pty Ltd,
PO Box 337, Bergvlei 2012, South Africa

British Library Cataloguing in Publication Data

Fitzgerald, Julia
    Desert queen.
    Rn: Julia Watson   I. Title
    823'.914[F]   PR6073.A865

    ISBN 0–7126–9584–2

Typeset and printed in Great Britain by
WBC Print Ltd, Bristol

They that love beyond the world cannot be separated by it.

William Penn

Contents

PART ONE

Mishaal's Daughter

The inhabitants of the desert are sounder in their minds and bodies than the sedentary people who enjoy a softer life. Their skins are clearer, their bodies purer, their figures more harmonious and beautiful, their characters more moderate and their minds sharper in understanding and readier to acquire new knowledge than those of sedentary people. Compare the gazelle, the ostrich and the antelope with their counterparts who dwell in settled countryside. The former have more shining furs, more harmonious limbs and sharper senses.

Ibn Khaldun

Perhaps you dislike a thing and it is good for you, or perhaps you love a thing and it is bad for you. God knows, but you know not.

Qu'ran, II:26

Chapter One

It was unnerving to be colour blind when she had relished colour all her life. In her misery, the vivid flowing robes of her people seemed pallid and dull, their sun-bronzed faces leeched of blood and life, while Prophet, her father's horse, the fourth of that name, was a wan silver shadow against the once terracotta sand.

The desert looked grey to her, a parched, pewter haze, exactly like her heart, all emotion and passion wrenched from her by grief. At seventeen, she felt a hundred years old.

Husain and Mishaal, Amir and Amira of the Land of Mirages for thirty years, were both dead and now she, Zahra, must rule in their place. Oh, but she could not do it alone! She could not. Who was there to help her now? Old Nur had died the previous year, ancient beyond belief, crying out that she did not want to leave her adored master, the Amir, but Allah had taken her all the same. Nur had known it all, every detail of the old legend and her parents' part in it, and how Zahra's mother, Mishaal, had saved the Land of Mirages from drought and starvation.

She still could not believe that they were dead; her mother had always said that she could not live without Husain, but how could Zahra have known that there would be such a literal meaning to that statement?

3

Her homeland was lush and verdant, blossoming with fruit and flowers, abundant with dates, figs and nuts, olives and citrus fruits, wheat and maize. There were camels in plenty and purebred horses, some the progeny of the first Prophet himself who had borne Mishaal to her marriage celebrations.

Her land, Zahra's land, was fertile and beautiful as the fairest Paradise. For thirty years there had been water in plenty; the wells were filled with it, fresh and cool; the rains came exactly on time, laving the parched desert so that hunched little trees and bushes could unfurl, stretching out their withered branches to the torrent and gorging themselves in greedy delight. Then from the bitter earth would spring a multitude of glorious blooms, amazingly coloured in scarlet and crimson, sapphire, cerulean blue and sharp, rich ochre. Wherever the touch of Allah's fingers was felt, there would be an extravagance of flowers.

Zahra loved every feature of her land: the undulating sand dunes, ochre-gilded by centuries of fiery sun; the oases with their vital pools of water, havens for the travellers who sheltered beneath their slanting palms. She especially loved the wildlife – the brindled *fáhd* or wildcat, after whom her father had affectionately nicknamed her mother; the *er-rakham*, a white eagle; the *sweydia*, a small pied bird that flitted amongst the rocks; the *thob*, a desert lizard. Now they were all the joy in life remaining to her.

But she must not give way to fresh tears, for their time was past. How she had wept and mourned her parents, seeing always in her mind's eye her beautiful, green-eyed mother dancing in her famous peacock robe, her body still as lithe and graceful as a young girl's; or her father astride his horse, ebony eyes crinkling at the corners as he laughed. How could so much love and life and laughter be torn away almost overnight?

In a musk-scented casket in her tent lay Mishaal's

peacock robe. Zahra could not bear to look at it now but one day she knew that she would, that she would lift it out with her own hands, dress in it, and dance as her mother had done over so many joyous years. But the realisation seemed almost a betrayal, leaving a chill in its wake.

When Husain had fallen in love with her, Mishaal had been a destitute, homeless dancer, possessing nothing but the famous dancing costume in which she looked like one of the immortals, glorious, ethereal. Whenever Zahra had seen her mother in the peacock robe, she had been moved almost to tears by the beauty and sweetness of the sight. There was – had been – no one on earth as lovely and as graceful as the Amira Mishaal. Once there had been talk of her mother taking the marriage name of Nur Husain, or Light of Husain, but the people had requested that she keep the name of Mishaal, the name foretold in the old legend which had promised that she would be the torch who would light the way for the people of the Land of Mirages.

Zahra had loved her mother and father devotedly. How could she not have done? They were kind and selfless and tender to her, and she had flourished in their loving care, but it was difficult to be the only child of two who were a legend in their own lifetime, two so handsome and confident, relaxed and charming, where their daughter was shy and insecure. As a child she had doubted that she would ever share their self-assurance, their bright, outgoing nature, and she doubted it now, when they were dead and she was Queen in their place.

Although Beduin women rarely wore the veil, she had worn it since the burial. It suited her mood of withdrawal; behind it she could bite her lip or let her mouth tremble, weep or stifle her sobs, and no one would be any the wiser. It would not do for the new Amira to show that she was still heartbroken, that she had forgotten how to laugh and smile, how to take pleasure in life. The

5

official mourning period was coming to an end and there would be no further excuse for her to hide herself in her tent, begging an indisposition. Soon she must begin to live again, receiving the visitors who were eager to see her, and preparing herself for marriage.

There were two possible husbands of her acquaintance and she knew that she must make her choice between them soon. The Land of Mirages had been peaceful and verdant for thirty years because her father and mother had ruled not only wisely but with strength and authority. Now it was up to her to do the same, and it was unthinkable that she should do it alone. Her father had wanted her to choose her husband when she was fourteen, considering that even a little old compared to some Beduin brides, but Zahra had begged for more time. She had not wanted to end the idyll, the golden days of childhood. She had wanted to keep maturity and all its pressures at bay for as long as possible, knowing that when she married, there would be a son or a daughter arriving by the year and she would no longer be her father's darling, her mother's pet. It was not vanity which made her dread seeing her own children taking a place in her parents' affections, but fear of the future, of the unknown years ahead and what they might bring.

To love meant to be vulnerable, and Zahra was all too vulnerable already.

For the sake of her people, whom she cherished, she must decide which man would rule beside her. He must of course be approved by them, for their will was sovereign, and she must feel liking and respect for him. Already schooled in the paths of duty, she knew that the people's choice was more important than her own. If her husband offended them, there would be endless problems; if he offended her, she must learn to live with it.

Two of her keenest suitors had been elderly – perhaps it was their increasing years that had made them pursue

Zahra so fervently – but she could not take the risk of being widowed within months of marriage. An early widowhood for their Queen would unsettle her people, and she had no male relative to whom she could then turn for protection, according to the laws of the Prophet. She must marry a man who was young and strong, a man with wisdom and compassion, who was liked by her people and whom one day she could come to love. Above all, her husband must give her healthy sons and help her to raise them to perfect manhood.

The Amir Mahmed ibn Beydoun was the man who exactly fitted her requirements. The son of one of her father's oldest friends, he had often visited their camp and been made welcome there. He had a winning manner and the people liked him. There were no insurmountable difficulties to their eventual union that she could see. Mahmed's first wife had died in childbirth and he had not remarried. Like most Beduin, he did not have a harem of concubines. He had loved the wife who had borne him four daughters, and had taken no other woman before or since her death.

Mahmed was tall and broad-shouldered, lean and narrow-hipped. He was skilled at hunting and riding. Once Zahra had playfully raced him on horseback, watched with delight by her parents, and he had generously let her win before them. Afterwards she had dismounted, laughing, and he had taken her hand and lightly brushed her fingertips with his lips, his dark eyes burning with unfulfilled desires. At thirteen, she had been too young to understand, but now she knew what had been in his gaze. Mahmed had confirmed it when he sent his messenger to her within hours of her father's death.

'El Saiyid the Amir Mahmed ibn Beydoun desireth that Her Highness the Amira Zahra become his bride. El Saiyid vows that he will treat Her Highness with the respect and honour due her as daughter and heir of the

7

great Saiyid Husain ibn Rashid, and that he will guard and protect her father's lands against those who would advance unlawfully upon them.'

Zahra recalled the messenger's face more clearly than his words, for she had been so bowed down with grief that she had heard very little that was said to her during her first weeks of bereavement.

The man had been nearing sixty years of age, his face crinkled like the sun-bleached leaf of the *sumr* tree, and on the side of his long, curving nose was a mole the colour and size of a bluish-black berry. Scrutinising him further, repelled by him yet relieved to discover that something could take her mind off her inner agony, she had seen another berry-like mole protruding from the collar of his robe, and yet another behind his ear when he turned to leave her.

Later, she had wondered why Mahmed should have sent a messenger who was so physically repugnant – he should have realised a young girl would be repelled by such hideousness – but at the time she had thought little of it, unwilling to take any decisions, think any thoughts that would necessitate action on her part. She felt numbed and constricted by her loss, blind to her future, deaf to her fate.

Mahmed's lands bordered those of the Land of Mirages. Husain had been his overlord, as he was of all the Beduin of this country, and during his lifetime Mahmed had paid due reverence to him as was the custom. There had been no man before like Husain ibn Rashid nor would there ever be again, Zahra knew with a simple conviction. Mahmed's land was nowhere near as fertile and lush as the Land of Mirages – but then, none was. She could not expect her husband to bring her the manifold benefits which she, as Husain's heir, would bring him. That was understood.

Allah, the one true God, had blessed the Land of Mirages Himself, endowing it with the promise of

8

fruitfulness and wealth at the coming of Mishal, Zahra's mother. In Islam the male line was paramount and all blessings came via it, but here in the Land of Mirages, Allah had decreed that a woman would work the miracle that would change the country from a parched, waterless waste to the verdant Eden it had become under Mishaal and Husain. No other amirate was so blessed, nor so beloved of Allah.

Rising from her prayers, Zahra sat cross-legged on the scarlet and blue embroidered cushions that covered her couch. Her appetite was beginning to return, but it was subject to every whim and fancy that attacked her. The slightest thing could make the idea of food nauseating, and she would sip goat's milk only at the insistence of Freyha, her devoted attendant. Freyha, whose name meant 'The Joybringer', was the youngest of Nur's daughters and had been trained by her mother in the arts of loyalty, duty, and tender subservience. Freyha was Zahra's favourite servant, despite their age difference.

'Lady, you will eat now.' Freyha spoke firmly, quelling argument in advance. It was her duty to protect the health of this tender young girl, and she would do it, come what may. Nothing would distract or deter her from her vow that the Amira Zahra would live to the age when her own mother Nur had been taken, and that was eighty-six and eight moons. Few survived that long, but Nur had shown that it was possible.

All the Beduin had prayed that Husain and Mishaal would live unto their ancient days, but Allah had decreed otherwise, in His wisdom. Husain had died of a fever that he should have thrown off with ease, and his beloved had died a few months later of a woman's complaint that was mild. She had begun to pine the moment that he had ceased to draw breath. Freyha had seen it in her face within minutes, that determination to join him, the loosening of the ties that bound her to a

9

living world where he no longer breathed. From the day he died, she had barely spoken, and had left her food untouched. Freyha saw the same reaction now in Mishaal's daughter, and her heart was tormented.

If this rare and delicate plant was culled in its seventeenth year, what would become of all the Beduin who looked to her for guidance and guardianship, and what of their beloved Land of Mirages? It was a mighty burden to become Queen of the Desert at this tender age, but it was Allah's will.

'He must know best,' Freyha sighed to herself, 'for if He does not, we are lost, lost. . . .'

'Freyha, you are ashen. What ails thee? Have you not been eating properly?' There was a hint of a twinkle in Zahra's eyes, bright jewel green, which she had inherited, via Mishaal, from her American grandfather.

'*Ya Sitti*, I am eating well, unlike thee.' Freyha's eyes narrowed, concealing their dark carob hue. To her way of thinking, on the matter of food and its importance there was no room for humour or wit. Food was all that came between a man or woman and death; how could anyone, even her sweet, beloved mistress, jest about it?

'You are sour today, Freyha. What is on thy mind? Does old age press in too much upon thee?' The green eyes positively danced.

'Highness, you mock an old woman who would lay down her life for you.'

'I do not mock you!' Zahra reached out a slender hand to stroke Freyha's cheek reassuringly. 'You have been as a mother to me these past months.'

'I would never presume to take her place.' Freyha shivered as if a cold finger had pressed against her heart. 'She was beloved, a saint, and I am not worthy to follow her.'

Zahra did not reply for she knew this to be true. Her mother had been a saint, and would be worshipped as such by the Beduin now that she was gone. It was not the

10

custom of her tribe to honour tombs, as did others; instead, they preferred to honour the wombs of the living who would bring forth the next generation. But they would pray to the saints, the good and the holy who had wrought miracles in their lifetime, and who had ever wrought a greater one than Mishaal?

Cupping her face with her hands, Zahra closed her eyes as if in pain. She had done nothing to prove herself; she was unworthy, too. How did she dare step into her mother's shoes? She was a child, an ignorant child, and yet she must be Queen.

As if reading her thoughts, Freyha said, 'Husain became Amir at a far younger age than you, *Ya Sitti*. He was thrust into the place of king and lord before he had seen ten summers, yet he did not bend beneath his burden. He grew strong as a desert palm tree; he showed no fear, nor did he shrink from what must be done.'

'It doesn't help to remind me of that! Such tales only serve to convince me that I am too frail for what must now be done. I am not Husain, nor am I Mishaal. I am feeble stock, unfit to rule; a *sumr* tree dying because the water has ceased to flow around its roots.' Zahra's voice cracked into a sob.

'Zahra!' Freyha only used the intimate name in anger or alarm. Any man or woman might come to the Beduin ruler and call him familiarly by his first name, for he was their brother and they his. But those who loved most dearly, and were closest, preferred to use the regal titles to show their respect. When Freyha was angered by the girl she had helped to raise, she would address her familiarly as Zahra which was usually enough to bring the required result. 'Zahra, you will offend He who made you Queen; there will be penance to pay for this doubt that fills thy heart.'

'And what if Allah Himself put it there?' Malachite eyes met carob brown. 'Maybe He wishes me to doubt and fear, so that He can instil me with courage which I

11

shall prize as coming from Him. Would you question my doubts then?'

'Sometimes you are your mother to the life. Her eyes, her expression, her sharp wit!' Freyha's heart twisted. It was exactly the sort of argument that Mishaal would have used, with her unique way of looking at things, her constant challenges to received opinion.

'So you have said before, Freyha, but what of the girl inside? She does not resemble her mother; no, not in any way. She is pale and weak, she has no wit nor does she know what will become of her. Too much is expected of her!' Covering her face with her hands, Zahra fell silent.

Instantly Freyha was by her side, gathering her into her motherly arms.

'You need not return to public life yet. Say that you still mourn – no one will dare to criticise that. Send away the suitors and bide your time until you are eighteen. Should anyone find fault, say that Mishaal did not marry until she was that age. They dare not criticise anything she did.'

'You make it sound so simple, Freyha, but my conscience tells me otherwise. I must rejoin my people, rule over them and choose a husband. I cannot hide like a coward in my tent. I must think of those who are worse off; the ones who come in supplication as they came to Husain and Mishaal before me. How much longer can I go on turning them away?'

'A husband would divide your labours and take some of the strain off your shoulders – '

'That is not what I want!' Angrily, Zahra pushed Freyha away from her. 'I do not wish to be humoured and cosseted! I am ruler here, and ruler I shall be. Don't you understand, Frehya? No husband could ever rule beside me – *with* me – as Husain did with Mishaal. There will never be their like again. I cannot have what they had, and so I must do it alone. I think I always knew that, even as a child, but there was always the hope that

12

Mishaal would have sons and release me from this burden.'

'You will not take a husband?' Freyha sat back on her heels, her jaw dropping in amazement.

'Oh, yes, of course I will – but he can only be a *husband*, not my equal. He must not look to rule me.'

'I see.' Freyha pursed her lips doubtfully.

'But do you? There is no Beduin who is my equal. My father was King over all; now I am Queen. I could marry an amir or one of the wealthiest shaikhs, but it would not make him King beside me. A Muslim woman takes her husband's majesty but she cannot endow him with her own, is that not so?' Freyha nodded mutely. 'So whatever choice I make, my husband cannot be my equal. When the people come to my tent to beg help, they will come to see me, not my husband. They will want to talk with the daughter of Husain and Mishaal, not some stranger who has a right to be here only by marriage, someone who is unfamiliar with our ways. The people want their Queen, not some alien shaikh.'

Zahra rubbed a hand thoughtfully across her cheek. In her mind's eye she was seeing Mahmed beside her. Oh, he was a striking figure undoubtedly, but not of the renowned bloodline of the Prophet Mohammed or the great Queen of the Desert, Zenobia.

Would her people take him to their hearts as they had taken Mishaal, even though her mother had come from the lowest tribe, the Sulubba, and her father had been an infidel? No, it would need a sign from Allah, a miracle. . . . Zahra's mouth curved, partly in humour, partly in cynicism. There was no need for a miracle, not this time. Her land flourished, and had done so for thirty years. With God's blessing, it would continue to do so, and she was not lax in her devotions to him. She was a faithful adherent of the Most High and always had been; He would not fail her and she would not fail Him.

Mishaal had once told her of the time when she had

considered herself a Christian. She had called it her 'infidel summer', speaking of it with much head shaking and eye raising heavenwards.

'How could I think that Christianity was the religion for me, the worship of the one they believe to be the Son of God? How could I have taken that creed to my bosom, even for a summer's length? I was beyond reason, such a fool! God made me see the truth. He took me close to him, out of my error and into His ways, and that is why you, my little *jijim*, were born Husain's child.'

'Tell me more of the infidel summer,' Zahra had begged, but her mother had said that she was too young to know, and none of this must reach Husain's ears anyway. One day she would tell her daughter more... but she never had, for death had intervened. Briefly, Zahra had wondered what it was like to be Christian, to worship a man who had died on the cross and was said to be the Son of God. She knew that Allah had no son. Mohammed had never spoken of a Son of Allah dying on the cross and rising again to join His Father in heaven, but he had revered Jesus as a prophet, the greatest until he himself received his revelations from the angel Gabriel.

Suddenly, the decision having been made for her as if by another, she spoke.

'Give me three more days to collect myself, and then I will meet my people again. Tell them to come as they did in the days of Husain and Mishaal, and that I shall be here to receive them. Tell them I have not forgotten them.'

Freyha breathed again. 'And your suitors? You will see them, too?'

'Yes, even the suitors. Are there more?'

'Some have gone away. They had urgent business, so they said. There were five here yesterday.'

'The Amir Mahmed ibn Beydoun, has he been here?'

'He sent another messenger last week, and then a

14

third one yesterday. I am sure that he will come himself when he hears the news.'

'That Husain's daughter will choose her husband now? Yes, nothing will keep him away when he hears that.' Zahra clasped her hands together, having spoken with a confidence for which she had little foundation. Would Mahmed come himself, or send yet another messenger? Perhaps he had changed his mind altogether by now. Perhaps she had injured his pride by hiding herself away?

How she wished that Husain had chosen her husband for her before his death, then she would have been secure now, married and safe, not having to make this choice when her heart longed only for seclusion. With her father's blessing on a marriage, she would have accepted it without question.

As it was, she felt she was in a wilderness where she must find her path unaided. Perhaps her mother's infidel summer had been like this? If only she knew.

Chapter Two

The Amir Mahmed ibn Beydoun was twenty-nine years of age. He had loved his wife Mahia, but now she was dead. His daughters' ages ranged from three to twelve, and they were healthy, large-eyed girls whom he cherished, particularly Zuli, the eldest, in whose tent he now was. Zuli was so like her mother; she had the same dark hazel eyes and long straight hair that she had just begun to redden with henna.

She wore a robe of sky-blue linen edged with deeper blue embroidery, and her hair was loose around her slender shoulders. At her throat was a *kirdala*, the Beduin choker necklace, fashioned from bronze. From its tight neck band hung engraved cylinder-shaped beads, glittering blue gemstones and tiny turquoises, and on her fingers were rings of *aqiq ahmar*, *fairuz* and *aqiq*, carnelian, turquoise and agate. Round her ankles were *khalakhil*, anklets of silver hung with *zarir*, the bells whose tinkling sound was thought to repel evil spirits.

So petite and decoratively dressed, Zuli looked like a young bride prepared for her wedding night. Today had been her twelfth birthday and these were her festive clothes. All day there had been singing and rejoicing, and she had joined in the dancing with a light heart. After the death of her mother the previous year she had been low-spirited, but today had changed that. She knew that her father would soon take another wife. However much he had loved her mother it was not the Muslim way to sleep alone, and he would want sons. No Muslim man was happy to be without sons.

After the feasting was over, Mahmed had escorted his daughter back to her tent amidst a laughing crowd of his people, and his heart had grown full at the memory of his marriage night thirteen years before, when the lovely Mahia had been awaiting him within the dark recesses of the black tent. Mahia, his beloved, with her dark hazel eyes and the long, straight hair that had hung down to her knees. He had tangled himself most willingly in that hair, never wanting to be free. . . .

Mahia had come to him in scarlet cashmere with a gleaming white shepherd's cloak hanging from her shoulders by twisted gold cords. Round her neck and wrists and ankles were silver circlets from which small silver bells gently swung with a noise like the sweetest singing of a choir in Paradise. When she was just twelve years old she had been led into his camp on the back of a white mare that had never been mated. Behind her, on another white horse, lay the virgin fleece, a white lamb's skin, which all Beduin brides brought as a symbolic gift to their grooms.

When Mahmed had seen her, his heart had risen into his throat. He was mute with love and the finest, sweetest rapture of his life. He, too, had been a virgin, having felt no wish to deflower other maids while he waited for his Mahia to reach marriageable age.

After the simple but ancient ceremony of the sacrificing of a lamb, whose throat was slit at the girl's feet and its carcase given to an orphan, as was the custom, Mahia had ridden round the camp on her white mare, a slave walking beside her to announce to all who were gathered there that this was Mahmed's bride.

'See ye the bride of Mahmed! See ye this virgin bride! See Mahia's eyes and Mahmed's white camels! Oh, for the young lord and his virgin bride!'

17

Then Mahia had placed the virgin fleece on the couch where she would lie with her husband that night, and retired to the women's quarters to await her husband's summons. When he had called, she had gone to him instantly. And then, with her own hands, she removed the middle pole from the tent, placing it on the ground. The black goatskin sagged, but the other supports and the tent cords had kept it from crashing down. It was the recognised sign that a Beduin bride was with her groom.

Mahmed realised that his fingers were on the silver bells that hung from Zuli's bangle, and his vision was blurred. He was reliving his wedding night, and in his imagination, Zuli was his bride, his fair, hazel-eyed Mahia. There she sat, almost the age that Mahia had been, and so like her, so heartrendingly like her.... There was a tearing pain in his heart; he could not breathe or see or hear.

'Father!'

There were desert wastes and *simûms* between him and the speaker... as if every movement might be his last, he leaned closer, knowing what he wanted. With all his being, he wanted this to be Mahia, needed this to be Mahia, and so it was for he could not tolerate the truth: that his wife was dead and gone from him.

'Father!' The voice was tremulous, gasping, but it was Mahia's although she was not calling him by his usual names. She had called him her dark-eyed hero and her sweet-lipped warrior, but only when they were alone where no others might hear.

'Mahia, beloved, come to me now,' he whispered thickly, his body aching for release.

Snuffing the lamp, he lay across his bride, crushing her beneath him, heedless of her anguished struggles – all virgin brides fought a little, it was the way – imprisoning her mouth with his own and branding on it the passionate kisses he had repressed for nearly a year and could no longer hold back. She cried out, but Mahia

18

had done that too as he had pierced her maidenhead and he saw no difference between that night and this: it was all the same. This was Mahia in his arms, and now she was his again, joined to him, imprisoned beneath him as he panted over her. The wild gazelle was returned to its fold, the eagle brought down from the clouds, the white camel hobbled at his side, and all was well again.

Night becalmed the camp and there was silence save for the cry of a night animal and the snort of the camels where they were settled to rest. The moon was full, its penetrating rays silvering the black tents as Mahmed staggered from his daughter's couch like an old man. Breathing harshly, he leant against a bale of skins, struggling to regain his sanity, wondering where his conscience had been while he had deflowered his own daughter. Not Mahia! It had not been Mahia; but it was too late now. His body burned where it had sinned, stung and seared, but it was only right that it should be so. He had destroyed his daughter's life. She would never find a husband now. He had ruined her.

Not until some hours later did he realise the entire truth. Not only was Zuli ruined, but so was he if people learned of his sin. Mahmed the Warrior they called him, but he was as nothing now; he was the dirt and dust of ashes, the stones of the desert, and the parched land after drought.

Zahra had dressed with special care in a robe of sapphire blue cashmere that had been a gift from her father. Loose and flowing, it was caught at the waist with a white silk tassel. On her feet were blue kid slippers painted with blue, silver and gold leaves, and round her ankles were solid silver *khalakhil* which tinkled as she moved. She wore a head veil of ivory silk fringed with silver, and over her shoulders a cape of ivory wool woven from the finest fleeces of her own herds, its edges fringed with silver. At her throat and on her fingers

19

were sapphires and topazes set in filigree silver, and hanging from her ears were *halaq*, earrings of beaten and fluted silver set with sapphire and carnelians. Her mother had taken to wearing *shaf* or *khizama*, nose ornaments, in later years, but Zahra had not yet had her nose pierced. One day, perhaps.

For two days her women had been preparing the grand audience chamber where she would meet the Amir Mahmed ibn Beydoun, and the sound of their excited chatter and laughter had filled the air. The insidious sand had collected in every crevice and cranny, but they had dealt with it summarily. Bronze and copper vases and jugs were polished savagely until they glowed, and the trays that would bear the coffee and sweetmeats were rubbed until the reflection of the dishes and pots could be seen in them.

The woven tapestries that had come from Persia were taken outside and shaken and beaten. In the brash sunlight their colours dazzled, rich violet-blues and crimsons, deep golds and subtle greens fashioned into gigantic exotic blooms and mythical beasts that stalked through the vibrant foliage with fearful eyes and fearless hearts. There were matching covers and cushions for the couch on which Husain and Mishaal had sat to receive supplicants, where Zahra would now take their place.

There were tears when one of Mishaal's earrings was found, a silver crescent studded with turquoises. She had lost it many months before and all their searching had failed to find it. Now they knew why. The seam of a cushion had come undone and the earring had slipped inside. Gripping it in her palm so that the sharp metal bit into her flesh, Zahra had wept and so had her women. They all missed the lovely Mishaal, the shining spirit who had charmed them into contentment. How could she be dead, the one they had loved so much?

It had never been the custom to mourn over tombs

and weep bitter tears of loss, nor to take offerings to the grave of a Beduin who had died. Moving about so much the people could not have maintained such a custom; they must travel to wherever there was new pasture for their flocks. But Mishaal's tomb was different. There she lay beside Husain, who had loved her beyond all telling for thirty years of peace and prosperity, and flowers had sprung up all around their resting place. Rich scarlet, blue, and tiny white blooms like stars grew in the scoured, waterless wilderness where there had been no rain for four weeks or more.

Because of Zahra's grief, they had remained stationary since the burial. First one, then another of the Amira's household had visited the double tomb, none wishing the others to know for it was not the custom. Then Freyha had gone, her heart heavy, and she had come back shaking and crying out.

'Flowers! There are flowers round them as if they lie in Paradise on earth!'

Zahra had gone to see the tomb for herself, not believing one word of it for there had been no rain for weeks. The flocks had been taken to fresh pastures, and soon she would have to follow.

Going back to the burial place was traumatic. Her palms were dewed with sweat and yet she felt chilled, as if her clothes clung to her with ice upon them. There was the tomb, simple and makeshift in the Beduin manner, piled high with rocks and stones to keep out scavengers. Then she saw, piled upon the stones, *kirdala* and *khatim*, finger rings and Qu'ranic amulets, the silver engraved jewellery which carries religious verses inside the little silver cylinders called *hirz*. And next to these was a snowy fleece, obviously recently brought because barely a grain of sand lay upon it. These were offerings to her mother and father.

Zahra had not known what to do or say, and she had quite forgotten about the flowers until she sank down to

21

pray and saw them burgeoning from the thirsty earth, so fresh and dewy that they might have grown after days and nights of rain. Touching them, she had felt as if she were dreaming, for how could these be real? Yet they were, soft and waxy and moist to the touch. Her throat had tightened so that she could hardly breathe, and her breast felt bruised and crushed.

She had gone back to the camp in utter silence, returning no greeting, seeing no one who crossed her path. It was too much for her to acknowledge; she felt small and fearful enough as it was without this new possibility that she was the daughter of saints. Her sins were too great, her failings and inadequacies too well-known to her for her to be able to accept that it could be so.

It was said that the daughters of the handsome ones would never possess their beauty, nor the daughters of the blessed their grace, and it was true, she knew it was. Her parents had been both beautiful and truly blessed, and so she could be neither. It was Allah's will.

She continued with the preparations for Mahmed's reception, selecting Duraya and A'isha to make the coffee for the Amir when he arrived. Ceremonial coffee grinding and preparation was a fine art to the Beduin and only the most graceful and accomplished females were chosen to undertake this task before honoured guests. As both the women were young and fair, they would wear their veils so as not to distract the Amir's attention.

Chaperoning her mistress, for Zahra's reputation must be protected until her marriage, Frehya would sit crosslegged on a cushion a few feet away from the Amira, and her bodyguard would be at the entrance to the audience chamber, as always.

Incense had been burned overnight to purify the air and remove the scent of disturbed dust and unaired tapestries, and small copper dishes containing attar of

22

roses were placed at strategic points around the tent, to fill the air with the scent of summer blooms. The oil lamps hanging suspended from their gilded chains had been cleaned and polished, and wild beeswax had been rubbed into the carved cedarwood chests at each side of the Amira's couch. The tent flaps had been folded back and secured, in a welcoming gesture to the visitor.

He would be here shortly. His advance messenger had arrived and was taking refreshment, sherbet flavoured with orange flower water. The camp was restless. Even the camels were snorting and stamping as if they knew that this was a momentous day for their royal mistress. Someone had seen a large eagle circling the camp at dawn, and Khalid ibn Khalid, the Amira's seer, had announced that it was an omen.

On hearing this, Zahra had gone to his tent, for he was a dying man, and kissed his age-bruised hand. There was much to be said for choosing the oldest as wise men and seers, but the speed with which death claimed them swiftly robbed Zahra of their advice. Khalid was the fifth seer during her lifetime, and as yet she had no idea who would replace him. Some said that his brother was exceptionally wise, for his advice bore excellent fruit, but she did not like Beni ibn Khalid. He had sly, slanting eyes and she felt that his mind was on unsavoury things every time she spoke to him.

'*Saiydi*, the omens are good. Hashir saw a great eagle with the dawn, and a camel has given birth to twins who live when it was not her time to bring forth.' The old man's eyes were covered in thick white cataracts; he was virtually blind. The cataracts looked like white pottery they were so thick and solid. Zahra squeezed his hand again, feeling a tremor run through him.

'*Saiydi*, I saw your father born. I was but a youth, yet I knew that he would be great. The omens were powerful: the hawk that landed upon his father's tent and would not be scared away by the stamping of the camels and the

23

neighing of the horses, the dreams that his mother had while he was in her womb, these things told me that his name would be blessed.'

'And what of my birth, Khalid ibn Khalid? Were there omens then?'

The old man laughed, a faint neighing sound. 'You want more? Is it not enough that you are the daughter of the great ones? By that alone you are blessed and set far above others.'

'So there were no omens?' She had not thought that there were. Her mother would have told her had it been so. Omens were noted and remembered for generations.

'Your mother and father loved one another beyond sight of all others. They bore you out of that love, and you are strong and healthy. Are these not omens?'

'I would wish for something more reassuring.'

'Like all the young you want the moon and the stars, but the moon is cold as death and the stars would burn you to cinders. It is better to be content with mortal things.'

Gritting her teeth, conscious of the stench of sickness and approaching death around him, Zahra asked Khalid whom he would choose as his successor.

'All my life I have sought knowledge, as the Prophet ordained, and yet I cannot answer you this, *Saiydi*. I do not know if there is one who has the wisdom, and I hesitate to name one who is unworthy. It saddens me to leave you without a seer, but I can do no more.' The old man's face was sinking inward before her eyes but he rallied momentarily, clutching at her fingers, and saying, '*Saiydi*, there is an old saying: "If you hit your hand against a stone, then it will hurt." Remember it, remember it well.'

Not knowing what he meant, Zhara leaned closer.

'Khalid, will the Amir Mahmed ibn Beydoun make me a good husband?' she asked, her heart thumping in trepidation as she awaited his reply, but he seemed to be having difficulty capturing his breath. He was wheezing, and there was a strange rasping sound in his chest.

'Saiydi, it is the end for him.' Umar, Khalid's daughter, came to the seer's couch, tears in her eyes, and Zhara pressed the woman's hand before leaving the dying man with his children. He would not die alone. He had seven daughters and five sons, all of them living.

Was it a bad omen that the seer should choose to die on the day that she had decided to accept Mahmed? She shivered at the notion. It was a thought that she must cast off. Once she began this wandering, defeatist train of thought there was no end to it. She had become expert at self-torture. At times she wished that her mother had been obese and stupid, her father poor and ugly and without title, for then she could have been happy with herself just as she was.

Mahmed would never be alone with Zuli again, he had sworn it. And he must take the reins of his courage and woo the Amira Zahra with every ounce of his energy and charm. He had last seen her when she was thirteen or fourteen, and he wished she were still that age now. He had heard that she was rather plain; that she had neither her mother's radiant beauty nor her father's striking looks. It was said she had no particular talents, not that a wife needed any beyond the ability to cook and clean and bear sons. But as a queen would do only one of these, she needed some artistic skills. Perhaps she danced like her mother had done, calling down the spirits from Paradise so that she appeared immortal? Or maybe she could sing or recite verses?

He rode towards her camp with an unflinching reluctance. Even if she danced like a *houri*, and was blindingly beautiful, she would not be his Mahia.

Behind him, the riders jostled for a place next to their Amir. He did not reprimand them. They were like children, excited by the thought of his marriage to the daughter of Husain and Mishaal. It was an honour above all honours, and they were dizzy with self-importance at belonging to his tribe. Let them rejoice, for their happiness might be short-lived.

The Amira's camp was now in view, the low-slung tents etched black against the pale saffron-coloured sand dunes under a piercingly blue sky. Soon he would see her. Mahmed's damp hands slipped on the camel's rein and he felt a pulse throbbing at his temple.

The people had gathered to greet him and his followers with extravagant *salaams*, and there were shouts and gestures of welcome. Someone was playing a reedy pipe and the wailing sound floated on the air like the sound of a *jinn* singing. Within moments, a rhythmic drum accompaniment was added, instantly enlivening the proceedings. Mahmed breathed a little more easily as he dismounted.

A young girl came running forward with a tray of sherbet for him and he grasped a flask and drank deep of it, conscious of all eyes upon him. He knew that few excelled him in stature and strength. He had always enjoyed good health, was vigorous and needed little sleep.

Made hurriedly, the sherbet was nauseatingly sweet and he felt his stomach heave in protest. Taking a deep breath, he replaced the engraved flask on the girl's copper tray, then turned in the direction of the audience tent, distinguishing it by the streaming silk banners that fluttered from it.

There were anticipatory murmurings from the people around him as he strode towards the Queen's tent, knowing that he could no longer prolong what must come.

When he had accustomed his eyes to the change of light inside the tent, he saw her, the Amira Zahra, the one whom they already called Queen of the Desert though she had barely shown her face there and was

26

only recently Amira. What had she done to deserve this glorious, ancient title, the same one that had been given to her ancient ancestress, Zenobia? Nothing so far as he knew. Whatever honours she had been given were because of who rather than what she was.

His breath caught in his throat at his first glimpse of her, unsmiling and decked with jewels, as stately as Zenobia herself. Instantly he thought of the Jewels of Destiny, hidden centuries ago by that same Zenobia and rediscovered by Mishaal thirty years before. Anticipation speeded his step. The Jewels of Destiny were said to be beyond human price, the most fabulous gems and gold ever collected together. His fingertips itched to touch them, but she was not wearing them. Her decorations were those of any Beduin lady, silver and bronze, set with carnelians and sapphire and turquoises. Much to his disappointment, he saw no fabled emeralds from the mines of Queen Cleopatra, no crown of solid gold studded with huge rubies, no bangles and earrings gemmed with amethysts, sapphires and pearls.

His mind emblazoned with the thought of the jewels, he did not distinguish her face at first, and when he did he was disappointed. Mishaal had been a striking woman, one to be gazed after wonderingly. Many times he had tried to imagine her on his couch beside him, but he had failed. He had gauged so little about her that he could not even tell whether she was fond of bed sport or not, and he had always prided himself on being able to tell that of a woman, even if it had been only a superficial interest while Mahia was alive. Mishaal had been a woman of mystery and spirit. Who had ever known what she was thinking, what she would say next, how her mind ran? Certainly not he.

Zahra was dainty, it was true. She had tiny hands and feet, which appealed to him, and she moved gracefully. Her eyes were green, almost like her mother's and yet not – and in that difference supremely disappointing.

27

No, she did not compare with Mishaal. Her face was held stiffly, her mouth set tight which warned him she could be a vixen. She kept her eyes cast down and spoke in low tones so that he could barely hear her welcoming courtesies. Her complexion was fair, it was true, but then she had infidel blood and it was to be expected.

Sinking down on the proffered cushions, he watched as the two veiled women began to prepare his coffee, while he sipped the mint tea that Zahra had offered him. There was a heavy atmosphere in the tent, and she was doing nothing to lighten it. He felt ill at ease and ready to take offence; he would have done by now had she not been who she was. The guest in the tent was sacred and to be treated as such, yet he felt out of place here, unwanted.

She had been named for Venus, the morning star, yet she displayed none of the signs that one would associate with a woman born under such a sensual portent. That tight-lipped, shadowy face, the clenched hands, the tension that he sensed in her, boded no good for their future together. Yet did it matter? The bearing of sons was her purpose in life, and they would be his sons, heirs to the Land of Mirages. One day his son would be Amir here, as once the great Husain had been.

Had she been born below him, then eventually he could have put her aside and taken another wife, but this woman could not be abandoned. She would wish to rule beside him as her mother had ruled beside her father; she would wish to discuss every matter with him, and have her say upon each. He would be prepared to defer to her occasionally because of her rank and power, but not to submit like a woman if she should demand her own way at every turn and, from the look of her, that was how she would be.

Since the night in his daughter's tent, Mahmed had changed. It was a subtle change as yet, but it was made all the same. Before, he had considered himself a good

28

fellow, generous and indulgent with his loved ones, stern when the moment merited sternness but only for the sake of guidance. Now he was disturbed, his image of himself shaken and still reforming. A man who could do what he had done was not the kindly, indulgent and noble character that he had believed himself to be. He was less noble than he had thought. Yes, far less noble, if noble at all. . . .

'*Ya Saiyid*, it is something like four years since last we met, if I recall. How are your daughters? They are well?'

The Amira's voice was pleasant and he relaxed somewhat, yet her choice of words stung him. He had been thinking of his daughter and this woman had mentioned her at the same moment. Such uncanny perception disturbed him. He liked a woman to be warm and soft and fluffy as virgin fleece, not bristling with acuity. With a woman like that, how could a man go on as he had before? He must be forever looking inside himself, and that Mahmed did not wish to do. There were things in there that he did not wish to face ever again.

'*Ya Sitti*, my daughters are well and send their salutations.'

'You have four daughters?'

'I do, *Ya Sitti*.'

There was an embarrassing pause while they sat and listened to the grinding of coffee, the pounding of beans with a pestle and mortar, and the sizzling of water as it came to the boil. Then there was the clang of the heavy skillet as A'isha put it to one side, lifted up the heavy brass kettle and soused the coffee grounds and cardamom seeds with steaming water.

The rich, choking scent of fresh coffee billowed towards them, engulfing them. Zahra wished that she were alone, that she had never summoned this man, that she could sit in peaceable silence with her women and sip the coffee and think nothing save simple, womanly thoughts.

29

The Amir Mahmed was older than she remembered. Perhaps losing his wife had aged him? He was, it was true, broad-shouldered and upright in stance, and his face approached handsomeness, yet there was a cold aura about him which she could not identify. When she had seen him as a child and they had raced together, she had distinguished warmth and generosity, a willingness to let her win before everyone even if it meant that she made him seem a poor rider. Could this be the same man? She did not know what to say or do with him; he was different, and in his difference, frightening.

It was the first time that Zahra had held audience alone with a man, let alone one of such rank. Instinctively she felt that he should have made matters easier for her, or was she wrong to expect fatherliness from a prospective husband? Was the truth of it that she had been blessed with the most perfect father in all the tribes, and would look for him fruitlessly in every man after? Suddenly, urgently, she longed for her mother. Mishaal would have known what to say, how to guide her. Allah, but she ached for her to be near!

The ceremonial coffee drinking helped to pass the time a little more easily, as did the eating of the wild honey and sesame seed cakes which Zahra had made with her own hands. Yet she did not impart this information to her guest. Even that was too much to tell him about herself.

Where was Akhim with the *davoul*, and Khalid's son with the pipe? Music would lighten the sombre mood which had beset them. Clapping her hands, she gave the sign that the music should begin but it was some time before it did. What were those two young idiots about? As the music began, Zahra gave an almost audible sigh. She had been frightened that the Amir could hear her pulses pounding, the breath catching in her throat. Now he would hear only the pipe and *davoul* of her two most gifted young musicians.

30

The atmosphere brightened almost instantly, and then the Amir pushed forward a small casket which he gestured to Zahra to open.

'A modest token of my respect and esteem, *Ya Sitti*,' he explained, knowing that if this gift failed then his hopes were unlikely to be satisfied. But women were easily won with gifts of jewels and gold. Even Zuli had been soothed with a rope of carnelians set in bronze and silver.

Zahra opened the casket as if there might be a venomous snake within. She had seen the fabled Jewels of Destiny many times and by comparison other gems appeared like cold glass imitations. Mahmed had not tried to vie with her parents' treasure by producing a gigantic pearl or ruby. Inside the casket was a multi-stringed collar of minute and delicate seed pearls set in rich orange-yellow gold. They were highly appealing to a young girl, and Zahra's cheeks flushed with pleasure. So, behind that coldness, Mahmed had some sensitivity. He had gone to the trouble of selecting a pretty and unusual piece of jewellery for a highborn young woman when he could so easily have given her something ostentatious and vulgar. When she looked across at him, her mouth had softened and she was ready to alter her unflattering first impression of him.

Mahmed could not control the grin that broke across his tanned face. He had been right. She was like other women after all, and in learning this he could relax. If jewellery could sway her, then he had her in the palm of his hand. There might be a chance for their marriage after all.

Chapter Three

Akhim, and Khalid's son had been making music for almost an hour now, and the Amira was still deep in discussion with her guest. A'isha, Duraya and Salama had cleared away all the dishes and platters from the welcoming refreshments and were now preparing sherbet, scented and flavoured with orange flowers, which was their mistress's favourite. With this there would be bite-sized cinnamon and ginger biscuits, *rahat lokum* in rose, vanilla and orange flower flavours, and the ubiquitous dried dates and figs which sustained the Beduin right through the year.

Zahra had found that Mahmed was not chilly at all, merely intimidated by her beauty. He told her so ingenuously, begging her forgiveness for his distant behaviour when he had first arrived.

'It is awesome for a man to meet a woman who rules in her own right, but when she is so lovely, fair as the petal on the rose and the moon riding at midnight, then he is struck dumb and cannot speak what is on his mind. Believe me, *Ya Sitti*, I have never known a woman like you. You are one to remember for all time.'

Zahra had blushed – what woman would not have done? – but she realised that his compliment was quite within the normal scope of one amir's greeting to another. She had been well schooled in protocol by her parents, joining them frequently in their audience chamber as she was growing up.

'Our daughter and heir must know all that there is to know concerning the governing of our people,' Husain had said, his slender brown fingers resting lightly on Zahra's head as she gazed up at him adoringly. 'We cannot guarantee that her future husband will be wise enough to guide her should the need arise, and so she must know all that we can teach her.'

That had been the week following the death of Bahran ibn Rahman at the age of thirteen. He and Zahra had been promised to one another, and for three years they had corresponded in affectionate terms. Bahran was the son of the Shaikh of Rahman, the bosom friend of Husain, and naturally the one whom he considered most worthy to inherit the Land of Mirages via marriage to Zahra. For three years her future had been settled and secure, then Bahran had been bitten by a large scorpion which had worked its way into his slipper while he slept one night. Many scorpion stings were not deadly, causing sickness and physical upset only, but the larger creatures gave nastier bites and their effects could be fatal.

The Shaikh had beaten his son's body servants for not protecting their young master, but that could not save his son. He had died, racked with fever and vomiting, and it had been a merciful release. Zahra had wept when she was told, and shut herself away in her usual reaction to shock and pain. In deference to her grief, Husain had not suggested another husband in place of Bahran. The months had passed, and then the years, and with Husain and Mishaal in such excellent health there seemed no urgency about making another choice.

Poor Bahran. He had been a smiling, good-humoured boy and she had loved him in her youthful, tender way.

'*Ya Sitti* is silent. I hope I have not offended her?' Mahmed's voice brought her back from her day dreams

33

with a jolt. How rude of her to forget that he was there.

'No, there is no offence taken, *Saiyid*. It is just that I am unaccustomed to such flattery.'

'Not flattery, I assure you, *Ya Sitti*! You are fair as a summer's dawn, as delicate as the spring flowers that leap from the flood,' he lied boldly. '*Ya Sitti*, I wish us to be good friends, and if there is hope of more then I am thankful to the one true God for His indulgence.'

Go through this again? She could not! She shrank from a sudden mental picture of lines of men gathering to pay court to her, and the confusion that would overwhelm her in such circumstances. Whatever her first reaction to Mahmed, he and his father before him had been allied with Husain for many years and she had never heard her father speak an ill word against either of them. If anything, he had praised Mahmed as a perfect example of connubial bliss and fidelity, and said that such a state was what he most wished for his daughter when she took a husband. On hearing that, Mishaal had cried out that Zahra had seen more than enough connubial bliss between her own parents, and there need be no more talk of marriage as yet. She had pulled Zahra to her, holding her close as if to say, 'You will stay with me.'

Perhaps it was this dichotomy that was making her cautious now? Husain had wanted her to be safely wed but Mishaal had thought her best at home. Which view did Zahra favour?

'*Ya Saiyid*, it would be better if we kept to the purpose of this meeting rather than indulge in effusive praises.' She fixed Mahmed with her dreamy peridot eyes, trying to instil them with sternness but failing. 'There are matters to be clarified between us, and I would beg your tolerance of me in this.'

'But of course, *Ya Sitti*!' His carob-coloured eyes gleamed. Now came the crux of the matter, and it seemed that she was considering their marriage ser-

34

iously. In his delight, he forgot what he had told himself moments earlier, that an independent, intelligent wife would be more of a burden than a blessing. Mahia had been sweetly dimpled and amiable, making obeisance to him as if he were a sultan, and that was why he had loved her so unwaveringly. He abhorred sharp-tongued, dominating women; they were an offence before Allah, a thorn in the heel that pricked and festered and kept one's mind off gladness and contentment.

'*Ya Saiyid*, you are fully aware of my circumstances: I must choose a husband. I will be quite frank with you – it will not be an easy choice.' Zahra halted, blushing. She had meant to imply that she was reluctant to marry, but had given the impression that she was torn between him and one or more other suitors. 'I – I mean that I am not eager for this state. Things crowd in upon me so I must learn to rule in the place of Husain and Mishaal. To marry at this time will distract me from all that I must do.'

'*Ya Sitti*, it would be my honour and delight to guide and advise you in the coming months. I have been Amir for eight years and consider myself experienced enough to aid you in your considerably more complex and extensive burden.'

'*Ya Saiyid*, I do not consider my inheritance a burden!' There was that sharpness again, and the green eyes flashed emerald fire.

So, she could show spirit when she chose. There was more beneath that pallid, undistinguished façade than he had thought, but did it tempt? The place for a woman's spirit was on the marriage couch, not in daily life. What if she spoke to him like that before others? He would want to remind her of her place, and chastise her, but how could he do that to the Queen of the Desert?

Husain and Mishaal had obviously raised her to be proud, independent and arrogant, and Mahmed disliked

35

that intensely. It would be a matter of concealing his true feelings until after the ceremony, and then slowly but firmly re-educating her. She must learn her place in the home, whatever her worldly rank and position. There was not a happy woman in the world who did not defer to her husband by night and by day, and Zahra would do so before they had been married a year, he vowed. He would break her spirit and remould it with his own hands in the form and shape that he desired.

'*Ya Sitti*, forgive me for suggesting that your famed inheritance lies heavily upon you. I have four daughters, and I thought of their delicacy and their craving for lighthearted pastimes and made the mistake of assuming that Your Highness would be the same.'

'Perhaps I was five years ago, but I am grown now, in case you had not noticed.' Zahra's eyes were narrowed so that he could not gauge their expression.

'With respect, *Ya Sitti*, all those of the gentler sex care greatly for lighthearted pastimes: dancing and singing, and making verses and music, embroidering and choosing new robes and jewels. I would wish that my bride may feel that she can revel in such happy pursuits without the cares of her amirate dragging her down.'

'That is thoughtful of you, *Ya Saiyid*, but I am ruler here and must be seen to be so, as my mother before me. That is part of our covenant with the Lord.'

Mahmed gritted his teeth. That covenant! He had thought that it was nothing more than rumour. It was so alien to their religion that he could not bring himself to think about it. The very suggestion made his temper boil: that the wives of all future Amirs of the Land of Mirages must rule equally beside their men. What *jinn* had devised such a covenant? Yet they said that it was sworn before the one true God and that He had asked it of them. How could that be so? Allah believed that man should have law over woman. Did the Qu'ran not plainly say, 'Women have such honourable rights as obliga-

36

tions, but their men have a degree above them'?

'You are silent, *Ya Saiyid*. Have you not heard of the covenant?' Zahra leaned forward, the silver bells on her anklets tinkling. It was an almost ghostly sound, as if Mishaal were beside her in her dancing costume, the glorious peacock robe spread wide as if to shelter her daughter.

'I had heard of it but thought it a rumour,' Mahmed confessed, thinking it best that he speak truthfully about this at least.

'You know that the Land of Mirages was suffering from severe drought just over thirty years ago? All the wells and wadis and tributaries had dried up and there had not been rain for nearly a year. Men spoke of the old legend, and it was said that our land was cursed.'

'I know as far as that, *Ya Sitti*.' Mahmed bent his head as if respectfully.

'The Jewels of Destiny had been hidden for centuries. No one knew if they even existed, but my father was positive that they did. He wanted to find them and save his country. His people were thirsting and in rags, and the animals were dying from lack of water. Then he found my mother in the desert wilderness, and she led him to the treasure without knowing how or why. Together, in the temple of the ancient Mother Goddess, they found the jewels. And then the rains began. Ever since our land has flourished, and grown lush and green. Now we grow fruits and vegetables that would never have survived here in the past, and our beasts are the fattest and healthiest in Arabia. I grow white roses in my travelling garden, and who else could do that in the wilderness? It rains here frequently, and the climate is pleasant and comfortable. No one has suffered from lack of water since Mishaal led Husain to the Jewels of Destiny.'

'And the covenant, *Ya Sitti*?' His patience was exhausted. Such talk of curses and legends infuriated him.

37

How could they believe such nonsense? Why should Allah bless this one place and not others?

'Before the statue of the Mother Goddess, the One who once ruled here before Allah, the one true God, my mother swore that she would keep the covenant so that no Arabian woman under her jurisdiction would ever again suffer from the heavy hand of her husband or any other male relative. Women must once again have their rightful place, in honour of the Goddess.'

Mahmed flushed deeply. This was idolatry! The Prophet had cast out all the hundreds of false idols when he had brought Allah to his peoples, and to speak of them or give them honour was a sin against the one true God. How could she be Muslim while she spoke of this false idol?

'Ya Sitti, did you not say that Mishaal made the covenant with Allah? Now you say that she made it with the – the Goddess.' The name stuck in his throat, and the heat that had risen in his face and throat spread across his chest like a scorching poultice.

'Is not the one true God everywhere, Ya Saiyid? Wherever Mishaal made her covenant, there He would be. He was certainly there in the temple of the Mother Goddess for he guided the sword hand of Husain to destroy his enemies and free the Jewels.'

Zahra made as if to speak on, then fell silent. She knew what she thought, but no ordinary Muslim could be brought round to that way of thinking. She had read everything that existed concerning the Muslim religion and discussed it at length with her parents, who had ensured that she was educated to a high degree. All of them had agreed that the Goddess should never have been excluded from their creed. In his eagerness to abandon and condemn the false idols who had plagued their land in the sixth and seventh centuries, and his insistence upon the one true, male, God, the Prophet Mohammed had perhaps acted too hastily. A male God,

38

thinking like a male, behaving like one, calling his followers to slaughter in His name, was all very well, but what was there for women?

'Allah in an idolatrous temple? I find that difficult to believe, *Ya Sitti*.' Mahmed gave a little burst of breath as if to cast grave doubt on what she had told him.

'He is not afraid of the idolatrous temple, *Ya Saiyid*. He goes where He will and casts out his enemies and those who foreswear him. If He wished the Goddess to be abandoned, why did He ordain that the Jewels be hidden in Her temple vault, so that we should discover Her when we discovered them?'

'The Lord is great! Great is the Lord!' was Mahmed's way of escaping from a difficult theological question. This girl was too highly educated: she could argue points of religion in a way that many men could not. Perhaps the goddess had worked her poison into this girl's blood and she was no longer one of the faithful? The thought made him shudder. Were he a Sultan with a grand harem it would not concern him what religion his concubines were, but this was no concubine. She was a queen in her own right; she was to rule here for the rest of her days, and her children after. She would raise her daughters to be as proud and clever and difficult as she was, and therein lay inestimable anguish and loss of pride for him if they were his daughters, too. He would be laughed at, scorned, his authority within the family disputed.

The scent of fresh coffee saved them from what might have become the most embarrassing moment yet. True to Muslim custom, neither wished to plunge straight into discussing the reason for their being there together. It was an ancient custom born of the belief that *jinns* and evil demons must be misled as to the purpose of a meeting. They would lose interest if nothing of moment was raised and then, when they had drifted away to search for other mischief, the proper subject could be resurrected. It was a measure of the inexperience of

39

Zahra and the over-eagerness and unease of Mahmed that the matter of marriage had been mentioned already.

Kneeling before them, A'isha offered the engraved copper tray on which stood the steaming cups of fresh coffee, and tiny herb and spice squares dusted with sugar and snippets of date. The constant offering of refreshments to important guests was also the custom. It would not do to let a guest go hungry, nor to appear mean with the refreshments offered. Also, the amount and variety of the hospitality denoted the host's wealth and power.

Taking the proffered cup, and a handful of the fragrant, sweet squares, Mahmed ate and drank. It was extremely rude to rebuff what one was offered or to display a poor appetite. Great offence might be given by the rejection of hospitality, whether the gift was of food or drink or even a woman.

Watching in decorous and veiled silence nearby her mistress, Freyha wished that she could take to Mahmed. He was reassuringly handsome and strongly built, his face smoothly tanned and healthy yet with nothing of the weather-battered Beduin tribesman about him. He might have been a city dweller. His attire was spotless, plain, and gave him a distinguished air. Had he been wearing flashy, gold-embroidered robes, thick gold rings on his fingers and in his ears, and with a body doused in violet oil, Freyha would have known instantly why she did not like him. Husain had never worn gaudy robes or jewellery despite his eminence. He had always said that what was good enough for the Prophet was good enough for him.

She studied Mahmed's face behind the security of her veil, glad that she had worn it although Beduin women usually did not except with complete strangers. It had its uses, as Mishaal had often said, and this was one of them: to be able to examine and peruse a member of the opposite sex when it was necessary without his knowing

40

anything of the woman behind the concealing silk.

Mahmed had a strong-boned face, full of character. His eyes were somewhat small but set nobly, and his nose was strongly hooked in the Beduin manner. His nostrils were perhaps a little flabby but the mouth was broad and might be generous, the chin firm and deeply dimpled. Surely there was nothing in his appearance to alarm or repel, and yet she did not warm to him. There was a sense of crouching energy behind his courteous façade, as if he might suddenly leap into inappropriate action. A man of wild impulse then? She racked her brain to try and recall all she knew of him. Devoted husband, sadly bereaved when his wife had died so young; devoted father of four daughters; fearless warrior in skirmishes and battles with troublesome and invading tribes; breeder of a magnificent line of rare white racing camels whose beauty and speed were envied by all.

Was it the fact that he had not brought her beloved Zahra a white camel as a gift that was irking her? Seed pearls set in gold were pretty enough, but a child would have been pleased by them and her mistress deserved something more suited to her rank and maturity. The ability to select a gift that would delight a guest or ambassador was vital in one who would rule beside her. Yes, a white camel would have been far better. And, besides, Freyha would have loved to have seen one. Neither she nor her mistress had ever set eyes on such a beast.

Or was it perhaps the way that he packed his mouth with food so that her mistress had to look away from embarrassment when crumbs spattered his chin and his robe as he spoke? Pretty manners at mealtimes were most winning, and those who chomped and packed and spat out crumbs were unusually repugnant to a delicate young girl. She could forgive him there, however, for she supposed that he was merely showing his delight in the food, as should any courteous guest.

41

What else was there about him then? From long ago, she heard Rhikia's voice telling her something. Rhikia had believed that people were surrounded by colours that told whether they were good or bad. She could see them plainly, she said. But however hard she had stared, Freyha never could. How simple it would be if she could see whether this man's colour was good or evil, and what a blessing for a ruler to have that ability. Rhikia, Mishaal's foster mother, who had raised the Amira until she was sixteen, had died some years before, of great old age, and with her had died the gift of seeing the colours. Mishaal herself had been perceptive at gauging character, but after Zahra's birth some of the gift had faded.

There were those who would speak of the evil eye and flinch from such things, but not Freyha. If Rhikia or Mishaal had possessed such a gift then it must have come from Allah. She had hoped that the child might have inherited it from Mishaal, if inheritance of such a thing were possible, but it was not to be. Sadly, Zahra had never shown the slightest sign of such prescience.

Mahmed was indicating that he would like more coffee, and A'isha obediently refilled his cup, keeping her head averted as if in obeisance. She was overdoing it a little, Freyha chuckled to herself. The man was no Sultan; he was a local Amir of some wealth and importance but nothing too magnificent. How easily a woman's subservience went to a man's head and inflated his self-importance, not to mention another part of him!

And then her mind was upon the marriage couch. Whatever Mahmed was like by day, only Zahra would have to endure him by night. What if he were odious as a lover, impatient or abrupt, insensitive and unskilled? Having had but one wife and been faithful to her, he might well be ignorant of the arts of love, which would be disastrous for her darling mistress. How could a woman be happy when her husband could not woo her on the marriage couch? There, a woman needed to be tended

42

like a fragile blossom, with constant care to nurture her through the frosts and deluges and savage *simûm* that could attack her in the desert wastes outside. In return, she would be faithful and devoted, adoring and worshipping, but the man's tenderness and dedication must come first. Having listened to Mishaal's views on the matter for many years, Freyha could not think otherwise.

The musicians had begun their repertoire again, from the very beginning. They were willing youths but by no means as dedicated as they should have been. Zahra indulged them, for any child of Khalid's would always have a special place in her heart, and Akhim would have been an outcast but for his musical ability. He had been born without eyes. His mother had instantly disowned him, so he had been reared by a barren woman who had been glad of any infant in her arms. At four, he had been given a pipe to play, and within days was producing a recognisable melody.

It would appear that the first audience was drawing to an end, for neither of the participants seemed to have anything more to say. Mahmed was growing restive and barely concealing it, and Zahra ached to be alone. Having bidden goodbye in the Muslim manner, with palms joined together and head bowed in a *salaam*, Mahmed withdrew and the black tent fell momentarily silent.

'Sweet one, what ails thee?' Freyha clasped Zahra against her indulgent bosom as the Amira burst into sobs. 'He is not so offensive, is he? He has a fair face and body, and can be taught better manners at mealtimes!'

Stifled laughter could be heard. Zahra was shaking, not with tears but with sobs.

'Did you see the crumbs that fell into the neck of his robe? When he undresses, I vow that the floor will be covered with food!'

'A man can be a messy eater and still possess all the most necessary qualities, sweet one.'

43

'I know it, and I do not judge him on it. Perhaps in time I will indulge him and think fondly of his carelessness, but I cannot do so now. Not yet.'

'So you have decided that you will take him as husband?'

'I have, for all his errors. I cannot face more meetings like this, with the man on his best behaviour and myself having to judge him as if he is a prize horse. It dehumanises both of us!'

'Sweet one, you care too much; you are too sensitive as to others' feelings. *You* are the Amira. If you wish to judge the stars and the universe, then it is your prerogative. No one would dare judge you in return. By birthright you are above all.'

'I may tell myself that a thousand times a day, but it will not change what I feel inside, Freyha. Oh, it is agony to be young and unsure! Allah, if only I were thirty and had ruled for many years!'

'Don't wish the years gone, my heart. Allah in His benevolence will guide and instruct you. We all start out frightened and filled with dread. It is our lot.'

'You have never been filled with dread in your life, Freyha, so do not pretend that you have! You have all your mother's toughness and sureness of spirit. She would sit alone in the wilderness with her herds for hours and never flinch from the stalking predators. I heard tell that she had once killed a wildcat with her own hands when it attacked a lamb.'

'There are many stories about Nur, but how many are true I cannot say. If she did kill a wildcat then she never told me.'

'She cared for Mishaal when she first came to our tents – when the people were wary of her and thought she was a strange thing from the city, when there was talk that she had the evil eye. Nur was not frightened of her when others were.'

'Nur was sensible and perceptive. She had seen the

44

way Husain looked at Mishaal when he first brought her here. Evil eye or no evil eye, she knew what would come of it, and she was right.'

'Oh my mother, my mother!' Zahra began to weep, her body shaking, and Freyha pulled her closer.

'Zahra, put the past behind you, sweet and joyous as it was, and think of the future now. You must do it for your own sake, painful as it will be. Your parents made the past for you with their love and guardianship, and now you must make the future for yourself, as we all must. If the Lord wills it, within the year you will have a child who will be looking to you as you once looked to your mother and father, and you must be ready for its sake, my heart. You must be ready.'

A child of her own, when she was still so much a child herself? Zahra felt drained, exhausted by the thought. Yet for her people's sake, she must rally herself and do what must be done. The sooner the marriage was arranged, the safer for them all.

The uniting of Mahmed's lands with the Land of Mirages would provide a strong bulwark against the encroaching French who had colonised lands to the West and were said to be looking for new ground to conquer. God forbid that they should hear of the lushness and fertility of her own country, and in their rapaciousness descend upon it. That was what she dreaded most of all. Should they hear of it, and that its ruler was an untried young girl, they would attack, she knew. Mahmed had many warriors and many racing camels that could fight at speed; she would need those should any offensive begin. If not, troops would still be there to give her peace of mind. God knew, that was something she needed desperately.

PART TWO

The Passionate Warrior

Nomads lead an isolated life, undefended by walls. Hence they look for protection to themselves alone. Always armed and watchful, they are ever on the lookout for any sign of danger, being full of confidence in their own courage and power. For courage has become one of their deepest qualities and audacity a second nature to them.

Ibn Khaldun

Now is the hour for the dauntless spirit... now for the stout heart.

Virgil

Call now; is there any that will answer thee? and to which of the holy ones wilt thou turn?

Job, 5:1

Chapter Four

The French Foreign Legion was formed on 10 March 1831, under the sign of Pisces whose subjects are happy to wander the world and live a rootless life of exploration and adventure, concealing their identities as a fish hides deep on the ocean bed.

Algiers had fallen to the French in 1830 and they rapidly discovered they needed a special force ferocious enough to police their new colony, hitting upon an ingenious method of doing so and ridding France of its villains and wild men into the bargain. All those men in France itself considered undisciplined and unpredictable were invited to join the new Legion and, at a stroke, their homeland was freed of an unmanageable problem and the new territory had its law enforcers. Many of the men had fought in Napoleon's Army of the Peninsular and had been struggling to survive on half-pay since that war had ended. Now that there was a King of France again – Louis-Philippe – soldiers who had fought loyally for Napoleon were viewed with distaste.

Not all the Legionnaires were French, of course. Many came from foreign lands, rendered stateless by wars or boundary disputes; some were fearless fighters who could not wait to forge into action again; others were fleeing justice and glad to have this escape route.

The most generous person could not have called them

anything but an unsavoury rabble. Unschooled, rough and raw, it had been the task of their commander, Colonel Stoffel, to batter them into shape. Within two years, they had earned their first regimental colour which bore the legend, 'The King of the French to the Foreign Legion'. By the time there were some five and a half thousand Legionnaires, Algiers stirred itself to retaliate. With three thousand horsemen, the Amir of Cascara, Abd-al-Qadir, attacked Oran, to find himself facing the French Chausseurs and the Legionnaires of the 4th Battalion, Spanish veterans from the Peninsular War.

Amazingly, despite the Arab brilliance at fighting on horseback, the Amir's men were defeated. One year later, the Spanish Fourth Battalion joined with the Italian Fifth Battalion to take Arzew, and then Mostaganem. By 1834, Colonel Bernelle was in charge of the Legion when they took Kolea, near Algiers. For the next few years, the Legion would be fully occupied in the Spanish Carlist War, during which their numbers were decimated from five thousand to five hundred.

In 1837 two newly formed battalions of recruits were dispatched to Algeria to lay seige to Constantine which had withstood a similar attack the year before. A fortified city, Constantine held out for four days before the Legion breached its walls and poured in, engaging in vicious hand-to-hand fighting until the citizens were defeated.

It was not all warmongering. The Legionnaires took part in some more peaceful endeavours, one of which was the building of a road between Boufarik and Douera, which was known as the Legion's Road for years afterwards.

But the gift of a new road could hardly assuage the discontent of those who had been ruthlessly conquered and constant vigilance against Arab insurrection was the Legion's lot. For nearly a decade it was forced to cross and recross Algeria, over and over again, to keep the peace by force of arms. Building forts and keeping roads and routes open was as important as dealing severely with rebels. Finally, all were subjugated save for the freedom fighters of Kabylia, hardy mountain men who had resisted all attempts to conquer or civilise them since Roman times.

Leading the Legionnaires, his looks as dark and exotic as the Arabs' themselves, was Mayne Amyan, Captain of the Dark Battalion, so called because of its secret work in spying and vanguard missions. Captain Amyan had acquitted himself bravely in sixteen such secret missions for the Legion, and had been awarded the Military Medal. He considered it the crowning glory of his five-year military career.

Born of a half-French, half-Arab mother, and an Irish-American father, the Captain was something of a hybrid but was not alone in that. The Legion was awash with such crossbreeds. He bore his father's surname but was not entitled to it as his parents had not been married.

For the first twelve years of his life he suffered hellishly for his lack of legal parentage. His nickname in the village to the north of Algiers where he was raised had been 'The Bastard'. Until that age, he was schooled as an Arab, raised and treated as one, finding no comfort in the fact that others who were illegitimate did not receive such castigation. It was his infidel blood that was hated and feared in that insular place. His skin was a little lighter, his eyes a golden hazel colour, flecked with blue-green, and he was shunned for it. The villagers thought he might produce terrifying *jinns* out of his sleeves, or cast the evil eye upon them.

Two days before his twelfth birthday, his mother died. She had not been strong since his birth and there had been money for only a meagre diet, lacking in nourishment. No one had come to aid her in her last hours and Amyan had nursed her himself, wondering why he could

51

not weep as she gasped out her last breath, her fingers gripping his hands as if she would take him with her.

For nearly a month he had hidden away in their wattle and daub hut, not daring to venture outside. His mother could not protect him now should the children crowd up on him and throw stones. He had buried her body at midnight, digging deep and piling her grave with stones to keep away the carrion and the hyena. She had said little about his father, and he now considered himself an orphan. When he had recovered a little from the shock of her death, he packed a few belongings into a bundle and prepared to leave the village. No one would stop him, he knew. All would be glad to see him go, except those who had enjoyed stoning and spitting at him.

He had the makeshift door of the hut open when the rider bore down on him. Fearing bandits, he stepped back and slammed the door. When he heard the foreign voice outside with its lilting, easy tones, he thought that it was a *jinn* come to hack him to pieces. He crouched frozen into place beneath a pile of rags as the door creaked open and the *jinn* stamped into the room.

'Hamda, where are you, Hamda? Do you remember me, honey? Damnation, where is the woman?'

Shivering with dread, Amyan recognised his mother's name but nothing else. Was this the *jinn* who had caused her death, and was he now coming for her son?

'Hamda, where are you, damn it?' To its evident annoyance, the *jinn* had trodden on some mouldering remnants of food that had lain on the floor of the hut for weeks. It was trying to scrape them from its boots and Amyan thought of dodging past, out into the fresh air and safety. Then the dust and stink of the rags got the better of him and he sneezed helplessly with a force that would have sent him reeling had he been standing upright.

Within seconds, the *jinn* had him by the scruff of his neck, tugging him out of the mess of rags and staring at him with fierce blue eyes that seemed to sear his face and body.

'You are Hamda's son?' The man was talking in Arabic and so Amyan could reply.

'Allah defend me! I am Hamda's son,' he quavered.

'And where is she? I sent a message that I was returning. Did she not get it?'

'My mother died two full moons past, *Effendi*.'

From terror, or perhaps from relief at finding that he was not going to be cut into shreds, tears had filled Amyan's eyes, tears for his mother that he had been unable to shed until that moment. He wept and wailed and sobbed, while the man looked at him askance, his fair eyebrows creased in annoyance.

'A cry baby,' he sneered. 'Jesus, Mary and Joseph, my son's a cry baby!' Then he relaxed his hold on Amyan's robe and the boy collapsed to the floor, still sobbing.

'When you've stopped that wailing, you can tell me your name and how she died.'

While he waited, the man who was not a *jinn* but Amyan's father sat at the door of the hut and smoked a long-stemmed white clay pipe, as if seeking solace from its contents. Finally, Amyan was ready to speak.

'I am called The Infidel Bastard,' he gulped, his throat tight from crying.

'That's no name, boy. What did your mother call you?'

'Yusuf, *Effendi*.'

'That's no name for any son of mine! My grandfather was born in Tipperary but he made his home in Maine, and that's what we're going to call you, boy – M–A–Y–N–E – just a mite of a change so that people will see we can think for ourselves. Now, how did your mother die, and why are you living in this hovel? Tell me, did she not get the money I sent?'

'Money?' Mayne did not know what the man was talking about.

'Did she not speak of me to you?'

'I knew only that my father was not one of the faithful, and that I was hated for it!' Mayne glared at the blond stranger.

'So the cry baby has some spirit, thanks be to Mary! Look, boy, I sent payments regularly, as I promised her I would when I left. I wrote twice yearly and sent the money with carriers. Did you never see one of them arrive and give money to your mother?'

'Never.'

'Jesu.' The man sighed gustily. 'And she never told you that I would return for you both one day?'

'No.' The boy's mouth trembled slightly, but his eyes were dry now. He would never weep again, he vowed in that moment. Let others weep, not he.

'I have been prospecting for gold. Do you know what gold is, boy?' Mayne shook his head. 'I wanted to make your mother rich and dress her in silks and pearls. I have them with me in my saddlebags, and an outfit for you, boy, a proper shirt and jacket and breeches, and a hat and boots like American boys wear. Jesu, I had not expected this.'

And then it was time for Daneyard Amyan to weep. He lost himself in grief, sitting slumped against the door, impervious to the boy's attempt to soothe him by raising a doubtful hand towards his father's blond hair.

Before an hour had passed, the boy was washed and dressed in the strange, ill-fitting suit and the clumsy, heavy boots that sagged from his toes like weights. Daneyard had not expected his son to be so scrawny and small, but then he had not known that he had been half starved for years. The hat fell off repeatedly and was eventually returned to the saddle bag. In its place Mayne wore a scarf, swathed Beduin fashion. One day he would learn to wear a hat without thinking twice about it, but that day had yet to come.

Everyone had gathered to watch the *kaffir* take his son

away. No one spoke; no one bade them goodbye. The man held his back very straight as he rode, his blond head high, and Mayne found himself emulating the proud posture, even if he was sitting behind his father on the same horse and had to clutch his hard stomach to prevent himself from falling.

The sea journey nearly killed him. It seemed to go on for years, and Amyan believed himself condemned to the Muslim hell. He moaned that he was dead, that the *jinns* were choking him, that he wanted his mother – but there was only Daneyard to soothe and cajole him, to bathe his feverish body with cold, wet cloths or fetch the bowl when his son retched again. The worst was over within three weeks when somehow Amyan adjusted to the ship's rolling motion. Malnourished and weak as he was, he swore that he would never suffer like this again, that he would find out how his father could weather stormy seas and arduous desert journeys as if they were nothing. What had forged that tall, hard body and that steely spirit?

When he asked his father this, Daneyard burst out laughing.

'You would say Allah, my boy, but I say the good Lord made me as I am.'

'But there must be something that you have done, Papa. Did you pray in a special way to be like you are? Did you eat special food?'

'Son, I did neither, as far as I know. A good diet, yes, that is essential, but a thousand men may eat the same diet and each one turn out differently.'

'Was it special prayers then?' The boy waited eagerly for his father's reply.

'No, not special, just the usual Catholic ones that I have been teaching you to say at night.'

'Papa, you told me that Catholics do not believe in forn-fornic-ashun.'

'Yes, I did say that, son.'

55

'And you told me that forn-fornic-ashun was a man and a woman having a child out of wedlock.'

'Yes, that's right.' Daneyard knew what the boy was getting at, but he let him struggle on, trying to explain himself in a mixture of Arabic and English. For all his puniness, he was a bright, quick child. Indulging him now would not help him to make the massive adjustment to a new language and a new life in America.

'Papa, were you and Mama in wedlock when I was born?'

'Your Mama would not marry me, son, and that's the truth of it. She said I was a *kaffir* and she would go to Hell if she married me. I had hoped that she would agree to the ceremony when we reached America and she saw how good life could be there.'

Daneyard paused for a moment, his voice choked with emotion. 'You will like your new home, Mayne. It's what we call a ranch, with horses on it. We shall sit beneath the trees and watch the sun coming up or going down, and you shall ride your own horse. Blueberry cakes and corn on the cob and big beef steaks will soon fatten you up! One day you will be as tall as your papa – all the Amyans are tall. They say that the sky and the stars are in our blood. We're always reaching up you see, searching for bigger and better things.'

Mayne was silent for a while, letting his father's words sink in. Then he tugged at Daneyard's sleeve and said, 'Will they call me infidel bastard in Maine, Papa, like they did in the village? Will you stop them from throwing stones at me?'

Daneyard flinched as if a stone had struck him, and then he pulled the boy close and muttered through gritted teeth that he would kill anyone who tried to harm an inch of his boy.

The smells and sounds and hubbub of their first days in Maine would stay with Amyan forever. He had never seen forests, or such wild country before. Everywhere he looked there were trees. He despaired of ever feeling at home there, for the people were tall and fair and either spoke in the easy, rolling, lilting way of his father, or in a strange, fast-spoken language that he could not decipher. His father said that it was French.

They worshipped the Catholic Lady and her Son, and at first Mayne was scared of them, the sweet-faced Lady with the tearful eyes and the bonny, smiling child in her lap. He feared the statue might suddenly come alive and leap out at him. Gradually he learned the full story of Mary and Jesus and the Father in Heaven, and came to accept if not to love them. Secretly, in his heart of hearts, he yearned for the harsher creed of Allah, the one true God, but it was better that no one knew that. He learned early on to be secretive, a lesson that would stand him in excellent stead in later years.

There was a memorial service for his mother at which everyone patted his head or squeezed his hand, especially the women. In their extravagant silk gowns, and bonnets with enormous brims into which silk flowers were stuck, they looked like herbaceous borders on legs. While others pretended to mourn a woman they had never known, Amyan stood beside his father and laughed inside to think that two of the herbaceous borders were in urgent pursuit of his father. He loathed them both. Now that everyone knew that Daneyard was free, they were scheming to marry him off.

Miriam Carlyle smelled like a rose garden, but Amyan did not like her for all that. She beamed and nodded at him and patted his hand with hers, murmuring of becoming his dear Mama, but he always pulled away. He might be small for fourteen, but he was not going to be pawed around by foreign women.

Annabelle Dilworth, Dolly to her mother and sister, was very pretty. She had bright blonde curls and smiling blue eyes, but she too hugged Mayne uninvited and begged him to have a word with his father on the subject of her becoming his Mama. For answer, he curled his lip and ran off to mount his horse. They galloped off into the forest and did not return for a day and a night.

He met the search party as the moon shone white in an ebony sky, lighting all beneath it. He heard the men's voices calling his name and did not want to go to them. He wanted to stay free, out in the wilderness. He did not want another mother, nor did he want to grow up.

A few days later his father took him aside.

'I have only seen you cry once for your late mother, God rest her soul, but I think you loved her deeply, Mayne, and the hurt of losing her is still inside you, festering.'

Mayne hung his head. How would he know whether that was true or not? He knew nothing. He was an ignorant infidel bastard.

'You cannot speak of it to your own Papa? Then let me tell you, son, you are still mourning your mother yet you don't say any prayers for her. You never go to the church except when I force you to, and you skip your prayers at night unless I superintend you. I know it is not the Muslim custom to make a big thing out of death, but you are part Amyan, remember, and there are bound to be feelings inside you that you inherited from me and our forebears. If I were you, son, I would try a few prayers for your mother and get myself to the church more often. When the day comes that you have to choose a wife, she'll not be wanting a man who shuns God.'

Mayne was stunned. Choose a wife? Never! He wanted the freedom to go his own way. Wives were women who were ignored and neglected and left behind, like his mother had been. Any woman who married him would be treated just like that. It was a lesson he had learned well, branded deep into his heart.

The years passed and outwardly he became the archetypal American youth. He could ride any horse; survive long weeks alone in the beautiful wild forests.

58

When he was there he became Yusuf again, a wild boy without master or discipline, in tune with the earth and skies, the land and the wild animals that roamed it. He would not kill a beast, however dangerous, unless it threatened one of his father's horses, and then only with regret. He considered himself the interloper on the animals' territory. They had every right to behave as nature intended them to.

He had grown to feel affection for his adopted homeland, alien though its climate was, adjusting in time to the long winters with their flaying winds and eye-blotching blizzards. He enjoyed the crackle and wince of ice beneath his boot, the dense muffled silences of the snow-covered wastes. There was nobility and grandeur in the distant view of white-peaked mountains; sudden piercing joy in the sight of a dart of glowing fur against the pervading whiteness, the sombre, echoing howl of the wolf.

Summers were all too brief, fitful and almost accidental, redolent with the odour of fish in the seasonal obsession with the catch. This was the time for lobster, sweet and succulent, followed by his favourite blueberry pie baked with a thick, tan-coloured crust.

The blaze of summer was all the sweeter for its shortness, the bright days punctuated by the rasp of the saw and the crashing timber of pine and fir. Mayne's father had money invested in sawmills as well as the fishing industry, but the savage winters put paid to both pursuits for part of the year.

Standing over a dead mountain lion one day, looking down at its velvety pelt, snarling mouth and fierce teeth, Mayne felt the tears welling in his eyes. He was alone and could have cried, but he fought the impulse back. Tears were irrational. What good did they do a man? A woman could get what she wanted with them, and frequently did, but not a man. He had filled this superb creature with bullets only to save the young foal now

59

lying, panting and shocked, a few feet away from him.

Was it his own wild nature that he saw in the lion? The hair on the back of his neck stood up and he looked cautiously around him. He could sense another cat, the dead one's mate, perhaps. The ridge of smooth, buff-coloured rock ahead was obviously their home and he the intruder.

The horses were restive, whinnying and stamping their hooves. He'd have a stampede on his hands if he did not take care. He scanned the rocks and saw it, a smaller cat, honey-coloured; a female without her male, just like his mother had been.

The tears dried in his eyes. Naturally women suffered; it was their lot. His right to a father had been denied him by his mother. She had chosen to stay in her home village, living as an outcast, and he an outcast with her.

Because she had refused to marry Daneyard, their son could never inherit Dane's Way. One day he would have to stand by and watch as a half-brother took over the ranch and the land, and the beautiful horses of Arabian descent that populated it. One of those wretched, rose-scented women would produce the half-brother when his father had decided which one he would marry, and that would be the end of Mayne Amyan's sovereignty. He could stay on as overseer, however, for his father had told him that such a provision would be in his will, and there would be a sum of money sufficient to keep him and a wife in comfort for their lifetime.

'I shall not be marrying,' Mayne had announced gruffly.

'Young men sometimes say that but, believe me, you will one day. When you do, you can have the ranch house out by the yellow rock – I shall make sure it is all legal, son.' Daneyard had paused to puff on his long-stemmed pipe, clouds of smoke wreathing his head.

'I shall not need it.' Mayne did not want to think of his father's death. There was still the acute but unacknowledged pain of his mother's dying. The thought of death left him terrified and helpless. Whenever there was mention of it, he became gruff and rude and cold.

Daneyard covertly examined his boy through the clouds of tobacco smoke. He was growing taller and had filled out. His skin looked more sun-burned than Arab but his eyes were a strange colour, hazel, oddly flecked with blue and green. Where the hell the boy had got those, Daneyard could not say. He seemed to recall Hamda saying something about her having French blood. She had been the offspring of an Arab girl and a French soldier, she believed. Perhaps that was where the blue-green flecks originated? Not that it mattered – the boy was his now and would remain so.

On the day that his father married Annabelle Dilworth, Mayne stood in the little wooden church and thought of the cat he had killed, that magnificent beast dead at his feet, and seriously considered shooting Annabelle Dilworth. Why not? Even dead, the cat was worth ten thousand of that greedy, conniving bitch.

In his mind's eye, he conjured up an image of Annabelle Dilworth being attacked by a mountain lion, screaming as the great curved claws tore into her face and neck, and blood spurted out to stain her wedding gown. The cat bit and scored and scraped and very soon she was lying on the floor, a blood-soaked pulp. Mayne grinned then, and everyone thought that he was happy to have a new mother. He kept on grinning throughout the dancing and feasting afterwards, even when his new mother asked him to dance with her.

Everyone clapped as they danced around the barn. Then, as the music halted and Annabelle Dilworth beamed up at him, he swept her out through the doors to the cloud-hung darkness outside where he kissed her as a man would kiss his new bride. Horrified, she squirmed and slapped him in disgust but he would not let go. He was aroused, fiercely and obviously. There was fear and

61

dismay in her eyes as he pushed against her thighs, wanting to tear away her skirts and enter her, take her for his own, make his son hers so that one day his own child would inherit what he could never have.

Finally she freed herself, pushing him away with loathing.

'Mayne Amyan, you must never come near me again, d'you hear? Blessed Mother, if your father ever found out about this he'd beat you until you screamed! You dumb head – you stupid, ignorant dumb head! Now you've spoiled everything!'

He cared nothing for her feelings or his betrayal of his father. He had shown her that he was not a child to be pawed and manipulated. He was seventeen, and should have been heir to Dane's Way. The bitterness festered inside him, stinging, lacerating, blighting his life. It had taken the sweetness from him, the promise of the good-natured, easy-going man that he might have been, and in its place was an ache for vengeance and the determination to make everyone suffer for what he had lost.

He had expected some sort of retribution from his father, but none came. Then he realised that Annabelle had not spoken and he thought he knew why she had stayed silent: she was afraid of him. The realisation had made him exceedingly happy, and blind to the truth that Annabelle genuinely cared for his father and wanted nothing more than to make a warm and happy home for the man who had spent all his life adventuring round the world, and the boy who had been raised in harrowing circumstances through no fault of his own.

Annabelle was thirty and had waited eight years for Daneyard to settle down and face the truth that his exploring days were over. He was nearly sixty when he finally married, and what a man of thirty could manage on horseback in the harsh and arduous Maine climate could not be done by one feeling the first twinges of approaching old age. Lovingly, Annabelle devised remedies for his aches and pains, and cooked healthy, wholesome food to strengthen him. Daneyard had a very sweet tooth and had fallen into the bad habit of snatching a sugared cookie or a handful of fudge candies instead of sitting down to a proper snack. As a result, his teeth had suffered. The worst of his toothache was lulled by the determined application of clove oil but it was obvious that a tooth would have to be pulled eventually.

'You cannot live in a stupor of alcohol and crushed cloves for the rest of your life, my darling,' Annabelle scolded him lovingly. 'You will have to go into Draper and have that tooth taken out, or its badness will spread and harm you.'

'Have it pulled, you mean?' Daneyard queried.

'Is there any other way of removing a bad tooth?'

'I don't fancy that, honey.'

'Fancy or not, you will have to do it! Otherwise it will be an inflammation, and the doctor ordering you to bed. Is that what you want?'

Daneyard feared being bedridden slightly more than he feared having a tooth pulled and so, grumbling and complaining bitterly, he prepared for the journey. Mayne was to drive him in the carriage because he could not tolerate the jolting of a horse while his tooth was throbbing so painfully.

Annabelle packed them food for the short journey, avoiding Mayne's eyes as she had done since the wedding dance, and then they set out with Daneyard driven in the carriage as smoothly as Mayne and Old Mary, their most peaceable grey, could manage.

The pulling of that tooth was to change their lives. None of them would ever be the same again, and Annabelle would have the rest of her days to regret the way she had ordered her new husband to the surgeon's.

Daneyard turned deathly white and lost a large

amount of blood, but that was nothing out of the way for it turned out that the tooth had an abnormally deep and twisted root. On the journey home, he lay down in the back of the carriage, urging Mayne to rouse him when they were within sight of Dane's Way for he wanted to sit up beside his son as they entered the gates. He did not want Annabelle seeing him lying weak and pale like an invalid.

Mayne obeyed, as he always obeyed his father, and Daneyard was sitting up and smiling as Annabelle ran out to welcome him back. He seemed lively at supper-time, taking a tot of rum to ease the pain in his gum, but for the next two days was pale and morose and not his usual self at all.

At the end of that week, Annabelle knew for sure what she had suspected for the last two weeks: she was to have a child. She wanted to tell Daneyard but feared Mayne's reaction and so kept back the news.

At three in the morning, on the Saturday before Daneyard's sixtieth birthday, 4 June, he woke with a jolt to find that he could not move his left arm and leg.

A light sleeper, Annabelle awakened instantly at her husband's start. When she lit the lamp she saw at once his staring eyes, the twisted mouth and the motionless limbs. Sweat broke out on his forehead as he tried vainly to move.

'Lie still, my sweetheart. Lie still and we'll get the doctor.'

'Noth' b'done. Noth' b'done,' Daneyard mumbled, feeling as if his mouth were full of pebbles.

Clutching his cold, paralysed hand, Annabelle cried out that she would not listen to such nonsense. He would get well, she would see to that.

Mayne rode for the doctor, galloping through the night, the shadows from the hills drowning out the pallid moonglow. He rode solidly for four hours, only to find that the doctor was out delivering twins forty miles away. Having no option, he borrowed a fresh horse and went after the doctor, but on his arrival it was obvious that the mother was in desperate condition and could not be left.

Striding through the pine trees that surrounded the clapboard house, Mayne battled with himself. He loved his father and did not want him to die. Yet if he lived he would give that fortune-hunting bitch an heir for Dane's Way while he, Mayne, would remain nothing more than an overseer for the rest of his life. If his father died now, then Mayne would have a secure, respectable position, and no one would dare look down on him again.

That was what he feared most: the loss of power and position, the humiliating reversion to having nothing – no name, no rank, no inheritance. For this prospect he had only his mother to blame. He felt no compassion for her in her desperate choice: she had put her religion before her son's legitimacy, loving her creed more than her child.

Mayne almost leapt out of his skin when the doctor stepped up behind him.

'There are some nights when I wish I'd become a gold prospector or a railroad builder – anything! – rather than have the power of life and death in my hands only to find that it's no power at all. Nothing I've learned was able to save her.'

There were tears in the doctor's eyes and he did not seem concerned that Mayne would see them.

'She died?'

'Yes, and the infants, too, a boy and a girl. Born premature, too small to survive. No lung power, no vitality. She was only seventeen, poor girl. Jesus Christ, but sometimes I wonder what it's all for and why the hell I ever chose this profession!' Then, as if remembering why Mayne was there, he said, 'What's wrong at the house? Not your mother?'

Mayne flinched at his use of that title but said steadily,

65

'No, my father. He can't move. He woke early this morning and could barely speak. He had a tooth pulled a few days ago, could that have caused it?'

She made him go, he was thinking. *She* forced him to have that tooth out and now it has killed him. A whiteness like snow blindness descended on him, a void where no emotion or hope could exist.

'A tooth, you say? No, like as not it's the apoplexy, lad. It comes to us all, and your father's no longer young and has led a tough life, by all accounts.'

'What is apoplexy?' The bright void was growing, sweeping in and around him, numbing his hands and feet and making his skin creep.

'A fragility in the blood vessels of the brain. If one bursts, blood pumps out and causes the paralysis. Shame about your father – such a vigorous man.'

The rest of the journey was silent, the doctor half-dozing at times and having to be jolted back to wakefulness by Mayne before he fell out of the saddle. It was early evening when they reached Dane's Way. Its master was already dead. He had died at four-thirty that afternoon, in his wife's arms.

Chapter Five

'God help the tribe who has no seer.'

Zahra thought of the words of Khalid ibn Khalid as she took her seat for the first audiences of the day. The old man had died some weeks ago and no one had stepped forward to take his place. Usually, there was a boy who would display signs of the gift and then the seer would raise the boy himself, teaching and guiding him, but there had been no such child this time, and there were still no signs of one. If a tribe had no seer, how could it read the omens and portents, and defend itself against the oppressive evil of the desert spirits who were constantly seeking to overthrow and destroy those who were undefended?

Zahra had held some twenty audiences now and her confidence was growing. She had not known what to expect when she began. It was possible that there would be distrust of the young female who had taken the place of Husain and Mishaal. It was customary for the closest male relative to inherit and, if Husain had possessed one, then he would have been Amir now in her place. Amiras who ruled in their own right were few and far between, so how could the people know what to say to her, or she to them?

Husain had been treated with reverence by his peoples. They would sink to the ground before him and kiss the hem of his robe before telling him of their troubles. Mishaal had never been lost for words in her life, and as the Beduin had considered her an immortal who had fallen from the stars to deliver them, she had suffered no problems because of her sex. Most Beduin women were accustomed to taking a place in the background where they would quietly go about their tasks while the truly important business was handled by the men. Despite her enlightened upbringing, Zahra knew that all the women who came to her now would be similarly accustomed to a female taking the lower place, and thus might find it strange to be consulting a woman.

Her stiffness during the first two or three audiences had been nothing more than nerves. What would they think of her? How would they react? No one was more surprised that she when she discovered that she was skilled at solving people's problems, having a way of cutting through the tangled circumstances surrounding them to lay bare the basic difficulty. And, having given some dozen men and six or seven women a clear way out of the trouble in which they had found themselves, Zahra felt altogether more relaxed about her own position. It was the loftiness that she did not like, the being held above others when she felt that she had done nothing to deserve it. She wanted with all her heart to serve and help, and now she was beginning to see a way that this could be done.

This morning her first supplicant was a middle-aged woman with a downturned mouth and deep-set acquisitive eyes. Zahra knew what the woman was like before she spoke. She was one who had spent a lifetime gathering possessions and putting them before others.

'Ya Sitti,' the woman began, her voice wheedling. 'I am here because my family have been cruelly unkind to me. My son took a third wife and she does not like me. There have been harsh words and my belongings have been pilfered. My best robes and my jewels have been taken for the new wife, and she sneers at me when she wears them. *Ya Sitti*, I no longer have any standing in my son's eyes and because of this, others are treating me harshly, too.'

'I am sorry to hear this.' Zahra bided her time, letting her first impressions of the woman harden. There was something else besides greed and self-seeking reaching her, but she could not immediately identify it. 'It is always sad to hear that a son does not honour his mother after all that she has done for him.'

The woman did not rush to tell Zahra of all she had done for her son. Instead, she blinked rather uneasily and compressed her thin lips.

'You may return to your son and give him this message from me: the Amira Zahra wishes to inform him that a loving and caring mother must never be dishonoured, or her belongings taken from her without her permission. Do you have that message clearly? Tell him that, exactly as I phrased it, with particular emphasis on "loving" and "caring".' Zahra smiled benignly.

The woman had changed colour and her tongue was darting in and out of the corner of her downcurved mouth.

'*Ya Sitti*,' she breathed, 'I cannot tell that to my son.'

'You cannot tell him? Why not?' Zahra leaned forward as if shocked.

'I cannot, *Ya Sitti*, because – because I have not been a loving and caring mother to my son!' The woman's head was lowered now and she was twisting her hands abstractedly. Zahra had never seen anyone so restless at an audience: the mouth, the head and hands, shifting and darting feverishly.

'You have not?' Zahra queried, leaning forward in her seat.

'I have not, *Ya Sitti*. I – I abandoned the boy when he was a child. I – I left him with a stranger while I went to – to find work.'

69

'If you were poor, then Allah will have forgiven you for desiring to make money to keep the boy.'

'I – I never did send any money, *Ya Sitti*.' Now the words were gushing out. 'For ten years, I did not send word to him or money for his keep. The woman with whom I had left him died of a fever and he was put out on the streets by her cousin who wanted to sell her house.'

'But you searched for the boy until you found him, and you were truly sorry for your errors and made it all up to him?'

'No, *Ya Sitti*, I – I did not even know what had happened until I met a relative by accident in the city and he told me that he had been searching for the boy himself when he heard what had happened. It was a year before he was found and he – he had been misused by those who had stolen him.' The woman's hands were twisting frantically now and a nervous tic in her cheek was jumping so that her eye gathered into crinkles and then fell open again.

'How old was he by then?'

'Thirteen and a half, *Ya Sitti*.'

'I see. And how had he been misused?'

'He – I cannot tell you, *Ya Sitti*, it is not decent!'

'He must have suffered terribly, thinking that he was deserted and unloved, and then being misused by villainous strangers.'

'Yes, *Ya Sitti*, you are right! Oh, it is all my fault and I deserve all that is meted out to me. Allah, forgive me!' The woman threw herself full-length before Zahra and kissed the hem of her robe repeatedly.

'If you will return to your son's home and give him the love and care that you denied him in his youth, then I am sure that he will stop being harsh with you and no more of your belongings will be taken.'

'Allah bless you, *Ya Sitti*, for you have taken a great burden from my heart! Allah bless you!'

When the woman had gone, Zahra felt exhausted and

yet elated at the same time. Could it truly be so easy to help others, or was she treading a dangerous path in thinking that she had the gift?

That night, Freyha looked at her so piercingly that she was forced to comment on it.

'Have I grown two heads that you stare at me so keenly, Freyha?'

'You are becoming a woman, my sweet one. The past few weeks have made you blossom like herbs after rain.'

'Only herbs, not radiant white roses?' Zahra's green eyes twinkled.

'I say herbs because they have healing and curing properties, my heart, and roses, while they refresh the soul, have no use beyond that.'

'If I can refresh one soul a day, then I will be more than content.' Zahra sipped her orange flower sherbet absently.

'Yes, but refreshing does not cure, and you, my heart, have the gift of Solomon.'

The sherbet jolted in Zahra's hands and a spreading stain darkened her terracotta-coloured woollen robe.

'The gift of Solomon! Allah, but you love me too much, Freyha, and raise me to the dizzy heights. I am no Solomon.'

'Who else would see into people's hearts, into their deepest fears and self-deceptions, and show them the mirror of their soul?'

'Nonsense! I merely watch them carefully and see the truth in their faces.'

'If the truth is there so plainly, then why have others not seen it? That so-called mother who came here bewailing her son's mistreatment: I vow that she had never admitted to herself for a second what a cruel woman she had been, and yet within minutes she was blabbing it all to you.'

'It was because she had kept it inside herself overlong and that was the moment for it to free itself.'

71

'No, my heart, it was not that.' Freyha was busily dealing with the sherbet stain in her practical manner so did not see the expression on Zahra's face.

'Then what was it, Freyha?' Zahra's heart was pounding in her chest and a fierce light seemed to burn behind her eyes.

'I have looked all these months for some sign of it in you,' Freyha was saying, sitting back on her heels to survey her charge. 'I thought, "She must have it for she is their child and how could it have escaped her? He was the wisest and she the most blessed, so their daughter must have inherited something of it." And yet I saw nothing, and I was heart sad that Allah, in His wisdom, had not gifted you with what a young Commander of the Faithful most needs.'

'And what does he need, this Commander of the Faithful?'

'Your mother had it. She was a visionary. They say that during her days alone in the desert with Husain, they saw the most miraculous mirages and it was Mishaal who caused Allah to send them. She was the instrument through which He worked to bring redemption to the Land of Mirages.'

'She never told me anything about the mirages.'

'If you have the gift, and I think it is growing in you now, then you will find out one day without another's help.'

'Oh, Freyha, your imaginings are wild today.'

'If I am right, and I think I am, then you will learn, my heart.' Freyha nodded vehemently, then added on an entirely practical note, 'This gown will have to be changed or it will stain permanently.'

Zuli was growing thin and her face was pale. Mahmed wished that he knew what he could do to help her, but he was lost. The truth was that he could not keep away from her tent. Because it had become difficult to find

72

hours alone with her during the day, he had given his younger daughters their own tent and could now stay overnight with Zuli when he wished.

He loathed himself for it, but he was powerless to resist the terrible temptation. When he stepped into her tent, he was stepping back in time and it was Mahia who waited in the lamplit gloom for him, Mahia who held out her arms to pull him close and kiss him with her rose-scented mouth.

Zuli seemed uncritical of him; she did not blanch or fight any more. She seemed to have accepted her new rôle, and for that he was grateful. He had loaded her with gifts: new robes and jewels; painted caskets that smelt of sandalwood; her own delicate porcelain coffee set, very old and rare, with fragile dishes from which to sip the coffee. Yet she was losing weight. He could feel her delicate bones when he lay on her, and that worried him.

As he palmed the softness of her breasts, feathering kisses down her neck, she would respond affectionately, sighing out loud and throwing back her head. That aroused him even more so that some nights he took her before she was ready. He could not help himself; he was accursed. This was how it had to be. He had no strength to stop himself.

When she wept and bit her lip, he would soothe her and rub her little body until she regained heart. He loved the smell of her for, like all young girls, she liberally applied her favourite scent, the rose oil that he brought her from Abeesha.

Tonight, he was in need of solace as he crept into her tent. He did not know when the Amira Zahra was going to give her consent to their marriage, and he felt insulted. Men were making fun of him because he had spoken of the marriage as if it would come to pass any day, and now it was said that the Amira had changed her mind. In the world he might feel a miserable failure, but

73

in Mahia's arms he was the greatest warrior hero ever born.

Zuli was coughing in her sleep when he reached her, and he woke her with passionate kisses. She trembled as he pushed back her sheepskin covering and stroked her belly and thighs to coax her into desire. He could not wait; he must have the exultation that he always felt when he was joined with her.

She gave a little cry, almost a yelp, as he opened her slender legs and hooked up his robe to free his erection. He pushed himself into her roughly, eagerly, feeling the deliciously familiar sensations begin as he entered her narrow body, needing her so desperately that tears filled his eyes as he came to his savage and lonely climax.

She was weeping, too, and when he had recovered himself he saw how upset she was and felt a pang of regret.

'My fair one, why do you weep? I love you, you know that.'

'It is not right! You should not come to me like this. I am spoiled; no man will have me now. I am betrayed, Father, betrayed.'

She had never accused him like this before, and he went cold, his fingers hooked in the air, immobile.

'I will have thee, fair one. Who else do you need?'

'You are my father, not my husband! And I – I am with child. I am betrayed!' Bursting into noisy sobs, Zuli clung to her father, alternately clawing at his shoulder then kissing him on the neck.

'You are with child?' His eyes were blank.

'Yes, yes! That is what happens when men and women lie together, Father. Did you not know?'

'How shall I explain this?'

'Tell them the truth. That you lusted after your own daughter and made her big with child.' Bunching her fist, Zuli pounded it against her father's cheek, then kissed the same place penitently.

74

'I cannot do that, it would ruin you. But there is a way. You must confess the truth: you took a lover who is the father of your child.'

Zuli began to laugh hysterically. 'And where is my lover, Father, this boy who got me with child? Shall you invent him, say that he was a *jinn* who took advantage of me when I walked in the wilderness?'

'I shall think of some way out of this, *mahbub*, be assured.' Then, the first shock over, he took her slender little hand and placed it low on his belly where it began to stroke and coax as he had taught it to do, until he was erect again. Then, urgently, he pulled her beneath him, gasping her mother's name as he always did in the moment's heat, spilling his seed inside her in mindless, blazing ecstasy.

The hospital had become her greatest interest, taking her mind off many of her problems. Should the badgering thought come into her mind 'Shall I marry Mahmed, or not?' she would concentrate instead on the children's hospital and its patients.

The Beduin did not like physicians. They preferred to put their hopes of a cure in Allah, and treat themselves where possible. Husain had tried to coax them into Western ways, but there had been great resistance. It was not easy to convert a people who believed that sickness and accidents came from the evil eye rather than physiological causes. They would set one another's broken bones with dexterity, and yet the healed bones would often be crooked afterwards. The lavish use of camel dung and urine, and charms to defend against the evil eye, were the mainstay of their medical care.

Knowing all this, and having seen the results of such 'care', Zahra had ordered the building of the children's hospital. At first there had been warnings that it would stay empty, for what Beduin would bring his or her child to a place which had a permanent roof and beneath which the child must be left? The Beduin cared for their own; they did not leave them in the hands of strangers.

Zahra had reassured the doubters. Nurses would be selected from Beduin women who were without family and were willing to tend sick infants and children. Messages would be sent out amongst the tribes that such were needed and she herself would choose from their ranks, paying the women's keep and supporting the hospital and its inmates with her own money. Should anyone wish to offer sheep or camels in payment for the recovery of a child the gift would be accepted, the beasts sold and the *drâhim* put into the hospital's coffers.

'The hospital will stay empty, *Ya Sitti*,' one elderly man had warned, shaking his dry, wrinkled finger. 'No Beduin will desert his sick child.'

'If the mother or father wishes to stay and care for their child, then there will be provisions made for them to do so, but they must comply with the rules of the hospital,' Zahra said gently but firmly.

'These women who will care for the sick – what if they are of bad blood and their taint harms the children?'

'I shall select them personally, by recommendation and interview,' Zahra replied, seeing the man's mouth open to complain again and then clamp shut. He could hardly say that he thought his Amira unsuited to judge for that would be an unforgivable insult, yet there was no doubt that this was the thought in his mind; she could sense it.

'Who will heal the children?' another man asked. 'Is there to be a doctor from the city?'

'I have sent word to Abeesha and three other cities that two good doctors are required, and these too I shall interview myself.'

'They will be of the faith?'

'Of course.'

As there seemed to be no other queries, the little

76

deputation had departed and Zahra was alone at last. She was weary. The night before she had barely slept. There was a recurring dream that came sometimes twice a week and it frightened her. In it, she was standing before her peoples, all of them amassed to make obeisance to her as the new Amira and their rightful Queen. And then, as the ceremony began, there was an icy, gusting wind and her clothes were almost torn from her. She could see from the watchers' eyes that they were seeing her as she truly was, not great and regal but small and weak and scared. From this dream she would jolt awake, beaded with sweat, unsure of where she was in the darkness.

Although she was carefully building her own inner temple in which she could rest, be herself and grow strong, she still had overwhelming doubts about her worthiness and abilities.

The hospital would soon be completed, the construction work undertaken voluntarily by the hundreds of men who had answered her call. It was an hour's ride from her camp, and within easy travelling distance of other Beduin camps in the area. An oasis and four wells would provide the water it required, and within the new courtyard of the hospital was a special well of exceptionally sweet water which would be kept for the sick children.

The building was a simple one, constructed of wattle, mud and sand packed together to form a hard crust that would exclude the burning sun. Treated sheepskins would hang at the windows to keep out the flies and mosquitoes, and on the baked earth floor were placed the pallets for the children, each with its sparkling cotton sheet and a goatskin for warmth.

If the men were over enthusiastic with their skills, or lack of them, Zahra said nothing. Here and there were odd bumps and cavities in the wattle and daub, and the floor was not as smooth as it should have been, but at least the haven was almost finished. Soon, she hoped, the first patients would arrive.

She worked from dawn to sundip, day after day, overseeing the workers, ordering equipment and furnishings, examining workmanship and supplies to check that their quality was acceptable.

Then there were the interviews, which were more gruelling than she had anticipated, mainly because she knew how appalling it would be for everyone concerned if the wrong women were picked as nurses. She did not want any of the patients to be beaten or neglected, or receive no comforting when they sobbed, as sick children were apt to do.

Day after day, she interviewed the women. Only one appeared to be lacking in enthusiasm for the proposed work, yet enthusiasm was not enough. Her nurses must be honest and sincere and trustworthy, and genuinely love children. It would be madness to consider any other sort of woman.

Zahra prayed constantly for guidance and the courage to complete her first major task, and she prayed too that the people would come to the hospital and not let their children continue to suffer in the black tents.

One of the women stayed in her mind long after she had been dismissed. There was no way that she would have taken on this one, whose name was Mediha, for she had an unfortunate skin eruption that prevented her from being considered. All the same, Mediha had a pleasant manner and showed intelligence and kindliness when she was questioned.

'You say that you have had experience in nursing sick infants?'

'Yes, Ladyship, many infants. I was widowed when I was seventeen and my husband left me without money or a home. The rent had not been paid and the landlord put me out into the street. I had two choices then, Ladyship, either to find honourable employment or to –

to lower myself in a way which I could not name before you, Ladyship, for it would be offensive to your ears.'

'I am aware that these things happen, Mediha,' Zahra put in gently as the woman flushed painfully. 'Do please go on.'

'I was truly fortunate in that my neighbour's son was sick of a fever and she could not nurse him because she also was sick. She was near her time with another child and suffering badly.'

'So you nursed the sickly child?' Mediha nodded. 'And the child recovered?'

'Thanks be to Allah, he did, and it was said that I had a gift for healing the sick, but I assure you, Ladyship, I have never claimed such a gift. Whatever good fortune I have had has been given to me by the one true God and only He. I have never boasted or bragged, nor would I ever do so.'

Watching the woman, Zahra was sure that she was sincere. She was also modest, and that was admirable in itself. Yet there was the skin eruption – rough, red scales with a silvery tinge to them across the woman's face and neck, her hands, and her feet where they showed beneath the hem of her robe. Zahra had seen such eruptions once or twice before and knew that they were not contagious, but they looked so alarming. Who would wish to leave their sick child with such a disfigured woman?

'You still have employment in Abeesha?'

'I do, Ladyship. People know that I am reliable.'

'Then why did you come all this way to apply for work?'

'I am desert born, Ladyship, as were my mother and father before me. I find the city oppressive; the ways there are different, the people grow angry over nothing and find fault with the slightest unwelcome behaviour.'

'But you have a good reputation in the city, and continual employment there?' The woman nodded, and

79

Zahra felt a flood of relief. Had Mediha been restless or sharp-tongued, inexperienced or lacking in respect, then she could have dismissed her without a pang of conscience, as she had been forced to dismiss others, but she seemed eminently suitable apart from her skin condition. If there was employment for her in Abeesha, then the dismissal would not be so painful for either of them.

'Mediha, I am impressed with you, even in these few short moments that we have spoken, but I must be frank. There are many, many applicants for work in my hospital and the large majority are without present employment, or suffering intolerable living conditions from which they must escape. If I gave you a place, then I would be depriving someone of work which they sorely need. Do you understand?'

'Ladyship, it would be demeaning for me to go back to the city and say that I was not good enough to be hired by you. People would say that I am a failure at my work!'

'I doubt that, for your reputation is sound enough from what you have told me. However, there is a way you could answer them. I shall give you an official letter – no, it does not matter that you cannot read for others can – and this will confirm that I wish you to continue your work in the city where it is urgently needed. Will that satisfy you?'

She did not have to make such a gesture, but she would be happier if she did. And so was Mediha.

'Ladyship, I am honoured! A letter from you, Ladyship! You have such kindness in your heart.' The woman fell to her knees and kissed the hem of Zahra's robe, an act which always made her feel uneasy and unworthy but which she did not interrupt this time.

Spring was passing, taking with it the last of the heavy rains and the sweet refreshment of the bright green pastures, the blossoms and flowers that adorned the desert as if by some magician's spell. The Land of Mirages never suffered prolonged drought, as did other desert areas, but the rains would not be heavy again until late autumn. It did not matter as the wells were fed from underground streams, and there were plentiful oases after thirty years of Allah's providence.

One day, Zahra asked for some of the hospital well water to be brought to her so that she could taste for herself if it was as sweet as rumour had it. Finding that it was, she felt a sudden raising of her spirits. Children had fallen sick from drinking dirty and brackish water; she had seen it happen herself when she was visiting the camps of her people. Now they would have fresh water that tasted light and smooth, and it would help them to get well.

Ten more women to be seen before nightfall! Her shoulders ached and the memory of her dream came flooding back to her. She was not worthy. Soon they would all know, and her plans and dreams would be shattered.

'My heart, you should rest. Send the women away for tonight,' Freyha begged her.

'When they have walked all these miles to see me? I could not do that. Send them in one at a time, and then sit close by and we shall discuss them after they have gone.'

Two of the women were clean and neatly dressed. Zahra always looked first at their nails, because if they were dirty then it meant that the women's hands had not been properly washed for days and that displayed a careless, impious nature. Washing was commanded by the Prophet, and was always to be undertaken before the daily round of prayers. If nails were dirty, then either prayers had been neglected or the Prophet's laws ignored. Either way, the offenders were not fit to care for other people's children.

'You are called Dafaq?' she asked the first woman,

81

who nodded eagerly. 'Tell me about yourself, and why you are here.'

'I am widowed and unhappy in my brother-by-marriage's house, Highness. I have no children and they judge me on that. My late husband's sister has seven sons and it pains me to see them running about when I have none of my own.'

'Yet you wish to care for the children of women like your late husband's sister?'

Dafaq flushed and said that it would not be the same, for there would be no emotions involved.

'You would not feel compassion for the sick children then, but only stony-heartedness?' Zahra's inquisition was penetrating.

'Oh no, Highness, I would care for them with all my heart.'

'And what if your sister-by-marriage brought one of her sick children into your care at the hospital?'

'I – I would treat him the same as all the others, Highness.'

Zahra must be more tired than she knew, for she could not make up her mind about this woman. She liked the look of her, but there was confusion in her thoughts.

Freyha was at her side before she even knew that she had gone deathly pale.

'My heart, you must rest now! Woman, the Amira will see you tomorrow. Go to the tent of Hamida and you will have food and a couch for the night.'

'No, they have travelled for days to be here,' Zahra protested feebly.

'And you have been on your feet since sunrise, my heart. Now come, your couch awaits you.'

The thick white fleece had been shaken in readiness and she sank into it gratefully. She was asleep within seconds while Freyha kept watch over her.

Her mistress was killing herself with work because she did not have a husband to instruct and guide her. A husband would say 'No, you are not riding to the hospital today, you are too weary,' and she would have to obey. Women were sometimes foolish and wilful; they truly believed that they knew best and yet only harm could come of such intransigence.

Freyha knew now that she wanted the Amir Mahmed to marry her mistress. He was strong and bold; he would make her rest when she needed it and, with Allah's will, he would get her with child and then she would live like a woman should, in the soft mellow sweetness of the expectant mother. Freyha wanted that for her beloved mistress more than anything else. Marriage brought nothing but blessings to a woman, and even an Amira could not ignore her true destiny. Queen she might be but she was a woman first, and the perils of forgetting that were becoming all too obvious.

There was the risk that Mahmed would take offence at her delays and arrive in force to take her as his bride. After thirty years of peace under the rule of Husain, the people were growing restive, she had heard. The French threat was growing, for these were invaders who wished to conquer as much of the Arab lands as possible. Mahmed's forces and his famous racing camels would be vital should there be an invasion by the French or any others. She knew that instinctively although she had never been one to involve herself deeply in men's matters, for men's matters they were. She felt this despite her love for Zahra's mother who had been as wise and strong as any man.

The truth was that her daughter was not. Oh, she had the same perception, and it was growing daily, but she did not have the physical stamina nor the sheer toughness of Mishaal, and Freyha feared that she would never possess the eternal elements required of a successful Amira. It was not enough that the people loved her – and Zahra was loved, that was obvious. No, she must be able to inspire valour. Men must be willing

83

to die for her cause should there be wars or invasions. If they were not, then the invaders would snatch an undefended Land of Mirages. Freyha feared that her mistress could never inspire the deeds of courage imperative in times of battle.

Apart from the occasional half-hearted skirmish on the perimeters of their land, there had been no full-blooded battles for three decades and the Beduin warriors had grown indolent and over confident. Mahmed would rouse them to their former strength; he would drill them and test them until they were fit to defend his land and Zahra's, and then Freyha could stop her constant fretting.

A thought came into her mind which she at first dismissed. If she could send a message to Mahmed, telling him the true state of affairs – that her mistress truly wished to marry him but was assailed by doubts because of her youth, and that he must visit again and woo her as tenderly as any lover – then the marriage could take place before the summer was out.

Curling her fist, Freyha pressed it to her mouth, her heart racing. Dare she do it, over her mistress's head? If she swore Mahmed to secrecy, then it might work. Zahra would not know that her handmaiden had sent for him.

Her sleeping mistress had the smooth, serene face of a child who slept without a care, and that was how Freyha wished it to continue. She was positive that Husain and Mishaal would approve of their daughter's union with the strong and handsome Mahmed, and that she would be working as their agent in encouraging the union.

And that was the moment when she decided that the message must be sent, for all their sakes. It was only later that she realised, to her dismay, that she had come to her decision without praying to Allah. Then she tried to pray regarding the wisdom of her decision, but learned nothing. All the same, she was confident that what she was doing was right, and that Zahra's mother and father would have done the same were they still alive.

Creeping out of Zahra's tent, she went to the scribe and told him what she wished him to write. When he had written, she gave the scroll to Jabal, her cousin's son, and commanded him to ride to Mahmed's camp with all haste, in the service of his royal mistress.

Chapter Six

'You killed him!'

Mayne faced his stepmother, his mouth twisted with rage. He was tall now, nearly six feet, and broad across the shoulders where strength was vital. His fists were bunched, muscles knotted in readiness to strike out.

Annabelle, swathed in black, felt her mouth quiver involuntarily. She had been without her beloved Dane-yard for nearly a month now and this rage had been simmering in his son all that time. Feeling it like a palpable barrier between them, she had slept badly and barely eaten. She still had not revealed that she was with child and she dreaded the time when it would begin to show.

What would he do, this vituperative young man with his foreign temperament and vengeful ways? She had made sure that she was never alone with him. Katy or Molly were always close by whatever she did, stolid, resolute and devoted maids, but she had not told them that she was with child either, because she feared that word of it would get to him, the one she feared.

In his father's will, he had been given life rights to a home and a position at Dane's Way, and he had made sure that everyone knew it. He had also told anyone who would listen that Annabelle was there only by his indulgence and that he could drive her out whenever he chose.

Now it had come, the first accusation, and she could barely believe her ears. Shaken and sick at heart, she could not reply for long moments, and when she did, her own words horrified her.

'You vicious bastard, leave me alone! Do you think you helped to make his last years happy, with your scowls and your moods?'

The hazel eyes darkened, filled with murderous fury, and Annabelle stepped hastily back, feeling a small bone in her foot click at the sudden movement. But she would not weaken, she would not!

Uncurling his fists, he grasped her arms and jerked her backwards and forwards until the pins in her hair began to shake loose and the room was swaying about her.

'No one calls me a bastard, you bitch! You fortune-hunting, scheming bitch! You were after his money, but it should have been mine, all of it. By God, I've earned it!'

'By law it's mine, and thank God for it. What do you know of running a homestead and the companies? You're just a brat – a lawless, violent brat!'

She had expected him to strike her but instead, to her alarm, he clamped his mouth on hers. She could feel her fear and anger melting and melding into longing and desire for him. She could not fight it. It was shocking and scandalous and yet she fell against him greedily, hungrily, their bodies crushed so close that their hipbones jarred. He was roused as he had been when he kissed her on her wedding day, and so was she, running with moisture and aching for his entrance, longing to feel him punishingly deep inside her.

Then when she had abased herself, let him know the truth of her crazy longing, he thrust her away from him and glared into her face.

'I called you bitch and I meant it. Now I can add another word: whoring bitch. You are a whoring bitch, Annabelle Amyan. Any man could have you and that is why I shall not.'

Then he was gone, vanished outside into the forest wilderness that he loved, and she was left slumped against the carved chest where she had fallen.

The situation was intolerable for them both. When she lay in bed at night, instead of yearning for her lost Daneyard, whom she had truly loved, she burned for Mayne to be making love to her, even though they had insulted one another beyond all possible redemption of their relationship. She had only to think of him and the moisture began running between her thighs, hot and welcoming, and he could have had her there and then if he had come into her room.

For three weeks she barely saw him. She knew he was probably in the hut in the lower mountains where he loved to spend time in the summer, amongst the trees and the wildlife. Once she had thought him a normal boy who needed nothing more than a mother's love to make him into the honest and noble young man that Daneyard's son must surely be. But now she knew better. His other blood, the foreign taint, had taken him over and he was not to be trusted.

She had never seen him mourn for his father; he had not gone to the funeral, and had not been seen in the church. He had wanted all the wealth and power that his position as Daneyard's son would give him, but there had been nothing deeper. He did not have a heart. If he accused and insulted her, then it was because he was vicious by nature and loved to taunt and distress.

She had hired some new hands, and there was always a man nearby on guard these days. When Mayne returned from the woods, he would get a shock. He would never be alone with her again, even if secretly she burned for him.

Two days passed and then he rode in, taking up his place in the cabin by the yellow rock where he cleaned and swept as thoroughly as any woman and brought a narrow bed, chairs and table, crockery and curtains to turn the lone, empty cabin into a home.

On the first cold night he lit the fire, and when smoke gushed out of the chimney and he watched it twisting its way into the moonlit clouds he felt an exultation that he had never known before. This cabin was his own, his very own, and no one could take it from him. He would be here for life, year upon year upon year, and she would not be able to do anything about it. And, if he chose, one day he would have her, take her where she stood and fill her with his seed. Then his son would inherit Dane's Way, and he could die knowing that. But it would have to be soon so that she could pass the child off as Daneyard's, otherwise the plan would be useless.

In his vengeful fury he did not think of anything but getting her with child. That tormenting longing made him erect every time he thought of it. There was no one to use meanwhile, no halfbreed girls into whom he could empty himself. He burned for Annabelle, waking in the night and, in his mind's eye, going up to the house, bursting into her bedroom and taking her repeatedly until he was voided of all desire.

One night he crept into the house, but when he saw the tall, hired hand standing in the corridor outside her room, his stubby hand on his gun belt, Mayne backed away. So she had hired a guard to keep him away, the bitch. He would make her pay for that!

A few nights later, hearing a crackling in the undergrowth outside the cabin, he jolted awake and crept to the window, pushing the nose of his gun through the flap of hide that kept out the draught. There was no moon and it was some time before he saw the dark shadow approaching, creeping up to the porch. She had sent one of the hired hands to kill him!

Standing silently behind the door as it slowly swung open, he raised his gun in readiness to smash it down on the man's head – and then he saw that the figure was small and slight, and only the padded cloak it wore had given it the appearance of solidity. Instantly he clamped his hand around her mouth, tugging her close against his belly so that her buttocks pressed into his groin. There he held her, revelling in the feel of her soft, rounded body arousing him to fiery hardness.

She tried to bite him but he laughed, and when he finally freed her mouth and pulled her round to face him, his lips were on hers before she could speak. He knew what she had come for, and he was going to give it to her.

The bunk was narrow and hard but they barely noticed. He took her within seconds, and she was ready, welcoming, warm and moist. She gripped him tightly, her knees hooked around his waist. Moaning his name, she bucked against him and he lost his virginity in the most searing, mind-shaking moment of his life, thrusting into her, four, five, six times before the uncontrollable, searing orgasm took hold of him as Annabelle squirmed and clawed, gripped and squeezed him until he was drained.

They lay still for barely a few moments, and then he began again while she crooned his name, pulling his head down to hers, thrusting her hips up against his, thrilling at the lusty, primordial impulse they were sharing. She knew that she could enjoy every second without fear that he would get her with child, and he was positive that he would impregnate her this night.

She could not stop herself from going to him. She had to know what he was like, to join with him and fulfil her yearnings, but first she had seen the doctor and he had confirmed that she was three and a half months' pregnant. She had wanted to wait until the pregnancy was well advanced so that there would be no risk of Mayne thinking the child was his. She wanted to have this night and enjoy it without any unpleasant repercussions.

Five more times he had her before dawn's light, and he

was sure now that she would be with child. How could he have failed? He had put everything he had into her, and it must bear fruit. She was stupid – all women were – and he had got what he wanted. She had been unable to resist him, and no doubt there would be other nights like this when he would use her in the same fashion.

Annabelle crept back to her bedroom on shaking legs, her body stiff and sore. There were bruises on her breasts, and love bites on her neck and thighs. She had wanted him, and she had had him. Now she could go ahead with the rest of her plan.

Within the week, she would be holding the small soirée that would be attended by her neighbours and the doctor, to which Mayne, too, would be invited. There she would announce that she was in an interesting condition, as it was called for the sake of modesty, after which she would give the date of the expected birth of her child. Then she would smile at Mayne, sweetly and innocently, and tell him that he was to have the pleasure of a half brother or sister to dandle on his knee before the year was out.

She could play at revenge, too.

Silently, swiftly, in the ebony fold of night, the man snaked his way along the sandy earth, the glittering curved *khanjar* in his grasp. He was going to kill, to slaughter, to end a life, and in his mind's eye, the victim was the one who had cheated him of his birthright. Swooping, he put the *khanjar* to the astonished man's throat and plunged it deep, slicing through windpipe and artery, then letting the corpse slump to the ground so that he could move to the next man.

They were on the perimeters of Kabylia, he and his troops, the Dark Legion as they were called, and within the past half hour they had put to death twenty guards. He had trained his men in the Arab ways, the silent, secret shock tactics: the ruthless blade in the throat, or the garrot, a method brought from the depths of Arabia where men would smoke hashish until they were imbued with superhuman powers to murder. From the hashish, they had acquired their name, assassins.

He had lived amongst the Arabs for two years, going right back to his roots, immersing himself in the Arab way of life so that he could shake everything that was American from him. He never wanted to think of America again, or the twin boys who were now heirs to Dane's Way in his place.

He had smoked hashish once only, feeling no benefit from it. If men needed to dope themselves until they could kill, then let them. He could kill ruthlessly, icily, without the need of any stimulant, but there must be an excellent cause for it. He would not kill needlessly.

When he had seen enough of the Arab life, relearning the language and living on their food, he had begun to travel. Perhaps killing was not the answer, after all. Somewhere there must be what he most needed, if only he knew what that was . . .

He had tangled with women. He had enjoyed the experiences in the main but as they were all prostitutes, they expected money for his attentions. If they genuinely enjoyed his favours, he never knew. They were adept at writhing and moaning and scratching his back and saying that he was the biggest who had ever been inside them – but as they all said that, he was apt to consider it merely their selling talk. What did it matter as long as he got what he needed, that explosive fulfilment that swept the misery and tension from him so that he could breathe more easily and feel lighter of spirit for a day or two?

Dananir intrigued him more than the others. She was young and sweet-faced, and he was one of her first customers. He was not penniless, for he had his life income from Daneyard's will and it was enough to keep a man in reasonable comfort. As he wanted less than that, he had enough to buy the things that truly mattered to him and, slowly, Dananir became one of these.

She was the first woman for whom he had felt affection since his mother's death, but she was in bondage to an Arab usurer for her father's enormous debt. Her father was a gambler and owed the usurer a small fortune. Dananir was enslaved to help pay off the debt.

When he learned the circumstances behind her enslavement, Mayne vowed that he would free her. He did not have enough money to pay the usurer, but he could undertake other tasks for the man in payment for Dananir's freedom. Yet here he was on shifting ground, for the usurer was involved in every vice known to man and he made it plain that he wanted Mayne to commit murder for him.

'Why do you want this man dead?' Mayne asked, eyes narrowed. He was sitting crosslegged on a scarlet silk cushion opposite Ali Ben Hazir, the usurer.

Ben Hazir grinned broadly, his eyes dancing. He was draped in buttercup yellow silk edged with silver tassels, and his toenails and fingernails were darkened with henna. His cheeks were rouged, and his nose was pierced with a silver crescent studded with pearls. Mayne thought him quite the most repugnant sight that he had ever seen. It was obvious what the man was, but he owned Dananir until the debt was paid and there was no way out of that. Momentarily, Mayne considered the secret *khanjar* at midnight, buried deep in this unnatural man's back, but he was no coward. He had never killed anyone who was not armed and the aggressor.

Ben Hazir was eyeing him salaciously, his kohl-darkened lashes fluttering as he directed his gaze pointedly at Mayne's groin. It was plain that his thoughts were on something other than murder. Feeling his gorge rise, Mayne repeated his question.

Ben Hazir sniffed at the interruption, then leaned forward.

'If murder causes you qualms, then there is another way that you could pay off the debt. I need a bed companion.' The blackened eyelashes fluttered again, and, despite his massive size, Ben Hazir moved lightly and easily to Mayne's side, his red-tipped fingers delving between the young man's thighs.

'You are so beautiful. Your eyes are like opals, all those colours mixed together, blue and green and topaz. I long to kiss your mouth! Allah, but we could enjoy many hours of bed sport together!'

Mayne could move fast, too, and in less than a second he was across the incense-scented room and standing with arms folded, glaring at Ben Hazir, grim-faced.

'I came here for the sake of Dananir, and if you will not answer my questions then I shall leave.'

'No, do not go. I wish to gaze upon your beauty.'

'Then answer my question,' Mayne growled.

'Ishak Mubarah is the man you must kill, quickly and cleanly. There must be no trail to lead back to me. Can you do this?'

'You have not yet told me why you want the man dead.'

'He – he raped my sister.'

It was so unexpected that Mayne felt the usurer was lying. As if he would care who raped his sister . . . and yet he might, for the Arabs were vindictive in the matter of their female relatives' honour.

'Report him to the authorities, then.'

'And have my sister's dishonour made public? No, I could never do that!' Ben Hazir trembled.

'Would her dishonour be any worse than your own?'

Ben Hazir flushed. 'You are vile to say that. What do you know of honour and dishonour, half-breed? She was an honest woman, a virgin, and Mubarah defiled her. Now she can never marry. Who would want a spoiled woman?'

'Is that why you wanted Dananir in the same position?

She was a virgin until you forced her into bondage.'

'These things cannot be helped. Blame her father, he caused that. If I were soft on all those who owed me money I would be a pauper within weeks.'

'I am not prepared to kill a man for dishonouring your sister,' Mayne said bluntly. 'You will have to hire someone else.'

'Then Dananir stays with me for another year.'

'Perhaps, and perhaps not.' Bristling with anger, his jaw jutting, Mayne strode out of the room and down the stairs, past the lace-like carvings and the frescoes of men and women copulating in every position known to the human race. Here, in these painted rooms, were held regular orgies attended by the rich and the important in the city of Bakasir. Ben Hazir had them all in his power.

Dananir was tearful that night. As he held her slight, trembling body close to his, he thought of freedom and all that it meant to him, and would mean to her. She was sixteen and graceful as a lily, her knee-length hair gleaming with lotus oils and hung with seed pearls. *Eau de nil* silk draped her body and her bare feet were painted with henna to repel the evil eye. Round her ankles were silver *khalakhil* hung with tiny tinkling bells. She smelled of the violet cachous that she loved to suck.

'If he will not free me, then I shall kill myself,' she wept. 'My father has disowned me. He will not come to see me any more, and who will marry a whore?'

'I shall marry you, *mahbub*,' he sighed against her ear, knowing that he was not prepared for this but offering it all the same. Where now was the hard-hearted cynic who had despised the world and the ties of love?

'I could not let you marry a whore! Men would sneer at you, and the women would shun me. Would you want your children to be born from a prostitute's womb? There is disease and sickness . . . all the time, I fear it. I think: what if this man brings me infection, what if that man will make me sick?'

95

Mayne shuddered at the thought and said, 'You must choose your customers with care. Take only the young and the healthy.'

'I have no choice. Zou Zou chooses them, and if she thinks a man will pay enough, she asks no questions. She is very old and foul-tempered, and Ben Hazir holds her in high regard. She makes more money for him from this house than all his others put together.'

'I shall speak to her, make her see sense.'

'The only sense she recognises is the power of the *drâhim*. You could never compete with the wealthy men who come here and offer her more, so there it is, my heart. I am lost, lost!' Dananir began to sob again, flinging herself against Mayne's chest and drenching him with her tears.

He held her tenderly, trying to map out a plan yet finding his thoughts confused. Where was the ruthless man of action of a year ago? Had love softened him so much that he was feeble-minded? He loved her, did he not, and he had promised to marry her. And yet she was a *bintilkha'ta*, a fallen woman, and by the end of the year, when the debt was paid, she would have slept with hundreds of men. The thought made him nauseous, made him want to fling her aside and run away, but how could he when she needed him so much?

Women were the cause of all mankind's agony. When had a woman ever brought him happiness or peace of mind?

Her whole life had been coloured by the loss of the dancing girl, Mishaal, foster daughter of Rhikia. How successful their house had been in the Street of the *Jijims*, all those years ago, and how rich she, Zou Zou, would have become had she been allowed to sell Mishaal as she had wished. That stupid, clod-headed Rhikia! Her refusal had ruined them. She had been forced to sell the house, and a paltry price she had got for it.

Those had been the days of the terrible drought, but Zou Zou would have had enough gold to buy the sweetest water if only Mishaal had not eluded her.

She had forgotten how old she was, preferring to count gold in place of years, but she knew from her twisted fingers where the knuckles protruded like fat white pebbles, and from the nagging ache in her spine, that she should have retired long ago. Perhaps she would have done but for Ali Ben Hazir and his houses of pleasure. Life had been a vicious struggle until she had heard of him. Their first meeting had been almost like a reunion, two like minds recognising one another at first sight.

'I have an ambition to become the richest man in Bakasir,' Ben Hazir had said. 'I was informed that you know much about the proper running of bawdy houses.'

'I know all, *Effendi*, and there is nothing proper about it,' Zou Zou cackled. 'I know how to choose the fairest girls, how to train them in the arts of the courtesan, and how to ensure that customers are never disappointed.'

'Allah be praised! If that is so then I can leave it all to you, and turn my thoughts to other matters.' Like taking the boy, Sayd, to my bed tonight, he added silently to himself.

'You will pay me well?'

'If you gain the required results, you will be generously reimbursed. That is a promise, Zou Zou.'

Her heart had fluttered so wildly that she had been forced to sit down. Ben Hazir's servant brought them strongly-scented lemon sherbet and date sweetmeats that jarred her old teeth, and they celebrated their new arrangement.

That had been twelve years ago, and now Zou Zou was as wealthy as Ben Hazir had promised – but not nearly so wealthy as she yearned to be.

Now and again, she would dream of Mishaal and what might have been, seeing the peacock dancer swirling vividly before her in a dazzling combination of colours and creamy-pale voluptuousness. Zou Zou saw the men's eyes bulging as they watched, heard the clink of the gold coins they would pay to see the famous performance. Sometimes she would wake as she counted the dream money, seeming to feel it still in her hands, her mind reeling with delight, only to have the miserable, numbing truth of it hit her as the dream faded.

'Oh Mishaal, Mishaal, if only I had not let you escape me!' she would wail into the feeble dawn light, but there was no consolation to be found in tears.

When she had first seen Dananir, she was momentarily reminded of Mishaal. There was the same limpid beauty – oh, not the startling bright green eyes, of course, for no one else had ever had eyes like Mishaal's – a glowing, almost ethereal luminosity that brought Rhikia's foster daughter to mind. Perhaps the girl could dance?

But no, she could not, other than an awkward swivelling of the arms and a self-conscious rotating of the hips. Nonetheless, Zou Zou could not take her eyes away. Dananir would make her fortune, she was sure of it. Sweet young virgins were rarer by the year, and one must make the most of them.

As always, she kept a careful watch over her girls. There were various reasons for this, the main one being that the tastes of the regular customers must be catered for. The day would come when they, unlike the casual client, would be willing to pay more for the favours of the courtesan who had touched their hearts. At this tender euphemism, Zou Zou would cackle to herself. Hearts? What did hearts have to do with it, unless men had theirs in their sexual organs, which was more than likely.

Peering from behind the curtain that screened her chamber from the entrance hall, she would watch the men coming in and leaving, noting their faces, their expressions, and their names if she knew them – and which girl they were visiting. She noticed the tall one for the way he towered above the other men. There was something strikingly different about him despite his regulation plain robe. His colouring was almost Arabian, but not quite.

One evening she emerged from behind the curtain, leaning heavily on the stick that was now vital to her. She wanted a closer look at the man, whoever he was.

Old woman and fierce-eyed young man faced one another in the trellised hallway where bedraggled flowering plants and gaudy paintings of barely-clad women were arranged to create an atmosphere of ornamental decadence.

'You, what is your name?' Zou Zou croaked, discretion forgotten in the heat of her curiosity.

'What is yours, old woman?'

Mayne stood squarely before her, arms folded, face set and inscrutable.

'It is not your place to question me!' Zou Zou shrilled. 'What is your name?'

'King Solomon,' Mayne responded with a European bow, the like of which she had never seen before. 'And you, I presume, are the Queen of Sheba?' He raised one ebony brow.

It was then that she saw the colour of his eyes, and realised he was no true Arab. In that moment, she became convinced that he was a wealthy man. And so she began to spy on them: the fair young Dananir who was not settling into her work and who led them all such a dance with her tears and complaints, and the man who disguised himself as an Arab but was nothing of the sort. She could not help but think back to the blond, dashing American who had stolen Mishaal from the house in *Jijim* Street all those years before, and she resolved that no one was going to steal Dananir from her like that.

There was a peep hole into the girl's tiny room, and

99

through this old Zou Zou watched their activities for as long as her aching limbs would allow. The man was an ardent lover, tireless and yet tender. Unlike other clients he did not lunge at the girl, mindlessly intent upon self-gratification. First there were kisses and caresses, and always he would bring some small gift. Once it was a gleaming gold and green bangle; another time an almond-green veil. Dananir loved green and wore it regularly.

Listening, Zou Zou heard much of love and tender words, but little of anything about the man with blue-green flecked eyes, although his visits grew more and more regular. And then one night, just as she had suspected, she heard him talk of marriage, of stealing Dananir away from her. Dananir, who was making a small fortune with her innocent doe eyes and virginal airs! No one was going to steal the girl from her. No one!

When the man asked to see her, she was forewarned. He wanted to buy the girl so that he could marry her, and he expected her, Zou Zou, to agree, just like that!

Mayne had never liked the old hag. There was something unpleasant about her, a ruthless, mercenary quality. The fact that Dananir was frightened of her was enough in itself to tell him that she was offensive.

'*Sitt*, I have a proposition to put to you,' he began, wondering why she was grinning so, her shoulders shaking with suppressed mirth. Ignoring this, he continued: 'I love Dananir, and I want to make her my bride. I shall, of course, recompense you for your loss.'

'How much?' There was a pearl of saliva at the corner of the old woman's mouth.

Mayne named a sum the equivalent of two years' annuity. It was a generous offer, and he knew it.

The old woman screeched with laughter.

'She makes that for me in a week!'

'I do not think so.'

'Ah, but she does, and what would you know about it, anyway?'

Impetuously, Mayne named a higher sum, knowing that it would mean they must begin their married life in dire poverty.

'Not enough, not enough! If you want her, then you must pay me four times that sum, and give me a virgin to replace her. And she must be young and fair, mind. No tricks!'

'I am sure we can come to some agreement.' Mayne lowered his eyes to conceal the desperation which must be reflected there. The greedy old hag wanted her pound of flesh and more.

'We already have. Four times that figure and a fair young virgin to replace her. That is not much to ask.'

'It is when you do not possess it!'

'Then you should lower your sights, young man. Dananir is a great courtesan. She can do better than take you for a husband.'

'In this shoddy hovel? I think not.' Mayne squared his shoulders, balling his fists in frustration. 'Will you think over my offer?'

'I have thought it over, and turned it down. You cannot have her.' Zou Zou set her crumbling jaw, happiness coursing through her veins at the power she possessed. Dananir would stay in her grasp. It helped, in a small way, to make up for losing the peacock dancer all those years ago.

Mayne stormed from the house, plotting mayhem and murder in his mind while knowing that he was never going to free Dananir unless some miracle took place.

When he had gone, Zou Zou scrawled an urgent message to Ali Ben Hazir. She guessed that the young man would go to him next, and it would be safer if the situation were clarified.

'*Effendi*,' she wrote, 'Dananir is one of our most successful girls. Men pay highly for her favours. She will make you a small fortune before the year is out, so please, *Effendi*, do not let anyone persuade you into

101

parting with her. I, Zou Zou, beg this of you from my heart.'

Then, folding the paper, she called Halim, her young servant, and instructed him to take the message to Ben Hazir with all speed.

In desperation, his annuity spent until the next year, he had taken on any task: carrying secret packages and not caring what was in them; bearing love letters between wives and their lovers, or husbands and their mistresses; guarding a coffle of slaves being marched from the port of Banjir to Bakasir.

What days those were, riding beside the chained up men, some of whom were little more than boys, to ensure that none escaped. There was very little for the slaves to eat, but generous rations were provided for Mayne and the other overseers. After seeing the thin, cavernous faces of the slaves, he gave them all the food he had and spent the rest of the journey eating roots and chewing bitter herbs. He did not consider himself noble for doing this, as he was, after all, taking the men to a life of bondage. Some would be beaten and ill treated; others, the ones who were blessed with good looks or fair hair, would probably end up in one of Ben Hazir's male brothels. If they could adjust to such indignities, then their lives would be ones of relative ease and comfort.

His pockets heavy, he went to Ben Hazir and gave him every coin.

'You can release Dananir before the year is out. This is only the first payment I shall bring you in return for her freedom.'

Ben Hazir cackled merrily, stuck his finger up his nose and seemed very absorbed by what he found there.

'You will not see the girl again,' he said with a sniff, rubbing his finger on his robe.

'Indeed I shall! I'm going to her now.'

'You will not find her. She has gone.'

'Gone where? If you have moved her somewhere else I shall find her wherever she is, you cunning old bitch!'

'Bitch, eh? The first compliment you have paid me.' Ben Hazir belched raucously, and fingered his nose again.

'Where is she?' Mayne demanded, advancing menacingly on the scented usurer.

'Don't you dare touch me!' Ben Hazir squealed in panic. 'My men are in that room, and they will hack off your head if you come near me!'

'Where is she?' Mayne grabbed him by his oil-soaked hair and shook his head until his eyes rolled.

'I t-told you she is g-gone! Dead, you fool, dead! But I shall keep the money all the same. She owes it me.'

Mayne blanched. 'Dead? But she can't be! You're lying, you devil!' He shook Ben Hazir again, hearing the rattling of his teeth with savage joy.

'She k-killed herself. T-took poison. She cheated me, Ali B-ben Hazir. She cheated me!'

The room danced before his eyes. Dananir was dead, his delicate, sensitive little beauty! Something seemed to burst in his head, the agony piercing right through him. Bunching his fist, he hammered it into Ben Hazir's face, breaking his nose and wrenching out the silver nose ring so that the blood streamed down the man's rouged face. Mayne almost killed him then, felt his hand tingling to seize the hilt of his *khanjar* and commit murder with it as he had in the old, Godforsaken days. Then, by an almost painful effort of will, he controlled himself. If he murdered this pig, vile as he was, he would be executed for it. He would not die for such a villain.

Letting the stunned Ben Hazir crash to the floor, he scooped up his money and raced down the stairs.

In the black days that followed, he searched every one of Ben Hazir's establishments, asking questions and attacking those who would not answer, for he feared that

Dananir had been spirited away so that the usurer could continue to exploit her when his year was out. He would not admit defeat, or that she was dead; he could not. Nightly he dreamt of her, his little lotus flower, so petite and frail, so trusting and tender with him, her kisses like the brush of rose petals, her eyes sparkling with love for him. How long had he loved her? Barely three months, and now she was gone as if she had never been. Her father was back in Ben Hazir's gambling dens. One night Mayne had seen him there, his arm around a heavily-painted courtesan, his expression creased with such avarice that Mayne shook with revulsion to see it.

No one save him had ever cared about Dananir; no one. She was one of the lost, and now so was he.

He would have gone back to old Zou Zou, itching to crack her skull on a stone, but he heard that she had died. A thief had raided her room and stolen her savings, and the shock had killed her.

Later that spring, he found himself on the perimeters of the Sahara, near Biskra, where the French Foreign Legion was stationed during its epic struggle against the Berber clans. There had been ferocious fighting and their ranks were decimated. Recruits were needed desperately. In later years, Mayne never forgot the commanding officer who laughed in his face when he approached him with the intention of enlisting.

'Do you think I am an idiot? *Mon Dieu*, you're a bloody Arab! Get out. We want no spies here.'

Patiently, Mayne explained to the man that it was true that he had an Arab mother but that his father was Daneyard Amyan of Maine, America.

'And I'm the King of Timbuctoo!' the officer roared, getting up from his seat with a threatening movement of his hand to his sword hilt.

Bowing gracefully, Mayne said that he was delighted to meet His Majesty and would beg only one favour of him.

The officer grunted, then laughed out loud. Beneath his growling, bear-like façade, he was basically a good-natured fellow who enjoyed a jest.

'Sir, if you could see me in uniform then you would realise that this Arab robe I wear is only for the purposes of desert travel. I am no spy, nor are my sympathies with my mother's race.'

'Can you speak Arabic?'

'Yes, sir.'

'That might be useful... I'll tell you what I will do. We're seriously undermanned, and I haven't time to play the inquisitor with every recruit who comes to me. There won't be time to train you properly, either – you must pick up what comes your way. First, you'll be taken to the bath house, and afterwards given a uniform. Report back to me when you are dressed and ready. And remember that you will be observed and guarded at all times, until you have proved yourself. Is that understood?'

'Yes, sir.'

The 'bath house' turned out to be a hole dug in the sand, its sides banked with stones for easier access. At the bottom lay a battered tin bath filled with murky water. There was no soap. Mayne lay in the greyish liquid, wandering why he was there. He knew of the Legion. It had made its name in Arabia during the past two decades by conquering Algiers and colonising it for France, despite all the Arab attempts to regain it. Even though the Legionnaires of those early days had been raw, rough and ill-trained, they had beaten off Arab defenders who were skilled and determined. A young boy could not help but be filled with admiration for so much heroism in the face of a dastardly enemy, and so Mayne would have been had he not known that some of that enemy blood was in his veins. Reading reports of the French victories in Arabia, never had he wished so deeply that he was Irish-American and

105

nothing more. The regret and confusion were with him still.

He had gone back to his Arab roots, thinking that such a sojourn would show him where his loyalties truly lay, but the visit had brought him nothing but grief. As there was no place for him in America now, he knew that he must make his own destiny, tear up his roots and plant himself elsewhere. His skills would be appreciated somewhere, he was sure.

He glanced up to see that the guard who had been ordered to keep watch over him was sitting against a stone step of the bath house, snoring in the heat of the day. Mayne could have snatched his pistol and shot him through the heart had he so wished. And then he saw a slender Arab girl, carefully climbing down the stone embankment to reach him with a small dish of soap in her hand.

Grinning, he almost stood up to give her a hand. Then, realising that she might not appreciate such a greeting, he sank back into the concealing grey water. However, he soon realised that she was no shy Arab virgin but fully intended to bathe him with her own hands. Lathering the soap in her fingers, she began to rub his body, her palms slipping over his muscular chest and arms, his flat stomach, and then lower – but there he brought up his arm and told her to stop. He spoke in her own language and she jerked back in dismay, dropping the soap into the water.

'Did you think I was French? That's good.' He grinned and took her hand, guiding it to the soap. 'I wish you were commanding officer here.'

'What do you mean, *Effendi?*' the girl faltered, but he did not feel that he had to explain.

'How did you get here?' he asked, taking in her crumpled robe, her neglected and uncared for appearance, and the deep, badly healed scar on her neck.

'I was taken prisoner. The Legion men attacked me,

106

but your officer saved me from the worst that can befall a woman, Allah be praised.'

'You mean you're still a virgin?'

Blushing, the girl nodded and then her hand came unexpectedly in contact with flesh that felt muscular and hard against her hand. She gave a cry of surprise and the sleeping guard grunted and slapped his hand down on the butt of his pistol. Then, seeing that it was only the new recruit being bathed by the Arab prisoner, he sat back, watching through sleepy but prurient eyes.

Fully aware that he was being observed, Mayne urged the woman to soap his back and sluice him clean, then stood up, wrapping the towel around his hips. Within moments he was stepping inside the hut where the uniforms were stored, the guard panting along behind him and wondering why he had rejected the advances of the little whore. Perhaps he was otherwise inclined? If he were, then his inauguration 'ceremony' would be all the more painful for him, but that would be his own fault.

In uniform, the dull red baggy breeches and dark blue long coat with its tails buttoned back and belted by a bulky ammunition belt, Mayne felt reasonably dashing. Then he noticed that there was a bullet hole, its edges blackened with cordite, right through the breast of his coat. A spreading bloodstain had been so hastily patched over that its edges remained, like gory fingers pointing to his heart.

Back in the C.O.'s office, he stood to attention, his chin held high. His boots were pinching him, but they were the best fit he could find and he would just have to make do with them. Silence ensued as the C.O. surveyed him, bleak-faced, as if he were an offensive sack of ordure. Finally the man spoke, or rather grunted: '*Mon Dieu*, you do look French. Some of us are dark-skinned like you.' Stepping closer, he looked at Mayne's eyes. 'Those aren't Arab eyes.'

107

'No, sir. I had a French grandfather, I believe, but that is all I know.'

'What of your father. Did he have eyes like that?'

'No, sir. He had blue eyes.'

'American, you said?'

'Yes, sir.'

'Then why are you here? You are the first American to come to us.'

'He died, sir, and I had no legitimate claim on his estate.'

'A bastard, eh?'

'Yes, sir.' Mayne felt the heat of shame suffuse his chest and neck and face, and his fists itched to beat the man's face into a pulp.

'Well, there are plenty of bastards here – me for one. At least you know who your father was. I never shall.'

Mayne's fists unclenched as he looked at the C.O. properly for the first time. He had a good-humoured mouth and his eyes were twinkling as if he were highly amused by his lack of pedigree.

The man was a bastard, too, and spoke of it freely, even to a stranger. Mayne was among friends.

Chapter Seven

Mahmed was more determined than ever to speed up the marriage proceedings. First he had sent Zahra a delicate porcelain coffee set from Cathay. It was patterned with terracotta and indigo figures which held the twining stems of white blossoms in their hands. Then he sent a soft wool cloak from Kashmir, brightest scarlet edged with snowy white fur. Zahra sighed when she folded back the soft doeskin wrapping to reveal the cloak inside. She had never liked scarlet, it was for bolder, braver women than she, but now she would have to wear it or Mahmed would be insulted. Arab men were so proud and touchy, one had to be extremely careful with them.

There she stopped herself, the heat rushing to her face. Already she was thinking of him as a husband, one whose views and opinions must come first with her, but she did not want that! She wanted to remain free as she was now, guided only by Freyha and those of her advisers who had known her from birth and who loved her for what she was, and not because she was Amira of the fabled Land of Mirages.

The nurses had all been hired, and one of the doctors, too. He was a thin, stern man but came with a multitude of recommendations. Apparently he was weary of tending the rich, self-indulgent patients of the city. He wanted to help those who would normally be unable to obtain proper medical aid, who would die without his skills, or remain maimed or delicate for life. He spoke with conviction and sincerity and although there was something of the zealot in the way his eyes burned when he related his ambitions, Zahra felt that there would be little to fear from him by way of sudden outbursts. He was respectful towards her, and grateful that through her he could tend the Beduin. What was more, he insisted that Zahra took his savings and put them towards the cost of the hospital building.

'It is not necessary,' she insisted, but he pushed the money towards her, saying that it was a gift for the children and he would be unhappy if she refused it; and so, with a gracious smile, she took it.

Dr Abdulla ibn Hasa took up his post, sleeping in one of the rooms allotted to the medical employees, and within a month he was joined by the second doctor, Hamsa Ben Da'oud, who, experienced in the setting of injured limbs, had spent five years in Bakasir experimenting with new techniques for the healing of fractures.

When Zahra asked him why he wished to leave the wealth and comfort of Bakasir, he half-closed his eyes with a fluttering movement which she was to learn he always made when about to speak.

'In Bakasir I see always the rich and the indolent. And, Allah forgive me, I sometimes do not care for their fate. It is those who are injured through no fault of their own who have commanded my sympathy for some years now.'

'You are not saying that the rich are deliberately causing themselves injuries?'

'Ah no, forgive me for not making myself clear, *Ya Sitti*. But I have a special tenderness for those who cannot better their own situations, for children and the young generally, and for the poor and people who through ignorance treat their wounds with charms and fasting and then must suffer the injurious consequences.'

110

'Although some of my people do adhere to the ways of ignorance and superstition, through no fault of their own, generally the teachings of Avicenna are employed where they are known.' Zahra could not bear to hear her people criticised.

'Yes, Avicenna the Bokharan, who taught medicine in ancient times. I would hope that medicine has advanced since then, *Ya Sitti*.' The eyelashes fluttered furiously.

'So would I, but surely many of Avicenna's teachings are still valid? Was he not court physician at Ispahan, and did he not introduce the works of Aristotle to Islam?'

'I am not saying that he was not a great and brilliant physician and philosopher, *Ya Sitti*, but I do believe that I have learned certain things that Avicenna never guessed at.'

'Then I must of course ask you for proof, *tabib*, doctor.'

'And I shall be more than eager to give it, *Ya Sitti*. Let me tell you of a young girl who was brought to me with a deformed leg. No, she was not born with it but had fallen from her mother's knee as a child. Alas, the mother was sitting on a camel's back at the time and the child broke its leg in three places. All that was done could be done; that is, charms were placed round the child's neck and the continual chanting of Qu'ranic verses was carried out while a relative painted a Qu'ranic prayer on to a plate, then poured rose water over it until it dissolved the writing. This rose water was then consumed by the patient.' Ben Da'oud's eyes twinkled.

'When three days had passed and the child was still feverish, more relatives were brought in to pray, and an uncle stood at the door of the nearest mosque with a cup of water into which everyone who left the mosque was asked to breathe. Some were kind enough to say a prayer over the cup of water as well as to breathe into it. The water was then given to the child who drank it all.'

'And recovered?' Zahra asked, well knowing that Ben Da'oud was in fact poking fun at the Beduin ways. While

111

she herself, like her father and mother before her, had sometimes despaired of the people's predilection for superstitious charms and incantations, she had never spoken out against this practice. No one could hurry an Arab; in fact, haste was believed to be the work of the Devil.

'Sadly no, *Ya Sitti*. The girl, as girl she now was, was brought to me in a sorry state, with a leg which would never support her weight again. I operated immediately.'

'You operated? But what could you do? Was it not the will of Allah that the girl was crippled?'

The eyelashes fluttered again. 'Yes, I agree that it was Allah's will that the girl should be disabled, and yet was it not also Allah's will that she should be brought to me when I had been carrying out my bone-grafting operations for two years, with considerable success after the early problems had been conquered?'

'And what were these problems?' Zahra was fascinated by the man and his talk of operations and experiments. Until this moment, she had never realised just how much medicine intrigued her.

'Infection and fever, *Ya Sitti*, and the body rejecting the implantation of the animal bone introduced, because it is foreign to it.'

'The patient's body would know when a piece of bone was foreign to it? How interesting.' She leaned forward attentively.

'I discovered a little-known treatise by an Arab physician from Bokhara who had actually worked with Avicenna and had carried on with some experimentation that the master had abandoned. This man, Ibn Hassan – his name is all I know of him – carried out operations in ordinary everyday conditions, without washing his hands beforehand, and without wearing clean clothes. He also used an operating bench where former patients had been tended. Every time the result was suppuration and fever in the patient.'

112

'Is that not caused by the wound healing? Is it not natural for it to suppurate as it heals?'

'So we have thought for centuries, *Ya Sitti*, and yet how many patients with fever and suppuration survive? Indeed, very few. After two months of operating in the old way, and closely observing the results, Ibn Hassan then ordered the thorough cleaning of his operating room. The old bench was taken away and replaced with a new one that was scrubbed. The floor was cleaned and so were the walls, and whitewash applied to them. Then Ibn Hassan bathed himself equally thoroughly, put on a new operating robe and sandals, and insisted that the patient was similarly bathed and dressed in a clean robe before he was operated on. Any who refused were rejected. For two months, Ibn Hassan closely observed the results.'

Zahra's eyes were sparkling. 'And were they good? The patients lived and were healthy?'

'Sadly, although there appeared to be a slight improvement, fatalities continued as before, and that was where Avicenna lost interest in the experiments. But Ibn Hassan carried on, even though Avicenna himself died shortly afterwards. Ibn Hassan found out that one of his assistants had not washed properly. Thinking that the clean conditions were a nonsense and a lack of faith in Allah, he had not bathed and was wearing the underclothes that he had worn for days before. What was more, he touched the patients with unwashed hands.'

'So there is something dangerous in unwashed hands?'

'It would appear so, *Ya Sitti*, and while men will wash extensively before prayer, it seems that they will not do so before treating their patients. You know of cauterization?' Zahra nodded. 'It is often successful although it is an agonizing procedure. I have been pondering on this and I believe that the fire causes a similar cleanliness to thorough washing.'

113

'You would not advocate cauterization for all injuries, I hope? It is not suitable for children. They cannot keep still long enough for the heat to cure them, and who would blame them?'

'You are right, *Ya Sitti*, for the Prophet himself did not approve of it unless there was no alternative. No, I would advocate the thorough cleaning of everyone and everything that is to come in contact with the sick. And if you wish to know how the operation on the crippled girl turned out – well, she is now my wife. She walks almost perfectly and she has borne me a son.' The doctor's face glowed. 'It was said that she would never marry because of her deformity and she was shut away in the harem, coddled by the women and considered a sad and pitiful creature.'

'May I meet her and see the straightened limb?'

'But of course, *Ya Sitti*. I shall arrange it.'

When he had gone, Zahra pondered over the notion that thorough washing could keep wounds clean. In the desert, in drought conditions, many of the Beduin resorted to sand in place of soap, and camel's urine was used to bathe infants and to wash the women's hair. Scented with the herbs that were one of the mainstays of the camels' diet, it was not offensive.

As a race, the Beduin were hardy yet famine and poor diet frequently made them susceptible to disease, and fatalities in childbirth were high. Thankfully, because her lands were lush and fertile, there was plenty of food for its nomads, but in adjacent lands there was the constant problem of finding nourishment. If the grazing was poor, then the nomads must search for days to find fresh pasture, during which their animals lost weight and they had to tighten their own leather-thonged belts to try and quell their hunger pangs. She had heard of flocks dying of thirst and their nomads following suit, but such fatalities had not been known in the Land of Mirages for thirty years.

114

When she saw Ben Da'oud next, she must ask him two questions: would thorough washing before childbirth help to save the woman's life or was it only injuries that benefited from cleanliness, and what method of washing did he advise?

It was amazing how handsome a building of twigs, mud, clay and packed sand could look, Zahra thought as she surveyed the hospital. She had not considered white-washing it before, but now she would order it to be done. Both inside and out, the building must be as immaculate as possible. As she walked across the shaded courtyard, where men were planting acacia trees and small flowering bushes, she paused by the well and thought of another question she could ask Ben Da'oud: would this sweet water hasten the children's recovery from sickness?

Inside, the nurses' voices were raised, but when they saw their Amira they blushed and made obeisance. Gesturing to them to get up, she asked them why they were arguing.

'Ya Sitti, we cannot decide between us whether the very sick children should be placed amongst those who are not so sick, in the hope that they will receive benefits from the ones who are getting better, or whether they should be kept apart where it is more peaceful and yet lonely for them. We discuss this because Beduin children are not accustomed to being isolated.' The woman waited expectantly for her Amira's reply.

'And what do you favour?' Zahra asked her.

'Why, Ya Sitti, I favour that they be kept amongst the children who are soon to leave.'

'Ya Sitti, sick children need sleep and quiet, while children who are soon to leave will be more high-spirited!' cried another nurse.

'Yes, but those same high spirits can spread to the sick and help to heal them, Allah willing,' interrupted a third.

115

And then, remembering that she had not said 'Ya Sitti', she flushed painfully and begged the Amira's forgiveness.

'You are not my slaves. We are equal in this venture,' Zahra said, her voice firm. 'I want no obeisances when you see me. The simple mention of my title or name will suffice. You must not be distracted from the work you are doing.'

'Oh, but Ya Sitti, we could not call you by your name! We are not highborn, we are simple women from ordinary stock.'

'All those who came to my father's tent called him Husain, and all those who come to my tent may call me Zahra. Did you not know that the highest amongst you can be named thus even by the lowest?'

'No, we did not, Ya Sitti!' the women chorused. It would be a long time before any of them dared to call Zahra by her first name.

'As to the matter of where the sick children will sleep, I shall consult the physician who will be joining us in a few days' time. He is skilled in the treatment of the very sick, and his voice will be the deciding one on this matter. Is that understood?' Zahra surveyed the anxious faces before her.

'Yes, Ya Sitti,' they chorused again. She left them to resume her slow inspection of the rest of the building. There had been two rooms prepared for the physicians, but neither would be big enough for a married man so Ben Da'oud would have to be found another dwelling nearby. She did not want either of the physicians to live any distance away from the hospital.

There was a small room which would contain all the medicaments and ungents. Some had arrived, but many of the cupboards were still empty. Looking through the boxes on the floor and shelves, Zahra noted wryly that there was everything but soap, nor could she recall having signed any order for it. We live and learn, she

116

thought as she walked into the next room which was the nurses' rest room for those on duty.

Here was a bench for those who had come from the city, and cushions for those who preferred the desert way of sitting crosslegged. Some of the cushions appeared to be occupied.

Stepping silently towards the sleeping girl, Zahra tapped her on the shoulder. Bleary eyes opened, took time to focus and then gaped wide as the girl struggled to her feet.

'Aiee, *Ya Sitti*, forgive me! I-I was so exhausted that I had to sleep. We did not know that you were coming today!'

'That is all too obvious. And why are you so tired? What have you been doing?'

The girl bowed her head and shuffled her feet. 'I-I am working very hard for you, *Ya Sitti*, and my sleep has been disturbed.'

'I do not want martyrs here, only dedicated nurses!' Zahra snapped. 'Who else has been working at night?'

'No one, *Ya Sitti*.'

'You mean that you have been working at night alone here while the others slept?'

'Yes, *Ya Sitti*.' The girl coloured.

'That shows extraordinary dedication but also stupidity. What if you fell asleep over your patient's bed? What sort of nurse would that make you?'

At the sound of a footstep behind her, Zahra turned to see one of the other nurses.

'*Ya Sitti*, what has she been telling you? Whatever it is, it will be lies! She does not wish to be a nurse. She came here to get a free bed and food, and she cares for no one but herself. She has a man friend.'

'I do not. That is a lie, Salma!'

'Indeed it is not, *Ya Sitti*. She has a man friend and she is out with him at night. It is indecent and she should be ashamed.'

117

'Is this true?' Zahra faced the first nurse, who looked alarmed and pathetic, her hair uncombed and her face lined from where it had rested against the cushion.

'No!' the girl cried. And then, beginning to sob pitifully, she said, 'Yes, *Ya Sitti*, it is true, Allah forgive me! But the man I see is the one I am to marry – he is not a stranger.'

'Huh!' was Salma's reaction to this. 'Then she will be taking six husbands, *Ya Sitti*, for she has been seen with six different men.'

By now Zahra was burning with fury: that this girl had passed her rigorous interview technique, and that she had been using the hospital as a base for her promiscuity.

'Do you admit this?'

'Yes, I admit it, *Ya Sitti*,' the girl wailed.

'Look at her belly, *Ya Sitti*, it is swollen. A fine nurse she will make with an infant on the way!' Salma sneered.

'Do you have a home to go to?' Zahra asked, unwilling to turn the girl out if she had nowhere to go.

'Yes, *Ya Sitti*.'

'Then go to it, and Allah forgive you for deceiving me.'

Wailing, the girl ran out of the rest room in a flurry of tangled hair and crumpled clothes. She continued to wail as she gathered together her belongings and headed out along the track towards the distant city.

Watching her from the window, Zahra reflected that there went a girl who was willing to lie with any man who would give her money, while she, the Amira, did not wish to lie with any man because she greatly feared that she would be the one who would be called upon to pay the price.

Mayne Amyan's progress in the Legion was meteoric. He rapidly obtained command of the Dark Legion, the idea of which had been partly his. It was he who had put

118

the plan for an élite force to his commanding officer; he who had formulated the tactics that should be employed; and he who had personally selected the men who would fight under him. They were chosen for their swarthy skins and dark colouring, their agility and linguistic skills. They were men who could blend in with any backgrounds, wear Arabian clothes and look the part while speaking the local dialects. They were also ruthless and expert killers.

The first few days in the Legion had been easy compared to the months of basic training that followed: the forced route marches, laden with heavy gear; the running, and the strenuous exercises; the overcrowded conditions in the living accommodation. Dozen upon dozen of men were packed into each hut, the number rising with each new intake of recruits, the resultant clamour, bustle and babble of voices being virtually neverending. Fortunately for him, he was usually totally exhausted by night time, so he would sink into his narrow bunk and sleep as if bewitched, hearing nothing until dawn when the ordeal would begin again. There was no place for weaklings, for those with frail bodies or neurotic temperaments; the men who comprised the French Foreign Legion must be invincible, hard-bodied and quick-brained. That was why so many fell by the wayside during training.

Now Mayne knew why the recruits had been asked to sign their long-term contracts, the *Acte D'Engagement* as it was called, before being launched upon their basic training; they would have fled after days had they not been contracted to the Legion. As it was, there were those who wept in secret and had shuddering fits, and those who rebelled and were despatched to solitary confinement or lashed until they dropped. The senior officers were often harsh, sometimes brutal, for it was their task to beat and bully the new recruits into fighting trim. They must be capable of waging war in the most shocking conditions, and be prepared to die for their Legion.

Mayne survived it all, as he had known from the first that he would, but he made no friends. He had learned the hard way that close relationships brought pain, and that was something he wished to avoid.

He was rapidly promoted, held up to others as the pattern of the perfect Legionnaire – brave, bold, silent and uncomplaining – and then, after three years' service, without one day's leave during that time, he was given six months in which to prove himself at the head of the Dark Legion.

There were many sneers and ribald comments from his fellow Legionnaires: rumour of his working his way to the top via the beds of his commanding officers; of his being a coward and fleeing from the battle front. He ignored it all, and when he and his men took Kabylia after all other efforts had failed, he was the hero of the hour.

Since 1838, every attempt to conquer Kabylia had failed. From Roman times, the indefatigable, steely mountain men had repelled all invaders. They flourished in their natural habitat, the snow-veiled, treacherous mountains of Algeria which were also their natural defence.

Mayne was familiar with treacherous, icy heights and difficult terrain. His father's country had prepared him well. He led his tough, superbly trained troops in a vanguard action to Kabylia's core, high in the hostile mountains, ahead of the troops that would follow in full battle gear. They wore bernouses like Arabs, and with their dark skins and Arab headgear, the *kuffayia* and *aghal*, were easily mistaken for local men. Scouts who were expecting the red and blue of the Legionnaires' uniforms, and the gleam of their rifles, were taken unawares by what appeared to be their own countrymen surging around them in the darkness – until the sudden flash of *khanjars* wielded with merciless precision.

120

Before dawn, Kabylia was virtually undefended. It lay open to the support troops like a young and eager virgin as the Legionnaires would say later while celebrating their triumph. Mayne lost only three men, and two injured. He was aching and bruised from struggling with three Algerians who had tried to batter his brains out on a stone, but he was alive – and famous. Overnight, amongst all ranks, he became a hero, but in the newspaper reports of the conquering of Kabylia there was no mention of the Dark Legion. It was never mentioned publicly for what use was a spy column if it was no secret?

Mayne found himself the proud possessor of the first *Croix de Valeur*, a medal specially created for heroes of the Dark Legion. It was presented to him in person by Napoleon III on Mayne's brief visit to Paris, that fabled city of churches and palaces and beautiful, amorous women. Out of the three, there was no doubt that it was the beautiful women who intrigued him the most, and when the presentation ceremony was over with all its stiff formality, the regal, bearded monarch pinning on Mayne's medal with his own fingers, the recipient was away, down the dark side streets that were, so he had heard, awash with intrigue and sexuality.

The first female to accost him was petite and heavily painted with her hair bleached so excessively that it stuck out around her head like a nimbus of parched wool. She was squeezed into a scarlet gown with very little bodice and the hem tucked up into her belt over one hip so as to reveal a shapely white-stockinged thigh encircled by a rose-trimmed garter.

'*M'sieur, pourquois pas? Essaie!*' she murmured, thrusting her half naked breasts against Mayne, who gently pushed her away.

'*Où est la maison de Sophie Brieille, s'il vous plaît, mam'selle?*' he asked the girl, prising her audacious fingers away from his groin. She was pretty in her own artificial way, but he had been given the name of one who was skilled in the more superior arts of Aphrodite.

'*Je vais vous ramener chez moi,*' the persistent female coaxed, but Mayne told her that he had no time to stand gossiping on street corners, at which she fluttered her eyelashes and demanded: 'Who needs to speak?'

Laughing, he slipped away from her and began knocking on doors, one after the other, until he was face to face with Sophie Brieille, or rather her prim-featured maidservant. The hallway was filled with the scent of violets, the walls draped with mauve silk, the carpet a rich, deep amethyst. Ahead of him was a flight of stairs that led, he knew, to Paradise. But first he must wait his turn.

After striding up and down restlessly for some time, he perched on a small gold-painted stool and duly waited, finding his thoughts returning to the day he had first met Dananir. How different had been the surroundings then and how different the country, but she had been the same as this woman, a courtesan, albeit an unwilling one. After Dananir, he had vowed that he would never pay for a woman again, but he was young and virile and it had been eighteen months since he had bedded one. Now his palms were moist with anticipation and his clothes clung to his body as if he had been running in the desert heat. Roughly, he brushed the dampness from his face, and then a door creaked open and the scent of violets became stronger.

Briefly, he saw a man's back as he was led through a discreet rear doorway, and then the prim-faced maid-servant was standing before him, bobbing a dainty little curtsey and gesturing to him to follow her. He was erect before he reached the third stair.

The entire room was decorated in shades of mauve and amethyst, and flowers decorated every available surface. The bed was vast, draped with mauve silk and gold fringing, and on it lay a woman of about thirty with

122

long golden hair draped around her on the pillows. She wore a transparent robe of soft violet silk and through it he could see her full breasts, taut against the material. As he came closer he could see that her eyes were a rich topaz colour, her mouth full and generous. Her complexion was a smooth, unblemished ivory; her teeth slightly uneven but sound.

She held out her arms in welcome. Because he was young and starved of love, he was inside her within seconds. Almost as suddenly it was over, and he was apologising for his embarrassing speed.

'You do not have to apologise to me, Captain Mayne. I am here for your delight, for as long as you need me.'

'I am no boor, *mam'selle*. I would hope that you would receive some enjoyment from this dalliance.'

'Shall I be frank with you, Captain? There is no such thing as enjoyment for the *horizontale*. She is bought and paid for, and she is used, and then used again. Are you married, Captain Mayne? Most of my clients are. There is something about marriage that brings out the wildness in a man, but not when he is with his wife.' Sophie Brieille laughed silkily.

'No, I am not married, *mam'selle*.'

'Is that through choice or accident? I would think that you would make a splendid spouse for some romantic woman. Have you not had women pursuing you for years?'

'My career has not allowed for it, *mam'selle*. I have been in the deserts of Arabia for the past three years, and before that I was in America.'

'An American made love to me once. He was very skilled, but he wore animal skins and the smell of them was nauseating.'

'I would prefer not to hear of the other men you have known, *mam'selle*.'

'As you wish, Captain. For tonight, there is no other man in the universe but Mayne Amyan.' And then, as if she had not spoken, she said, 'Do you know Alfredo Martinez well?'

'No, we are not intimates. He recommended you when he knew I would be in Paris.'

'Give him a message from me, will you? Tell him that Sophie would like to see him again, and that she has not forgotten him.'

Mayne's eyes narrowed. The last thing he wanted was to have to think of one of his fellow Legionnaires bedding this perfect creature, for it would destroy the illusion that she was there only for him.

'Shall we continue? That is, if you are not missing Martinez too much?' he said tersely, and took her in his arms.

The second time he lasted longer, pausing to revel in the silky sensations of her pearly, scented flesh against his hard brown body, the sensuousness of her full, curved lips on his starved mouth. She was as well versed as his fellow Legionnaire had promised; there was nothing she had not learned about pleasing a man. She could stretch out the moment of anticipation for hours, until his groin was white hot and throbbing for relief, and then, when he believed he could last no more, she lowered her mouth to his hardness and carefully, expertly, began to lick at it with her strong little tongue.

Then, just when he thought that he would explode, that he could not survive such pulsing ecstasy, she would pause, smiling up at him with her teasing, topaz eyes, and he did not know whether he was glad or sorry that she had stopped. Drawing in a shuddering breath, his face flushed and his eyes glazed with passion, he urged her on with the beautiful, intolerable torture.

And so it continued until his heart was banging against his ribs and he knew that he could not hold out a moment longer. But it was Dananir's name that he sighed as his orgasm engulfed him, and Dananir's face that he saw in his mind's eye.

124

He was there for the rest of the night, as arranged, and when he woke his body ached but his head was clear. When he found the woman with whom he would spend the rest of his life, she would be one who had eyes only for him; she would see no other men, nor think about them, and he would know that, waking or dreaming, she loved only him.

Chapter Eight

General Lazare Baronne of the 2nd Foreign Regiment stood up to salute Mayne when he entered the reception room, although he was of lesser rank. Mayne, startled but pleased, saluted back. Even though more than a year had passed since Kabylia, he was still very much the hero, it would seem.

He had met the General before, and liked him. It was obvious that the feeling was reciprocated for the officer was beaming.

'I asked you to come here because I have a vital request to put to you, Captain Mayne. What the Legion needs today are ingenuity and valour, and who possesses them in greater measure than the hero of Kabylia?'

Mayne felt himself colouring and tried to control it with little success.

'We are in difficulties. You will have heard of the desert area that they call the Land of Mirages?'

Mayne nodded. Lectures on various parts of Arabia were *de riguer* for the Legionnaires, to familiarise them with the land they had partially conquered.

'It is singularly lush and generously provided with water. There is a brand-new hospital there which we need. However, there is a female in control there.' The General scowled at such a notion. He had never been a supporter of the Salic Law of France which allowed inheritance through the female line. In fact, he had

126

joined the Legion because he despised such madness. 'She rules for no other reason than that she has no male relatives. It seems outlandish to me. I thought these Mohammedans kept their females underfoot. I have never heard of a woman ruling in Arabia, have you, Captain? Your mother was from these parts, was she not?'

'From Arabia, yes, sir, but not from Algeria. As for women ruling Arabia, that is not unknown. There was Queen Zenobia, who bravely stood against the Roman invaders, and Queen Semiramis who was of Syrian stock, if tradition is to be believed. It was said that she was so radiantly beautiful that all men who gazed upon her became her slaves. Then there was Maqueda, Queen of Sheba, who worshipped the Sun God until she fell in love with King Solomon and was converted to worshipping the God of Israel.'

'You are well read, Captain, yet I particularly do not wish to hear talk of Arabian queens defending their land against invaders. You came to mind immediately I heard what was required in the Land of Mirages. You have Mohammedan blood, you can pass for an Arab, and I am told that you speak the language. Is that correct?'

'I do, sir, although I have not for some time.'

'What would you say if I told you that you were to be given *carte blanche* to go on a mission that should, God willing, bring all the riches and benefits of the Land of Mirages to the French Crown?'

'I would be intrigued to know more, sir.'

'This is top secret, of course, but we plan to take Bahraud, and from there we shall invade this woman's country. That is, if she does not hand it to us on a plate.' The General gave a rasping laugh. 'Naturally, we would wish to spare life and limb, and we would like the acquisition to be easy for us after the years we spent struggling to take Kabylia. Algeria has cost us dear, one way and another. This Amira is young, eighteen or nineteen only, and she is a Beduin. They are freer than

127

their city counterparts, and frequently go unveiled…
but of course you will know all this. I mention it because
it should make her far easier to approach. I am told that
she holds regular audiences for her people, and that any
of them can come to her for assistance at any time, so
you should have no trouble in getting to her.'

'You wish me to dress Arab-style, sir? Take on a false
identity?'

'I am not too sure. I have thought about it for some
days now and it appears to me that an Arab would have
easier access to the woman. But, on the other hand, a
man in our glorious Legionnaires' uniform should have
an effect upon her which should work entirely in his
favour, Captain.' The General winked, slowly and
deliberately.

'I am told that she is arrogant, which is what one
would expect of the daughter of the Amir Husain ibn
Rashid and the Amira Mishaal, and no doubt because of
this she believes herself to be one of the mighty. No
doubt she has been pampered and spoiled and never
wanted for anything since she was in her cradle. It is
unlikely that she will ever have heard a sincere word in
her life so your task should be easy, Captain. Woo the
woman. Flatter and cajole her; tell her that we wish to
give her country all the aid possible; that we can provide
her with doctors and medicaments and will build more
hospitals. We can provide anything she might need –
agricultural experts, child specialists, new roads, anything she wants. We want the Land of Mirages soon, and
many lives depend upon it.'

'What is the Amira's name, sir?'

'Zahra. It sounds a harsh name to me, but then Arabic
is not the sweetest tongue.'

'Zahra. That is Arabic for Venus, the morning star. A
pretty name even if it does not sound so to your ears.'
Mayne could still bristle when anything Arabic was
criticised.

128

'Ah, you would think the language sweet, being born here. Forgive me for speaking against it. You do not look Arabic in that uniform and I tend to forget your origins.'

'I have spent my entire life trying to do that!' Mayne wanted to shout, but he clamped his lips together.

'You wish me to persuade the Amira Zahra that union with France will bring her untold benefits?' he said instead.

'That is it in a nutshell. We have a spy or two in her camp, but little has come of that yet. Basically, I want you to convince this high-nosed beldame that we are God's gift and should be welcomed with open arms. When we are on her land, we shall of course claim it for King and Crown. By then it will be too late for her to defend herself. Charm her, promise her anything, lie if you have to. I am sure it won't be the first time that you've lied to a woman, eh?' The general laughed coarsely.

'Charm her, promise her anything, and if necessary lie to her? Are those my orders, sir?'

'They are, Captain.'

'And when do I set out on this mission?'

'You have three days to put your affairs in order, Captain. Everything has been prepared: your horse, baggage, maps, provisions for the journey. There will be a camel waiting for you deeper in the desert at the Oasis of Rajab, and from there you will proceed Arab fashion. I take it that you have ridden a camel before?'

'Yes, sir.'

'You will of course be given written orders, which you will be required to destroy when you have memorised them. Now, are there any questions, Captain?'

'No, sir.'

The General stood again to salute his subordinate as he left. Mayne heard the door click to behind him as he walked away down the echoing, whitewashed corridor.

Even he, accustomed as he was to the sapping heat, was

finding the climate oppressive. The Land of Mirages was supposed to be lush and well-watered, but as yet he had seen nothing to substantiate this.

One night, lying curled in his goatskin, he had heard the distant thudding of hoofs in the sand and waited tautly to see whether the riders would come his way, but they had not. Far on the horizon, astride an elevated spine of night-dark sand, he saw the ebony silhouettes of camels and their riders, and guessed he was witnessing a Beduin raiding party returning to camp. What he knew of the Beduin was small, but it was believed that they would never attack in darkness for that would offend against their code. Raiding parties must behave according to rigid rules of combat, rather like the medieval code of chivalry.

Mayne lay deep in thought, sleep eluding him after his glimpse of the Beduin. The feeble excuse for a moon was brocaded by dark, scowling clouds and he could see no stars. Desert nights were legendary for their spectacular, starry beauty; that was, when there was a moon to see them by. Two days more and he would be at the Oasis of Rajab, where fresh provisions and the *dhalul* awaited him. His memory of camels was not too fond; smelly, stubborn, humourless and grotesque, they were prone to ill temper and to biting but Mayne could ride them easily, as could any Arab worth his salt.

He grinned to think that here he was, willingly donning the Arab character again. Once, in the days when he had found it necessary to deny his maternal heritage, being ordered to live as an Arab would have caused bitter turmoil within him. Now he was a hero, thanks mainly to the skills inherited from the Arab side of his parentage, an irony that had not escaped him.

Briefly his thoughts lingered on the Amira Zahra, the high-nosed young woman who was the reason for his lonely quest. Once, as a boy, he had seen a splendid camel train passing through his mother's village. The people

130

had all come out of their houses to gape at it.

'The Amir Husain is on that horse,' his mother had told him, 'and in that litter hung with veils is his wife, the Amira Mishaal. Usually she would ride beside him, but now she is great with child and so she rides in comfort.'

'Who are they?' he had asked in boyish innocence.

'The greatest in the land. He is the Lord of all the Beduin and she is the one they call The Torch who will Light the Land. Long ago, when their country was impoverished and there was no water, the Amira made a covenant with Allah and He gave them everlasting water and the richest jewels in the universe.'

His mother's face had crumpled at the thought. She would have given anything for just one of those fabled pearls but she had shown no envy of the Amir and his wife, only a deep despair that caused her to fall silent for days afterwards.

It was possible that the Amira Mishaal had been carrying her daughter Zahra when Mayne saw that camel train pass by, and the notion pleased him for some reason.

Eventually he slept, waking to a glittering frosty dawn in which he was unable to drink his water because the contents were layered with ice. The sky was an anaemic peach colour, and the desert looked as if it had been limned with platinum. Stamping his feet on the ground to speed his circulation, Mayne ate a few mouthfuls of chilly oatcake, but they went down badly without a drink. After the previous day of skewering heat, he would never have dreamt that the dawn could bring such frostiness. He tried to think back to his Arabian days and what the weather had been like then. As a child, he had hardly noticed the fluctuating temperatures, and later, when he had been trying to reclaim his roots, he had noticed everything but the climate.

Looking around him, seeing nothing of the usual desert colours, orange shading to rusty hues then deeper

131

sun-baked terracotta, gilded dunes with the sapphire palanquin of sky arching above them, he could not stop himself from shuddering. Not from fear, for he was a stranger to that, but from the unexpectedness of it. The chill was eating through his desert robes even though he was wearing a woollen *kuftan*, and that he found distinctly odd. Even in the icy heights of Kabylia, he had not felt the cold.

His horse seemed slower, almost bemused, but he put that down to the cold, too, and as he mounted he tried to jerk the beast into life with his heels.

Three hours later he was laughing at the memory. Now the sun was high and stark in the sky, scorching his face and hands and causing the sweat to stream from him in uncomfortable trickles. His horse seemed to be itself again and it was time to think about food. Forgetting that his water bottle would be defrosted by now, he tilted it carelessly to his mouth and drenched himself with lukewarm water. That made him roar with laughter, which was just as well for he had only a mouthful or two left now and still a day and a half to get to Rajab. With luck, there would be a well somewhere, or a wadi rushing with water after rain. It always rained in the Land of Mirages, they said. It was God's Bounty.

Lunch was more of the solid, heavily salted oatcake, and a piece of cheese that was almost singing from the heat. He had to hold his nose as he bit into it. At Rajab, he would take on suitable desert rations, not this attempt at sailor's food. Dates and figs, and *laban* would keep him fit. He loved the sour milk that was thickened in leather pouches until it was a solid yoghourt. It provided excellent nourishment and fluid at the same time. He should have asked for it at the start, but how could you tell a General that he has misjudged your requirements?

At first glance, the track ahead appeared stony and barren, but he knew from past experience that there would be small flowers lurking between the rocks, and

132

acacia bushes in the hollows where rain was trapped. He spotted *dhorur* and *ra*, which the nomads boiled and used to treat stomach upsets, and tiny blue, scarlet and sunny yellow flowers. It was then that the tranquillity of the desert began to steal over him, and he felt a warm rush of feeling, a sense of being at home. Strange, when he had fought his origins all his life, loathing his half-breed status, his stupid Arabian mother and his lack of wealth and power.

Yet what was power? The authoritative hand to wield in justice, the mercy to forgive, the wisdom to judge rightly and according to God's laws....

Mayne blinked. The heat was making him sleepy and words were coming into his head unbidden. Next he would be seeing one of the famous mirages which had made this land a legend. He grinned to himself. Mayne Amyan see a mirage? That would be the day. He was the most unimaginative, down to earth person that he knew.

Also unbidden, his thoughts flew back to his Dananir. She had dabbled in the arts of astrology and had told him that his sign was that of the Bull, stoic, fearless and unimaginative. He had not been able to argue with that – despite not believing one word of her mystical nonsense – for her words described him perfectly. Then she had gone on to say that those born under the sign of the Bull were sensual and passionate, and fond of money and possessions. He knew that he had a passionate nature, but money and possessions had always evaded him unless one could call a modest log cabin a great inheritance.

Suddenly he no longer cared. Out here, in the wilderness, he was a different man. Envy and bitterness were falling away from him as if they had never been.

They had founded a new medal just for him, the *Croix de Valeur*, and the Emperor of France had pinned it on his breast with his own fingers. It had been the greatest moment of his life but what did it signify? What was the value of worldly achievements? Where had he read, 'Verily God giveth beyond measure to whom He will'? It was in one of the *suras*, but he could not recall which. He had read everything that he could set his mind to when he had returned to Arabia, read and absorbed until his thoughts were reeling.

Every man came to dust in the end, he had concluded, but if he were fortunate he would first achieve something that would inspire those who came after. Mayne would have liked a wife, and a son or daughter to leave behind him, but there seemed little chance of that now that he had dedicated his life to the Legion, signing away his freedom. His future was mapped out: he was a Legionnaire, and his importance to the Legion was inestimable. Out in the world, he would lose that status and become nothing again, a half-breed nonentity. He could not take that step, but what woman would marry herself to the rootless wanderer he must remain? How he longed for roots, yet looking back it seemed that so far he had deliberately uprooted himself from what measure of security he had been given. Perhaps he was more like his mother than he knew; perhaps he was doomed to destroy his own happiness, piece by piece?

Halting, he gazed around him at the brazen desert. The sun had bleached it mercilessly, leaving it arid and barely able to support life. Yet in the distance, poised like a golden figurine, stood a gazelle. Mayne marvelled at its taut, quivering beauty, the fragility of the slender limbs which it seemed a puff of air might snap. His heart wrenching at the sight, he gazed until his eyes burned, feeling at one with the sublime creature, as if its breath were in his lungs, its heart beating in his breast, and his thoughts went back to the wilds of Maine and the mountain lion that he had been forced to kill there. He felt again, more profoundly than ever before, that these beasts, God's animals, were His particular creations,

134

special, beloved, and that it was they who had truly inherited the earth, not man with his ruthless, mercenary drive.

He wanted to pray, but the ability had almost left him after years of disuse. He wanted to vow to God that he would never ever again harm one of His most perfect and innocent creations, be it gazelle, Arabian horse, or camel. They had more right on this earth than he or any man.

Was this what his version of forty days in the wilderness had done to him, placing him even more firmly on the side of the animals? Eyes twinkling, he rode on.

There stood the hospital: sparkling, pristine – and empty. Only three children had been brought into it in all these weeks. One had a twisted leg, the next a mysterious, recurring fever, and the last was strangely small and shrunken for her age. Hamsa Ben Da'oud was already preparing the first child for preliminary tests, and Abdulla ibn Hasa had formulated a nourishing broth for the undergrown child, despite her mother's protestations that she had always been well fed. Both the doctors were in their element, and so were the three patients who were receiving devoted round the clock attention from the hospital staff.

Impatient to see Hamsa Ben Da'oud at work, Zahra had come to the hospital on that fine morning of clear skies to do just that. She wanted to see the miracles of which he had spoken, for miracles they had sounded to her. Crooked limbs straightened and healed, lame girls made whole again. How had he achieved this?

Today she would be meeting Hamsa Ben Da'oud's wife, and the young patient with the twisted leg. Both were expecting her, but she had given orders that there must be no panoply surrounding her visit.

135

Dismounting, she looked fondly at the building. She loved it more each time that she saw it, not because of its architecture, for that was humble, but because of what it represented for her people: healing; straight new limbs; recovery from fever; a new beginning.

Hamsa Ben Da'oud was waiting for her in the entrance, his eyes sparkling. In his hands were a pair of soft brown slippers which he handed to the surprised Zahra, requesting that she put them on 'Until we know more about the problem of contagion. If the hands carry it, then why not feet?' Surprised, but in agreement, Zahra kicked off her riding boots and donned the slippers. Next, she was presented with a bowl of hot water and a small ball of crude soap, and this time he did not need to say one word. When she had washed her hands and dried them on the clean square of linen presented to her by one of the beaming nurses, Queen and physician entered the sick room where the child awaited them.

She was very young, with huge, dark eyes and a mouth that was quivering from nervousness. Sitting beside her on the bed, Zahra soon put her at her ease, taking her damp little hand and holding it as if they were old friends.

Not until the child had relaxed and begun to smile would she allow the *tabib* to show her the twisted limb.

'See, *Ya Sitti*, how crooked the bone is? I do not think that the child was born like this, as her mother claims. I think there was some accident, a jarring of the bone that hindered its normal growth.'

'Will that make your procedure easier or more difficult?' Zahra asked, trying to keep dismay from her voice at the sight of the deformity. To think that this child might have been forced to struggle through life on her twisted limb, trying to keep up with her fellows and wondering why she was cursed to hobble while others could run. And when the time for marriage arrived, who

136

would want a wife who could not labour as others did?

In that moment of realisation, she made a vow: any child who came to the hospital suffering from a defect such as this, whether or not they were entirely cured, would hold her interest for life. She would have husbands found for them, or wives as the case may be, and she would do her utmost to ensure that all went well for them.

'I shall have to break and reset the bone in three places, *Ya Sitti*.' Hamsa Ben Da'oud had lowered his voice so that only she could hear. 'I have an elixir that will take the pain away while I work. The child will know nothing. I cannot rush the procedure; it will take months. It would grieve me if the child were only partially cured and had to be sent back in that state to its mother and father.'

He looked her in the eye and she wondered what rumours he had heard.

'She will stay here until she is cured,' Zahra said firmly. 'What of the grafts you mentioned. Will she need one?'

'Only if parts of the bone prove weak and I do not think they will for her bones are strong elsewhere. She has been fed well even if she was allowed to injure herself as an infant.'

'You said that the jarring of the bone had caused it to grow crooked. Will it not wish to continue in that way even after you have reset it?'

'With rest and care, I hope that the growth will become normal again, *Ya Sitti*.'

'But you cannot say for sure?'

He looked uncomfortable. 'No, I cannot, *Ya Sitti*. I have much to learn, these experimentations are only in the early stages. But with Allah's help I shall be successful, and with each new patient I shall learn something that I did not know before.'

'I wish you every good fortune, *tabib*. You have my full support.' She liked the man. He was willing to admit that he did not know everything, and how many physicians would do that?

Saying goodbye to the little girl, who was now smiling happily, Zahra followed Hamsa Ben Da'oud to the private rooms where Yabila, his wife, awaited them. The room where she stood anxiously in readiness was rich with colour. Bright blue and rosy red hassocks and hangings, embroidered by her, had turned a plain, white-washed dwelling into a cosy and attractive home.

Yabila herself was small and walked with a slight limp, but that was nothing by comparison with the ugly deformity that had plagued her in her youth. That, too, had been caused by a fall, Zahra remembered. No wonder that the *tabib* was so involved with his first young patient, so determined to cure her.

Yabila wanted to sink to the ground and kiss the hem of Zahra's robe, but the Queen pulled her upright.

'I have been eager to meet you, Yabila. Your husband has told me of how he met you.'

'My husband is a fine, good man, *Ya Sitti*! Never has there been such a fine, good man!' Yabila's eyes glistened. 'I was a helpless cripple, doomed to imprisonment in the harem, yet without a husband to call my own and without children to lighten my heart. Then my husband was sent to me by Allah, and my new life began.'

'I am very happy for you, Yabila. You have a son, I believe?'

'Yes, he sleeps, *Ya Sitti*, but I will waken him if you wish to see him.'

'That will not be necessary, thank you.' Zahra smiled. Wake the baby indeed!

'Do you wish to see my legs, *Ya Sitti*?' Yabila made as if to hitch up her *kuftan*, but again Zahra said no, that would not be necessary. Before, she had wished to see the results of the *tabib*'s work, but now, in the privacy of his home, there was something almost disrespectful in

138

asking a woman to bare her limbs for a stranger.

Yabila hastened out to fetch refreshments, and Zahra could see that she walked almost normally. When she returned with a tray laden with delicacies, they sat down together like a family. After Yabila had recovered a little from her nervousness, they talked of the ordinary, reassuring things of life, growing more at ease with one another.

Later, Zahra would look on it as one of the most pleasant days since her mother and father had died. Making good friends: what better way was there to spend a few happy hours?

Zahra had considered various courses of action to bring in the patients, knowing that even if she brought an Imam from Abeesha or Bakasir to bless the building it might have little effect on her people. Superstition and fear were more likely to keep them away, four walls and a roof being seen as a trap by the nomads who viewed their beloved wilderness as their natural habitat. Zahra had known this all along, of course, yet she could not have sick children being treated under the open skies, or crammed together in an airless tent.

Finally, she summoned her *katib*, Abidul, and ordered him to write messages to all her shaikhs and chiefs, telling them in glowing detail all about the amenities of the new hospital: that it was free, that families might stay nearby while their children were ill, and that there were new and successful treatments available there.

Abidul, an aged man who had been Husain's secretary before Zahra's, wrote assiduously for two days, long, elaborate letters to every shaikh in the Land of Mirages, yet all the while he was tut-tutting beneath his breath. He had never approved of women being given a free hand, and now he was seeing the results of the Amira's hasty and thoughtless plans. Had she married the Amir Mahmed eighteen months ago when he had been so

139

eager to unite his lands with hers, then none of this nonsense would have happened. An empty building that was hated and feared, all those doctors and nurses brought here, and now without employ. His mistress would be laughed at throughout the length and breadth of the country.

She should take a husband, and soon, for it was against the laws of God that a woman remain unmarried. A husband would temper her wild whims and give sensible counsel, and children would calm the highstrung temperament that was so like her mother's at that age. He had always had his doubts about Mishaal. Oh, she had made their land wealthy and well watered for thirty years and more, but she had ruled equally with Husain, and sometimes she had insisted that her wishes be paramount above his, and that was wrong in Abidul's eyes, very wrong.

'The beauty of man is in his intelligence, and the intelligence of woman is in her beauty.' That was a Sufi saying, and he agreed wholeheartedly with it. A woman was beautiful and soft and scented because that was what Allah had planned. If he had wished her to be ruler and commander, then he would have made her muscular and tall like a man, and fashioned hairs on her body.

Abidul put down his pen wearily. His great-granddaughter Amaliya would have his evening meal waiting for him, couscous and ground meat followed by dates mashed to a paste because of his loose teeth. His belly rumbled at the thought, and he speeded up his shambling gait. As he approached their tent, he smelled the couscous steaming and his nose twitched. She was an excellent cook, Allah be praised, and, another blessing, she was patient with him.

Once seated, Abidul tore into the food, cramming his mouth so that couscous dribbled down his untidy moustaches.

'Was the Amira sad at heart, Grandfather?' Amaliya

asked as she refilled his coffee dish and placed un-leavened bread before him.

'Sad? Why should she be sad?' Abidul mumbled, never having considered that his mistress might be downcast at the failure of her hopes. Women who planned without asking counsel of a man must learn that failure was unavoidable, otherwise they would begin to behave in the most lawless manner and disaster would follow.

'Because the hospital stays empty, Grandfather, what else?' Amaliya sighed at her grandfather's slowness.

'It does not suit the Beduin, so why should they come?'

'Grandfather, that is heartless! Would you not take your sick child to a *tabib* if it would save her life?'

'I would.'

'Then why should the Beduin not do the same?'

'They would not do the same because they are Beduin, my child, wanderers, the roofless ones who flourish beneath the skies and the stars but not beneath plaster, stones and twigs!'

'If a child is sick then it is not flourishing, is it, Grandfather?' Amaliya said with incontrovertible logic.

'If a child is sick, then that is Allah's will.'

'Are you saying that Allah would instruct us to neglect our children when they are ill; leave them to die when help is at hand?'

'No, of course I am not saying that! Let me finish my dinner, child. You are as argumentative as your mother was, and you will give me indigestion and I shall not be able to sleep. I have written letters all day and now you want me to argue with you!'

'I only wish that we should be agreed on something as important as the saving of a child's life, Grandfather.'

'Why? Why should we be agreed? You have no children to fret over. Worry about them when you have first found a husband.'

'Jaria is with child.'

'Jaria, already?' A piece of mashed meat went down

141

the wrong way and Abidul began to choke uncontrollably. Jaria was his favourite great-granddaughter, a lovely creature with slanting honey-coloured eyes and skeins of black hair. Beside her, Amaliya seemed heavy and clumsy. Jaria had married only three months before and now she was to be a mother, and he – he would be a great-great grandfather! In the middle of his choking he began to gasp with joyous laughter, and between Amaliya's slapping him on the back and his own riotous glee, he almost passed into the next world. But not quite, for he was determined that he would live to see Jaria's son born.

Zahra was having the dream again. The people were coming towards her to greet her as their queen, and then, before them all, she felt her robes slipping away and there she stood, naked and ashamed.

She woke with a sickening jolt, her eyes smarting with unshed tears. She had built the hospital out of love and care for her people and they had rejected her gift. Once more she was the unsure and doubting girl of eighteen months before, mourning her parents and positive that she would fail as her people's leader. She knew what she should have done. She should have married Mahmed months ago, and consulted him about the hospital. The Beduin hated speed and innovation as well she knew, yet she had forged ahead when she should have moved more cautiously.

The darkness was scented with lamp oil and sandalwood, and she could hear Freyha snoring gently on her couch. Lately, her dear friend had complained hardly at all to her, not even giving way to the brief outbursts of temper that beset even the most loving companion. Freyha was trying to shield her from the truth. They all were. She had dreamed a dream, and planned a plan that no one but herself had wanted.

142

PART THREE

The Oasis of the Stars

Tell me, what is Destiny preparing?
Tell me why we two have drawn so near?
Aeons since, you were my sister, sharing
Kin with me, or else my wife most dear.
Everything I am, my every feature,
You divined, my every nerve could thrill,
Read me at a glance – no other creature
Knows me as you know, nor ever will...

Goethe (1749–1832)

Chapter Nine

The Oasis of Rajab was much like any other oasis. There was a small caravanserai housing the men from a camel train, and a meagre pool framed by frayed and wind-battered date palms. Mayne saw that his horse was fed and watered and made comfortable for the night, and then he turned in.

Wild shrieking woke him, the terrified, bone-numbing wailing of a woman in dire trouble. Somehow her screams had intruded into his dream, and the woman who had been dancing seductively, entwined by multi-coloured veils and some strange, shimmering material that he could not identify, began to withdraw from his dream-vision, stepping back into the shadows. He was aware of a bereft feeling, a deep sadness that cut into him. Then, as the shrieking became louder, he woke.

It was a night storm, the tortured vehemence of wind and sand rising eerily, insistently, so that no one could possibly remain asleep. Men were already awake, and looking at one another askance. As the roughly-hewn shutters slammed and creaked, someone leapt up to resecure them. There was sand in everyone's mouth. It tended to be there even when there was no wind; in the desert, it was inescapable.

Yawning, longing to be back in his seductive and sensual dream, Mayne got up and looked out into the heaving darkness through a crack in the shutters. Richly silvered by the moon, the scene that met his eyes was spine-tingling.

The date palms seemed to glow as they bent and dipped before the wind, their fluorescent brightness standing out against brilliant, bronzed sand that hit the gaze with its powerful ochre hues. The water was shining, too, a ghostly, glowing luminosity of rich, dark lamé, and as he watched, he could have sworn that ripples began to part the water's surface, growing deeper and wider until something broke through them. Straining his eyes, he saw that it was a slim, elongated shape of deep, shining silver, like well-honed steel.

A blade, curving and sharp, dazzling in the moonlight, was spearing out of the water!

Mayne closed his eyes disbelievingly, then looked again. There was the same silver-frosted scene, and there the glittering blade suspended an inch or two above the water's surface as if by a spirit hand.

A desert *jinn*, that was what it was. From the beginnings of time they had tricked and confused desert dwellers. He was still dreaming, of course, there was no doubt of that, even though the blade now began to sway smoothly, gently, towards him until it was no more than an arm's length from him and he could see the inscription upon it. He was trying to make sense of the Arabic legend, suddenly knowing that it was imperative that he should read and understand it, but someone was pulling at his sleeve, and he heard a man's voice urging him to stand back. Turning, bemused, he saw the one who had spoken staring at him as if he were crazed. Two more men stood waiting to hammer a board over the shutter crack to keep out the storm. Looking down at his feet as he felt them crunching in grit, he saw a mound of sand that must have blown in while he was standing there. Sand covered his clothes and face. Still not understanding what had happened to him, he glanced

146

quickly back into the storm before moving away. Outside it was pitch dark, and the night was a nightmare void. There was no silvery light, no blazing moon, no ethereally glowing blade.

Of course not. How could there be? He wanted to grin but there was no humour to form the laughter. He had been asleep on his feet; that was it. Indeed, what else could it have been?

'The well, *Ya Sitti*, the well!'

Zahra stared at the woman who had rushed into her tent, her robes crumpled and sand-stained from travelling.

'What well is this?' she said coolly, fearing more criticism.

'The well at the hospital, *Ya Sitti*! It is run dry! Overnight it has happened, and we know not why! Yesterday, it was full as always, and the sweet water was drawn up as it is, fresh every day for us. Today, when the women went to draw it up, there was nothing to draw! Nothing! All had gone. We stared down into the depths and could see no sparkle of water, nothing but bare stones, *Ya Sitti*! Allah, it is a curse, a curse!' Weeping, the woman had sunk to her knees before Zahra and was using the hem of her robe as a kerchief.

Gently disentangling herself from the clutching fingers, Zahra tried not to panic. Wells running dry . . . the ancient legend . . . her mother. As these thoughts swirled in her mind, her body became taut, chills trickling down her spine. But she must not panic. Wells had run dry before without its being the hand of Allah. And yet, even as she tried to reassure herself, she knew with chilling certainty that she was wasting her time. This was the hand of Allah; she could feel it, sense it. What had she done to offend Him that He would take away the water from His beloved Land of Mirages, the land that was His most favoured place on Earth?

147

She had angered Him, she knew it. She had gone against the Qu'ran, thinking that her lone way was best, when she should have married and borne sons to secure her country's heritage.

'Ya Sitti!' The woman was tugging at her hem again, her face swollen and spotted with tears. 'What shall we do? Allah has turned His face against us. We are accursed, we shall all die! What shall we do?'

White-faced, Zahra remained silent, her throat constricted by fear. She did not know what to say or do; she was numb. She had taken it all for granted, as they all had: the wealth, the plentiful water, God's bounty, and now the day of reckoning had come.

She had agreed at last. His face alight, Mahmed took her in his arms and they kissed for the very first time. He was more than pleased with the result. Soft and tender, her mouth opened as his kiss deepened. He could feel her slender body fluttering a little in his embrace as if she were overwhelmed with passion. Perhaps she was not such a cold thing after all? Anyway, he would be able to teach her all the many arts of love that she knew nothing of as yet. Ignorant little virgin, he would show her there was more to love than she had ever dreamed of!

Zahra managed to stay still while he kissed her, forcing her mouth open and plunging his tongue deep into her mouth, although his temerity made her shudder. Yet she had no choice. She must make amends as swiftly as possible, live her life as Allah had intended, marry and unite Mahmed's lands with hers, and bear the sons who would strengthen the inheritance of Husain and Mishaal.

She had thought that she would quite enjoy a lover's kiss, but she was not enjoying this one. It seemed to last eternally and she was growing tense and breathless. When she tried to push Mahmed away, he crushed her closer, and she could feel something rigid and hard

148

pressing against her thigh. As she became aware of it, it jumped against her, once, twice, as if it had a life of its own. Heat suffused her cheeks and she yearned to be able to scream at him to go and leave her alone to gather her broken thoughts.

'Allah, give me courage,' she prayed silently, 'give me courage,' but she feared that she was not to have her prayers answered. She was quaking inside, and filled with dread. There was no escape for she had just told Mahmed that she would marry him, that he could set the date and she would prepare for it. How delighted he had looked and how he had hastened to embrace her, despite his coolness and lack of enthusiasm on previous visits.

Now she wished that he would be cool again, for he was continuing to kiss her and his square brown hand was squeezing her breast, pressing and kneading and pulling as if he believed that she would be driven into a frenzy of ardour by the insensitive, almost painful assault.

With fortitude she bore it all, calling to mind the hospital well, and the news that had arrived during the week of further wells in Pujabur and Rabnaik that had dried out, along with two oases hitherto renowned for their fertility and excess of water. Now that she had said yes to Mahmed, she hoped with all her heart that Allah would smile on them again. To show her penitence she would return to womanly tasks, to stitching and sewing silk prayer mats, to embroidering robes and slippers for those she loved, and reading the Qu'ran for longer hours than before. If she lowered her head and veiled herself, perhaps Allah would cease to notice her and all would return to peace and tranquillity.

'Zahra, sweet Venus star, we shall be so happy together!' Mahmed murmured in her ear. 'You are unsure of yourself now, and that is fitting for a virgin bride but soon, very soon, I shall take you to the marriage couch and make you a woman. You will not regret our union, my heart. Our lands shall unite and we

149

shall know nothing but contentment. I do not ask that you should say you love me as yet but time will bring that certainty to you, and then I shall delight in the words I crave to hear.'

Zahra looked up at him, astonished by this lengthy and romantic outpouring. Before, Mahmed had always seemed a quiet, sometimes morose sort of man. She had obviously misjudged him sadly, but then, her judgement was far from perfect. Now the truth was dawning. In her ignorance she had condemned Mahmed because she had not been ready to see the facts. He was a little lacking in eloquence, it was true, but that did not mean that he was an unfeeling monster. He had sworn that they would be happy together, and, as that was what she now needed and wanted more than anything, she believed him.

Mayne's camel was a game beast. For the past week it had survived on roots, herbs, and the occasional mouthful of camel's thorn, while he had subsisted on a single pouch of *laban*. The oases where they were to have restocked had dried out, unbelievable though it seemed.

The residents of the second caravanserai had appeared at his shouted greeting, their faces pale and shocked. They looked at him so strangely that he almost felt he should not be there, as if this were not the place where travellers had been succoured for decades.

Eventually, they let him in, but with none of the famed Arabian spirit of hospitality. Silently, they brought him bread and dates, and an aged, wrinkled woman sat before him to prepare his coffee, steaming and fresh.

As she poured the steaming water from the engraved copper pot into his dish, she muttered prayers beneath her breath as if she feared that the brew might be noxious. When he asked her what was troubling her, she looked away, catching up her veil and tucking it firmly into place so that only her old, weather-dried eyes were visible.

150

'Why are you all so unhappy, *Sitt*? This place is like a tomb.'

'Our days of happiness are finished, *Effendi*. Three days ago my son, Jabal, went to our well and found it . . .' Her voice cracked and she paused, gasping for breath. 'He found it dry, Allah forgive us for our sins! He found it dry, the great oasis of Kahabi, dry! The water has gone, the water that has nourished travellers for year upon year upon year!' Bowing her head, the woman began to sob, Mayne's coffee forgotten.

'*Sitt*, I am sorry to hear of your misfortune, but do they not say that the Land of Mirages shall never run out of its supply? Perhaps this is some temporary shortage and the water will return soon?'

'Return soon? Never, it will never return. I, Kira, know it! I am old enough to remember the dreadful times when all the wells and the oases ran dry, and we starved and wore the same thin rags for months on end. Do you know of those times, *Effendi*? But no, you are far too young.'

'I have heard of them, though,' Mayne assured her.

'That was before Husain found his Mishaal, the Peacock Dancer. He fell in love with her but she would not have him at first – oh no, women can be blind to true love even when it is under their noses. Many months it took before she would admit that she, too, loved him, and then at last the rains began, and they rained in a great deluge, on and on, for week after week, until every well and every wadi and oasis was overflowing, and all the underground rivers swelled, and the sweet fruits grew on the trees, and we knew that we would never go thirsty again.' Kira sighed shakily, and Mayne's heart went out to her.

'So why should you fear the return of the drought, *Sitt*? Did it not rain the night before last?' He really was not interested in this old woman's ramblings.

'Yes, but it did not fill our water pool. It is slowly

151

emptying, and there is nothing that we can do about it. After the full moon, we shall have no water left and our lives shall be finished. How could we survive out here without water? We shall have to journey to the city and struggle for a living there, but we are desert folk and city life is poison to us.'

'Old woman, leave the *Effendi* alone. He is not to blame for our troubles. Forgive her, *Effendi*, she is distressed at the family's misfortune.'

The speaker was the man who had opened the door of the caravanserai to Mayne. Thin and haggard, he too looked as if he might burst into tears at any moment.

'My sympathies are with you,' Mayne told the man, out of courtesy to a host. 'I shall pray for you.'

'You are one of the faithful?'

Mayne did not reply immediately. He, one of the faithful? In truth, he did not know what he was, being something of a hybrid, first Muslim, then Catholic, then Muslim again, and since then cleaving to no faith.

All the same, he nodded to the man. 'Yes, I am one of the faithful.' And as he said it he felt a lifting of the heart, despite the gloom that surrounded him and the plight of these poor people.

As he finished his dinner, he reflected on his past. He had never taken completely to the Catholic religion; it was so very different from that of Arabia, where Jesus was considered one of the Prophets of Allah but not the chosen Son of God. To adhere to Catholicism had meant that he must try to reverse all that he had learned in his childhood, and he had tried for a time, warming to the Mother of God, if not to the Trinity.

What he had learned of the North American Indian's religion had appealed to him more, with its vivid, energetic worship, the belief in the great sky spirit and the intimacy with nature and the earth. That was what a religion should be: all-encompassing, whole, complete. Yet there was much to attract him back to Allah, and if

152

he should be pulled in that direction, he would not resist.

'Where do you journey?' It was the old woman again, come to collect his empty dishes.

'Wherever the path leads me,' he replied obliquely, having no intention of imparting any information to anyone.

'Those are the words of a Sufi,' the old woman responded, pausing in her clearing, 'yet you do not wear the woollen robe.'

'I am no Sufi, old woman.'

'Yet you speak those words, placing yourself in Allah's hands so that He can direct you where He will.'

Mayne shrugged. He did not have to explain to anyone. What was more, he was suddenly bone weary and he knew he had a hard few days' travel still ahead.

He slept like a babe until dawn when he had a dream that woke him instantly. The woman was dancing again, draped in her shimmering dancing robe of multicolours, swaying and gyrating as if she were lighter than flower seeds borne on the breeze. She affected him deeply. He wanted to reach out and touch her, see if she were real, hold the shimmering robes to his lips and kiss it as if she were a great queen or goddess, but the closer he approached, the further away she drifted. Her face glowed silvery white as if there were a lamp beneath her flesh. Then she vanished, receding to a piercing white pinpoint of light, and it was then that he woke with a sensation of despair at her leaving.

Lying on his roughly-woven straw mat, his goatskin pulled around him, he reflected on the dream. It was not unusual for a man of his appetites to dream of a woman, but this was no sensual *houri* come to tempt him as he slept and incite him to arousal. This was a dream-spirit of far deeper dimensions, awakening an altogether higher part of him.

Dawn was slowly brightening the whitewashed room, giving it the opalescence of a pearl, and in his mind's eye,

153

on the wall opposite, he saw the swaying, undulating dancer, her arms coiled above her head so that she took on the form of a rearing serpent. But this was no vicious, deadly snake. The memory of the shimmering beauty of his vision brought the tears to his eyes, he who had not wept for years and who had vowed that he never would again.

Sadness filled him as he left the oasis. It was like parting from a friend. The inhabitants stood at the door to wish him Godspeed, *salaaming* with their heads bowed low.

Mayne decided that having thought of little else save his mission for the past month, it was not unnatural that he should dream of an exotic dancer. The Amira's mother had been famous for her dancing, and that must have put the notion in his head.

He reminded himself of what his Commanding Officer had told him. The new Amira was young and quixotic, very headstrong and determined to go her own way. She had refused to marry the one man who could unite and strengthen her lands with his, and there was fear that she would be overthrown by a stronger power. And there the General had beamed happily.

'The Beduin fear the invasion of their Mohammedan rivals and enemies; they do not envisage a foreign power conquering them, but it is now virtually certain. One way or another, we'll have that land and all its riches. The Amira considerably weakened her position when she offended her advisers and countrymen by insisting upon staying single. That is not considered a natural state for a Mohammedan woman, y'know.'

'I know, sir,' Mayne had replied. The General's knowledge of his origins seemed to wax and wane by the minute.

'Yes, yes, of course y'do. Remember that she is a virgin, and accustomed to excessive courtesies. You will have to use them all or she could take offence and throw

154

you out. That must not happen, d'you hear? We are depending on her wealth to reinforce us in our efforts to maintain our grip on Algeria. The cost of maintaining a force there is astronomical, and money does not grow on camel's thorn!' The General had guffawed at his own joke.

Later that afternoon, Mayne saw the camel train. Knowing that his face was burnt dark ochre from the sun, his clothes outright Arabian, and his command of Arabic superlative, he greeted them as if they were his own countrymen. Camel trains were often the bearer of news and gossip. When they halted to take refreshment, he was invited to join them, and after much quaffing of coffee and trivial talk that did not interest him at all, sure enough out came the gossip.

They were taking bolts of silk and a casket of black pearls to the Amir Mahmed, it transpired, his betrothal gift from the Amira Zahra.

'Then she has agreed to marry the Amir?'

'Yes, Allah be praised. It was the wells drying out that hastened her decision.'

'The well at the oasis a day's ride from here?' Mayne asked.

'That too has run dry?' His informant paled. 'No, I did not know of that, Allah protect us! Many wells have stopped giving water during the past two moons ... the Amira is distraught. Naturally, she believes that it has been caused by her reluctance to marry the Amir Mahmed, but now she has agreed, we pray the water will return. Do you know of the old legend?'

'No, what old legend?'

'Centuries ago, the Queen of the Desert, Zenobia, ancestress of Husain and Zahra, concealed her jewels in the desert when she was fleeing from the infidel, the worshippers of pagan gods. Until thirty years ago they stayed hidden, and it was said that if a non-believer touched them first, then all the wells and wadis of the

Land of Mirages would run dry. Instead, Mishaal found them, in an ancient ruined temple, a place where idols were worshipped in the days of Zenobia. Bravely, she faced the idol, so that she could retrieve the Jewels of Destiny and give them to Husain. Then the wells began to fill again, and the wadis and the oases, and thus it has been, God's Bounty upon us, for thirty years.'

'If the legend said that a non-believer finding the jewels would cause the great drought, why then did it have to be Mishaal? Could not Husain have found the jewels?'

The Arab bunched his fist, shaking it back and forth in front of his cheek as he screwed up his face with delight.

'Ah, but you see, it had to be a female who touched them first. Allah does not reveal all His mysteries at once. Mishaal was the one who would be a light for her peoples. After she found the jewels, the darkness fled and we have basked in the light of Allah for thirty years.'

'And what do they say of Zahra, daughter of Mishaal? Does she have any place in the legend?'

'There is no legend for her, the wayward one. She has offended her peoples; she has refused to marry and beget heirs to carry on the blessed line of Husain, and she will not listen to the advice of her ministers. Now Allah has shown his disgust and is taking our water from us!' More fist shaking, this time with both hands and no laughter.

Mayne listened, astonished. The woman sounded beyond all reach. In her short reign she had managed to offend everyone, and go against all the customs. Arab ways were firmly entrenched, it took decade upon decade to begin to alter any of their firm beliefs, their deep-rooted customs, and for those who attempted swift change there was frequently an unhappy end. Men fared badly enough in such attempts, but for women to try them would inevitably lead to disaster.

156

'When is the marriage to be?'

'As soon as the Amir returns from his journey. He is seeking a she camel that is white as the tusk of the elephant, for he wishes to breed it with his racing camels that are famed throughout Arabia.'

'He knows of the white camel, you mean, or is this another legend?'

'Both, *Effendi*, both. He has heard much of the camel that is white as the tusk of the elephant, and now he has heard where it is, he wishes to obtain it. His bride will ride to her wedding on it, when it is found.'

So Mahmed was away, and the wedding would not take place until he returned with this famous camel.

'How far will his journey be?'

Suddenly the loquacious Arab became suspicious, and, ignoring Mayne's question, returned to mundane gossip about the weather and the food that was now being served to them, and nothing that Mayne could say would make him return to the subject of the Amir's journey. So he would have to guess how long he could stay safely in the Amira's camp, that was, if he could not extract the information from her when they met, but at least it would give him a stay of execution.

At the use of those words, he suddenly felt chilled. Stay of execution? It sounded like someone's death knell! With all his heart he hoped that it would not be his.

Chapter Ten

Having obtained details of the whereabouts of the Amira's hospital from the leader of the camel train, Mayne decided that he would view it before heading for her camp. Everyone in the land knew of its failure, it would seem. Once the well of sweet water had run dry, the *atib'ba*, the physicians, and the nurses had deserted the building. It was already said to be an immoral place, ill-omened and unlucky to those who resided there, so the leader of the camel train had told him.

One of the nurses had indulged in fornication and when the Amira had banished her, she had spread the tale that all the nurses accepted men into their quarters at nightfall. What mother would let her children be nursed by such *bintilkha'tas*, women of low repute? They might have their childish illnesses cured only to contract worse ones!

The sad, white, empty shell stood baked by the desert sun, a ghost place of glories that would never be. He did not stay there long. It was ill-omened as they said; he could sense it.

On the way to the Amira's encampment, he briefly dismounted and stood in the shelter of some sloping dunes. There he stripped off his desert gear and attempted to bathe himself in a miniscule puddle of water mixed with sand. Afterwards, he donned his

Legionnaire's uniform, which had been carefully rolled into his saddle bag, and combed his hair. It had grown longer during his weeks of travel, contrary to the Legionnaires' custom of keeping their hair clipped close to the skull, and he trusted that he would now present a more winning appearance to a woman accustomed to the Beduin men with their flowing locks.

Having got the better of his thick dark hair, he donned the white *khépi* of the Legion, squared his shoulders, and once again assumed a military stance. In the past weeks he had relished the freedom and comfort of the Arab robes and his uniform felt rigid and constricting by contrast, but he knew that he must wear it. His mission was to impress, to charm, cajole and gently coerce. If gossip were to be believed, he could not be arriving at a better time. The Amira's morale was low; she was in a weak position and would be more malleable. She must listen to him and see the sense of what he said.

The spiralling twists of smoke from the campfires hazed the horizon with charcoal grey, behind which the afternoon sky was fading from cerulean to palest speedwell. Timid clouds drifted across the blue, unsure of their reception, eventually to evaporate. Mayne watched it all as he rode, marvelling anew at the majestic face of nature and comparing the terracottas and oranges, the burnt yellows, carob browns and gilded hazels of this exotic scenario with the colours that he remembered from his days in Maine: the silver and pearl white of the snow, battening against the eyes so that everything became a pallid, platinum haze; the unearthly blue mauve of the distant mountains, their crowns iced by snow; the colours of autumn, orange-bronzes, bright golds, lemony greens changing to burnt sienna, rich apricots, and fiery deep scarlets, and he felt a painful pang of longing for the America that he would never see again, and the father who had given him so much and yet so little.

The camp was coming into sight, stretching for acres across the wilderness. He saw the lowslung black tents of the Beduin, the camels, goats and horses, the men, women and children all going about their accustomed daily routine. It was a tranquil scene of entrenched domesticity, and his heart twisted within him at the sight. Once he had lived not unlike this, knowing no better. It had helped to make him what he was, for good or bad.

'Bed the woman if you have to,' the General had said. 'Perhaps that is what she is short of. *Mon Dieu*, eighteen and still a virgin! I would not object to taking your place, Amyan. But woo her first, for God's sake, I do not want to have your death on my hands!'

'Bed the woman if you have to.' Mayne grinned to himself as he rode into the camp. Yes, he might just do that if she were beautiful, although wooing a virgin was not his idea of seduction. He liked his women to have courage and spirit, but they must be amiable, too. The Beduin women were too indomitable, too serious for him.

Men ran towards him, grasping his camel's reins, shouting up at him. He had expected guards to stop him long before he reached the camp but security seemed lax. He was being questioned, but only half-heartedly. The camp was ripe for plucking, it would appear.

After telling them his name and rank, and that he wished to speak to their Amira, he was instructed to wait. Then he was left standing for an interminable time while the afternoon became early evening, and the sudden onset of dusk descended.

Squatting down in the sand, he considered what he would do if he were not received into the royal presence. He had been given suitable gifts for the Amira, and these could be given to her servants and passed on to her as a promise of things to come.

They were valuable trinkets, pretty things that would

160

tempt any female, and he knew that her curiosity would be piqued when she had opened the packages, and she would want to meet the envoy from France.

Dusk became night and a passing servant caught sight of him. The man looked askance for a moment and then, with profuse apologies, ushered him into a small, empty tent.

'A thousand pardons, *Effendi*. We had forgotten about you.'

The tent smelled of goats and more goats, and the food that he was brought comprised goats' cheese and more goats' cheese, but it was better than sleeping on an empty stomach.

Sinking on to the goat-scented pallet, he chewed on the heavily crusted cheese, washing it down with the sickly-sweet fermented date juice. When he asked for water, the servant looked even more horrified and hurried away without replying. So much for desert hospitality!

That was only the beginning. Three days later he was still in the tent, having had his lifetime's fill of goats' cheese and *nabidh*, and he was boiling with fury. How dare the arrogant bitch keep him hanging about like this? He had sent her the first gifts – pearl bracelets, earrings shaped like gazelle's antlers studded with tiny diamonds, and four garnet rings – but she had sent them straight back. What temerity! Next he had sent her a written message, carefully composed and flowery with flattery, and that too had come back, obviously unread.

'Is the Amira sick?' he had asked the man who brought him his daily abominations, as he now called his meals.

'*Ya Allah!* No she is not sick! Why do you ask, *Effendi*?'

'She refuses to see me, to take my gifts, to read my letter.'

'That is Allah's will, *Effendi*. . . .'

'I see. Then the Amira is in direct contact with the

161

divinity?' His sarcasm was wasted on the man, who shrugged and went away.

The fourth day dawned and Mayne considered aborting his mission but quickly changed his mind as sunlight beckoned. She would have to see him. There was no way he was going to let her evade him, the haughty bitch! His hands tingled. He fantasised flinging her over his knee and slapping her bottom until she screamed, then he would shake her until she agreed to do whatever he ordered. It was a heady fantasy, but it could go no further than that. She was in control here, and he must never forget it.

At mid-morning, a man came for Mayne, ordering him to present himself at the banner-hung tent of the Amira. As he waited inside, conscious of his dishevelled appearance, he set about straightening his uniform, tugging down the hem of the jacket, fixing his belt neatly around his hips and smacking the creases from his dull-red breeches. There was a speck of dirt on his boot and he was bending down to remove it with a wet finger when the curtain to the royal audience chamber was pulled back and the scent of full-blown roses billowed out to meet him.

Naturally she would be full of womanish wiles. She would be decked in silks and jewels, smelling like a rose bower, and calmly expecting him to forgive the insult of being kept waiting for nearly four days. Clenching his jaw, he straightened up and followed the womanservant into the holy of holies.

It was a colourful room, decked in bright Persian tapestries depicting fawns and gazelles and fair maidens combing their long golden tresses. There were vast, silk-embroidered cushions, gleaming golden oil lamps suspended from delicate chains, and cedarwood chests carved with patterns of coiling vines and blossoms. He felt almost drowned in the brilliant hues and the multitude of scents; they were an assault upon the

162

senses after the bald ochres, duns and bronzes of the desert wilderness. He steeled himself inwardly, scanning the opulent audience chamber for the one whom he had come to see. He would not have put it past her to be absent, to keep him waiting yet again, even if in more opulent surroundings.

Then he saw her, and his blood turned to water. How small she was, sitting there crosslegged in Beduin fashion, heavily veiled in rich sapphire blue silk. First he noticed her minute hands, almost bare of ornament, then her smooth, creamy forehead from which tiny ebony hairs drifted backwards into the confinement of her head veil. Seeing that her face too was veiled, he cursed. All he could see were her eyes but as he approached her he could discern their colour, a most un-Arabian green, a rich and dazzling malachite. He thought of the set of jewels in the second casket – rings, earrings, collar and bracelets, all studded with malachite in filigree silver – and he cursed himself for not having offered them first. She would be as vain and gullible as any Western woman, of course.

An elderly woman who watched him as closely as if he might turn into a twist of smoke at any moment, bade him stand before the Amira, which he did, and then a cushion was brought for him and he was given permission to sit. Having done so, he brought up his eyes to meet her malachite gaze and his mouth filled with water.

She had removed her face veil. Perhaps she had decided that he was harmless after all? His jaw went limp. If he had tried to speak, the words would have died on his tongue. His pulses throbbed, and a fierce blush coloured his face and neck. Sweat beaded the collar of his uniform jacket.

There are some moments that are beyond the human capacity for words, and into this silent void something quite unexpected enters and out of this is fashioned destiny.

163

She was like an exquisite little idol, so graceful and diminutive that he wanted to laugh out loud. She could not be real. This was some figurine they had placed there to trick him. How could any living woman have such velvet-cream skin, so smooth and glowing, and such a full, curving mouth, rosy from nature's blessing and not from artifice. And those eyes ... they were the eyes of a sorceress, mesmerising, stunning. He was enchanted, doubly enchanted, and all his prejudices and preconceptions evaporated, whisked away into the hemisphere. She was beauty, radiance, divinity, bliss!

'Captain Mayne, you wished to see me?' Her voice was like temple bells singing out across fresh, pure air. He wanted to worship at her shrine, adore her, deify her.

Struggling to collect himself, he croaked out his greeting. He had written his letter to her in Arabic, so she knew that he was cognisant of the language, and now he spoke in that tongue, telling her his reason for being there. On behalf of the French Foreign Legion, he was representing His Imperial Majesty, Napoleon III, Emperor of France, who wished to make an alliance with the Land of Mirages.

'With the land itself, and not with its Amira?' she responded, her mouth quirking, and he wanted to laugh out loud again. A woman with a sense of humour! A rare jewel indeed.

'With Your Highness, of course, if it would meet with Your Highness's favour.' Speckled blue-green eyes met malachite and could not look away.

'You are very direct, Captain.'

'You wished to know why I am here, Your Highness, and so I told you.'

'You speak my language, Captain. Does that mean that you are familiar with the ways of Arabia?'

'It does, Your Highness.' He knew that it was disgracefully rude to stare at her as he was doing, but he could not wrench away his gaze. He wanted to memorise

164

her face, imprint it on his mind for eternity. And those slender little hands, the skin so white and yet gently gilded by the sun, the fingers small-boned and sensitive, the knuckles very slightly wider than the rest of the bone which told him that she was vulnerable and deeply emotional. Dananir's hands had been like that.

'That is why your Legion sent you?'

'It is, Your Highness.'

'Yet you came alone, without a deputation? I would have expected a procession of your fellow soldiers at least, laden with caskets of jewels and gold.'

So she can be bribed! he thought gleefully, then saw the twinkle in her eyes. She was teasing him.

'They will follow, Your Highness, if Your Highness gives her agreement to the treaty that His Imperial Majesty wishes to make with you.'

'I see, but we have plenty of time to discuss this matter. Would you care for refreshments, Captain?' Before he could answer, the Amira clapped her hands together and four attendants entered, bearing vast oval gold trays on which were piled a variety of sweetmeats and cakes. Then two more women, draped in blue-green robes, began to prepare the coffee, heating the copper kettle over a trivet and grinding the beans so that their pungent odour filled the tent.

Seconds after, two young men entered the audience chamber, heads bowed, took up their positions in the rear of the tent, and began to play reedy, haunting music.

A scene from the Arabian nights, thought Mayne, suddenly filled with the sweet, rushing happiness he had not felt for years, if ever.

To show that he was an honoured guest, the Amira passed him his porcelain dish of coffee with her own hands, and he was invited to take his choice from a selection of sweetmeats. As he did so, their eyes met again over the gold platter. Sitting there, coffee in hand

165

while balancing a gold plate on his knee, he felt like a boy again, diffident, unsure, and yet content to recognise, in all its true, bright detail what had been missing from his life all these years.

Dazedly, he thought, 'You are the one I have been waiting for all my life,' and tears prickled behind his eyes, startling him. 'Idiot!' he told himself silently. 'Idiot. You're here to twist her round your finger – not let her do that to you!'

'If she capitulates, and signs the treaty, then you will have earned yourself a lifetime's fame and fortune, Captain,' his General had said. 'If we invaded the Land of Mirages, we would have the whole of the Arab world on our backs, but if she treats with us, then we shall have Arabia behind us. No matter what we do after the treaty is signed, the very fact that Husain's daughter trusted us and united with us will be paramount. The idea is to steal through Arabia bit by bit, using her country as our base. It will supply us with everything we need for the next step of our invasion, and no one will suspect our plan until it is too late.'

Remembering these words, Mayne gritted his teeth. They were poisonous, treacherous, but he would not have expected anything else from one of the most ruthless commanding officers of the Foreign Legion. The Legion was famed for its toughness and brutality; men with tender hearts and generous sympathies would not survive an hour there.

'When you have refreshed yourself, I would like to introduce you to some of my people. Have you ever been in a Beduin camp before, Captain?' Mayne nodded. 'So you will know something of our way of life?' He nodded again. 'We are renowned for our hospitality. Every guest is holy; even if he has only drunk one dish of coffee, he cannot be harmed. We take our laws from those that the Prophet Mohammed gave us in his *suras* in the seventh century. Do you know anything of his life?'

166

'A little.' In fact he knew a great deal, but he wanted to hear her voice again, those silvery temple bells singing out across the clear, fresh air.

'Mohammed ibn 'Abdallah was orphaned when he was an infant, and was adopted into the Quraish tribe of Mecca where his uncle raised him in desperate poverty. It would seem that his life was without event until he reached the age of forty, by which age he had achieved many hours of deepest meditation in the caves near Mecca. Married by then, to a rich widow, he felt obliged to proclaim the absolute unity of God, and to speak against the worship of false idols, of which there were many in his day. Much money was made from the idolatrous ceremonies at the sacred *ka'ba*, so naturally there was resentment when Mohammed denounced these.'

'But apart from that growing resentment, there was little reaction to his words,' Mayne continued for her, his eyes sparkling.

'So you know of this?' The Amira bit into her lower lip as colour flooded her face. Mayne grinned, unable to stop himself. He could listen to her voice forever but he had no wish to deceive her.

And then he realised what he was thinking. He had no wish to deceive her, and yet his entire mission was built on deception! Was he not there for the express purpose of tricking and cheating her, talking her into agreeing to what she believed would be a treaty of friendship when in fact it would be the end of her sovereignty in her own country? His throat dried as he realised that he would have to act as he had never acted before, and tell lie upon lie if he was to be successful. Yet it must be done. He had his orders, and he had never defied them before.

'Yes, I know of Mohammed's early days,' he said with a smile. 'I know that he was treated very much as Jesus Christ was treated: ridiculed, sneered at or, ignored. Then he had to move away from his home because of

167

local objections to his preaching, and eventually, after having been almost killed by the Meccans, he fled to Medina where he spent some time in gathering a group of followers. In 630 he was strong enough to return victorious to Mecca, the great new Prophet of the religion that he fashioned with the help of Allah and His angels.'

'You are very well informed, Captain. What do you think of Mohammed and His God? Do you have any views upon Islam?'

Mayne wavered only briefly. He had studied Islam for over two years during his sojourn in Arabia where he had delved into Sufism, admiring its honesty and directness, yet the Path had scared him with its puritanism and extremism, the demand for absolute obedience to one's religious master, undertaking to do whatever he decided was good for one's soul. Obligatory to the Sufi were the wearing of the saffron orange robes to show that all must be the same externally, and the carrying of the staff and bowl, the only requirements of the wandering religious. They were to remind the supplicant that the Sufi order was dedicated to work and authority, as represented by the staff, and spiritual and physical nourishment, as represented by the bowl.

Mayne had been all too conscious that he desired something, but he had not known what it was five years ago. Sufism had intrigued, but not commanded him; nonetheless, he had ventured a little way along its path.

'What religion do you practise, Captain? You speak our language as well as any true believer.' Her little face was alight, shining with an inner brightness that he knew he would never possess. Her religion obviously meant everything to her, which was as it should be. He was suddenly ashamed of his maverick beliefs.

'I was raised in Islam by my mother, and afterwards I became familiar with Catholicism.'

'The Cult of the Virgin Mary? I know very little about that. It is totally different from Islam. And which of the two did you prefer?'

'A trick question,' he thought, 'be wary how you answer.' She was weighing him up, yet again he did not wish to deceive her.

'Islam was everything I needed when I was of Islam, and Catholicism was everything I needed when I was of the Christian world,' he said cryptically.

'You speak in the past tense. Are you not still of the Christian world? France is Catholic, is she not?'

'For the moment, I am of Islam again. This journey has brought it all back to me: my childhood, my dead mother, my hopes and dreams as a boy.'

Of being wealthy and renowned, of having the universe at my feet, the stars and moon my servants, the most beautiful women at my command. . . .

'Does your father still live?'

'He died a few years ago.'

'So we are both orphans!'

'Dangerous ground,' he thought. Too much in common would make him even more sympathetic to her and her cause. Reminding himself why he was there, he tried to stifle all emotion.

'I believe that I must congratulate you on your intended marriage to the Amir Mahmed ibn Beydoun?'

Closing her eyes, she threw back her head. 'Yes, congratulate me for I shall need it! But no, I should not speak like that. Mahmed is a good man and he will be a good husband. It is the will of Allah that a woman should have a husband to guide and advise her, did you not know?' There was a bitterness in the temple-bell voice.

'That sounds to me the business of a father, not a husband. Love should be lighthearted and tender, not weighted down by the advice of aged ministerial husbands.'

'*Ya Allah*, but you are right! Tell that to my advisers,

will you, and step well back! My future has been mapped out for me, and I am not allowed to have any say in it.'

'But you are Amira, Your Highness, daughter of Husain and Mishaal.'

'They were the blessed ones, not I.'

Sadness robbed the beautiful eyes of their brightness and his heart ached for her. Striving for detachment, he said, 'I find it hard to believe that some of their gifts have not been passed on to their daughter.'

'Perhaps they have. I am wilful, and I desire to go my own way, just as my mother did. I have a head filled with wild notions, just as my mother did. I speak out of turn, as I am speaking now, just as my mother did. But you see what worked for her does not work for me. She was unique, and very special. She came from the lowest of tribes, the Sulubba, but she was never treated with contempt. She brought thirty years of riches and peace to these lands, and everyone knew that Allah loved her, that He worked through her, so they listened to her as if she were a saint. Perhaps one day she will be, if she is not already. People go to pray where she and my father are buried, and flowers grow there even when it is not the season for them. I saw them myself.'

The haunting green eyes were dreamy, and more than anything in the world he wanted to take her in his arms and kiss away all her fears.

'Fool,' he thought, 'remember your mission! You are here to win her over to your side, not to be turned into a puppet who obeys her every whim.' Yet he knew that something almost frightening had happened within moments of his meeting her. He felt two things: that she was the most exquisite, adorable creature he had ever met, and that he had known her all his life, and perhaps in lives before that. There was a tie between them that he had never felt with another woman, a feeling of rightness and confidence, as if he could support and love her always from this day forward.

And that was what he wanted to do, with all his heart. Curse his mission! Curse the General and his hero's reputation in the Foreign Legion! What were they when he had found the love of his life?

'When girls are young and untried, they imagine all sorts of things. They imagine that they have the ugliest noses ever created, and that they are so fat, or so thin, that no one could ever love them. They are filled with doubts and racked by moods. That is all part of growing up,' he attempted to reassure.

Suddenly the sad eyes were piercingly bright and the gentle sweetness had faded from her lovely face.

'A lecture in growing up from the good Captain! I would never have survived without such advice, be assured. How would I have gone on if you had not come here and told me this?'

She spoke cuttingly, but he was not cut. Instead, he grinned for reply and said beneath his breath, so that her attendants would not hear, that he had other matters to discuss when they were alone.

'I have no wish to be alone with you! How could I trust you? You came here out of the blue, you represent the enemy who has invaded Algiers, and now you lecture me on growing up!'

'The Emperor deeply regrets the events of his invasion of Algiers, and he now wishes to form an alliance with Arabia. Naturally, as you are the most important sovereign here, he came to you first. If you will treat with us, then others will follow and the Emperor will be able to make recompense for his regretted invasion.'

The lies tripped lightly off his tongue. Had he not rehearsed them throughout his journey, speaking out loud to his silent *dhalul* who had stared back at him cynically, chewing on camel's thorn and pawing the sand with an impatient foot?

'Surely withdrawal would be the surest recompense?'

'That is what the Emperor plans, Your Highness.'

171

'He does? After all these years of making inroads into Arabia and strengthening his position, sending in new Legionnaires like yourself to conquer my fellow countrymen and even ruthlessly conquering Kabylia, now he wants to retreat and make friends?'

'He does, Your Highness. That is why I was sent here, to pave the way for a peaceful withdrawal.'

'Truly I cannot see how a withdrawal can be anything else! Everyone would welcome it. No one would object, or insist that your troops remain where they are.'

'That is true, Your Highness, but would there not be bad feeling left behind after they had gone? The Emperor does not wish his name to be blackened. He wishes to leave behind him a strong treaty, and in such a document he will clarify his intentions. He will offer financial compensation for any damage done, for the upset and distress he has caused your countrymen, and he will – '

'Captain, time is passing and I have other commitments.'

It was the curtest form of dismissal. Pulling her veil across her face, eyes lowered, she looked like a diminutive statuette carved from ivory and sapphire, distant and unreachable. There was nothing he could do now without offending protocol. Already her attendants had risen and were waiting for him to do the same so that they could escort him outside. With a profound feeling of loss, he accompanied them, glancing back once as he came to the heavy curtain that served as a doorway. She was still sitting there, head bowed, silent and still.

Feeling bereft, he stepped outside the *majliss*, the reception room, and into the piercing midday light of the desert where the heat assailed him, pounding against his thick uniform. Replacing the *khépi* which he had kept tucked under his arm, he returned to his allotted tent and sat down to consider his next move.

172

She was silent for the rest of that day, despite all Freyha's attempts to question her. The stranger had done it, the dashing stranger in the foreign uniform, the man with the blue-green eyes and the brutally handsome face. His eyes had looked into her heart, judged her correctly and perceived the truth, and she did not know how to react before such perception.

When he had gone, she had no appetite, no interest in anything else, although there was a deputation waiting to congratulate her on her forthcoming marriage, and to give her wedding gifts from the chief of a neighbouring tribe. She could not keep them waiting and so eventually they were brought into her *majliss* and she welcomed them with smiles that did not reach her eyes.

The gifts were beautiful: a samite robe of deepest green edged with encrusted gold embroidery, matching slippers and a veil of the finest spun gold silk, shimmering with multi-hued lights. And for Mahmed, a robe of date-coloured brocade embroidered with silver, and a pair of matching slippers.

Yes, they would make a perfect married couple in their robes and slippers, hands joined but not their hearts. No, never their hearts.

When the audience was over, she knew she would have to escape the confinement of her tent. Riding alone in the desert was one of her greatest joys, but her guards grew furious when she attempted it and it had become necessary for her to slip away in secret. Queen she may be, but she had less freedom than the lowest desert nomad.

Saying that she must rest, she retired to her private quarters and instructed Freyha not to disturb her. Then, slipping off her robe and veil, she pulled on Turkish-style *shalwar*, baggy trousers in soft linen, and a knee-length shirt-style robe, tying a knotted silk belt around her waist. Tucking her hair up into a *kuffayia*, she secured it with an *aighal*, the cord to hold it in place.

Her mirror revealed a small boyish figure which she smiled happily to see. Then, gently raising the flap at the rear of the tent, she escaped, heading for the enclosure where the horses were kept, running in delight to her favourite, Ya'bub, Swift One. Ya'bub was a descendant of Prophet, her father's horse. She was beautiful, the colour of the rich ochre sands in the deepest desert, with a gilded mane and tail that swished and frothed at sight of her. Having gently kissed her cheek, Zahra led her up and down to get the blood flowing in her limbs, and then leapt on to her back, saddle-less, urging her out into the wilderness.

The horse's speed created the illusion of a cool breeze around her. She galloped into the desert, towards the lonely and isolated oasis where she could be alone with the tangled thoughts and wild imaginings that had disturbed her since she had spoken to the handsome Legionnaire.

Too bad if her guards raged at her when she returned. She was Queen and would behave as Queen despite their blandishments. Not even marriage to Mahmed was going to change her. Nothing would. She was Zahra, daughter of Husain and Mishaal, and the world would have to change, not she.

Chapter Eleven

The Oasis of *Njun*, the Stars, had been Mishaal's favourite stopping place while out riding. It had been here, eighteen years before, that she had felt the first labour pangs that had warned her she was about to give birth. Husain was angry with her for riding so far against his wishes when she was with child, but had she not always done what she wanted to do, and succeeded at it beautifully?

Zahra was born after a short and easy labour, and Mishaal had recovered fast, although it was a bitter disappointment that the child for which they had waited for so many years was a girl. Perhaps infants understand more than people guess? Perhaps, while lying in her mother's arms one day, Zahra had heard her father say that he regretted she was not the male heir he craved. Perhaps he had raged against fate, and the infant, hearing it all, had thought, 'I am not what they wanted. I have failed them.'

Tingles danced down her spine as she imagined the scene, and the effect it might have had on her as a child.

The Oasis of the Stars was still watered, she saw with relief as she dismounted, leading Ya'bub into the shelter of the palms. The small oval pool shimmered its welcome and suddenly she was aware of how hot and dusty she was, and how appealing the water looked.

When the first news of the drying out of the wells and

oases had reached her, she had thought instantly of the Oasis of Stars but shrank from sending a servant to check if its waters were affected. She could not have borne the knowledge that her beloved oasis was doomed. She did not know whether its waters had dried temporarily, to return at the announcement of her marriage to Mahmed, but she was relieved and delighted to find the pool still there, fringed with palms, the *sumr* acacia trees, and the dozens of brilliantly coloured flowers that clustered gratefully at the water's edge.

It took her only moments to strip off her dusty clothes and plunge into the pool's limpid depths while Ya'bub grazed contentedly nearby. The water folded around her like liquid silk, cozening her body, making her flesh sparkle. She splashed about in the blessed coolness for a while then looked up with a grin at Ya'bub's snort of surprise when some small creature fled from the grasses she was chewing. Bronzed coat flaming in the sun, Ya'bub had the appearance of a mythical horse, a Pegasus perhaps, with her small, high head, slender neck and supple, autocratic body. How marvellous it would be if Zahra could leap on her back and fly off into the clouds, to freedom and a happier life.

A single tear trickled down her cheek and she rubbed it away furiously. She was not one to be maudlin, not these days, anyway. The days for tears were long over, as she had so often told herself; now she must fight.

The oasis had won its name from its primary position in the desert. As dusk settled, so many bright stars could be seen directly above it that it was said they all journeyed to this point so as to stand guard over the Amira Mishaal as she rested, for on more than one occasion Mishaal and Husain had slept in the oasis overnight as if to recapture the glorious desert days before they were married.

Oh, for a marriage like that, with such surety of love and direction, such unity! Knowing she would never attain that blessing, Zahra would have preferred to do without a husband. She knew that every day she spent with Mahmed she would be judging their relationship by that of her parents, and finding it sadly wanting. There had never been a happier, more devoted husband and wife than Husain and Mishaal, and there never would be again.

The water lapped around her comfortingly and she patted its crystalline surface so that cooling droplets showered her flushed face. Then something caught her eye and she looked up to see a young antelope approaching the water's edge. Normally, they were the shyest and most reclusive of creatures, never venturing near a human, but this beast was different. It had a golden-fleshed body, slender and delicate as glass, and its sharp, central horn jutted proudly from its head.

When she had first seen it, months before, she had thought at first that it possessed two antlers, because that was what she had expected to see. Then, as the animal came closer, she had seen the truth. There was only one twisted horn rising from its pale gold forehead, and that was white as goat's milk.

In rapt disbelief, she watched the delicate beast lower its slender neck to drink from the pool, as unafraid as if she were not there. Eager to see how near she could get to it, she had moved carefully through the water so as not to startle it, and raised her hand to pat the beautiful pastel-gold neck. Amazingly, the animal had not shied away but had continued to drink for a while before raising its head to look her straight in the eyes, as it was doing now.

The beast's eyes were a deep and infinite blue, so rich and yet so calm that she felt all the tension and fear draining from her body at sight of them. Gently she cupped its chin in her palm, feeling the creature's soft, warm flesh, the bristle of its hair, the pulse which marked the flowing of its life blood.

177

'Beautiful creature,' she whispered. 'Why have you come here again today? Did you want to see me?'

The single, twisted white horn was as spotlessly clean as when she had first seen the animal. Closer inspection had shown that it had only ever had one horn. There was no sign of a wound where a second had been lost. Gently, she touched the twisted horn, wondering at its coolness, while the beast stood obediently as if it were her slave.

Slowly, always fearful of frightening it away, even though it had joined her at the Oasis of Stars many times, she pulled herself out of the water and seated herself at the pool's edge. Immediately, the antelope came to her side and lowered itself as if it would kneel before her. But instead, it lowered itself on to its side and, before she knew it, the small, exquisite head with the single, snowy white horn was resting in her lap, and the long-lashed eyes had closed as if the beast wished to sleep.

Zahra had no wish to disturb its slumber. Marvelling at this uncharacteristic behaviour, and taking it for the omen that she was sure it was, she stroked the beast's silky head for some time, and ran her forefinger along the twisted horn. It was too small for a deer, with only the one horn instead of two. It had none of the deer's terror of human contact, inculcated in the race from years of being hunted.

She could see the pulse beating in its neck, the tiny golden hairs on its chin, the dappling of the skin that was a slightly deeper gold in places, its small, neat hooves free of dust and sand. It was so clean, so pristine-looking. She sighed to see such tranquil beauty and, as the minutes passed, began to understand something.

This was, in its own small way, a miracle: her first miracle. Fate was decided by omens; a large dark bird flying overhead, a strangely shaped cloud in the firmament when a child was born, a star falling in the heavens; vivid, unforgettable dreams would be translated by a seer as the promptings of fate. What would Khalid ibn Khalid have made of this if he were still alive? If only she could have asked him.

There she sat, sun-dried after bathing, the beautiful creature's head in her lap, the palms dipping and bowing above them, the scent of roses suddenly filling the air. How she loved their scent! None grew here in this lonely oasis, yet always their idyllic odour hung in the breeze. The branches of the acacia trees nearby shivered in a sudden gust of wind.

Zahra's hair had dried by now, a thick dark glory that flowed down her back and across her shoulders, draping her like a cloud. To the watching man, it was like a scene from a medieval tapestry, the Virgin and the Unicorn, in brilliant, multi-hued beauty, the ebony and the ivory, the golden and the ochre, all blending to form a chiaroscuro of colour that could not fail to affect an observer.

Mayne had ridden out on his camel, needing time alone to think. Seeing the oasis, he had approached it to let his camel drink, but the beast had halted stubbornly and refused to go nearer so Mayne had dismounted and walked on foot. There was a stillness about the place that impressed itself upon him. He had expected to disturb birds and animals, cause the usual flutter of wings and scurrying of tiny feet, but there was only an eerie silence. Then he saw the Arab horse grazing, an exquisite beauty, quite the most splendid mare he had ever seen. Next he saw the sheet of glittering water shining like a mirror, and then, reflected in it, the young girl with the glory of ebony hair and the small, slender beast with its head in her lap.

His heart stood still and then pounded into life as he saw the reality rather than the reflection. The young girl had cupped her chin in one palm and was leaning towards the water. Her eyes were closed, as were those of the beast in her lap. The scene was so achingly lovely that he gazed upon it for a long time, anxious to commit it to memory for ever.

He withdrew slowly, anxious not to disturb them, but his boot cracked on a brittle twig and the snapping sound broke the enchanted moment. Together, girl and beast opened their eyes. The animal scrambled to its feet and fled, but not before Mayne registered with amazement that its second antler had not been hidden by the girl's hair, as he had thought. It did not have a second antler. It had a single horn, like the unicorn of ancient myth, the unicorn that would trust no one but a virgin.

He shook his head to clear it then glanced towards the pool again. The unicorn had gone, but the girl was still there. She was white-faced as she rose to her feet.

'Who said you could come here?' she cried imperiously, drawing her hair around her to conceal her nakedness. 'How dare you intrude!'

'I'm sorry. I was looking for water for my camel.'

'Where is he, this camel? I can see no camel. You came to spy on me. Everyone knows that the French are lewd and depraved!'

'They do? But I am not French!'

'You wore their uniform this morning.'

'Yet I do not wear it now, as you see.' He was wearing his desert *kuftan*, loose and enveloping. 'The Foreign Legion is multinational. There are men from all over the world in it.'

'And they are all lewd and depraved!'

He could not stop himself from laughing. She looked so small and helpless, little more than a child. She stood quite still, hoping that her hair was concealing her nakedness when in fact he could see one dusky, rose-pink nipple and the dimple at her hip. At first he had not been able to imagine who she was, this girl fashioned from ancient myth, but now he knew. There was no mistaking those distinctive eyes. God alone knew why she was there alone, without her guards, nursing a beast

180

that surely could not have been a unicorn? And yet there she was, the Amira Zahra herself, in the guise of a water nymph.

'Not so, Your Highness, not so.' Without thinking, he took a step closer.

'Stay away!'

'What are you going to do, scream? You are here alone, and if I wished I could take advantage of you.' His eyes glittered meaningfully.

With all his heart he wanted to do just that, to crush her in his arms and make her little virgin body his own, thrust deep inside her and see her cheeks grow flushed, her eyes glaze with passion. Heat burned in his groin and he knew that he was erect with frenzied excitement. Too many weeks sleeping alone had affected his self-control badly.

'So much for your treaty of friendship, Captain. You came here to take me prisoner. Admit it now, admit it! Did you think that my people would not ride after you and hack you to pieces for daring to touch me? You will regret this until your dying day.'

'I would never regret kissing you, Your Highness.'

Madness possessed him; he knew that he was behaving more foolishly than he had ever done in his life, even with his stepmother, but he could not stop himself. He must have her in his arms, he must feel her mouth beneath his, her breasts and hips crushed against him, her legs wrapped round him, urging him on, for he knew with certainty that she would react exactly like that if only she could forget the fiery pride that made her beat her fists against his face and neck. She was screaming, but when his mouth halted her screams, she seemed taken aback, the breath knocked from her body, her arms falling limply by her sides.

He thought that she had fainted, but she had not. Suddenly she was fighting again, but fighting to hold him closer, clutching and clinging to him and returning

181

his kisses with a directness and a savagery that took him aback.

'You little wretch, you wanted this all the time, didn't you?' he gasped, seeing the glint in her slanting eyes, feeling her laughter bubbling, and then she was pulling him down on to the sand so fiercely that he lost his balance. He should have been the hunter but it was she who had trapped him, he realised now, as her searing kisses stimulated him unbearably. Before he knew it, she was kneeling over him, forcing her kisses upon him while tugging at his hair to hold his head still, squeezing his hips with her knees as she lowered herself over him so that he could not move.

'You thought I was a weakling, did you not? You thought that I would be frightened of your challenge and run away. Well, now you can see how wrong you were, Mayne Amyan! I run from no one, not even he who would rape me.'

'I would never have raped you!' he gasped through the tangled cloud of her hair, the rage of her kisses.

'You do not need to. I am going to rape you. Ever since I saw you riding into my camp I have wanted to do it!'

'Then why in the name of Allah did you make me wait nearly four days to see you?'

'Because I was promised to another man, and because I did not know what to say to you while my blood seethed and my flesh screamed out that it must join with yours.'

'Dear God, you kept it well hidden from me.'

'Before my people, yes, but not now. Now I can be myself, and I want to taste the truth about a man before I become a prisoner for life. I want to know what it is like to lie in the arms of a lover by choice and not because of politics. Do you understand me?'

'Yes, I understand you, but what of the consequences? What will your husband say when he finds that you are no longer a virgin?'

'How will he guess? I shall get him drunk and he will have no memory of the marriage night.'

'And you will have forgotten me by then?'

'Yes. Shall you not have forgotten me? You will have gone back to your troops and on to your next mission, and I will be just one more female who bedded with you. Is that not the truth?'

'*Allah*, no, I do not want it like that! When I saw you, I saw the woman I could love as I have never loved any other, the one I want for all time, the one who will warm my nights and cool my days, my companion in the desert beneath the stars, the one whose mouth will always soften beneath mine and whose body will always cleave close.' He halted, astonished at the force of his feelings for her.

She was silent, her arms linked like a chain around his neck, and then he was taking control, rolling over on top of her and pressing kisses on her neck and breasts, her soft, creamy belly and the ebony triangle below, the ark where he would make his covenant. Dappling it with worshipful kisses, he prepared it for his onslaught, and when he thrust against her she retaliated with equal passion. And so they made their first attempt to unite, pausing to gasp for breath when it failed. She was a virgin, though determined not to remain one.

At the third attempt there was victory, and such an excess of passion that they were all but overwhelmed. The ecstasy was almost unbearable. Their hearts were pounding, the sweat dripping from their bodies, and their minds in glorious unison. It was like the most blissful fantasy, and surely it must be that for how could he, Mayne Amyan, be making love to the Amira of the Land of Mirages? Could he really be scything deep into her moist, responsive body and kissing her so possessively?

He had never felt such unendurable passion. He felt as if he might explode, burst into a thousand slivers of

183

silver light and never reform into a man again. She was writhing against him with such bold determination that he knew he could not hold out much longer. Voluptuous sensations bombarded him, feelings and impulses that he had never known before, and control was fast slipping away...

'My Legionnaire,' she gasped huskily, 'my very own Legionnaire, and all for me.'

'Yes, all for you, my darling,' he groaned as his control vanished and orgasm consumed him, his body convulsing against hers with a furious intensity that silenced him for long, fiery seconds.

When he had recovered, he saw her gazing up at him, a smile curving her lips, her hands resting gently around his neck.

'So you got what you wanted, Legionnaire, like all of your kind, brutal and self-seeking, putting your own desires first and caring nothing for those of others.'

'Call it that if you will, but I would prefer the truth to be told. Amira, you are the most extraordinary woman I have ever known. You fill me with such longing that I lose all control, and for that I must beg your forgiveness. But it is only because you are so beautiful. You must have driven mad every man who ever saw you!'

'If so, they concealed it well.'

'Mahmed must adore you.' Swift, searing jealousy overwhelmed him. He felt sick at the thought of any other man making love to her, calling her wife, getting her with child.

'He has never said it. If anything about him impressed me, it was his lack of enthusiasm. It has taken him nearly two years to make a definite offer.'

'And you did not do anything to put him off?'

'Well, perhaps I did.' Her green eyes danced with laughter.

'I can see now why they talk of you as the one who makes her own laws.'

184

'They do? I have not heard that before.'

'Normally, would you not have been promised to your future husband by the age of three or four? Arabs like to have their destinies mapped out, especially where heirs to such territories are concerned.'

'I was promised as a child, but the boy died. I begged my mother not to send me away and she wanted to keep me with her, so time passed and I remained unwed. Then they died, so suddenly and sadly, my beloved parents.' Tears gemmed her lashes, but to her surprise, she found that she did not mind weeping in front of this man. As he stroked her brow and dried her tears with his kisses, she opened to him as a flower to the sun, and within moments they were tightly joined together again, clutching, holding, and now it was her turn to reach the heights.

Oblivious of the baking heat of afternoon, the sudden swishes of breeze that swelled and dropped, the occasional cries of a bird, they loved and loved again, and it seemed as if the little oasis visibly flourished, the palms thickening with dates, the buds bursting open on the graceful, widespread bushes, the water glimmering more brightly than it had ever done before, fleet, silvery fishes racing through the depths like arrows. Time stood still, and if there were any desert *jinn* nearby then they were amiable ones who looked on lovers with delight.

The lovers slept, and when they woke the stars were gathered above them in clusters of sparkling platinum fire, joyously guarding the two who were plighting their troth while there was a shimmering moon, a sharp white crescent piercing the indigo sky as if it were a brooch pinned there by the Sky Goddess, Nut.

Hands linked, the lovers saw nothing but one another as their mouths joined for the final, sweetest time before they must return to reality.

Then he told her of the legend of the unicorn, of how it could only be enslaved by the virgin who was untouched

185

by man, and that it was a symbol of innocence and great purity of heart and spirit. During the telling, he saw her eyes cloud over.

'I did not know why the gazelle came to me like that and made me hold it as if it were my favourite hound. Nothing like that has ever happened before. It has visited me often, but never come so close.'

'I think it came to say goodbye to you, my lovely one, after eighteen years of abiding fidelity.'

'Goodbye? But I do not want to go back! I want to stay here like this forever. I am not made for queenship, my Legionnaire. I should have been born to some ordinary Beduin, not the highest of the high.'

'Your people love you. You could never think of leaving them, surely?' He thought of all that had eluded him during his lifetime – position, name, inheritance, respectability – and how she possessed all those in abundance and yet did not want them.

'I am not my mother's daughter. The burden is too heavy. I would rather have been born a goatherd's child to live in some hovel in the wilds.'

'Dressed in rags and with bare feet?'

'I have less than that on now!'

'That is true, but I feel that you are more than a little favourably disposed towards silks and fine jewels.' He thought of the camel train that was winding its way towards her camp, laden with the second stage of the gifts sent to her by the Emperor Napoleon.

'They are not everything in the world!'

'Do you say that because there has been so much emphasis on the Jewels of Destiny since your mother found them?'

'You know about them?' Her eyes sparked warning emerald fire.

'Who does not?'

'Yes, maybe you are right. But my father and mother raised me to know what matters most in life, and that is love – true, abiding love. Then comes charity to the poor, and then the quest for knowledge, all according to the laws of Allah.'

'Would you not say that Islam would put the quest for knowledge first, then charity, and then love?' He raised one dark brow.

'Maybe, but I would always put love first.'

'Because you have less of it than of the other two?'

'Maybe. You are very perceptive, Legionnaire, but why should I tell you what is in my heart?'

'Little sphinx!' Gently, coaxingly, he kissed her face, first her creamy eyelids, then her apricot-pink cheeks and straight, small nose, her tiny pointed chin, and finally her tremulous lips. 'I love you now, and I want all the gods to hear it, yours and mine!'

'There is only one God!'

'And He is the God of Love.'

They kissed again, knowing that soon they must end this idyll and return to the camp, reluctant as they were.

'What shall we do, my Legionnaire? Shall we pretend we barely know one another and that this day never happened?'

'That would be the best plan, Your Highness.' Getting up, he bowed formally to her as if they had just met.

'How shall I conceal what is in my heart?'

'You have had a lifetime's practice, Your Highness.'

'Oh, Mayne, I wish we need never part. I wish I were to marry you!'

'An infidel, a *kaffir* non-believer? Your people would rise up against you!'

'But you are not that, are you? You have Arabian blood, and speak warmly of Allah as if you love Him.' Clinging to Mayne's hands she gazed up at him, wishing with all her heart that she could change fate by the sheer force of her longing.

'Remember what the Prophet said: "Do you think you love your Creator? Love your fellow creature first."'

187

'You see, my Legionnaire, you can quote the Prophet! Oh, my people would take you to their hearts, I know it!'

'A penniless stranger? A pauper wearing the uniform of a foreign power? And what would your Mahmed say? He would pursue me unto death.'

'I can find some way out of it, I know.' She set her jaw resolutely.

'There is no way out of it, my little queen. You have your life mapped out for you, and nothing can alter that. We must be thankful that we had this day, these few sweet hours.'

'My infidel summer,' Zahra whispered against his cheek, and then, as he hugged her closer, she closed her eyes as if in pain, knowing that one thing was sure. She would never see her unicorn again.

PART FOUR

The Royal Betrothal

I have spread my couch with carpets of tapestry, with striped cloths of the yarn of Egypt. I have perfumed my bed with myrrh, aloes and cinnamon. Come, let us take our fill of love until the morning; let us solace ourselves with love.

Proverbs, 7:16, 17:18

The Lord shall make the rain of thy land powder and dust: from Heaven shall it come down upon thee, until thou be destroyed.

Deuteronomy, 28:24

Chapter Twelve

Several days later the camel train still had not arrived, to Mayne's frustration. He imagined it lost on the journey, the imperial gifts stolen or strewn around in the desert wilderness by careless thieves. Even he was unsure what the Emperor had sent, and just a few days' residence in the Amira's camp had shown him that she had everything a woman in her position could possibly desire.

Of what use to a desert queen were basqued jackets with bell sleeves and *engageantes*, cage crinolines ballooned by whalebone frames, and frilled lace headcaps? He had thought them excessive for women in Maine who liked to think themselves well versed in the very latest mode, even if it meant being unable to sit comfortably in a chair or sweeping china off tables when their basilica-shaped sleeves took on a life of their own. No wonder slow and cautious movement and a delicate manner had become the ideal of feminine beauty! It was difficult enough for drawing-room ladies to sport the latest modes without attempting to force a desert queen into them.

All the same, the bestowing of the gifts would give him a genuine reason to be in her company, and anything which did that would be more than welcome.

How discreetly they had behaved since returning from the Oasis of Stars, the Amira arriving some time before Mayne to allay suspicion that she might have been alone with him. That evening, he had been formally invited to dine with the Amira's advisers, surprising them with his knowledge of Arabic and Arabian customs and not turning ashen when roasted sheep's eyes were presented to him. They, the special delicacy kept for favoured guests, were a mark of honour which he ate with visible enjoyment even if they were not his favourite fare. To be treated with honour: had he not sought this all his life? Yet now that he had it, all he could think of was the luscious, desirable girl who had lain in his arms that day.

The Amira had not attended the *al fresco* feast, which had keenly disappointed him. What he truly wanted was to have her sitting beside him by the camp fire, the flickering firelight dancing across their faces, the stars open-eyed above them, the moon drenching them in its transmuting silvery rays.

Her advisers were elderly and wizened desert sages, and he was all too conscious of their sharp scrutiny of him throughout the meal. One of them had lost an eye at some time and the earnest gaze of his single remaining orb was almost more intolerable than the double gaze of the others present. It was like being analysed by a Cyclops who might pounce at any moment.

Mayne hid a grin. These were his lovely Zahra's chief ministers and he must respect them, even if they were opposed to her plans to rule alone and build life-saving hospitals. No one had ever speeded up the rate of Arab progress, and no one ever would.

In true Arab fashion, it was very late before he was asked to state his reason for being there but he courteously repeated what he had told the Amira and the advisers listened intently, saying very little at first. Thinking that they were unimpressed and would coldly refute his offer, relief gushed through him. Dear God, but he did not want his beloved to have her lands invaded by the Legion! She would be either a prisoner or an exile, or both, and their love would be finished. Yet what future did it have anyway? He was an alien; he could no more marry her than disobey his orders.

'You talk of bringing physicians and modern medical care to our land, but we have very little occasion to use such methods,' one of the ancients put forward. 'The power of Allah is sovereign here, and He will heal whom he wishes, whatever is attempted by so-called modern methods.'

'That I know, *shaikh*, but even Allah says that He will help those who help themselves. Perhaps it is now His will that modern methods are brought to the Land of Mirages? Is it not true that many infants and children die here annually because there are not the physicians to heal them?'

'If they die then that is Allah's desire and none may interfere with it.'

'I do not deny that, but what of the wives who die in childbirth? Physicians can save them, too, and their newborn infants. Do none of you have wives whom you cherish and wish to see produce healthy sons with as little suffering as possible?' He surveyed the elderly faces fully aware that at least one of them would have taken a young wife recently.

'Is it not true that the *kaffir* women who have the attendance of these modern physicians also suffer greatly in childbearing, Captain Mayne? There is no ideal world where everyone survives untouched. For some, great travail is God's intention.'

'Nonetheless, the latest medical care can help a great deal,' Mayne rejoined, but there was little conviction in his voice. Where now was the icy ruthless Mayne Amyan of old? All he could think of was his beloved and the hours they had spent together in the Oasis of Stars, an enchanted time when reality had fallen away; when all that had mattered was the force of love.

193

He did not try to summon the old Mayne. He knew he would have been wasting his time. Today he had become a soft, malleable creature, easily swayed, dreaming of love nests with roses round the door, of love-filled hours with the woman of his dreams, and their blissful future together.

All his life, he had forfeited what he had most desired, and now he was yearning for something that could never be his under any circumstances, a woman of a different race and creed, a desert queen who was already promised in marriage to one of her own kind. As the cold realisation of his plight turned the contents of his stomach to jagged rocks he longed for the freedom to retire to his tent and mourn his loss.

The moment arriving at last, he took his leave and sped into the darkness of his goat-scented haven where he tore off his uniform and sank naked on to the lumpy, sheepskin-covered pallet that was his bed. There, for over an hour, he attempted to talk himself out of his romantic reverie. It was over. As he had not taken advantage of her, he need feel no pangs of conscience. She had leapt into his arms to taste the fruits of what he now sourly called free love before she was married off to a man for whom she had not the slightest affection. A loveless marriage. God protect him from such a bitter fate.

Tossing and turning for an hour resolved nothing. Again he reminded himself that he had actually done her a service that afternoon, and that was why she had flung herself into his arms. What was more, while he had foolishly talked of love, she had not. And, indeed, why should she?

He struck himself savagely on the forehead with the palm of his hand, cursing himself beneath his breath. He had behaved as if he were under some enchantress's spell, falling into her arms, telling her he adored her, that he wanted to make her his wife. That impetuous

194

behaviour was so far removed from his real self that he wondered if the dry, baking heat had somehow affected his mind.

There was an old Arab saying: 'A stolen kiss is not easily returned.' They had both stolen kisses that afternoon, none of which could ever be returned.

Turning, he thumped his lumpy pallet with a bunched fist, and then thumped it again. Sighing, he got up and pulled on the loose bernouse-style robe that was his preferred mode of dress, and within moments he was heading out beyond the camp on foot, walking beneath the wilderness of wide-eyed stars and tenderly soft moon, wishing that he were anything but an impoverished Legionnaire, a 'missionary' who had come to bring disaster on the Amira and her tribe.

Reflecting on the irony of the fact that he had come to enchant but that it was he who had been enchanted, he strode through the basalt darkness, guided only by the stars. In this flat, wide expanse of open desert, they seemed to be very low and quadruple the number that he would normally expect.

A verse came into his head as he walked, something by Fuzuli.

'My lover's unheeding, the Sphere is unfeeling, the times are not well; My luck's bad, my foe's glad, I've much to complain of but no one to tell.

'The warmer the sun of desire burns, the less is the shadow of hope; Frustration's the master and schemes are its helots to rule and compel.

'The road to his grace twists through dead-ends and pitfalls; a stranger I come, An innocent dupe to receive whom the world lays its lure, casts its spell...

'Our dearest ambitions lie hidden like tunes in the string of a harp; The cup of delight is inverted like bubbles which emptily swell.'

He had always enjoyed the satisfying rhythm and

balance of the poem but somehow the lines sounded hollow now, taunting him with their bitter truth. He wished that he could blame his black mood on the sheep's eyes, but it was love that had stricken him, robbing him of all sense.

'I am not in love with her!' he shouted at the moon, picking up a stone and throwing it fiercely into the ebony void. 'I am not in love with her! I shall forget her after this, I swear it!'

Burning with the heat of anger and frustration, he halted, and it was then that he realised he was not alone. He had been so involved with his thoughts that he had not heard the crunch of sandals on the ground, nor the rustling approach of a watcher who obviously stood close by, but he heard their laughter, and he flinched at what they must think of him for cursing at the moon.

Light and taunting, the laughter continued after he had fallen silent. In fact it continued just long enough to impress itself indelibly on him. Someone was laughing, almost crowing, at what he had just said; someone who was only a few yards away. And yet he could see no one, however hard his eyes strained to pierce the night.

'Who's there?' he shouted, again and again, but there was nothing now save the uncanny stillness of the darkness, not even the patter of animal's paws or the shriek of a night bird. He would have given anything to have heard such familiar and comforting sounds, but there was nothing save an abyss-like silence that tore at his nerves.

Desert *jinns*? Mayne grinned in derision. He did not believe in them, powerful and palpable as they were to the Beduin. It must have been an animal panting heavily; what else could it be? Dismissing it thus, he almost convinced himself that it had been some beast of the night. If only it had not sounded so human, so like someone of indeterminate gender laughing at him. . . .

He had been lying when he swore he did not love her.

196

He had known that, but how had they? *Allah*, but the desert night was giving him the shivers. Back in his tent, he would sleep like a stone until dawn. When he awoke, refreshed, he would continue with his mission, the sweet talking and charming that he had been selected to perform, the silver-tongued convincing and persuading. And when he had succeeded he would be out of there as fast as that creature that had fled on his approach to the Oasis of Stars.

Stepping into his tent, he drew in his breath. Before it had stunk of goats but now all he could smell were roses; heavily bedewed blossoms, freely blooming. Had someone been there in his absence, looking for him? If so, it could only have been one person, and he cursed himself for not having been there to welcome her. His body betrayed him the moment that he smelt that heavenly odour. He thought immediately of her smooth ivory body, the full, bell-shaped breasts, the tiny waist and sensual, swelling hips, and that glory of cascading ebony hair streaming round her slender shoulders.

Erect, his groin throbbing with fire, he knew that sleep was about to evade him again, and that there was nothing he could do but punch his bed and swear into the darkness.

It was a wooden horse, or so the accompanying letter described it, calling it a 'Draisienne' and explaining that it was named after its inventor, the Baron von Drais de Sauerbrun. As Mayne unwrapped it to reveal the circular wooden wheels with spokes, the movable steering contraption and padded saddle covered with rich scarlet velvet fringed with gold, he was left speechless. What city-bred mind had decided that a desert queen would welcome this so-called Draisienne?

Zahra stood gazing at it in confusion. What sort of gift was this from the Emperor of France, a wooden horse that had to be pushed while she walked along beside it?

She did not understand it at all. Why should she abandon her beautiful Arab mare to walk along beside an ugly wooden *khail*?

Mayne, still perplexed, but aware that he would have to teach the Amira how to conquer this weird wooden beast, read and reread the accompanying letter. The Draisienne was for the Amira's sole pleasure and enjoyment, and there were detailed instructions on how to ride it. The scroll addressed to him, and multiply sealed, was innocence itself. Even if someone had stolen it, and could read French, they would have learned nothing about the truth of his mission. There were separate letters for the Amira and her chief ministers, and these he handed to them immediately, Zahra retiring to read hers at her leisure.

Thankful that she had left him to puzzle out the Draisienne by himself, he returned his gaze to the wooden horse, and as he considered its proportions and how he would attempt to conquer it, he tried to visualise the Amira riding it before the astonished eyes of her elderly ministers. Had it been the Emperor's intention to make her look a fool? If so, he could not have chosen a more appropriate offering.

Slowly, he reread the instructions for riding the machine and then, while the Amira was in her tent reading her letters, he climbed on to the padded saddle and let the Draisienne roll itself down a nearby slope. It moved easily, but even through the padded saddle he could feel the joltings of the wooden wheels. All the same he was determined to master the machine so that he could show the Amira how to ride. What a golden opportunity to be in her company, in all innocence, while assisting her in the mastery of this ultra modern invention.

His second attempt at steering set the cumbersome wooden wheels sinking into loose sand, and before he knew it, he had come to a jolting halt, jerking forward on the saddle and almost being flung across the handle bars. Bursting into laughter, he heaved the wooden horse out of the choking sand and placed it on a flinty slope. This time, as he careened along, he felt the impact of every stone and pebble juddering through the wooden wheels and jarring his bones. This was an invention most definitely created for smooth city roads.

A little later, hearing the crunch of feet, he turned to see the Amira's bodyguard advancing towards him, faces fixed in their accustomed expression of reverence. Behind them, looking even more minute and delicate, came the Amira herself, her eyes twinkling as she took in the scene. Mayne stood with his *khépi* tilted over one ear, his boots and breeches dusted with sand, his hands rubbed raw by the handle bars of the Draisienne.

Bowing, he affected an ambassadorial smile, but as their eyes met there was no need for such pretence. Veiled and draped in voluminous robes his beloved might be, but her eyes told him everything that he yearned to know.

Next moment, he was trying to explain how to ride the wooden horse, explaining that it sank in sand, rattled the bones when running over stones and pebbles, and had to be pushed along by the feet in the most ungainly fashion unless it was placed at the top of a slope.

'Are you advising me not to try it out, Captain?' Her green eyes twinkled with mischief.

'Certainly not, *Saiydi*, that is for you to decide, but I would suggest that you tell your people to go about their business while you master the wilful beast.' His blue-flecked topaz eyes danced.

For a moment, to tease him, she looked as if she would not consider this, and then, to his delight, she ordered her guard and her followers to withdraw until she summoned them. Only the woman with the piercing eyes, Freyha, remained to chaperon her mistress.

The next few hours were among the happiest of his

life. First he showed Zahra how to select the correct type of ground for riding the Draisienne, only to promptly sink deep into the sand himself, where he remained stuck, roaring with laughter, while she pointed at him and burst into peals of laughter herself. Even the steely eyed Freyha, who obviously viewed him with suspicion, tittered behind her veil.

Having heaved the contraption out of the sand, Mayne looked around for a more suitable section of ground, deciding on one where the stones were smooth. Then he leapt into the saddle with great agility, beaming from ear to ear, set the contraption on its course and bounced crazily over the stony surface, so that his *khépi* tipped down over the other ear.

Zahra roared with laughter, bent double in hilarity, then straightened up to clap him as if he were a fairground act, which was exactly what he felt like at that moment.

'Tell me, Captain, what does a desert ruler do with a Draisienne?' she called out.

'Why, she rides it on ce-re-m-m-oni-al-l-l oc-c-a-s-ions-s-s!' Mayne called back, every bone in his body vibrating as he rode over an unexpected patch of jagged flints.

Zahra burst out laughing again, throwing up her hands and wiping the tears from her eyes. Even the usually silent Freyha was shaking with amusement.

'Now, it is my turn, Captain,' Zahra called.

'I would rather that you observed my skills a little longer, *Saiydi*!'

'What skills are those, Captain?' Zahra challenged, stepping forward to place a proprietorial hand on the Draisienne's handle bar. Plainly she thought that she could do better, and so, *salaaming* courteously to placate the watching Freyha, Mayne let her have the wooden beast.

She had been quick to learn, for she immediately

200

selected a smoothly sloping area of ground, seated herself on the saddle without any help from Mayne, and pushed herself off. For some yards the Draisienne rolled along quite sedately, and Zahra grinned widely, shouting back over her shoulder. 'It only takes a little skill, Captain, as you see' before the front wheel lodged between two stones in a patch of soft sand and she was jolted forwards towards the handle bars, her skirts hampering the movements of her legs so that she could not save herself.

'Yes, only a little skill, *Saiydi,*' Mayne rasped as he leapt towards her, catching her neatly in his powerful arms before she hurt herself on the handle bars.

He held her momentarily, aware of the shocked intake of breath from the waiting woman who stepped towards them hurriedly, only to be ushered away by the Amira.

As they enjoyed one another's closeness, Mayne's arms locked tightly around her waist, their gazes meeting almost fiercely, and with a deep yearning, he inhaled the delicious scent of roses that seemed to spill from her body, saw the fine, gleaming strands of shining ebony hair where her head veil had been tugged back from her forehead. Her lashes, long and straight, looked like miniature wings, shielding the heady beauty of her malachite gaze. For now, they were downcast, perhaps because she had hoped to outdo him with her riding skills and had failed, and he longed for them to rise and reveal those wondrous eyes, radiant with an inner beauty he had never seen before in a woman, not even his lovely Dananir.

Strictly speaking, she was no classic beauty, certainly her features bore no relation to the effigies of Greek and Roman goddesses, but she had more, far more. There was vitality and innocence, and an ancient, timeless wisdom submerged in the striking green depths of her gaze, and he knew again, as he had in the Oasis of Stars, that he was lost, hopelessly, eternally lost. Whatever she wanted, whatever she asked of him, he would do, if it meant damning his own soul unto eternity.

'Captain, I shall try again.' Her voice was firm and yet husky with unspoken emotion.

Shakily, he put her at arm's length, their eyes still transfixed, and when he let his arms fall from hers he was stricken with a sense of emptiness. She had been created for his arms, and he for hers. They were meant for one another. They were meant to be lovers for the rest of their days.

Zahra was more practised at concealing her emotions than he, for she leapt astride the padded saddle once again, as if she did not have a care to trouble her, and then, by pushing her slippered feet along the ground propelled herself into movement. The Draisienne rolled along quite reasonably well for its longest journey yet, Zahra appearing to have conquered it, when it suddenly sank into soft sand and came to a violent and jerking halt.

Alarmed, he ran to catch her before she came to any harm, but she was smiling broadly as his arms caged her protectively to prevent her from flying forwards, her eyes glittering with mischief, and he knew then that she had deliberately embedded the wheel in sand so that this would happen and he could hold her again.

'Captain, this wooden horse is more wilful than the most unpredictable camel.' She spoke loudly for the benefit of Freyha who had come running up in fear and was now standing staring at them in puzzlement, unsure whether to be frightened or enraged.

'*Saiydi*, you are a most brave and courageous rider and I am sure that you will be able to handle the Draisienne superbly by the time you wish to employ it for ceremonial occasions.' He tried to keep a straight face.

'Captain, will the Emperor be furious if I keep his gift for more private occasions such as this?' Zahra's green eyes were winsome, her fingers still tightly clutching

202

Mayne's arms, her hips pressed against his so that he felt an answering throb in the pit of his stomach.

'The Emperor need never know, *Saiydi*.'

'You will not tell him then?'

'Not if Your Highness does not wish it.'

How could he bear her closeness for much longer without crushing her mouth beneath his and tearing aside her blue silk robe so that he could caress her pale, tenderly soft breasts, her smooth flat stomach and the heaven that lay beneath it? Now there was such a fiery heat in his groin that he blessed the bagginess of the Legionnaire breeches. If the watchful lady-in-waiting observed his arousal, her mistress would be torn away from him in seconds. If only she knew what had happened in the Oasis of the Stars when he had made this radiant creature his.

'You are very generous, Captain, and I thank you.' Her fingers dug deep into his arms, telling him that she knew he was aroused and that she wanted him, too. There was a glaze of pink on her cheeks and her eyes were slumbrous with desire. Her breath smelt of the sweetest, freshest flowers.

'*Saiydi!*' It was the waiting woman, her face red with anger, eyes darting fire. She glared at Mayne with such venom that he would have moved away had not Zahra's fingers remained clamped around his arm, her expression imperious.

Coolly regal she commanded her servant to stand back, and then, eyes bright, she allowed Mayne to assist her on to the padded seat once more, and then she was pushing the heavy, cumbersome contraption into movement, urging it on as if it were a reluctant camel, and away she went down the slope, head flung back and veil swept up and off by the breeze, freeing her cascade of luxuriant black hair.

Watching, feeling his heart do a crazy somersault, Mayne was consumed by a longing to be alone with her

203

so that he could bury his face in that fabulous ebony mane and make love to her as he had done at the oasis. How much longer would it be before they could be alone again, chained blissfully by one another's arms, imprisoned together by their passionate love?

God, but he was thinking like a lovesick swain! Where she was concerned, he was feeble as tissue; he would do anything to make love to her again, to join with her firm and fragrant little body in the ecstasy that had transported them at the Oasis of Stars. Was there nothing that he could do or say to change their fates, hers to be married to some unloving Arab Amir, his to return to the Dark Legion to renew his *Acte D'Engagement* and spend the rest of his service gaining meaningless medals and honours?

'Dear God, if there is a God,' he whispered, 'let her be mine soon. Fashion a miracle for us, for that is what we shall need. Fashion a miracle for us, Lord!'

But he knew that he was wasting his breath. Her fate was sealed, and so was his. They were as far apart now as they had been before they met, and no amount of loving, longing and yearning could change that.

'Captain, I seem to have conquered the beast!' Zahra called out as she drew the Draisienne to a lurching halt and waited for Mayne to help her dismount.

'Perhaps Your Highness would care to come riding again tomorrow?' he asked, his voice low and husky.

'Yes, if we go on horseback!' she whispered back, and then she was smiling up at him as if he were some courteous stranger. After they had placed the Draisienne flat on the ground, which was probably the best place for it, he escorted her back to her tent, Freyha hurrying behind them, muttering beneath her breath.

At the entrance to the tent, Zahra bowed her head as if in distant and polite goodbye and he bowed low in response like some gallant courtier of olden days, gaining a fleeting impression of her bright, laughing

eyes and look of longing that equalled any he himself
could have given.

That night, he lay awake for hours, hoping that she
would somehow come to him despite the watchful eyes
of her women and her bodyguard, but the night
remained silent and without event. Sleepless, he burned
for her, aching and throbbing, yearning for her tender
little body in his arms, her smooth pale thighs beneath
his own. Finally he lay on his belly, attempting to crush
out the demon of longing, but it was hopeless. Nothing
could cure him but his Zahra, his Morning Star.

Dawn was transforming the black sky into frosty
silver when he finally began to sink into an exhausted
sleep, and then, just as his lids were closing, the phrase
'wooden horse' jolted into his mind and he woke cold
with shock.

The Emperor's letter had not been so innocent after
all. Quite openly he had called the Amira's gift, 'the
wooden horse', calling to mind the gift that had been
sent to the Trojan camp during the wars of the same
name. How joyously the Trojans had taken in the gift,
treating it as a bountiful offering from their enemies,
refusing to heed the warning of the discredited pro-
phetess, Cassandra, who had cried, 'Beware, the horse is
full of armed men!' Then, at dead of night, the men
concealed in the horse's belly had climbed out and
opened the gates for the invader to enter and conquer.

The Draisienne had been a symbolic gift, the fore-
runner of the enemy who would invade and conquer the
Amira's camp and her people.

'Jesus, Mary and Joseph!' His father's favourite exple-
tive was on his tongue. He, her lover, was to be the
instrument of her downfall, the bringer of the wooden
horse that would cause her defeat and subjugation. How
clear the Emperor had made that today, and for a
moment the face of Napoleon III came into his mind,

205

adorned by its stately moustache and elegant beard. Maybe Mayne would be heaped with honours for bringing the Land of Mirages to the French Crown, maybe he would be given titles and land and earn himself eternal royal gratitude, but he wanted none of it.

All he wanted was his darling Zahra, his *mahbub*, his beloved, the one who had lanced the bitterness fermenting in his soul and enabled him to turn his face to the sun.

Chapter Thirteen

'My heart, I saw what was in your mind today, and it is wrong, so wrong! He is a *kaffir*, a non-believer, he has come here to represent his Emperor, not to entangle himself with the daughter of Husain and Mishaal!'

Freyha stood, hands on hips, surveying her mistress who sat combing her long, ebony hair.

'Will you not answer me, put my mind at rest and tell me that I misunderstood? Tell me that you did not desire him out there today. Tell me so that I can sleep well tonight!'

'The heart is not always governable, Freyha.' Zahra's voice was choked, her face concealed by her flowing hair. 'Sometimes we are swept away by our longings.'

'Only if we are weak! You can withstand his spell. You must, for all our sakes! When Mahmed hears of this, he will beat you – '

'No one touches the daughter of Husain and Mishaal, no one!' Zahra flared. 'And no one will tell Mahmed, for no one knows, do they?'

'And how do you think I learned of it? I saw it in your eyes, blazing from your face. You think you love this *kaffir*, but you are misled. He is not for you. Soon he will return to his Legion, and he will forget you as he forgets the *simûm* and the harsh sun of the wilderness.'

'Freyha, tell me one thing: has my promise to marry

Mahmed made the wells fill again and the rivers run? Yesterday, did not three men come from Abeesha to say they were already fearful for their water supplies, and that every oasis between here and the city had run dry, just as it did thirty years ago? Today, more came from Bakasir to tell the same tale. I thought that Allah wanted me to marry Mahmed, that He was angry because I stayed single. I thought that once He knew that I would agree to our lands being united, He would let the waters run freely again, but it has not happened. Why not, Freyha? That is what we should be discussing now, not my feelings for the *kaffir*.'

Freyha's mouth fell open but no words came. It was true that she had been more shocked by what she had learned today regarding the *kaffir* and her mistress than she had on hearing that more oases were now arid. But was she not right to put her mistress first? Was that not her rôle in life? *Allahu il'alim*, but she had always done her best for her mistress and now she was trying to protect her, as any mother would her wilful daughter. Oh, for a father's hand to come down heavily upon her mistress now and show her the error of her ways!

'You cannot distract me from what must be said,' Freyha pressed on. 'If you would marry Mahmed to please the Lord, then why do you lust after the *kaffir* now? Do you think that He will forgive you for betraying Mahmed? Perhaps that is why more wells run dry!'

Zahra stared at her askance. 'I have not betrayed Mahmed. Where is he, that reluctant bridegroom? For nearly two years he failed to summon up the courage and ask for my hand. What do you think that did to my self-esteem? It very nearly destroyed it, Freyha!'

'You, the great one, Queen of the Desert, ruler of the Land of Mirages, have no need of the flattery of others to bolster your self-esteem.'

'Nonetheless, I do! First I am a woman, and only then

208

am I a queen. Have you never understood that, Freyha? Was my mother not the same?'

'She was faithful to your father for thirty years!'

'She loved him. I do not love Mahmed. I am making a political alliance for the good of our land, and that is bad enough without this castigation from you.' Flinging her comb aside, Zahra plunged her face into her hands.

Instantly Freyha knelt beside her, contritely plucking at her hands and kissing them.

'Sweet one, forgive me, but I fear for you. If they should discover how you truly feel, it will mean disaster. Send the *kaffir* away now, tonight, before it is too late. Before Mahmed finds out. I beg you with all my heart!'

Zahra forced a laugh. 'What do you think Mahmed will do? Sew my maidenhead back in? It is too late, Freyha, far too late. I have given all that I had to give to the *kaffir*, and there is no going back now.'

'*You are lovers?*' Freyha was ashen-faced.

'We are lovers.'

'When? *Where?*'

'Does that matter? It is done, I assure you, and no one must know save yourself. You will promise me that?' Green eyes pierced into carob brown, until the latter had to look away, her mouth quivering.

Freyha was shaking uncontrollably as she replied: 'I shall never tell anyone, you have my promise on that, but what if *he* finds out? How will you keep it from him? He has a ferocious temper!'

'He will not be the first man to drink himself insensible on fermented date juice. I shall ensure that the *nabidh* he is given is especially strong, fermented overlong, so that it sends him to sleep on the wedding night. Next day he will think that he has done what he should have done, and that will be that. I shall behave as if he is the greatest lover in the land, and he will never suspect a thing.' Zahra's voice was toneless.

'My heart, you tread on shaky ground.'

209

'Not for the first time, dear Freyha, not for the first time. Will it be any shakier than the building of a hospital and the hiring of physicians that no one wanted, or the insistence that I stay unmarried? The first mistake was the hardest to make, but now I am quite an expert at these things. Believe me, I know what I am doing.'

'They say that Mahmed greatly prizes fidelity.'

'Then I shall remind him of that if he ever wants to take another wife!' Zahra tossed her head.

There was another deputation the next day, five bedraggled, sand-grimed men and a child. They had come from the Oasis of Kujab, which was in the opposite direction from Abeesha, and they had a terrible story to recount.

Shivering as if he had an ague, their leader knelt before Zahra, tears welling in his eyes.

'Highness, they are all dead! We are the only survivors. Once we were wealthy and flourishing. Our oasis was filled with travellers and the caravanserai was renowned for its comfortable beds and good food – and then all gone, like a seed borne on the *simûm*. The water failed, and we know not why. There has been no rain for seven weeks, if not longer. There is the underground river which usually serves us well during a few weeks of drought, but not this time. Our travellers left us, but we were not alone. Death was with us. Soon the first ones began to die of thirst. My wife and father died of it, and then my daughters. Ten more of my friends died before the next moon, and now here you see all that is left of us.'

Tears came into Zahra's eyes, too, and she held out her arms to pull the small child close. He had the hollow, hunted look of a wild, broken animal trapped by a falcon, and her heart ached for his motherlessness.

'Leave the boy with me and I shall raise him as my own,' she said, and the man flung himself lower on the

210

ground, kissing the hem of her cornflower blue robe repeatedly and blessing her name.

'What is your name, child?' she asked, her voice trembling slightly.

'Karim, Your Highness,' the boy quavered. 'But I do not want to leave my father!'

'Of course you do not. All of you shall have a place here in my camp. Homes will be found for you, and perhaps wives, too. We have widows here.'

'Highness, Allah will bless you for this kindness!'

'Then thank Him, and not me. I wish you all happiness with us, and if you should have any problems come to see me personally.'

Karim turned to follow his father and then, turning back, he managed a watery smile at Zahra who smiled back. Dear God, she thought, there was nothing more heartwarming than making people happy.

Outside, the father turned to his son and their companions and said: 'You see, I told you she was Husain's daughter. She has his great heart and his generosity. I never did believe the rumours that she was cold and wilful. How could anyone say that of her? I shall bless her name wherever I go, for the rest of my life, and you will do the same, Karim, if you wish blessings upon your head.'

'I will, father, I will.' Gripping his father's rough, dry hand, Karim followed him towards their new beginning.

That night, Zahra dreamed of her mother. For months, she had yearned to dream of her, longing for the sweet reassurance that such an experience would bring, but her wish had not been granted. Now, when she had accepted that such a dream would never come, there was Mishaal, radiant and beautiful, reaching out her arms to hold her close. How she longed to step into her mother's embrace and cage her tightly, so that she could never leave again, but it was not to be. In the dream, Mishaal's face was lined with anxiety, and she seemed burdened down with misery.

Through the mists that swirled about them, Zahra called, 'Mother, my mother, wait for me, wait for me!' but Mishaal was already drifting away from her on the mother-of-pearl mist, turning as she was almost out of sight to call back: 'There is a non-believer in our land, an infidel, and you have been entertaining him as if he were one of us. Beware, my daughter, beware if you love our land!'

Zahra woke with a cry on her lips, and Freyha was beside her instantly.

'Have you dreamed bad dreams, my heart?' Brown fingers clasped pale ones tenderly.

'I dreamed of Mishaal! I tried to hold her but she would not stay. She warned me!' Zahra closed her eyes tightly and then opened them again, trying to clear her mind. 'She said there is a non-believer in our land, and . . .'

'You must send him away for his presence is offending God?'

'Yes, I suppose that was the gist of it.' Zahra stared unseeingly into the darkness.

'And you will obey?' Freyha waited tautly for her mistress's reply.

'When the time is right.'

'You will not do it now?' Freyha gasped.

'I cannot.'

'You cannot? But Mishaal has come to you in a dream. What more proof can you want that she is unhappy about the *kaffir* being here? You must listen to her!'

'He will be going soon, anyway. Do I have to remind you of that, Freyha?'

'But if Mishaal has told you that he must go now, then go he must. She has always known what is best for her land.'

'My land now, Freyha, *my* land, and I must make the judgements that are needed for its welfare.'

212

'So you will not listen?'

'I do not wish to speak further of this, Freyha. Sleep now, and I will do the same.'

Closing her eyes, she thought, 'Even from the grave, my mother knows what is happening here and comes to warn me, and yet I cannot heed what she says. I love him. From the first moment I saw him, I loved him, that was why I kept him waiting for our first meeting. I knew my life would never be the same again. It was like this for my mother, too, in her infidel summer. She could not fight it either.

'Please, let me have this happiness now, Lord,' she prayed, 'and later I shall make amends. Just these few days, dear God, and then I shall do whatever You ask of me.'

They spent the next day together, Zahra proudly showing Mayne round her camp, introducing him to her people. He met the bright-eyed, mischievous children and their shyer, sometimes veiled mothers, who said little while their Amira spoke to them, explaining the reason for Mayne's being there.

The men were courteous and reverent, answering their Queen's questions in detail and *salaaming* to Mayne as if he were someone of great importance, but he knew that they behaved like this only because their Amira was present. The Arabian welcome for the non-Muslim could vary between outright hostility and persecution, to generous greetings and open hospitality.

He watched with interest their reactions to Zahra. It was obvious that they cherished her, because they were overwhelmed with delight when she spoke to them, the proof evident in their shining eyes and flushed cheeks, and the way that the women caught at the hem of her robe when she passed them by, showering it with their kisses. To them, she was as sacred as her mother and father had been, born of the long line of Husain, right

213

back to the Prophet Mohammed, and doubly revered because of that.

He felt a sudden pang, thinking of his own hybrid past, his lack of descent and heritage. Beside her, he was nothing; he owned nothing and he came from nothing.

He saw women grinding grain in a stone quern, kneeding it with water in readiness to make the flat, unleavened bread that resembled pancakes. It was flung expertly from left hand to right and back again repeatedly before being baked on a hot stone in the fire.

He saw children reciting Qu'ranic verses watched over by a learned *shaikh*, a title given not only to Muslim chiefs but to elderly men who were highly educated. The children chanted the verses in sing-song fashion, their voices strong and vibrant, while the *shaikh* watched them with a pleasure he did his utmost to conceal behind a mask of sternness.

The children were clean and healthy, their robes tidy, little calico caps spotless and their hair finger-combed neatly about their ears.

'*Saiydi*, the children are learning fast!' The *shaikh salaamed* reverently before Zahra. 'They know that their Amira wishes them to be the cleverest children in the land, and so they work hard at their lessons.'

Zahra smiled broadly, knowing that it was flattery but with a measure of truth. She did want her people to be soundly educated. There was nothing worse than languishing in ignorance. It was a barrier between a man or woman and God.

'*Shaikh*, this is Captain Mayne Amyan of the French Foreign Legion. He speaks English and also our own language, and he is here to bring news of a treaty between our two lands. I am sure that he would like to talk to the children, if you do not mind the interruption?'

'I am proud to give my permission, *Saiydi*.' The old man greeted Mayne in surprisingly good English, which for a

214

time Mayne himself used before they switched to Arabic.

The children proved shy when approached by the visitor, but Mayne asked them about their lessons, their brothers and sisters, and their future plans.

'I wish to be a *shaikh* one day,' one boy said, making his tutor laugh.

'You will have many years before you can assume that title, Ali. It is only for those who have studied for many decades.'

'That is what I shall do!' Ali responded, his eyes sparkling.

'God's blessing be upon you,' the old man smiled before introducing Mayne to a small, thin boy called Karim, who had only recently joined the children.

'Sadly, Karim lost his mother in the drought, and his sisters, too, but his father is safe, God be praised. They arrived here yesterday, and when I tested the boy I found him an apt pupil. He cannot yet read or write, but the signs of future understanding are there. I thought it best that he join us immediately, even though he is lamentably thin.'

'*Salamun 'alaik!* Peace be among thee!' Mayne said to the boy who gave the required response in a lacklustre voice. '*Wa-'alaik issalam!* And on thee be peace!'

The *shaikh* looked surprised. 'You gave the Muslim greeting. You are a believer?'

'My mother was, and I suppose that more than a small part of me is also.'

'Yet you wear a foreign uniform?'

'The Legion is a mixture of all races and creeds.'

'Do you worship in the required manner?'

'I confess that I do not.'

'That will offend the Lord.'

'I am sure that He does not notice what I do,' Mayne said with a disarming smile.

'He notices even the sparrow that falls.'

'Pray for me, *shaikh*, if you would,' Mayne found himself saying much to his surprise, aware of Zahra's astonished look at his words. Why had he asked it, he the happy half-believer, the one who was so sure that he needed no creed? Did he care what God thought of him? He never had until now.

'Come, Captain Mayne,' Zahra said in her most formal voice, 'we will go on to see the women at their weaving. Thank you, *shaikh*, I am delighted with the boys' progress.'

The weavers sat giggling together as their fingers agilely twined the woollen threads around their spindles, fashioning brightly coloured rugs and cloaks of sapphire blue, scarlet and sunshine yellow. On seeing the Amira they leapt to their feet to *salaam* and then returned to their seats at her request.

'We make as much as we can of all that we need, even though we are far from destitute, Captain. The wool is collected from the sheep, goats and camels, and woven or spun into rugs and hangings like these you see here. They make excellent wedding gifts, too, and a girl will usually make what she requires before she takes a husband.' Her green eyes fixed his meaningfully. It was not easy to keep their mutual attraction hidden, and Zahra managed it only by keeping her eyes away from Mayne's as much as possible.

Having admired the work of the weavers, they passed on to a group of women who were making Qu'ranic charms out of turquoise and terracotta-coloured beads, linked together with thin silver wire.

'These are to protect against disease,' Zahra explained. 'Each will have a Qu'ranic verse engraved on the flat silver disc that hangs at the base of the necklet. Every child is given one. Sometimes they are lost and that is considered very serious.'

Next they came to a group of men who were cleaning guns and cartridge belts. Mayne saw to his surprise that they were reasonably recent models, and looked to be in excellent condition.

'Are these for hunting?' he asked Zahra, who raised her brows at the question.

'They are for hunting and for defence.'

'Defence against whom? I thought there was peace here in your land?'

'There is, but it is safer to be prepared for all eventualities.' She did not meet his eyes.

'Would you use these guns against an invader?' It was a stupid, asinine question and he knew it the moment it was out of his mouth. Of course she would do just that. Did he expect her to stand by and let her enemies conquer her without a fight? Arabs were ferocious and tireless in battle and that was why he was here, to prevent such a reaction when the Legion moved in.

'Guns are necessary when invaders decide that they wish to annexe land that belongs to someone else. Surely you, as a soldier, appreciate that?'

'Of course.' He had the grace to flush. 'It is just that everyone here seems so amiable, so unfamiliar with the ways of aggression.'

'That is because we have had peace for three decades, Captain, but we have not been blind to what has been happening elsewhere in Arabia, believe me.' She met his glance squarely, and he knew that he should be feeling deep shame at the deception he was practising. Yet if he allowed himself to think like that, he would have to abandon his mission, disobey his orders, and return empty-handed to his commanding officer.

He could lie, of course, say that there had been no opportunity to befriend the Amira and her people, claim that they were hostile and violent, but what cause would that serve? They would send another emissary, and more gifts, and fate would have its way despite him. The Land of Mirages would be decimated, as planned, and its wealth misappropriated by the Legion in their Imperial

217

Master's name. And he would have to try and live with himself afterwards.

'Captain, did you not hear me? We are a peaceable people and we make alliances where others would make war. In that we differ from others of our countrymen, but that is because we *are* different. We have a special place in the heart of Allah.' Zahra smiled dreamily and he could almost have believed what she said, if he had not been a half-believer.

Next they watched women making yoghourt; first taking fresh milk and heating it, then leaving it to stand with some of the previous day's yoghourt in a leather pouch. One woman was squatting beside a goatskin which had been sewn into an oval shape and suspended over two poles. Her work involved pushing the leather bag to and fro until the contents thickened into butter.

'We eat a great deal of *laban*. It is an excellent source of nourishment.' Zahra looked closely at Mayne, the dreaminess gone. She seemed to be trying to read his mind, for those ancient-innocent eyes were searing right through him. 'It was my mother's favourite food. She survived on it for weeks in the desert before she married my father.'

'Your mother is still spoken of with reverence.'

'And always will be! Did I tell you that she was one of the Sulubba tribe? They are the lowest of tribes, and normally a woman born of their ranks would have no chance to marry a man of a higher tribe, but my mother did.' Pride filled her voice. 'They serve as trackers and hunters, they mend pots and dishes and make saddles for the higher ones, and their women dance and sing and compose verses for entertainment. They say that the women of the Sulubba are the most beautiful of all, and wealthy men frequently take them as their mistresses but rarely as their wives. There is something else that they say about the Sulubba.'

Zahra had stopped midway between two groups of
218

women, where no one could hear her speak except Mayne.

'They say that they are sorcerers and sorceresses, that they can make magic, cast spells and even put the evil eye on those who offend them.'

'And did your mother do that?'

'She bewitched everyone who ever set eyes on her, but not purposely. She certainly bewitched my father. He had only to see her to know that he would love her for the rest of his days and beyond.'

'Then you must have her skills, for that was how I felt when I saw you. Have you bewitched me, *mahbub*?'

Zahra's face was flaming, and now there could be no pretence that she was not affected by the closeness of the foreign emissary. Anyone watching would know that she was. Trembling inside, she craved his arms tightly wound around her, fettering her for life.

'We must not speak like this where my people can see!'

'When I saw you sitting there like a maiden from centuries ago, with your unicorn resting in your lap and your hair trailing over your shoulders like spun silk, I knew that my first feelings about you were right. I had not been mistaken. Zahra, I love you and I always shall.'

Pain swam through her arms, the pain of keeping them by her sides when she longed to braid them around him, imprisoning him so that he could never leave her. Only the utmost self-control kept her mouth from trembling and her eyes from meeting his. This was madness. How could she have thought that denying him would be easy?

'Nothing can come of it, I told you that!' she hissed beneath her breath, imagining every eye upon her when in fact her people were happily going about their business. 'You must forget me. I belong to another, and if he should hear what has happened, then he will kill you – and me.'

She added the last two words despite believing that

Mahmed would never dare harm her. But she wished to impress upon Mayne that he must not come near her again. Even so, her heart ached as she warned him. Did love mean having to lie, having to warn and threaten and keep one's distance? *Ya Allah*, but she had dreamed of enjoying a love like that between her mother and father, consuming, searing, sweetly shackling, but now it was here and she dared not take it. She dared not!

'Sorceress, I am yours and there is nothing that either of us can do about it,' Mayne hissed back.

That evening, when they had eaten and the formalities were over, the dishes cleared away, Zahra excused herself for a few moments, leaving Mayne to reflect over his final dish of coffee. He had spent a perfect day in her company, with more quiet contentment than he had ever known in his life. It was a weird feeling, this sensation of happiness, and he did not know whether to trust it. Why should he, when he had long been resigned to doing without it? Briefly, with his Dananir, he had enjoyed something approaching bliss, but that had evaporated overnight into tragedy. Now he must face that this love, too, would be brief, gone from him all too soon, and that his own willing treachery would be instrumental in destroying it, as he had destroyed everything else that was precious to him.

Had he ever truly been a ruthless villain? Once he might have been, but not now. Once he had killed and executed without compunction, hungering for fortune and position, for recognition and power, but now he saw them as mere empty vessels that would never contain true love.

What was he going to do? Usher in her downfall, stand back while her lands were commandeered for the French and her riches swept away into imperial coffers? If she knew the true reason for his being there, she would loathe him for ever more and he would deserve it.

He put down the coffee dish whose contents tasted like sand in his mouth, and it was then that the first wafting notes of the flute came to his ears and he looked up, expecting to see the musicians.

In the lamplit interior, which was bathed in rose-gold light and scented with incense, rose and cinnamon, he saw the most enchanting sight of his life.

Zahra had not worn the peacock robe since her mother's death, although she had been allowed to try it on, very carefully, as a special treat when she was a child. The robe had of course been left to her, and now, radiantly in love, she wore it in the full bloom of womanhood, wore it for the first time in her very own right, as Zahra, Queen of the Desert, not as Mishaal's shadow.

The flute and the *davoul* echoing her swirling steps, she bowed and dipped and rotated so smoothly on her bare creamy feet that she appeared airborne. Extending her arms above her head, she twined them round one another until palm met palm and thumb met thumb, and then she parted them, extending them to either side of her, forefingers touching thumb tips, the rest of her fingers spread fan-like while her body curved and swayed enticingly.

Mayne, watching, felt his mouth go dry, his heart temporarily thump into an uneven rhythm that shook his body. Sweat broke out on his forehead and palms and he could only gape. Was this vision real? How could anyone possess such unearthly beauty? If she had been created by some magician's spell, woven from heath flame and moondust and firefly light, she could not have been more entrancing.

She wore what he supposed must be the famous peacock robe, an intricate design of iridescent sapphire blue, warm jade greens, cerulean and indigo, formed in the shape of peacock feathers that rustled crisply like leaves pursued by the wind, and when her arms rose, the

221

broad wings of the robe swirled out behind her like a peacock's proudly erected tail. On her ankles were tiny gilded anklets hung with bells that went chink, chink, chink, almost eerily, making the hairs on the nape of his neck tingle. Was this the woman he loved, or some sorcerer's greatest creation? He could barely breathe. His fingers were shaking, his throat choked with emotion. She looked so young and sweet and fair, so innocent and trusting as she danced, swooping and gyrating on her bare creamy feet with their delicate, lacy pattern of henna that he knew he was lost all over again.

What were disobeyed orders compared to the preservation of the beauty before him? How could he ever have considered endangering her for one second? She was all that he had ever wanted, or would ever want. If they were the poorest and most destitute lovers who had ever lived, then he would love her until the day he died, and beyond.

As he fell in love with her all over again, he was no longer the ruthless Legionnaire, the man who had tried to create a new identity for himself with deeds of bravery. He was a man who loved a woman, and she was the rarest of the rare, beautiful and shining with humour and kindness and wit, a woman who had not seen herself truly until she looked into his eyes, just as he had not seen himself truly until he looked into hers.

God – or Allah – had brought them together, now he was sure of it, and in that moment he vowed that no man would separate them.

Later, when the air was scented unforgettably with musk and rose incense, she lay with her head in his lap, gazing up into his blue and green flecked eyes and knowing that if she died that night, she would die the most contented woman in the universe.

222

Turned low, the lamps swung gently on their gilded chains, casting monstrous shadows on the walls. There was an intimate atmosphere in the tent; it was a haven where they could think of nothing save one another. The servants had been sent away, and only one guard stood at the entrance. He was Joab, a black-skinned mute, sold into slavery as a boy when his tongue had been removed so that he could never let slip secrets. Husain had freed him after he had been taken during a raiding party on a tribe who were dealing in slaves against his wishes. Having chosen to stay and serve the Amir out of gratitude, Joab was one of Zahra's most devoted attendants.

'Do you know what the Beduin believe?' Zahra touched her hand to Mayne's cheek, delighting in the feel of his fingers as he took it to press her palm against his mouth and kiss it passionately. 'They believe that the desert wolf can understand what humans say because he was once human himself, and was owner of all the goats and sheep, but because he committed a terrible sin, he was changed into the form of a wolf.

'Sometimes a shepherd will draw a circle round the animals he guards, to keep the wolves from harming them, and while he draws it, he says, "The circle of Solomon, son of David, is between thee and me. If thou breakest it, Allah shall break thee."'

'Nothing about the desert creatures would surprise me. How they survive in this climate is beyond understanding.'

'And what of this desert creature? What do you think of *her*?' Gently Zahra pulled his face down to hers, her eyes molten emerald in the lamplight.

'I think that she is the hardiest of creatures and yet beneath it all the most tender and vulnerable, that her heart is the most generous I have ever known, and her courage inestimable. The French have a word for it: *formidable*.' Caressingly, he kissed her arched ebony

223

brows, then her forehead and each high, strong cheek-bone.

'Do you think that we might be turned into wolves for our sin?' Suddenly there was something that might have been fear in her eyes. 'And for the rest of our lives be outside the charmed circle? I could not bear that!' She took a little gasping breath.

'Not even if we were together?' He squeezed her hand. 'No, I think it is more likely that I shall draw a circle around you, and recite the same charm. "The circle of Solomon, son of David, is between the world and us, and if anything should break it, then Allah shall break the world, but not us, never us, my beloved."'

Then he took her in his arms and the furious melting fires of love entrapped them.

PART FIVE

The Forsaken Princess

Perhaps I lived before
In some strange world where first my soul was shaped,
And all this passionate love, and joy, and pain,
That come, I know not whence, and sway my deeds,
Are old, imperious memories, blind yet strong,
That this world stirs within me.

George Eliot (1819–1880)

I feel
The link of nature draw me;
            flesh of flesh,
Bone of my bone thou art...

Milton (1608–1674)

Chapter Fourteen

Zuli had never been more miserable in her life. Her servants had been told that she had given her virginity to a secret lover, and now she was in disgrace. Before he had gone to put down the insurrection in Bakasir, her father had given orders that she was to be kept a prisoner in her tent, and there she had been for weeks. Hardly anyone spoke to her now save her old *da'da*, the nurse who had tended her and her sisters from their birth, but even she looked at Zuli with sad, reproachful eyes.

Her father had convinced them all, she thought bitterly. No one would believe her if she shouted out the truth, not that she could ever bring herself to do that. After all, he was her father and she loved him, despite the anguish and suffering he had caused her. Not understanding at first, she had believed him when he said that all fathers did this with their daughters; that it was a well-kept secret but common in all families, although it was forbidden to discuss it. In fact, he said, the whole subject was taboo, and that was how it had always been.

Desperately lonely and unhappy since her mother had died, she had not argued, accepting and being glad that her father sought her out so much. Once she had haltingly asked when it would be time for her to marry, and he had grown so angry that she had never dared raise the matter again.

He had given her so many gifts that her tent was crammed with them: cedarwood chests; embroidered deerskin slippers sewn with emerald and silver silks; robes of apple green and quince yellow, deep ochre, sky blue and rose pink; caskets piled with jewellery that she constantly put on and took off in her boredom and loneliness. And then there was the dancing costume of fragile lemon silk, transparent and beaded with topaz crystals that glittered in the lamplight when she danced for her father. He would watch her avidly, his eyes overflowing with emotion. How awkward she had felt dancing without musical accompaniment, for, of course, this had been secret, as were all their love-making sessions.

Not at ease in revealing robes, she was far happier in her everyday ones of woven wool or linen, her mind empty of any cares save those of daily life.

Yes, she loved her father, for how did one stop doing that? But at the same time, she hated and feared him for what he had done to her. She was by no means aggressive or fiery; it was in her nature to be passive and gentle, to take what life sent and not to complain. She would have made a perfect wife and mother. As it was, she directed all her grief and torment inwards, where it twisted and congealed so that she felt all the guilt, the burden and the blame. She wanted to love her father in the way that she had done until two years ago, and because that love was now tempered, she felt the guilt and not he. If he had ever suffered a qualm of conscience he had kept it totally hidden, while she suffered on and on.

She looked at other girls' faces, wondering if they too were feeling as she did about this taboo subject, wondering if they were happy and content when their fathers took them on their couches, or whether they felt the mixture of love and hate, disgust and tortured desire that she did. If only she could break the taboo and speak of it to others! But she could not be the first, and well she knew it.

She had hoped that her father's absence would give her some time to gather her thoughts and usher in a little peace of mind, but how could she do that when her swollen belly jutted out in front of her by night and day? Poor child growing within her. *Ya Allah*, make it a boy! she prayed continually, desperately opposed to bringing a daughter into the world to face the same racking conflict.

If this were the natural way, why then did she feel so riven? But perhaps she was not natural? Perhaps she had abnormal feelings and desires and Allah was punishing her for them? If she had been grateful for her father's arms around her, in her motherlessness, was that a crime? If only she knew! What if she were not meant to enjoy those times with her father, for enjoy them she had in the beginning, before realisation had begun to affect her and she had conceived their child.

If this were the normal way of things, why were there not more unmarried girls with child? Unlawful child-bearing was outlawed and virtually unknown in her tribe, as among all the Beduin. To be virgin on one's wedding night was of paramount importance. Why then did fathers take their daughters' virginity? Or perhaps it was all a sham; perhaps the insistence that girls were virgin on their marriage nights was understood to be an empty custom? If only she knew!

Her head was throbbing and the low backache that had disturbed her sleep was beginning again. She had endured this, on and off, for three weeks now, but had been told by her *da'da* that she was not yet ready to give birth. There was another month and a half before the child was due.

'What if he comes early?' she had asked, but her *da'da* had said that it would not be. She knew the signs. Had she not been present at the births of Zuli and her sisters?

The backache made her nauseous and the throbbing in her head was like a bee's drone, distant yet ever present, so that she longed to thrust it away as she would a stinging insect.

The suffocating heat of the tent was intolerable and her appetite had vanished long ago. She had struggled to drink milk and eat *laban* and dates because she was urged to do so, but she had frequently vomited them back up again. She knew that she had lost a great deal of weight, but she was not concerned about that. The bulge that was constantly beneath her eyes was reassurance enough that all was well physically, while at the same time it was a continual reminder of her unhappiness and how sadly her life had changed since the night of her twelfth birthday.

'The Amir will be back after the full moon,' her *da'da* reminded her, face solemn. 'You must eat well so that the baby is healthy, or the Amir will be angry with me and ask me what I was doing while he was away.'

Her nurse had taken to referring to her father as 'the Amir' ever since it had become obvious that Zuli was with child without the blessing of marriage. Before that, in private conversation, her nurse would call him 'Mahmed', or 'your father'. If only she knew the truth!

'I cannot eat. The food makes me sick.'

'You say so to gain attention for yourself! The food is good, and your infant wishes to eat. If you do not eat, then he cannot. You must think of him before yourself.'

'It would be best if he died!' Zuli cried, her voice agonised, and then she burst into a torrent of tears because whatever else she wanted, she did not want her child to die. Young and desperate she might be, but she loved her baby already. When he came, he would be hers and she would love him without hesitation or doubt. It seemed to her that in relationships with men those two were always present, but not with the child born of one's

230

womb. She could not wait to see her son's face. In delivering him, she would deliver herself.

The pains began that night, strong and insistent, and when she saw her nurse's face, she knew that the baby was about to arrive.

'How long?' she whispered, terrified in the still darkness of her tent, surrounded by her jewels and robes and the plethora of gifts that could not comfort her now.

Her *da'da* shrugged. 'By dawn.'

'All will be well?'

'It is in the hands of Allah. Pray to Him, not to me, child. Rise, and I will dress you in your delivery robe. It would be better if you squatted so that the child has free entry into the world.'

She had seen her father's famous racing camels give birth, and his horses and goats and sheep, but not a woman. Her mother had suffered badly when her sisters were born, and she had been kept away from the tent at that time.

Dizzy, and taut with fright, she found the squatting position painful. It made her lower back feel as if it were splitting apart and her knee joints soon began to ache.

'I must lie down,' she beseeched, but her nurse was adamant that the child would not come if she did that.

'He will think himself not welcome and will refuse to be born. Hold this in your hand and you will be safely delivered.' She pushed a Qu'ranic charm into Zuli's palm. 'Pray! I told you to pray!'

The next few hours were terrifying, with such pain and fear of the unknown that Zuli sobbed instead of praying, her nurse slapping her hands in reproof of such stupidity so that the ache in her fingers was added to her agony.

'He does not want to come!' she wailed.

'It is the full moon, only a few more hours. He waits for that.'

'But you said by dawn!'

'It may be later.' Her nurse shrugged.

How cold her nurse was these days where once she had been a doting *da'da*. All the blame was heaped on Zuli, who had done nothing to deserve it. Or had she? Which was right in the eyes of Allah: to love her father and long for him, or to feel a frigid coldness when she was in his arms? She had felt both, but surely one must be right and one wrong?

'Think on what you are doing, child!' Her nurse's voice grated against her ears. 'Ah, I have never known such a stubborn and wilful one as thee!'

At that, Zuli burst into tears again, and when the contraction came it caught her unawares. Already too tense, she screamed loud and long as her body was racked with agony.

'He is not welcome, and he knows it! Who but a sinner would fight her own son's birth?' Zuli felt wiry, iron hard arms forcing her upright again from where the contraction had driven her down onto her couch.

The tent was swaying around her dizzily, and she knew that she was about to vomit. She called out for the bowl, leaning over it wretchedly until her stomach was empty of what little she had eaten. Then, gasping, she collapsed back on to her couch and lay as if unconscious. She did not hear the voices at the entrance to the tent as the women of the tribe asked if her nurse needed help, and were sent away by the old woman who prided herself on her knowledge and skills. To accept help now would be to admit that she was too old, too ignorant, and that she would never do. She would die first – or her patient would.

Dawn came, and mid-morning, and Zuli wept for her mother and at last thought that she was there in the tent. Through a gathering mist she could see her face, so beloved, so tender, the smiling mouth and loving eyes. She held out her arms beseechingly and even the indomitable old nurse was shaken at the expression of longing on the girl's racked, sweat-streaked face.

More voices at the entrance to the tent, blurred and thick and distant yet at the same time punishing to her eardrums. Zuli thought that her father had returned and she sat up, crying out his name and then weeping again. But it was not Mahmed, although he was indeed on his way back to her, the insurrection put down, the thieves and rebels slaughtered and the precious milk-white camel in his possession. The camel that the Amira Zahra would ride to her wedding.

A band of vagabonds had grouped together and attacked a camp and then another, burning tents and raping women. The attacks took place only on the perimeter of Mahmed's land but they concerned him all the same. If he had not given the rebels a show of his might, they would have come ever closer. In battle he was pitiless, inflexible and savage, yet the opportunities to display his skills were rare these days. He had almost welcomed the chance to defeat the bandits, except that it would take him from his Zuli.

'It is not the Amir, but he is returning,' her nurse said, exasperated at her charge's wailing. 'Get up child, and let the infant out, for he will never come while you lie on your back like that.'

'Get up? I cannot move!' Nor could she see properly. The tent seemed dark and there was a strange, un-pleasant odour in the air. 'What time is it?'

'Evening.'

'The full moon is tonight?'

'Tonight.'

'It is not safe to bring forth a child at the full moon. You told me that yourself.'

'Allah will watch over you. Now get up. Here, lean on me and let your knees bend so that you are near the ground and the babe has not far to fall when he comes.'

'I shall not let him fall! I shall catch him!' Zuli sounded hysterical.

233

'When he comes.' The old nurse was sceptical. She had her suspicions but would not voice them. She had massaged the swollen belly and probed it with her fingers but she had felt no movement. The infant was stuck high up in the womb, and they said that these were the worst births. If it had been full term, then the infant would have descended in readiness for the world. *Ya Allah*, the Amir would beat her when he returned if there was not a living son to show. This was his first grandchild, even if its mother had brought disgrace upon them.

It was midnight when the old woman knew that she would have to accept help. Outside the tent were younger women, eager to step in where she had failed. Her wrinkled knuckles dug into her mouth, the old one retired to the other side of the *qata* that separated Zuli's couch room from that of her living quarters, and there she stayed, drinking deep of *nabidh* and praying that it would drive away her wakefulness so that she could forget her failings.

Mutterered voices came to Zuli's ears and then a scream, long drawnout and ear-cracking, and then another. She heard someone say that the infant was the wrong way round, its feet coming first, or trying to, and that a knife would be necessary if they were to save the mother.

Silence, and then the stinging smell of scorching metal as someone dipped a blade into a flame before cutting into her. Then came the worst screams she had ever heard, so close to her that they might have been coming from her own mouth – in her fever she did not realise that they were doing just that, and she clamped her hands to her ears to shut them out, but nothing could. It was the will of the Lord, blessed be His name.

She was burning hot, her body drenched in sweat, and when the blade cut into her, swiftly and surely, to open up the birth passage, she was momentarily shocked into

234

silence before fainting away. When she came round, her hands went straight to her belly. It was still swollen but the shape of it had changed. It did not feel right now and she feared for her son.

'Help me!' she croaked, and the three women turned to her at once, their eyes distended. Had they thought that she was dead? 'I must have water!'

When the water was brought, she could barely swallow it and then the pain began again for they had managed to move the child an inch or two but no more and it was still lodged inside her. For an hour they let her rest and then it began again, the terrible pain that tore through her as the *khanjar* bit deep, another cut being made in the birth passage, but still the child was stuck.

'She is so small!' someone whispered, thinking that she could not hear in her stupor.

'She should not have taken a lover and shamed herself and her father!' another hissed back.

Then fingers were digging agonisingly deep into the birth passage, trying to grasp the infant's body, and someone cried out 'Allah be praised!' for the contact was made and the child began to move at last.

Zuli felt sick again and vomited into the bowl that was brought hurriedly. And then the rending pain began, the sensation of being torn apart. It was intolerable but thankfully brief, and when it ended she heard the cries of her son.

'He lives!' one of the women said, leaning over her, eyes shining, and then the babe was swaddled and placed in her arms and she could hardly see him for her tears. He looked exactly like her father, but she did not care. He was her son, her child born of her body and she would love him until she died!

Then they slept solidly, hour upon hour, after which she held the infant to her breast and he began to suckle, which was a miracle considering the ordeal they had both been through. As she felt the convulsing pains in her

235

womb when he took his feed, she cringed, but was this not nature's way? A woman must bring forth her children in pain and suffering as the Lord had decreed, and she must be thankful that she had her son alive in her arms.

Weak though she was, such a soaring happiness broke inside her that she had to bite her lips to keep from crying out. Her son! Her darling son! She would call him Badr, which meant Full Moon, for he had come at the time of the full moon, safely through the valley of death she had brought him.

When Mahmed arrived, he feigned joy at being a grandfather but his shame cut deep. When he entered his daughter's tent and saw her waxen, haggard face, he winced. Then he saw the sleeping child, heavily swaddled so that only the tiny, crinkled scarlet face was showing. He saw himself in that face and his stomach churned. He could not look at that every day, knowing how the child had been conceived, reminded of the crime he had committed. He could not! And so he told the watching women that the child was a child of shame and immorality and, lifting the infant high in his arms, he showed him to his mother for the last time.

'Here is the result of your sin, my daughter! You conceived this child in an unlawful union, destroying your chances of marriage with any man when you lay with your lover and deceived your father!'

'He is my son, Father. My son, Badr!' Zuli wailed, holding out her arms to take the child.

'No! He is the child of your sin. You have shamed our house, daughter, and the sin must be punished. He will be raised by a foster mother in Bakasir. There was a woman there who had lost her child and was grieving deeply. He was killed by the bandits. Would you keep the child from his new mother? Here, kiss your son and wish him Godspeed on his journey.'

Zuli screamed out in horror, unable to believe what was being said to her, tears bursting from her bewildered eyes, but she was not allowed to hold Badr for more than a few moments, and as she looked across the child's head into her father's narrowed, dark gaze she saw there such disgust and loathing, such hatred and revulsion, that she wanted to die. What else was there left to her now?

Time meant nothing any more, nor did the breeze or the sun. She had said goodbye to this world when Badr was taken from her. Weeping for hours, she had felt her life draining from her with tears. Her little son, her Badr, her full moon, and she would never see him again. If she could not see him, then she would see nothing. When her father came in to ask how she was, she would not reply. She had no strength to speak but lay there limply as if she were already in her shroud as she longed to be. She would be shielded from her agony when she was dead; she yearned for it.

'Zuli, I love you. All will be well again soon. You will marry and have more children and they will bring you joy. I am not such a cruel man, I think only of your honour. While I was in Bakasir I found you a husband, a man who is willing to take you although you have shamed yourself. He will arrive for the betrothal feast before the next full moon, and you will like him. He is young and very handsome. Also he is rich. He is a prize indeed for you in your position, and you must give thanks to the Lord.'

It was not strictly true, for the man was aged and physically deformed, but Zuli must be married off before Mahmed took Zahra as his bride. When he had been a child he had toyed with children; but now he was a man and he had put off childish ways.

When she did not speak, dumb in her misery, he took her hand and said that she would be having a new mother, for he was to marry Husain's daughter soon. It was all arranged and he had but to present himself at the ceremony.

'You must hasten and recover your strength so that you can be there at the feasting. When you are strong, you can ride on the milk-white camel that I brought from Bakasir for my bride,' he promised.

Turning her head away, Zuli felt the breath fading from her as if there were no air in the tent, yet there was a soaring exultancy where there should have been pain in her lungs. At last she had what she wished: Death was coming to release her. What else was left to her if she could not have her Badr? She had said that his birth would deliver her, and it had. Soon, she would be free.

'Zuli!' The last sound she heard was her father's shocked voice crying her name, and then there was a soft and tender fluffiness enveloping her and a swelling, silvery light of welcome as she drifted out of the physical world towards the only escape left open to her; the place where one day, if Allah were good, she would hold her Badr in her arms again, hear him chuckling as she sang to him, and it would be as if they had never been parted.

Chapter Fifteen

'Honey, you shouldn't be hiding that talent away!' In his happiness he felt more at ease with his origins than he had ever done, remembering the endearment that his father had used for his stepmother, and using it himself for his own love.

Zahra smiled broadly as she sat beside Mayne. Tonight she had danced for him a second time, and he was still open-mouthed at the spectacle. She had felt more accomplished, her body lither and more controlled, and she remembered the days when she had sincerely believed that she was a poor dancer by comparison with her mother.

'Would you want me to dance for other men as I did tonight, Captain,' she said with mock formality. 'Do you want other men to lust after me, as they lusted after my mother when she was a dancer in the Street of the *Jijims*?'

'Perhaps not.' Willingly conceding defeat, Mayne took her hand, thrilling as he always did at the feel of her silky, tender flesh against his weather-roughened fingers.

'I dance only for the ones I love. Before, I danced for my mother and father, when we were alone together, and my father would smile and nod happily at my efforts but I always knew that he was comparing me to my mother and finding me lacking. When my mother

239

danced, the angels came down to watch and the birds ceased their singing. They said that the wild beasts would not kill their prey while she danced, and that the whole world dreamed until the last note of the flute.'

'And what of your wild beast? The one I saw you with at the oasis? You were not dancing and yet he was lying in your lap like a pet dog.'

'I do not know why he took to me as he did. Perhaps it was because I am the daughter of Mishaal.'

'You think he knew that, my darling?' Mayne's eyes shone, the blue-green flecks rich and bright in the rose-gilt lamplight.

'Perhaps.' She shrugged, looking away.

'Honey.' He used the endearment again, marvelling at how well it suited her, her skin tone, her sweetness. 'When I first met you, I thought you were the most self-important little thing I'd ever seen. I was warned that you were proud and arrogant and that you did exactly what you wanted and heeded no one. That was why they chose me to come here, because I have a certain reputed knack with the ladies.' He grinned apologetically. 'I expected tirades and terrible scenes and the need to exert all my diplomatic talents, for what they're worth.'

'And I have made not one scene! Mayne, I have disappointed you, can you ever forgive me?' she teased. 'But if you insist, then I am sure that I can lose my temper and throw this jar at you.' Lifting an enamelled ornament, she moved it threateningly towards her lover. Laughing, he caught the jar and put it to one side, and then she was in his arms, fire to fire, passion to passion, as it always was with them. In a collision of like minds and like bodies, heat engulfing them as they kissed, they clung together fiercely as if they might at any moment be parted forever.

'Beloved, we cannot take the risk again. I sent Freyha away, but she can almost read my mind. She would know what we had done.'

240

'The oasis? Would you meet me there while she sleeps? I shall keep watch for you as you journey.'

She laughed softly. 'No one would harm me, beloved. Remember, I am Queen of the Desert, Husain's daughter. All the wild things know me.'

Wondering, he held her at arm's length. 'Can you not see your own uniqueness, *mahbub*? You say that you cannot dance like Mishaal, and the people do not love you as they loved her, but I have seen no sign of it. Who else but you could say that the wild beasts would not harm them?'

'Did you not hear their complaints against me as you rode here? My ministers, although they are aged, have their fingers on the heartbeat of my land, and they say that I have offended many by what I have done or not done since I became ruler here.' Suddenly the light had gone from her face and sadness shadowed her eyes. 'I have failed my people and I know it. God knows it, too. Has he not sent back the drought to make that plain?'

'My darling, you can't please everyone, however hard you try. When you stayed unwed, it frightened the men because they saw their own women staying free and living their own lives without them, and nothing terrifies a man more than thinking that his woman might act without consulting him.'

'Does that frighten you, Mayne?' She looked at him, her face serious.

'No, but then I am not the average male. I would want my woman to think and act for herself. It would be different if I were insecure and lacked confidence.'

'And you think my people do?'

'Some of them undoubtedly will. Arabs cling to custom more ferociously than any other race, but I do not have to tell you that. Had I not spent some time in the most modern country in the world, America, then I would feel the same. How could they change things now? It would cause them too much agony. They would not be able to do it.'

'And what of my hospital? I built it only for their good, and they would not come to it. How did I go wrong there, my love?'

'Custom again. It takes time for the Arab to grow familiar with new things, the Beduin most of all. City dwellers are frowned upon by your people who see them as immoral and avaricious, yet the city dwellers would have accepted your hospital gladly.'

'So you think I should have made a gift of it to Abeesha, perhaps?'

'Possibly.'

'But I wanted it for my own people, not for strangers!'

'Let the city dwellers use it first, and when word spreads of its benefits, the Beduin will follow.'

'There has to be somewhere for all the French physicians and nurses to work when they come here.' Unwittingly, she scorched him with shame.

Truly, he was under some enchantment. He had forgotten that he had come there to lie and cheat and deceive. For her and her people there would be no French doctors, no modern medical aids and medicines, because the Emperor had never intended to send any except those who would treat his own Legionnaires. The Draisienne had been meant to impress the Amira with France's amazing modern inventions so that she would sign the treaty without hesitation. Instead they had spent a day trying to master its temperamental and unpredictable ways. It had been a happy day, and one during which he had decided that he would never carry out his orders.

'Oh, Mayne, when you talk like that you sound more of a believer than I do! I did pray, but He did not listen.'

'He did, I am sure of it. Perhaps you did not give Him time to work? You must have faith, my little one, you must have faith. To believe that you will fail is lack of

242

faith. The devil tricks you into thinking your plans are wrong and that you are a fool, but you are not. You love your people. Do you think they are stupid enough to disregard that? I have seen adoration and reverence shining in their eyes when they look at you, or talk about you. Do not turn your back on them because you do not want to see the truth!'

He was gripping her by the shoulders, almost painfully, and trying to instil in her a proper sense of her own worth. She must see that what he said was true, or she would continue to languish in this hinterland of doubt and blame.

'You have only your own fear to be frightened of, *mahbub*, nothing else.'

'I have nothing to fear save fear?' She giggled helplessly, then leant against him, clinging like a child, knowing with all her heart that what he said was true, and that was why he had been sent to her.

Midnight came in a bedazzlement of stars, the full moon blazing in their midst. From a distance, the stars above the oasis of that name did not seem especially thickly clustered, yet the moment they stepped into the enchanted circle of palms and *sumr* trees around the water's edge, Zahra and Mayne could see such a glorious multitude of them high above in the sky that they were breathless. Kissing and clinging together, they heard the eerie sounds of night: a fox barking, lone and mournful with no one to love him, and the night insects twittering and humming like tiny birds, a continual chorus that buzzed hauntingly in their ears.

Mayne's hand touched the gift that his beloved had given him when they dismounted. It was cool against his palm, almost shiveringly cool, and he could not help but think of the man who had once owned this legendary weapon, known as the Sword of God.

Many centuries before, Zahra had told him, a meteorite

243

had crashed into the desert, leaving a vast crater where it had fallen. Men and beasts had been killed by the impact, buried beneath the rubble. When their first terror had died, Hamid ibn Husain, Zahra's ancestor, had gathered some of the meteorite to fashion a sword from it, so that he could say he truly ruled by the command of the Most High. The celestial weapon was bluish in colour and streaked with silver; it was also surprisingly light despite the fact that it was some two and a half feet in length. Later, ornamentation had been added, and a Damascus silversmith had designed a hilt for it, and a gold-embossed scabbard, the finest artist available fashioning a Qu'ranic charm to be engraved into the blade.

'It is given to the heir on the day that he becomes ruler of the tribes,' Zahra said, her eyes blazing with emotion. 'I give it to you, Mayne, the man I love above all others.'

Shiveringly cool was the feel of the metal against his skin, as slowly, caressingly, he removed the sword from its scabbard to examine it closely, sensing in its smooth metal the mysteries of the skies and the planets, all the knowledge of the universe. Suddenly he remembered with a jolt the strange vision he had seen at the oasis during the great sandstorm: a sword, a glowing sword, rising from the spilling depths of the pool, some strange script emblazoned on it that he could not decipher at that distance.

'Mishaal used to bathe in this pool,' Zahra was saying, smiling at him. 'She said that the waters were like those of the Oasis of the *Jinn* where she once stayed with my father. They were always talking about their happiest days together, especially their time in the desert before they married. They told me everything except for one thing. My mother would never talk of the weeks she spent in the desert before my father found her. She knew a foreigner, apparently, an American, but I only learned a little of the story; she would say no more.

'He claimed to love her, but he put the Jewels of Destiny first. You see, they were concealed in a hidden place, in the temple of the Pagan Goddess, and when the American worked the spring that would reveal them, there was a rock fall and my mother stood directly in the path of the falling stones. . . .'

'And the American rushed to save the jewels and not your mother?'

'Yes, that is exactly what happened. How did you guess? Ignoring the treasure, my father rushed to save her, even though he believed that the rocks would bury the jewels forever, as the builder of the concealed vault had intended. He did it in spite of the fact that our people were desperate then, dying of thirst after months of terrible drought with all the wells running dry and no money to buy food from outside. Despite all that, he chose my mother.'

'And the American?' He waited to hear what she had to say about this man who in a way resembled Daneyard Amyan, for he too had placed the acquisition of personal fortune before the woman he loved.

'He was killed by the rockfall, as Allah had intended, I think. That is truly what you call *nasib*, destiny.'

'Was your mother very upset? Did she love the American more than she loved your father?' In a way, his mother had been like Daneyard, too, for she had placed her religion before the man she loved. Two errors that had blighted his life and which would ensure that he never made the same mistake himself.

'She might have thought she did, but when my father chose her above the wealth of Queen Zenobia, she knew where her future lay. She never spoke to anyone in detail of those days with the American before my father found her, but she referred to them once. She called them her "infidel summer". And this is my infidel summer with you, my beloved.' Tears spangled her eyes as she raised her mouth for his kisses.

245

Behind them, unseen, the water glowed, rubified by the crimson-tinged moonlight. In the depths of the water, the silver fishes plunged and swarmed, and the earth beneath the lovers trembled as if with a glorious excess of passion.

They were oblivious to it all as they sank to the soft, fresh sand, tearing aside one another's robes and pressing flesh to flesh, voracious to be joined, to be as close together as was possible.

When Mayne drove himself between her thighs, groaning in his delight and longing for her, Zahra gave a little whimpering cry, like some diminutive creature that is helpless in the talons of a predator, but this was no violent, unfeeling assault; this was heart meeting heart, and soul meeting soul, melding themselves into one united spirit that could defend itself against all the world's evil.

She was luscious as silk in his arms; he would never be able to get over the feel of her tender, rose-scented flesh, the odour of incense that emanated from her robes when she moved as if she were sanctified, a holy woman. He grinned to himself at the thought, for no nun had ever responded to a man with such fervour, such single-minded ecstasy, yet she had an unusual dual quality that he found both disturbing and thrilling. When he had called her unique, he had meant it. He had known enough women to be able to judge her correctly, and in judging her, he was beginning to understand himself.

All his life, he had gone from woman to woman, searching, but never finding all that he wanted for the simple reason that he had never known what it was that he sought. Now he did, for in loving everything that Zahra was, including her strange ethereal quality, he had found that he was capable of loving and being loved, just as she was.

Silvery tingles were scintillating through Zahra's

246

body, touching her limbs with fire, setting her skin ablaze with desire. To feel her lover deep within her was to glory in the most thrilling gift that God had given her, and she was revelling in the sensation. Her lover was strong and generously built and he fitted deep inside her, touching every part of her, caressing, inflaming, rousing her to such glorious frenzy that her senses rioted and she almost had to beg him to stop, unable to bear such sweet agony.

How could she have survived all these years without him, thinking that a solitary life was for her? She had surely been bewitched by *jinn* when she had thought that, for now she knew that she was made for love, *his* love.

Closer, deeper, she pulled him into her, moaning his name, feeling him touch where no man had ever touched before, locking her legs round his broad, muscular back so that he could not pull away even had he wanted to, while her arms braided him tightly to her and she begged him to come even closer, if it were possible. Such extraordinary sensations were possessing her that she twisted her head from side to side, arching her back and crying his name out loud, feeling the sensations starting at the pit of her belly, thronging there fervently before they would pitch across her body, consuming every muscle, every pore, until she knew of nothing and was nothing but her oneness with him.

Moonlight, starlight, peace, the sanctuary of their haven surrounded them. If they could have stood aside and watched themselves, they would have seen that their bodies shimmered slightly as if bathed in a light that came from the earth and not the clouds. It ringed them, encircled them, like a cameo, so that they were immortalised in their passion.

The moment of ecstasy came, and Zahra gripped her lover ferociously. As he spilled his love inside her, both felt the deepest and most profound intimacy yet, the commingling of their souls, the touch of spirit to spirit as God intended true love to be.

After, lying contentedly with Zahra's head on his chest, Mayne gazed at the firmament above. He had spent many years of his life in Arabia, some of them in the desert, and though he knew it to be an extraordinary place in many ways, he had never before viewed it as magical. Yet now he did. From his vantage point he could see that the rest of the skies appeared empty of constellations, and yet above the oasis named for them they crowded so close together that little of the indigo sky could be seen. And how they pulsed, scintillating almost feverishly as if they were trying to impart some message to him.

Mishaal had bathed here, and they said that all the stars had gathered to watch her. Sure enough, there were the stars in their thousands upon thousands, directly above him, and in that realisation Mayne felt a tingling along the nape of his neck. Either the stars were always so multitudinous above the oasis, or else they had gathered in their trillions especially to watch him and Zahra making love.

He would have grinned had he not felt so suddenly vulnerable. Stars clustering to watch him? What crazy imagining. Then he looked down at the silky ebony head resting against his chest. He was no longer plain Mayne Amyan, adventurer and Legionnaire. Now he was the lover of the Queen of the Desert, and why should her firmament not assemble to watch her in her very own oasis?

'Mayne, you will never leave me, will you?' her whispered voice broke into his thoughts.

'Never, *mahbub*, never.'

'What shall I tell Mahmed? He will be greatly offended. He is a warmonger. That is why he breeds his racing camels, and that is why I thought that marriage to him would doubly protect my land.'

248

'You think that he will make war on me? On what grounds?' Still in the afterglow of love, Mayne was not thinking straight.

'On the grounds that you are an infidel invader and have stolen his bride. On the grounds that you have no title or standing, no property, no descendancy from the Prophet Mohammed. Oh, he could summon a hundred good reasons – if he needs any at all when he is in the warmongering mood.'

'There is only one valid reason: I have stolen his future bride.' Mayne pulled her closer to him protectively.

'Not his *future* bride. In his eyes, my acceptance of his proposal was binding. He has sent the first bridal gifts. We have but to name the date. Our people have been told.'

'Then they must be untold.' Mayne sat up, the coldness of the real world slapping against him hard. 'You are mine now, Zahra, and no one shall part us. I would die before I let Mahmed lay a finger on you!'

'Oh, my heart, I do not wish to see you endangered! What if he attacked you? I could not bear it! My heart would break. If anything happened to you, then I would want to die too!'

With tears in her eyes at the impossibility of their love, Zahra flung her arms around Mayne's neck and wept.

For a day and a night, Mahmed refused to believe that Zuli was dead. He sat beside her cold body, rubbing her hands and kissing her face, speaking to her as if she had only fainted and would return to him.

'The Amir is crazed with grief,' his people said. They too mourned the young girl who had been well loved until she had brought shame on to her father's house, although such public grief was usually reserved only for sons of the house. 'It will take him time to recover. If only his grandson had been born of a lawful union, then he could have found some comfort in the child.'

249

But Badr was already in his foster mother's arms in Bakasir, and would never again set eyes on his true mother or father.

By evening of the second day, Mahmed was becoming resigned to the truth, agonising as it was. His Zuli had died, and in her dying she had revived all the pain of Mahia's loss. The thought that he had caused Zuli's death was something that he would not acknowledge; Allah gave, and he also took. He had taken Zuli and it was not Mahmed's fault. Women died in childbirth all the time; it was God's will.

Zuli, Zuli! his heart cried out for her, and as he gazed on the pallid waxen features, the sunken eyes with the lids closed to him forever and the mouth pinched and tinged with blue, he felt such a surge of venomous rage that the joints cracked in his clenched fists.

She was gone from him, his darling, and now he had nothing.

When the messenger rode in, dust-drenched and exhausted, Mahmed refused to see him at first, so the man was given his supper and a couch for the night. Hours were to pass before Mahmed would rally and summon the man to him, but when he did, he would hear something that would stir him from his melancholy.

'*Ya Saiyid*, Her Highness the Amira is much taken with the French emissary. He has brought her many gifts and she is much pleased by them. She wears his jewels round her neck.'

'His jewels? The emissary's jewels?' Mahmed flushed darkly, his fists bunching in rage.

'No, *Saiyid*, the jewels from the French *malik*, the King who sent him.'

'The Emperor!'

'Yes, *Saiyid*, the Emperor!' The messenger's voice trembled slightly. He had never seen his master in such a violent rage except on the battle field. There he himself had seen the Amir hack to death twenty-five bandits

250

who had laid waste one of his villages and raped the women. Mahmed was known as Allah's Avenger with good reason.

'What else?' Mahmed growled.

'The Amira has let the emissary see her dance. On two nights she has worn the peacock robe of her mother, the Amira Mishaal, and in it she danced for the man.'

'*Istafarallah!* She did not!' Mahmed was on his feet, his face as bleached of colour as his robe.

'She did, *Saiyid*, she did! And then she placed in his hands the Sword of God, the Amir Husain's sword, and she said it would be his.'

'I do not believe this! She cannot give him that sword! It is for me, for the Amir of the Land of Mirages. Has she gone mad?'

'She is bewitched, *Saiyid*, or so they say. Bewitched by the *jinn* so that she thinks she loves this man.'

Mahmed let out an unearthly roar, causing the spy to leap back in fear.

'What is he like, this emissary? Tell me now!' Mahmed gripped the man by the neck of his robe and almost lifted him off his feet.

'He-he is young, *S-Saiyid*, less than thirty summers, and he-he is handsome. He has Arab blood, and his hair is d-dark. His skin is dark, too, but his eyes are l-lighter coloured – infidel eyes.'

'Handsome? He is handsome and young?' The spy nodded. 'And he has Arab blood?' The spy nodded again, gulping on the choking sensation in his throat. 'You are right. She is bewitched. He wears a foreign uniform whatever his origins.' Mahmed let the man fall, which he did, to his knees, a bone snapping loudly as he collapsed, a groan on his lips.

'Have they tricked me? Is this some double dealing?' Mahmed spoke his thoughts out loud. It was too much to suffer: the loss of his beloved daughter, and then the news that his bride was dancing for an infidel while he

251

was away keeping the peace and fetching her the white camel on which she would ride to her marriage feast.

'Has who tricked you, *Saiyid*?' the spy croaked through his pain. His legs were his one weak spot. He had been wounded in the knee during a battle where he had seen his master slaughter a dozen insurgents, and he had been bedridden for almost twelve moons afterwards. Now he felt the fragile bone giving way as if it were splintering wood, but he was too petrified of the Amir's fury to complain.

The Amir did not reply. Impatiently, he gestured to the man to go, which he did with difficulty, hobbling and crouching and unable to hold back the yelps of pain. When the tent was empty, Mahmed strode up and down, kicking footstools and hassocks, trays and dishes out of his way. Then he stepped up to the tapestries hanging at the rear of his audience tent and, letting out a ferocious growl, began to tear them down, heaving, tugging and wrenching until they lay in a pile at his feet.

Mahia had loved the pictures embroidered upon them, the undulating flowers and vines, the dog with its mouth wide open as it bounded along behind its young master, who wore the strange, outlandish costume of the land where the tapestries had been made: Arras, in France, the same country where this infidel's royal master ruled.

He would have his revenge. No man, believer or non-believer, would be entertained by his bride, even if she be Queen of the Desert. That she had danced for this infidel and feasted with him cut Mahmed to the heart. How dared she, the harlot! He would ride into her camp and take the *kaffir* prisoner. With great delight, he personally would castrate the man, and then hack off his head. No one, man or woman, was going to make a fool of him, and no one was going to taste the delights of his virgin bride before he did. When he had given his orders to his men-at-arms, he would ride with them to the Land of Mirages, and God help anyone who stood in their way.

Sending for his scribe, he instructed the man to compose a message that would freeze the blood of the *kaffir*, saying that he, Mahmed ibn Beydoun, was on his way to avenge the honour of the Amira Zahra, and that only by the death of the foreign emissary could this be done.

PART SIX

Temple of the Pagan Goddess

We shape ourselves, the joy or fear of which the coming life is
  made
And fill our Future's atmosphere with sunshine and with shade.

The tissue of the Life to be we weave with colours all our own,
And in the field of Destiny, we reap as we have sown.

John Greenleaf Whittier (1807–1892)

The tent on which free winds are beating
Is dearer to the desert's child
Than palaces or kingly greeting –
O bear me to my desert wild!
To seek a heart with freedom swelling,
A kindred heart in deserts wild.

Maysun, Beduin wife of the first Umayyid Caliph

Chapter Sixteen

Zahra was dressing when the message came. Having slipped on a simple white cotton robe, its edges embroidered with sapphire and plum-blue embroidery, she pushed back the hair that was streaming free around her shoulders. Leaning at an angle to look into the hand mirror that Freyha was holding out for her, she carefully applied the *kohl* to her eyes. In the desert, *kohl* was used by both men and women to protect the eyes against infection and the blast of the sun, helping to keep them cool. Taking a thin stick round which was wound a wrapping of fine cotton, Zahra dipped it into the *kohl* pot and then stroked it close to her lashes. The effect, as always, was to increase the luminous green glow of her eyes and to make her skin resemble the finest porcelain.

The messenger, who was not kept waiting overlong, was given mint tea to refresh him. When the Amira sent for him, she had donned a *kuftan* of plum-blue trimmed with silver, and a white silk headveil carefully arranged so that its corners swathed her shoulders like shining white wings.

Having flung himself to the ground before her, the messenger handed her the scroll of parchment which she read in silence.

As she took in the words, her fingers clenched

convulsively and the sweat broke out in beads on her forehead. She no longer had need of the Persian rouge that she had just applied so delicately.

Mahmed was coming to kill her beloved!

Waves of weakness attacked her legs, and the muscles at the back of her calves jumped and jerked beyond her control. Her voice shaking, she dismissed the messenger and then sank down on to a velvet hassock, shivering uncontrollably.

How had Mahmed found out? As far as she knew, he was still in Bakasir putting down the brigands, yet he appeared to know everything that had happened here and he said that he was on his way to murder Mayne and avenge her honour. Her honour! What had Mahmed ever cared about that, or anything else to do with her? He had been the most dilatory and reluctant bridegroom ever, and now here he was threatening death and vengeance. What was more, for him to have learned of her movements there must be a spy in her camp, and the thought of that sickened her to the heart. One of her people was prying into her private affairs, listening to gossip about her and transmitting it all to Mahmed!

In her mind, she went through those closest to her, trying to imagine any one of them betraying her, but none of them was capable of such treachery, she was sure. The young girls who waited on her were giggly and lacking in composure, but that was the same the world over with girls of their age. Would they spill details of her activities to Mahmed? No, of course not. And yet what if he had said, 'Watch my bride, care for her, and tell me everything she does for I love her deeply and wish to know how she spends her time.' The pretence of loving concern had enabled many a traitor to discover what he or she most needed to know.

Mayne was out riding in the desert, as he loved to do before the heat of the day gathered. She must ride after him now and tell him that his life was in terrible danger.

But where would he go for safety? Oh if only he had brought a troop of his Legionnaires with him!

Allah, what should they do? Where could they go?

She found him not far from the Oasis of the Stars. He was staring down at the Sword of God in rapt concentration. When he looked up at the sound of approaching hoofbeats, she saw that his eyes were wide and his face incredulous.

'*Mahbub*, if you had been here only moments ago! I swear this sword glowed with a life of its own. I had just taken it from its scabbard to look at it again for I have never had such a marvellous gift.' He grinned, his eyes filled with love for her. 'Thinking the light was a reflection of the sun, I turned so that my body would shadow the blade. But the glow was still there, stronger than ever. Do you think the light of the sun has played tricks with my eyes?'

'No, my heart. This place is not called the Land of Mirages because of the ordinary illusions caused by the heat, although there are plenty of those. Strange visions have been seen here before, omens and portents when there has been the greatest need of them.' Drinking in every detail of Mayne's face, she felt a violent pang of fear at what might happen to him when Mahmed arrived, knowing that she could not stand to see him harmed in any way. If he died, then she would die with him; it was as simple and straightforward as that.

'Strange visions, eh?' He was thinking of the glowing sword he had seen thrusting from the spilling water during the storm. A dream he had thought at the time but what if it were not? Returning the Sword of God to its scabbard, Mayne took Zahra in his arms and would have kissed her avidly if she had not placed a hand across his mouth. Then, as his brows raised in surprise, she handed him the message and watched as he read it.

'There is a spy in our midst. Someone has told

259

Mahmed everything, it seems, and now he will kill you. Oh, my heart, my darling. You must fly before he gets here!'

'I will fight him man to man,' Mayne growled savagely, but Zahra put her hand across his mouth again.

'No, he would fight like a madman, and he would have his men-at-arms with him, dozens of them. He is infamous for his battle tactics. Once I thought that would be of great advantage in defending my country against foreign invaders.' Her expression wry, she laid her head against his broad shoulder. '*Allah*, but you must get away before he kills you! You would have no fair fight against his hordes.'

'And where do you suggest I go? Do you think I would leave you to his mercy?'

'You must! If he kills you, then I shall ever be at his mercy! You must hide, but I could not think where until I was out in the desert. There is something about the wilderness that sharpens the thoughts. I thought of the temple where my mother found the Jewels of Destiny . . . there you can hide. There is no less a taboo on that place now for all that its treasure saved our land from destruction. My heart, would you fear the pagan idol, the Mother Goddess whose shrine it is?'

'I have never feared a woman yet!' Mayne grinned, assuming a nonchalance he was far from feeling. How could he bear to be apart from her, his little queen, his darling?

'She is not fearsome as was thought, or so my mother said. The statue of the idol is sweet-faced, and she smiles on us. It was there that my mother was crowned, in that very temple, when my father placed Queen Zenobia's coronet upon her head. They would not have lingered there had it been an evil place, would they?'

'I am not afraid of evil, my little queen, only of being parted from you, not having your mouth to kiss and your body to lie beside. My beloved, I think I knew before

260

you found me tonight that we were to be separated. When the light shone from the sword, I think I knew it then.'

Taking his face between her palms, Zahra gazed up at him adoringly. 'We have one last time together here, beloved. We must make the most of it.'

The oasis encircled them, nourishing, shielding, and never had the palms seemed more protective, the bushes and flowers more delicate and brightly coloured, the waters more silver and limpid. It was as if the oasis was bidding them goodbye. Dreading that it would indeed be that, that she might never see him again, there was a particular poignancy in Zahra's heart. She wanted to memorise every line of his face, every hair on his head, the deep blue-green flecks in his eyes that made the hazel in them seem almost golden by comparison, the curling black hairs on his chest, the swelling hardness of his muscles, the firm outline of his determined yet sensual mouth that showed his courage and strength of will. She loved and cherished every inch of him, and she knew that she would miss him terribly.

Unable to wait for him to take her, she pulled him close, hard against her thighs, opening her legs to welcome him and revelling in the voluptuous sensations that his entry brought her. When he was deep within her, she felt complete as never before, her doubts and anxieties vanished, her heart singing. He was all that she had been waiting for, all that she wanted and needed.

Since the day that she had first seen him riding into her camp, he had haunted her thoughts, dreaming and waking. She was obsessed by him, but it was a glorious obsession and one that she hoped would never be cured. Whatever time brought, whatever Mahmed did to them, they would always have these brilliant days of love and exultation to remember.

It was past midday and the heat was scorching, but they barely noticed. Above them the cornflower blue basilica of the sky deepened and widened, and the last little cloud vanished so that there was nothing but blue upon blue, down to the baking, bronze earth and the glint of silver where fragments of flint littered the sand. This was her world, her desert, and she loved it with all its hardships and isolation, as she loved the people who lived in it, her people as they had been her mother's and her father's before her.

'Let her choose her own husband when she is old enough, as I chose mine.'

Her mother's words returned to her, as clearly as if she was hearing them spoken beside her. The words brought tears to her eyes for that was exactly what she had done, and fate had cruelly conspired against them. If only she had not given her final word to Mahmed, if only she had stayed free, but even then the enormity of what she wanted to do would have stood in her way. To marry a man who was part *kaffir*, a stranger who had no wealth or title and no connection with her by way of blood, race or heritage, would have been anathema. She knew that her people would have been deeply shocked and refused to accept him, yet she would have married him all the same.

There was no passing of time in the Oasis of Stars, or so it seemed to them. The heat of midday remained, and there was no diminution as the afternoon wore on and they made love many times, marrying one another in heart and body and soul if not in lawful ceremony. Zahra had never known such ecstasy, nor had Mayne. They were the happiest lovers of all time, and in those few hours they experienced paradise.

Still the afternoon endured, the sun as high in the sky as it had ever been, and yet they knew that some hours must have passed. They had made love, dozed lightly in one another's arms because of the heat, then made love again and again, and now a fourth time, the last time, gentling and coaxing, lavishing love and silent promises

262

on one another, vowing that their souls would never be parted, whatever happened to their bodies.

'Honey, if I die, promise me something.'

'Anything.' There were tears in Zahra's eyes.

'Meet me in the next world. I don't care what our creeds say, that Christ insisted there would be no love and marriage in Heaven, and that you Muslims fill Paradise with dancing girls and gold and silver trees to reward the faithful. That does not bother me. Something tells me that our spirits will not just die, or exist in a loveless hinterland. Something tells me that we can be together again, wherever it is, so look for me there, my darling, look for me there as I shall look for you.'

'I promise, my heart, I promise!' she cried, then she flung herself into his arms to memorise the feel of him close against her body, for memory would be all her comfort in the days to come.

She had packed all he would need and brought it with her. As they set off, leaving the Oasis of Stars, it was suddenly cool though the sun still hung high above them. Travelling in the skin-flaying heat of midday would have been intolerable, yet now the air was almost like that of evening, pleasant and balmy before the sudden cold of night would enshroud them.

Zahra knew the way to the temple. She had always known it. In her father's audience tent there had been a map which had been copied and recopied by his scribe so that there would always be a version in good condition. As a child, she had been allowed to look at it, to memorise the names on it and to ask questions about the temple and the surrounding area that were so adamantly taboo. No one ever went there; no one dared. They feared devils and demons and the most evil and terrifying *jinn*. The Prophet sternly warned against idols, and in that temple was the massive, larger than lifesize statue of the pagan Goddess, Inanna, the ancient one. In Muslim eyes, she was steeped in sin and evil. Mayne would be safe there. No one would dare intrude in that place.

'He will never dare harm me,' she assured her lover. 'He may shout and make threats to me but he would never lay a finger on me. My people would not allow it. If he harmed me, they would hack him into a dozen pieces.'

'All the same, I feel I am leaving you at his mercy, and to do such a thing is alien to me. I shall never forgive myself, even if no harm befalls you.'

'I can handle the almighty Mahmed, believe me. I do not fear him, only what he would do to you!'

They rode on towards the temple, and the air grew even cooler. There was an unearthly light in the sky, strange streaks of thunderous indigo swirled amongst white striations like a pattern deliberately painted with an exuberant yet moody brush. The hours passed, and they rested and ate some of the goats' cheese and unleavened bread that Zahra had brought with her. There was plenty of water, she had hung leather bags of it all around her saddle, and they drank the warm, musty, leather-flavoured liquid gratefully.

Then the dark was upon them, taking them by surprise, and they decided to sleep where they were, under the shelter of some jutting rocks. Holding hands, they curled up close together beneath their goatskins while their camels rested nearby, their ankles hobbled so that they could not gallop away on some impetuous journey of their own.

Zahra's dreams were wild and distorted. She saw ugly shapes and indistinguishable figures reaching out to her, arms extended, fingers flexed, a chilling scenario for she could not see their faces yet she knew that they were hideous. Waking with a start, she cuddled closer to Mayne, pushing back the flap of goatskin that had fallen across his cheek.

Beneath the flap was a skull, bleached white, devoid of brain and flesh and features, eyeless, noseless, with huge clenched teeth that yawned wide to bite her.

Petrified, she began to scream, her body shaking, and it was her own scream that woke her, for she had still been asleep.

Mayne pulled her close, kissing her face, braiding his arms around her until she realised that all of it had been a nightmare. Eventually, she slept again, but warily.

Dawn woke them with a glowing white mist. It wreathed their ankles as they stood up to snatch some food and drink. They shivered and could not wait to be on the move. There was only one consolation. They were much nearer to the temple than Mishaal and Husain had been thirty years before. They had been forced to trek for days and nights to reach their goal whereas Zahra and Mayne need take only two days, all being well.

It was not an easy journey. There were changes in the weather like nothing they had ever seen before. There were dark glowering clouds yet without any rain, and they would feel sudden icy winds while the sun still scorched down upon them. On the second morning, they woke to find that three of their water bags had inexplicably split during the night and the water had run away in deep brown streaks into the sand. Now they had only one flask between them.

Looking at the lost water, Zahra wondered if someone was trying to prevent them from reaching the temple, yet she was as sure as Mayne that no one had been near them during the night. The bags had been safely beside them as they slept, and in the stillness of the desert they would have heard the slightest footfall. All the same, Mayne searched the area for footprints, but found none.

'Should we go on?' Zahra asked, her voice unsteady with fear. 'What if it is wrong for us to go there, and God is trying to show us that we should stay away? What if we offend Him by going there?'

'We go on.' Mayne's voice was steely. He did not tell her his plan; that as soon as she thought he was safe in

265

the temple, he was going to follow her back to the camp. He would assume a disguise and keep watch over her in the coming days. He had no option. He was not going to leave her in the violent clutches of Mahmed the Warmonger.

It was easy to believe, out there suspended in God's wilderness, that they were safe; that no interlopers could find them or harm them.

They were resting in the flesh-crisping flame of midday, reluctant to waste time and yet aware that driving themselves on in such a Beltane of heat would weaken them unnecessarily. For miles now they had not seen a living thing, not a bird nor a rat nor even the smallest of lizards. The sun was so livid that their clasped hands were pooled with sweat.

'If we were the poorest nomads, with rags on our back and our bare feet baked hard as the earth, no one would pursue us. We could live free as the eagles, even if we had nothing save poverty to offer one another,' Zahra lamented.

'Wealth sometimes brings unwanted responsibilities. When I was younger, I dreamed of riches and possessions. I wanted my father's lands and horses. For a time, I even wanted his wife.'

'Your own mother!' Zahra turned astonished eyes upon him.

'I express myself badly. She was my stepmother, and not much older than her rebel stepson. What a life I led her! She would have been within her rights to have kicked me out, but she knew how much my father loved me, so she kept patience.'

'Mayne, you have never told me of this before.' Zahra's fingers curled in his.

'There is something about the desert that brings back memories I thought I'd lost forever.'

'You should not forget anything. The past helps to
266

make us what we are today. I was a weakling until a few months ago. If I forgot that, then it might be so again.'

'You, a weakling? Honey, you are a child, an orphan! You should have more compassion for yourself. You have so much for others.'

'But they are worthy of it.'

'How can you tell? What makes you think that others deserve the compassion you withhold from yourself? You judge yourself too harshly.'

'Why not? I cannot fail the ones I love. They ask so much of me.'

'You give them more, so much more than they ever give you, honey.'

Almost angrily, he gripped her by the shoulders, looking down into her sweat-pearled face with its eyes that gleamed like viridian silk in the Beltane sun, the sharply delineated cheekbones standing out from the tender little mouth, the winged ebony brows that pointed so delicately to her smooth and creamy temples.

'You are being kind to me, my warrior, indulging me when I know that I do not deserve it,' she said, stubborn to the last.

'But I say that you do! Dear God, does this desert life not teach you anything? To survive in the wilderness you must face the truth, see life as it is, and not hide behind self-created veils fashioned from silly doubts and foolish imaginings.'

Tears glistened on her lashes and he knew that he had gone too far, but he had meant to speak only for her good.

'Forgive me, my darling, but I think of you in the years to come, and want you to rule in wisdom and contentment, not from behind a shield of self loathing. Others tend to judge you as you see yourself, and I want your people to see you as you truly are, with all your

267

generosity and selflessness and a heart that would never turn away from anyone in need. Do you hear me, you determined one?'

'I hear you.'

'And will you heed me?'

'I have always heeded every word that ever fell from your lips.'

'At last, some response!' Mayne cried, his eyes alight.

'But that does not mean that I always agree.' She lowered her eyes so he could not see their sparkle.

'Zahra, you drive me to distraction!' Pushing her from him, he leapt to his feet and headed deeper into the cleft of rocks where they were sheltering. Soon, the burnt-sienna rock was shoulder high, and then head high, towering above him like distended wings, their spines and creamy-rust layers of softer stone impacted between the older, darker rock.

How cool it was here. If he had known the cleft went so deep, and widened out like this, then he would have brought her here first, far from the flame-scorch of the sun. He would walk a while and leave her to cool her hot little heels. She was a firebrand, the most tempestuous spirit he had ever encountered, but one day she would learn. One day, with his help.

The blood of his childhood was flowing strong within him at that moment, reminding him of the days when he had ruled his ignorant mother. Women must have their wildness subjugated, or it will sear through the bonds of love.

There was such a tumult in his veins as memory gushed back that he did not notice the darkness descending, nor the scent of the *simûm* burdening the air. Women must heed their men; to ignore them was folly. If they went their own way unguided, disaster would follow. His fingertips tingling unpleasantly, he rubbed his hands on his robe, seeking to quell the uneasiness that was building up inside him.

268

He would not go back to her until she had seen the error of her ways; he would not, and no one could make him.

A low growl alerted him, the sound shivering throatily along the rock, funnelled down to where he stood. It was only then, as he looked up, that he realised that the blue sky was now cinereous, the air darkly, oppressively humid.

Framed against the mole-grey vastness, a wildcat crouched, thunder in its throat. Instantly Mayne was once again the rebellious boy who had killed a mountain lion's mate to protect a foal. Now here was retribution, its face dark-gilded apricot spotted with cinnamon, its eyes bright with murderous intent.

His fingers curling round the hilt of his *khanjar*, he froze, meeting the animal's livid, unblinking gaze, retaliation the first thought in his mind. Then his hand relaxed and fell from the knife's hilt. He no more wanted to kill this noble creature than he had the first; and certainly not to defend his own skin.

He felt clammy, his robe clinging leech-like to his back and arms, but this was the product of the humid air and not of fear. In his mind's eye he saw the beast leaping, saw the cleanly powerful swathe of feline muscles bunching, spreading, then bunching again as he went down beneath the brindled fur. Yet he did not move. Why should not one wild creature kill another, and there had never been a wilder one than he.

Still they surveyed one another, topaz eye to topaz eye, yet still the beast stayed where it was. Mayne did not move. This moment had the weave of destiny in it; he could feel the tingling in his spine. Whatever God sends, he thought, whatever God sends. Islam means submission to Thy will....

'Mayne. *Mayne!*'

The voice seemed to shimmer towards him as if from another world, breaking through the cinereous veil that encapsulated him. When he looked up, the wildcat had vanished as if it had never been.

Zahra threw herself into his arms, clinging to him as if they had been parted for months. As their lips met, the *simûm* retreated, to eject its sandy burden elsewhere. Suddenly the crevasse was filling with dappled sunlight, rose-gold, coppery light that drenched them where they stood, soothing, healing.

'I would not have killed it,' Mayne said firmly. 'I am the interloper here.'

'Killed what, my darling?' In puzzlement, Zahra gazed up at him.

'You did not see it?'

'See what?'

'The wildcat up on the ledge, about to pounce.'

'No, I saw nothing, my darling. The sun was in my eyes, anyway.'

'The sun?' He stopped, ice-cold twists racing down his spine. He was remembering the sloe-dark clouds, the abrasive scent of the approaching sandstorm, a pungent reek in the atmosphere. Yet Zahra had seen only sun.

'What were you going to say, *ya mahbub*? You look so strange, as if you have had a vision.' Gently, her fingertips traced his forehead, the scimitar curve of his cheek, the strong yet sensual mouth, and it was as if life-giving energy coursed from one to the other.

'Perhaps that's what it was, yet I could have sworn I saw a wildcat.'

'It is the heat. What else would you expect in a land famed for its mirages? We see what we most fear as well as what we most want to possess.'

'What we most fear?' Yes, above all things he dreaded killing one of nature's most beautiful wild creatures.

'What we most fear.' Her voice took on a musing tone. 'My father often called my mother little *fáhd* – wildcat – because of her strong spirit. Sometimes they would laugh about it; at other times, it was so true that it hurt

270

her. And when she was hurt so was he, for they were as one.'

'You are saying that the wildcat I saw just now was your mother?' His eyes twinkled.

'Hardly. But my thoughts have been on her since we spoke just now. I realised that we can argue fiercely, just as she and my father did.'

'And how did that make you feel, my wild one?' He pulled her to him tenderly. 'Did you resolve to put me right out of your mind?'

'Yes! I vowed that I would never think of you again, that I would never so much as allow you in my dreams. I swore that I would hate and loathe you until the day I died!'

She lied so convincingly that even he, the scholar of the double thrust, was momentarily fooled. The malachite eyes were wide, unblinking, glowing with veracity. Not a muscle twitched in her face.

'My love,' he began, his voice choked.

Eyes slanting, she let her control slip, laughter bubbling on her lips.

'See, brave Legionnaire, even you were lost for words!'

'You little minx, you fooled me!'

'And why not, Captain Mayne, why not? Should it all be on one side?'

'You knew?' His throat had tightened. There was a rushing sound in his ears.

'From the first; well, almost.'

'But how?'

'Would you believe that I can sense such things?'

'I would believe anything of you, but I do not see how you could have sensed what was in my mind. Besides, would you not have kicked me out at once had you known?'

'I did the next best thing – I seduced you.' Her eyes glittered with mischief.

271

'How like a woman!' Throwing back his head, he roared with laughter.

'You mean no man has ever seduced a woman to convert her?'

'But was it only for that? Did you embark on it without love in your heart?'

'As so many men would have done?' she countered neatly. 'No, my heart. I loved you at first sight. When you walked into my tent in that ridiculous, impractical headgear, and with those baggy breeches, I could do little else but love you madly.'

Mayne smiled bravely, remembering how he had swaggered in his uniform, so confident that he was the apogee of the romantically-dressed, handsome and dashing Legionnaire; so sure that he would need to do little more than smile to win his fair lady.

'So much for my pride and vanity,' he lamented, but she pressed a finger to his lips.

'Never have I known such a forthright and honest man, with such a natural modesty.'

'Yet you say you knew what my plans were when I came to your camp, so how can you call me honest?'

'Because you are! Because you could not go through with your mission. They misjudged you, Mayne Amyan, when they asked you to practise such deception. How could they have been so wrong?'

'Because they do not have you to advise them?' he hazarded, eyes glittering.

'You could be speaking the truth there,' she replied, straight-faced.

'Honey, I shall never deceive you again, ever. You have my heart, my soul, everything. I swear to you.'

Again she pressed a finger to his lips.

'I know. I feel what is in your heart. *Ya mahbub*, we have so little time left together. No one would find us in these rocks; they shelter us completely.' Her eyes were filled with an unmistakable meaning.

His eyes were lambent with passion as he crushed her to him. How cool the air was here, tempered to docility by the high rocks. No one would have known that it was only a little past noon.

Slowly, dreamily, she looped her arms around his neck, so that he was her willing prisoner, thrilling at the feel of his vigorous hardness pressing urgently into her belly. Their kiss was scented with all the herbs of the wilderness, spicy-sweet and evocative; they would never smell them again without thinking of this kiss, this place, this moment. Thyme and oregano, lemon verbena, rosemary and basil, drifting, swirling on the air.

In one graceful movement, Zahra swayed towards her lover as he lifted up her robe, deftly pulling it over her head so that she stood before him quite naked. Then, when he thought that he had the upper hand, she lunged at him, gripped the hem of his *kuftan* and peeled it up over his shoulders.

Awe-filled, he looked down at her adorable little body, so winningly curvaceous, plump where it should be plump and slender where he most wanted to cup it with his palms, and his mouth went dry.

'Heart of my heart,' he sighed, 'soul of my soul. Wherever I go, from this hour onwards, you will be with me, borne in my heart and my thoughts.'

'And you will be with me, my brave warrior. I think somehow you have always been there, even before we met if that is possible.'

Almost reverently, he caressed her breasts. They were pale as acacia honey and had the texture of silk velvet except for her nipples, hardening in welcome.

Eagerly she pressed closer to him, desperate for the sensation of his flesh on hers, the scent of him in her nostrils, the wildfire inside her which only he could summon.

She could barely wait as he flung their robes in a heap on the ground and pulled her down with him.

273

They were joined instantly, unable to hold back, such passions unleashed that they could not have been separated for any cause. There was such a vibrant reality in their desire that it seemed almost unreal, too much for the human mind to comprehend.

How perfectly they moulded together, hip to hip, thigh to thigh, breast to breast, mouth achingly to mouth, their bodies gilt-dappled by the lush apricot sun so that they looked brindled as wildcats themselves.

'My little wild one, when you are in my arms, I can believe anything, even miracles.'

'That we are here together like this is a miracle, *ya mahbub*,' she sighed, and he knew that what she said was all too true.

A warm trickling sensation was cascading along her spine, tingling, twisting, rousing her to fever pitch, and there was an ocean of pulsating warmth between her thighs. The feeling grew stronger, becoming almost overwhelming, a force powerful enough to consume and annihilate her so that she could be reborn in love. Wild as any barbarian, she locked her legs around his waist, moaning his name, urging him on, knowing that he would respond with every ounce of passion he possessed.

Aeons might have passed and they would have been oblivious. When hearts and souls cleave truly to one another, they escape time and all its burdens. Is that not what Love is for, the circle of Solomon that blocks out the world and all its trials?

It might have been made of fire or ice or both, that circle; they would never know, nor care, yet it was there, a powerful enchantment to protect and guard them.

'Fill me with your love,' she begged, her nails scoring his back. 'Give me our son so that I shall always have your face to look upon!'

'Our son.' The thought made him pause. Leaning on

274

one elbow, he looked down at her. 'If that happens, will you tell him about me?'

'Of course.'

'The truth?'

'What else?'

'What will you say?' His heart had slowed its thunderous pace. In his mind's eye he was seeing the boy, his hair dark as pitch, his eyes topaz with bright green lights, the little body sturdy and straight. His son, a bastard like his father.

'That his father was a brave warrior who loved me beyond reason.'

'What reason will you give him for his father's leaving?'

'Duty and responsibility.' Zahra clenched her jaw firmly.

'Fine-sounding words to adults, but no consolation to a small boy.'

'I know, I know.'

Suddenly she was sobbing, but he was kissing away the flood of tears and telling her that it was foolish to weep in such an arid place.

'He will be born of love,' he reassured her. 'How many can say that?'

Eventually her tears subsided, and they kissed with mounting desire. If they wanted a son, they must first create him.

Linked closely together, they let their emotions surge, their blood soar, and in their uniting were all their hopes and dreams and longings for the passionate tomorrows that they would never know.

There it lay before them, shimmering eerily as if painted on the heat haze that lay above the desert's surface. It was fashioned from the most dazzling white stone that either of them had ever seen, perhaps some variety of rare marble; they could not say at this distance. How

275

serene and proud it looked, and fresh and new as if only recently built. Remembering what her mother had told her, Zahra clung to Mayne's arm.

'My mother said that the temple was like new when she first saw it, every stone intact and no sign of ageing, yet it is thousands of years old.' Screwing up her eyes, she looked again, only to see the same shining and sparkling new building with its massive Romanesque columns.

'What do you see, my heart?' she whispered.

'An ancient white ruin with crumbling walls and pillars, saddened by neglect and pitted by the winds.'

'You do?' Zahra's voice quivered. So only she was seeing the magnificence of the temple as it had been in its days of glory and pomp.

Remounting, they rode on, the atmosphere thickening, the white of the stones ahead of them growing brighter as if lit from within by the darts of lightning.

'A storm is rising. We had better take shelter fast,' Mayne urged.

'I do not think that it is a storm, my heart. The air feels different, somehow tender and almost sad, as if reproaching me. Oh, it sounds like madness, I know, but it is what I feel.'

Mayne looked at her in surprise. She was swathed in her travelling cape, veiled across the head and face to keep out the sand that swirled everywhere, even when the air was still. All he could see were her beautiful peacock-green eyes, glowing like rich emeralds newly polished, alight with excitement and anticipation.

How he loved her, his little desert queen. She was the most noble and generous woman he had ever known, ever involved with the needs of others, constantly reproaching herself for what she saw as her failings, taxing herself so strictly and unforgivingly for acting anything less than perfectly while she would treat others with a tolerant and tender forgiveness and

276

understanding that she never allowed herself. Remembering how he had thought she would be arrogant and vainglorious, he gave a wry grin. Dear God, she was the most human and lovable creature he had ever known!

Now, even here in this desolate, taboo place, she felt the reproaches of times long past, judged herself harshly and allowed herself no quarter. And he loved her for it.

The atmosphere was heavier now, chokingly so, and Mayne shouted out that they should hurry for shelter in the temple.

'It is not a storm!' Zahra called back – too late. Urged on by him, Mayne's camel stumbled in a stony crevasse and he felt himself thrown from the saddle, crashing down on the hard rock before him to the sound of Zahra's screams.

There was total blackness for some seconds, then, as he regained consciousness, a stabbing, twisting pain shot through his leg. Zahra was kneeling beside him, white-faced, begging him to speak to her.

'I am – all right,' he groaned, cursing himself for his temporary clumsiness. The beast that had caused the trouble stood nearby, grazing steadily on camel's thorn, totally unhurt.

'Where is the pain, my heart? Oh, tell me! Where is the pain?'

'My leg,' Mayne grimaced. 'Jesus, Mary and Joseph, I think it's broken!' He had used that exclamation only once since his father died, but now it came to his lips involuntarily.

Tenderly, Zahra inspected the limb and as Mayne winced, she winced too, sharing his pain. 'I cannot feel bone jutting out so I do not think it has shattered, but you must not put any weight on it all the same.'

'Then how do I get to the temple?'

Zahra sat back on her heels. 'A litter. There must be some material to make one. I can tie it to the camel saddle and you will be pulled along in comfort.'

Searching, she found twigs and a few branches but nothing solid enough to support a man's weight. There was one consolation; the storm having evaporated, the sky was clear once more.

'There might be something in the temple, some poles to support the rug.' She looked towards the ruined building, now seeing it for what it was – old and lonely, desolate and forgotten – and in that moment of realisation, she knew that she need not fear entering it.

Before Mayne could answer, she was walking steadily towards the temple, her head held high, shoulders back, every inch the queen, every inch the woman he loved and cherished. Watching her disappear inside the ruins, he felt his heart jolt. It was as if the very walls, crumbling as they were, acted as a barrier between them.

Once she stepped through the massive Romanesque pillared entrance, she was in another age, another time, the dense silence that greeted her was almost palpable. Cautiously, she stepped through the portals, her move-ment stirring motes of swirling dust that spangled in the streaming sunlight like minute diamonds. Despite what her mother had said, she had expected a forbidding place of darkness, filled with fearful idols and effigies that would glower back at her from the gloom, latent with evil, but sunlight was gushing from on high, its life-giving beams directed on to a statue that stopped her in her tracks.

Her mother had described the sweet, tenderly smiling face of the goddess whose temple this was, the eyes that held such affection and a sharp and wise intelligence, but nothing could have prepared Zahra for the reality of it. In her religion, idolaters were despatched into the Fire of

Gehenna, for idols were sinful things, artefacts of *Shaitan*, the Devil, bringers of terror and abomination. She might be struck down even as she stood there before the statue, gazing up at it, so tall and nobly carved with its loving expression, soft, sloping shoulders and slightly raised hands. The goddess seemed to be gesturing, saying: 'Come to me, my daughter!'

Zahra's fingers went to the ornament in the shape of a coiled serpent at her neck. Mishaal had found it where it had fallen on this very floor when the statue had been overturned by desecrators centuries ago. Somehow, the serpent was connected with the Mother Goddess, but she did not know how or why.

'Come to me, my daughter.' She seemed to hear the words again, as if spoken softly but insistently in her ear.

Was this the work of devils, an evil enchantment? The back of her neck tingled, and she felt suddenly cold. Turning, she half-expected to see some vile manifestation behind her, but there was nothing save sunlight and peace.

Lightly she touched the statue's outstretched hands one after the other as if to reassure herself, then she found herself smiling. It was, after all, only cold marble.

Remembering why she was there, she began to search for two long, pole-shaped pieces of wood, finding an assortment of shattered pieces of carving. Having found what she needed, she hurried outside, feeling the burning desert sun smack against her face, tasting the dust on her tongue, the acutely blue sky almost blinding her.

Very soon, she had fastened a saddle rug between the two poles, binding them on tightly to form a litter. Mayne crawled on to this as best he could, wincing at the pain. Blood had soaked through his robe, fresh and scarlet. Zahra gasped when she saw it, but he dismissed it as a minor wound. Tying the two poles to a rope, she suspended it from the saddle of her camel and then led the beast towards the temple, the litter swaying and bumping along the ground, Mayne biting hard on his lips so that he would not cry out at the pain.

The journey did not take long yet it disturbed them both: Mayne because he felt himself helpless at having to be cared for by the woman he loved, and Zahra because she knew that she would soon have to leave him to return to her people. She could not risk Mahmed coming after her with his men-at-arms.

Somehow she helped Mayne through the temple entrance and towards the dark stairwell in the far corner, which led down into the vault where the Jewels of Destiny had been found by Mishaal. Her mother had described every step of their discovery so many times that Zahra felt almost at home there.

It was gloomy and unpleasant down those carved stone steps yet they had to descend them. Mayne could not be left in the open precinct of the temple. Haltingly, Zahra helped him down them, but it was an arduous effort and exhausted them both. At the bottom of the steps it was basalt dark, and Zahra hastily lit a torch, refusing to admit to her lover that she was icy with fear.

She cried out as the flame billowed around them, darting in orange shadows on the walls. Just ahead of them were the bleached, scattered skeletons of the men who had died there thirty years before, the men killed by her father in valorous combat, and one of them would be the American, the infidel whom her mother had once loved.

Clamping her lips shut, she looked away, but her face was leeched of colour. There was a lesson to be learned from them, she knew: never trust a non-believer. Was that not why the wells and the rivers had run dry again, as they had when her mother loved her infidel American? How close were the comparisons, as if history were repeating itself, as if women never learned their lesson.

Refusing to weep, she lifted back Mayne's robe, dreading what she would see. His leg was black with clotted blood, and there was a deep, jagged gash where a sharply jutting stone had driven itself into his flesh, directly to the bone. Taking the last of their water, she cleaned the wound as best she could, gently dabbing and coaxing away the clotted blood, biting her lip as fresh blood oozed in its place. When she had finished, she bound the gash with a strip of cloth from her own robe, tightly enough to impede the leakage of blood but not so tightly that she would stop the circulation.

'You are a good nurse.' Mayne managed a jaunty grin that twisted her heart. 'You should have built the hospital for yourself.'

'I did,' she grinned back, and then was shocked into silence as she heard a voice speaking, clear and authoritative, impressing its message with determination.

'The outcome of union with an infidel is death and disaster for you and our peoples.'

It was the voice of her mother!

But how could that be? Shivering, she clasped her arms around her waist, not daring to look up for fear of seeing some frightful apparition.

'The wells will all run dry again, the land will be forsaken by Allah! Can you not see? He is angered now, my daughter. Forsake the infidel before God forsakes our beloved land!'

'D-did you hear that?' Zahra gasped.

'Hear what? This place is silent as the tomb.' Mayne shuddered. 'I suppose I should not have said that as I have to make some sort of home here for the moment!'

'Oh, my heart, I shall never stop loving you! I shall never forget you!' Zahra flung herself into his arms, kissing him frantically, achingly, knowing that she could never see him again, that she must obey this command. She must return to her people and begin afresh with Mahmed, as Mishaal had ordered. They had dared to

281

throw a gauntlet in the face of fate, and now reality had broken in upon them.

Their rapturous infidel summer was over. They must never meet again.

Chapter Seventeen

Without water, Zahra felt sucked of strength within a few hours of leaving the temple, but her determination to be as far from Mayne as possible before Mahmed found her drove her on. With her knife, she dug out suitable plants, probing to locate the plump, water-filled bulbs which she shredded with the blade until the moist pulp was ready to eat, the residual moisture on her palms eagerly rubbed into her taut-skinned face. If she was lucky a bulb would yield a mouthful or two of water as well.

Her father had taught her this survival trick when they had ridden out together into the wilderness. In her present heightened state of consciousness, she could almost imagine him beside her as he had been in the contented days of her childhood. When he and her mother had particularly disagreed on some matter, Husain would invite Zahra to accompany him into the desert. How she had revelled in having him to herself alone, learning from him how to endure the privations of their land. Deliberately, they had left the areas that were verdant and water-filled, as if Husain had needed the challenge of nature at her harshest to revive his spirit. Or perhaps he had been recalling happier days, as she was now.

It was idiotic to weep when she was desperately short of water so she refused to do so, but her eyes were blurred as she scanned the vivid ocherous yellow of the shimmering horizon. She had dug up roots for Mayne and left them with him, having shown him how to shred the bulbs and extract the moisture. His leg had stopped bleeding and she had rebandaged it. She consoled herself with the thought that he was young and fit and would heal fast, but that did not console the empty, yearning pit that had turned her stomach into a void of despair.

Never to see him again; never to lie in his arms, her head on his breast; never to see his sparkling eyes filled with love for her, nor his flashing grin that made her heart turn over. Misery braided her until she could barely think.

While she huddled in the cold, profound darkness of the desert night, trying to sleep, she thought of all the things that could go wrong. His wound might become infected, causing him to burn with fever. He might lie in the temple vault for weeks, unable to move because of his weakness, and slowly starve to death until he resembled the skeletons that already lay there. Curling into a tight, shuddering ball, Zahra attempted to rid her thoughts of such horrors, but she had set herself an impossible task.

If she loved him, how could she have left him like that? How weak she was, and stupid, just as she had always believed. She was no more fit to rule her people than a goat; she was the greatest coward ever born!

Briefly, in Mayne's arms she had enjoyed a blissful interlude, finding courage and a pride in herself she had never known before, but that was vanished now. Allah had demanded that she prove herself fitted to reign in His beloved land; He had demanded that she give up her darling Mayne, yet the fact that she had obeyed Him made her feel no better. Was it not as cowardly to abandon one as it was to abandon thousands?

'Allah, help me!' she cried into the unforgiving darkness. 'Help me!' but there was no comfort for her that night.

When her camp came into sight, she was drained of all energy and feeling, her clothes sand-stained and crumpled, her hair tangled with sweat and dust. To look at, she might have been any beggar girl but she would get Freyha to fetch the hip bath and languish there in steaming, oil-scented water until some semblance of physical recovery returned to her. Her mental recovery would take far, far longer, she knew.

'Oh Mayne, Mayne, why did we ever have to meet? Allah protect and care for you,' she prayed for the hundredth time. 'I will do anything if You will heal him and get him safely back to his people!'

Then she saw it, and her mouth fell open. Gone from her audience tent were the banners that proclaimed her father's line and her own, ancient and sacred, their heritage from the Prophet himself. In their place streamed the colours of the Amir Mahmed ibn Beydoun.

Speeding on her camel, she reached the camp, ordered the beast to its knees, and flung herself to the ground. In seconds she was rushing into her audience tent, fury coursing through her veins.

The first thing she saw was Freyha sitting silently in a corner, her face utterly dejected. The second was the group of four guards, all dressed in Mahmed's colours, their broad faces brutalised by years of battle and skirmish.

And then she saw her future husband himself. He was sitting crosslegged at her father's carved chest wherein lay all the most precious documents of their heritage and lineage, the maps that showed the way to the temple of the Goddess, the details of their financial affairs, Mishaal's letters and account books.

'How dare you!' she cried, her anger firing her with an energy she had thought would need a sound night's

285

sleep to revive. 'That is my father's private cabinet. Who said that you could open it?'

Mahmed was on his feet instantly, taking in the sight of her, dusty and sweat-streaked, her hair tangled. His mouth was held in a thin, bitter line and his eyes were black with anger.

'The so-called Queen returns at last! How kind of you to remember your people, oh Queen.' He gave a mock *salaam*, and then, taking her by the arm, pulled her roughly towards him.

'You will not harm her, you will not!' Freyha cried out, but when the old woman rushed to try and protect her mistress, Mahmed pushed her away so that she fell to her knees. There was the feral spark of madness in his eyes. Zahra would never have believed this was the same man who had come to woo her, the man who had seemed so taciturn and ill at ease in her company, the one who had been so reluctant to marry her. This man was glowing with fury, taut with barely suppressed malevolence.

'How dare you enter my camp while I am absent! How dare you touch my father's property!' she challenged him furiously.

'Your father? This is his, is it? Then tell him to come and punish me for this intrusion – if he can,' Mahmed sneered.

'Devil!' Zahra lashed out, catching him a swiping blow on the nose with her curled fist.

Bellowing, he grasped both her arms and pushed her down viciously so that she was forced to kneel before him, her head lowered by the brutal weight of his hand on the nape of her neck.

'Whore, you have destroyed your honour and brought shame upon our peoples. Never again shall the house of Husain know the blessings of the one true God. Never again shall the house of Husain be revered!'

Despite the shattering pain in her neck, Zahra tried to

grasp Mahmed's ankle so as to bring him crashing to the ground. But he stepped back smartly and clicked his fingers for two of the guards to approach her. Before she knew what they intended, they had lashed her elbows together with cord and she was a prisoner.

Lying in the blackness of the vault, his torch long burned out, leg throbbing painfully, Mayne thought back over the days he had spent with his little queen. From this sad and bereft vantage point, every kiss, every embrace and tender word seemed no more than the fevered workings of his imagination. Had she really existed, that radiant and adorable creature, or had he created her because she was all for which he most yearned?

His belly was cramped with hunger, his throat clenched and gritty from lack of water. If he ever got out of this place of skeletons, he would consider it a miracle. Eventually, his eyes became slightly accustomed to the blackness, but not enough to see more than those things that were close enough to feel: the bulbs, the stem of the torch, his knife and the Sword of God. Running his fingers along it, he made a wry face. There had been such promise in its bright blade, such hope and so many dreams to fulfil when Zahra had placed it in his hands. Now it was nothing more than metal, a good weapon but dependent upon his own ability to wield it if it was to be any protection at all.

'Zahra, did you ever exist?' he sighed into the darkness. 'Was it all a mirage, beautiful and unforgettable, but a mirage all the same?'

After a time he slept, exhausted from loss of blood and the fever that was struggling to break in him. If he dreamed of the woman he loved and tragically lost, then it was some small and tender comfort.

Within three days she had lost the only man she would ever love, and her power as Queen of the Desert.

Mahmed was lording it as the new ruler, hastening the arrangements for their marriage, and sending out invitations to every dignitary, amir, shaikh, prince and minister in the vicinity. He would have married her without guests had he not wished to have many witnesses to their union and the fact that he was now the ruler of the Land of Mirages. The more people who saw the marriage and were witness to its legality, the more would refuse to come to Zahra's aid should she ever beseech them to.

He had been disappointed by her silence. After her first outburst she had sunk into a sullen misery and would not speak to him. He had been forced to send out all the invitations and to command the wedding preparations without her aid. Rare bolts of Persian silks were brought for Zahra to choose her wedding robes, and this she had done without one sign of enthusiasm. Yet she seemed resigned, he was pleased to observe, and he knew why.

She knew that no other man would have her now that she had whored with the *kaffir*. Just to have been alone in his company without a chaperon was more than enough to have destroyed her honour. Eventually, she would be grateful to Mahmed for taking her as his bride, and then they might find some semblance of happiness together – not that he considered this imperative. His dreams were still coloured by the loss of Zuli and he did not think he would ever love again. Where there had been love and desire for his sweet daughter, now there was only cold, hollow anger and the wish to avenge himself on anyone who tried to halt his progress.

Zahra had not been the only one who had received an emissary from the Emperor of the French. Unknown to Mayne, there had been another ambassadorial approach, this time to Mahmed. In the event that Zahra refused to treat with the Emperor, the French hoped that her new husband would coerce her into agreement. With this in mind, they had made him an offer which he could not refuse. If he rejected it, then they would take his land by force, sending in the Foreign Legion *en masse* and laying waste his amirate. If he treated with them, handing over the Land of Mirages into their control in exchange for an agreed sum of gold and jewels, then his own land would be spared.

Naturally, he would have preferred to keep the Land of Mirages and sell his own, but the French did not want a bleak and parched amirate like his. They needed food and water and the riches of his future wife's domain: the vegetables and fruit and grain, the sheep and goats, the plentiful cheese and *laban* which was excellent marching food, and of course the fabled Jewels of Destiny, or what was left of them after some had been sold to ensure that Husain's land recovered its former glory.

No one knew exactly what jewels were left, which was why Zahra had found Mahmed delving into her father's cabinet. Not that he had learned anything from it for there was no mention whatsoever of the gems. Nor had he learned more by scouring the many papers and scrolls he had found. But she must know, the sullen bitch who was soon to be his bride, and he was determined to discover the whereabouts of the gems: the fabulous ruby-studded crown that Queen Zenobia herself had worn centuries before, the emeralds from the mines of Queen Cleopatra, the enormous black pearls, the bright blue sapphires, the solid gold bangles and earrings, the collars and jewelled corselets.

He had hoped she would tell him where they lay so that he could secrete them before the French found them. Desperate men did desperate things, and Mahmed was desperate. The French emissary had arrived when the balance of his mind was disturbed, with his beloved Zuli barely cold in her grave. The knowledge that he could lose his amirate as he had lost his daughter had decided him.

If he had the jewels, then whatever happened he would be safe. He did not trust the French, but if they reneged on their agreement he could vanish with the rubies, pearls and gold and settle somewhere else. The Beduin were famed as wanderers and he would not be doing anything unusual if he moved on, although it would break his heart to leave his beautiful white camels behind.

Not that life was as it had been. Now that Zuli was dead he was utterly changed. His guilt was festering deep inside him, driving him on to commit ever more evil actions, and, like so many disappointed lovers, to replace emotional needs with material ones.

If love had been cruelly snatched from him for a second time, he still had his amirate, his camels, and the promise of riches to come. As for the woman who would soon be his bride, he cared very little for her; he had never found her attractive. She did not resemble Mahia or Zuli in any way. She was high-nosed and shrew-tongued, and her voluptuous curves offended him. He cared nothing for what became of her after she had given him what he desired. He would not even trouble to consummate the marriage; indeed, why should he taint himself with a harlot's immoral body? In the event that there were no jewels – Allah forbid! – he would take her back to his camp and she could care for his three remaining daughters. They were small and they needed a mother's care. She would never be free to be anything other than a mother to them; her days of monarchy, inept and blundering as they had been, were over.

She moved like a carved effigy into which life had been breathed, her limbs stiff and awkward, seeming not to belong to her, her breast aching from the effort, her spine tight and unyielding. If she had only known, then she would have stayed with Mayne, rallied her peoples and attacked Mahmed, but even if she gave the rallying cry, what grounds would they have found for attacking him? That he was an overbearing husband? Many were. That he sought more power than she? That was a husband's right. But if only she had known in time!

There was a heavy guard around her tent, and all the men were Mahmed's. She had no idea where her own guards had gone. Inside the tent, there was just herself and Freyha. No one else was allowed in unless Mahmed was present, and he rarely was. Zahra had no idea what he was doing or how her people were faring under his rule, but she could not put from her mind that spark of madness that had glittered in his eyes. Something had happened to him to change him so drastically. She wished she knew what it was, but most of all she wished that she could put back time.

Her tent was filled with sumptuous cloth and marriage attire. Diaphanous silks from Persia in rich, dazzling colours: crimson and tawny russet, kingfisher blue, plum red, plum brown embroidered with red-gold roses; glittering brocades in purest turquoise, rose pink, hydrangea blue, copper gold and delicate tangerine. Mahmed had not stinted her in this direction, yet she knew that he had given her all this only to impress the wedding guests as to his good intentions. If a bride was besieged with silks and gems and other generous gifts, how could she bewail her fate and sob that her husband was ill-treating her?

She stood silent and pale-faced for the fitting of her wedding robes while Freyha busied herself with pins and thread. Zahra's long flowing hair had been energetically brushed and looped around her head to allow for ease of fitting, and a mirror stood propped before her on the carved chest for her to follow the proceedings, but she rarely glanced in it. What did she care if her wedding robes fitted her or not? What did she care if she looked hideous in them? Without Mayne, there was nothing to dress for.

Separation from him would have hit her badly enough without this suffocating incarceration. Without her freedom – the gallops in the wilderness on her favourite mare, the dialogue with nature that so inspired her, the smiles and conversation of her people – she was so much dry tinder, lacking the flame.

However hard and diligently she prayed, there was no answer. She had obviously offended God and He was punishing her. She suspected that the punishment would be lifelong, and knowing that she had brought it upon herself was no consolation. From time immemorial lovers had behaved impetuously. Did Allah believe that she should have comported herself with the dignity of a wise old sage? Surely not! She was still so young. If she had indulged her dreams and snatched at happiness, who could blame her?

Nonetheless, God did. Her land was favoured, had always been thus, but now, through her intransigence, she had forfeited the blessings that had nourished and cherished it for thirty years. All of it was her fault.

Seeing the pain in her mistress's eyes, Freyha tried to cheer her. But there was nothing she could do or say to make the girl smile.

'Sweet one, when he has made you his bride, he will lose some of this anger. Then he will feel assured that he has you, and that –'

'And that my lands are his? Yes, I know.' Zahra wrapped her arms around herself, heedless of the pins which held her robe together. 'I can think of nothing else. I have nightmares about it. My lands will be his to do with as he wills, and it is no comfort to know that Allah brought this about.'

'Your punishment?' Freyha's carob brown eyes were reproachful. 'You think that Allah would bind you to a ruffian to show you the error of your ways?'

'What else? I told you, Freyha, I heard my mother, Mishaal's, voice in the temple. It made my neck tingle . . .

She warned me: she said that if I became the infidel's bride then our land would be accursed all over again. Have not the past weeks proven that? The deputations have come from every corner of the land. The water has gone from so many places.'

'And after your marriage it will return?'

'I am showing my obedience to the will of Allah. When I have shown my willingness to become Mahmed's bride, I believe that the water will begin to flow freely again and the rains will come. As soon as my mother put aside her infidel lover and went into my father's arms, the rains began, did they not? That is how it will be this time also.'

Zahra's face was white and strained, her green eyes dull and her nose sharp and pinched from losing so much weight. At the first fitting for her gowns, the pins had been carefully placed but now the seams all had to be resewn. Soon she would be little more than bone and a thin covering of flesh. Secretly, she was praying that Mahmed would be repulsed by her scrawniness on the marriage couch, and draw back from consummation. Only once had she seen him look at her with desire. At all other times it had been with polite interest only, and latterly with fury. Perhaps he still loved his dead wife? It was rumoured that they had been very happy – but that had been in the days when he was the Mahmed of old, not the quixotic, bullying savage who had made her his prisoner.

Suddenly she could bear it no more, this burden of conjecture, and tore the robe away from her to fling it to the ground. Mayne was alone and sick; he needed her. He had no water and only a few roots to subsist on. In her mind's eye she could see him wasting away in the darkened vault, her name on his lips. His sufferings were her sufferings. She wanted to die with him.

He must have been asleep. The parade of eerily

293

shimmering figures had drifted before his eyes one after the other, passing from the foot of the steps towards the pile of rocks by the entrance to the vault where the Jewels of Destiny had once lain. Strangely garbed in milk white robes, pleated and immaculately clean, carved belts around their waists, hair flowing free down their backs and wearing tall, square headdresses, the women had walked with care and reverence, carrying caskets in their hands. Were these the priestesses of the Mother Goddess?

Somehow he knew that they were, and that they were bearing to her vault the gifts that had been sent by her worshippers. One after another the small, shimmering figures did what they had come to do. Mayne heard the entrance to the vault opening, that whirring, buzzing sound, almost like a deep-voiced cicada, and then the priestesses would bend, placing their offering inside before closing the vault and withdrawing, still at that stately, reverent pace.

Yes, he must have been asleep because his eyes met the same darkness when they opened. It was like a pall of thick black velvet hanging closely before him. He was so sure that it was somehow tangible that he reached out to touch, but of course there was nothing.

Priestesses with gifts for their goddess. Well, why should he not dream of them? He was in the most likely place for such a dream. Yet they had seemed so very real. He could recall every detail of their pleated robes, their brown hands and feet, the delicate sandals with thongs criss-crossed around their ankles, and their faces of an Egyptian cast, noses rather pronounced, the eyes slanting and heavily outlined in black and turquoise. And those strange, square headdresses balanced on their long black hair. How on earth did they keep them on?

Eventually, after puzzling over the dream, he returned to the discomforts of reality. His leg was throbbing quite violently, and his throat could not have

294

felt more bruised and parched had someone clamped their fingers tightly round it to do him some injury. In the darkness, he had no notion of the passing of time. He might have been there for two or three or four days; he could not say. The hour was fast approaching when he would be driven by desperation to try and climb the steps to the upper precinct and search for food, but every movement was agony. Now he was sure that he must have broken a bone, yet careful probing with his fingers did not reveal a jagged edge, to his mystification. The bandage was dry; the wound was healing well, yet there was this almost paralysing agony when he tried to move. He was forced to drag his leg along behind him and so, rather than risk making the break worse, he had stayed where he was, hoping that time would do its work.

The fever had troubled him for a time then faded, but now he could sense its return. His head was swimming; his eyes conjuring up strange pictures in the blackness. When he felt his forehead it was cool, but that was no indication. His clothes were drenched with sweat, or was it only the dampness of the sunless vaults?

Hearing a sudden scraping sound, he froze in alarm, but it must only have been a lizard searching the upper precinct for food. If only he could get up there and find something to eat and drink. Once again, he summoned up his strength for the effort but the blood pounded in his head, the pain of his wound overcame him and he fell back, exhausted. He was weaker than he had ever been in his life – he, the one who had grown broad and tall on blueberry pie and lobsters in the plenty of Maine. Nothing had ever affected his health before. He had flourished even on the poorman's *pilaf* and unleavened bread during his two years without a roof over his head. There were times then when he had gone hungry from necessity, but he had never felt as vulnerable as this. Was this what love did to you, made you only half a man without your woman beside you? It was an unsteadying thought.

What was she doing now, his little queen? He wanted to call her to mind, yet the thought that she might by now belong to Mahmed brought nausea to his throat and quickly he pushed her from his thoughts.

He must have dozed again, for he heard the clash of swords and saw in the darkness a glowing blade wielded by an unseen hand. The same sword that he had seen during the sandstorm at the oasis, brightly shining, unknown words engraven on it. It bobbed and swayed in the darkness seemingly of its own accord. Was it really unsupported, or was it simply that he could not see its bearer in the blackness, nor those who were attacking him? Blade crashed against blade and, hearing a moan and the sound of a body falling close by, his skin prickled.

'Who's there?' he called out, yet already he knew that there would be no answer.

Then there was nothing save the shining sword and the sound of a woman's voice crying out in relief, followed by utter silence.

He did not believe in ghosts, although he had a healthy respect for *jinn* and who could blame him after his upbringing in Arabia? But this was something different; he could not put a name to it. Cautiously, he touched the Sword of God again, running his finger along its well-honed blade, tracing the inscription, drawing some comfort from its weight in his hand but knowing that he could never have used it in his present crippled state.

Drifting off to sleep again, he awoke chilled. He tugged the goatskin tightly around himself, shifting into a more comfortable position. He had fought not to think of her, but it was impossible. Now, in his mind's eye, came a vision of his darling, and the memory of a meal that they had shared soon after their first meeting. He had been surprised to find that she did not eat lamb or goat's meat; while others chewed on the succulent flesh, she dined only on fruit and *laban*, rice and vegetables. When he had asked her why she did not eat meat, she had smiled up at him.

'This was how I was raised by my mother. She did not eat meat, either. When I asked her why, she said, "If you want to be of the light, then you must eat the light." She would not touch the flesh of an animal that had been slaughtered.'

'That is unusual in an Arab.'

'Everything about my mother was unusual.'

'Do you not hunger for meat?'

'How can I hunger for something that I have never tasted?'

'Have you never been tempted to eat meat?'

'I cannot say that I have,' she had said with a shrug.

'What did your mother mean when she said that to be of the light, you must eat the light?'

'You would have to ask her that, I am afraid. She did say once that if we eat meat that comes from the misery and pain of the killing of animals, then we shall take upon ourselves their misery and pain, but if we eat plants and vegetables and fruit, then we take upon ourselves the sunlight and the warmth and benevolence of the earth itself.'

'That seems a good enough explanation to me.'

He could almost see in his imagination the dish of goat's meat before him, large, juicy chunks dripping with rosy blood, and his arm began to move to lift one to his mouth. Oh, Land of Mirages, indeed!

Come what may, he was going to make the effort to move soon. If he did not, his mind would give way, his muscles would waste, and he would never escape this abysmal place with its haunting and reproachful memories.

Some half day's ride away from the temple, Mahmed's men scoured the desert wastes for the one who had

297

dishonoured their master's bride. Having been ordered not to return until they found him, they were heavily stocked with supplies of water, large pouches of *laban* and goats' cheese. They would survive in the wilderness for weeks if necessary, or as long as it took to find the vile *kaffir*. None of them wished to enrage their master, for his temper had always been uncertain where his servants were concerned and of late he had become as vicious and temperamental as a wolverine protecting her young. Yet who could blame him after the way first his daughter and then his promised bride had deceived and cheated him? Had Zahra been any other, and not the daughter of Husain, their master could have ordered her execution by beheading, or the old, eminently satisfying method of stoning to death.

Women were wayward, wilful and immoral creatures; they had to be controlled and schooled by their husbands and fathers. Thus it was and thus it had ever been in Islam, as in the days of the Old Testament before.

The words of the Qu'ran were adamant: 'And say to the believing women, that they cast down their eyes and guard their private parts, and reveal not their adornment, save such as is outward; and let them cast their veils over their bosoms, and not reveal their adornment save to their husbands or their fathers.'

Queen she may be, but this woman had sinned; she had revealed her adornment to the *kaffir* and thus had made herself unfitted to rule. Everything she had done since her father's death had been an offence before God. She had stayed unwed; she had kept their master waiting for her reply to his proposal; she had not consulted with their master over the *kaffir's* mission, but had kept his presence secret so that she could fornicate with him. It was anathema to fornicate with the infidel, the unbeliever, and their master's bride had disported herself like a Salome.

Now her days of sinning and immorality were over,

and their master would reign in her stead. She had placed herself in his hands and so he had no option. But first, as their wedding gift to their master, they would find the *kaffir* so that their master could have his revenge with his own hand and present the *kaffir's* head on a platter as the central decoration at the marriage feast.

Then the days of this Salome would be finished, and all power would be in their master's hands.

Chapter Eighteen

And as for the unbelievers, their works are as a mirage in a spacious plain which the man athirst supposes to be water, till, when he comes to it, he finds it is nothing.

The little deputation could not understand what was happening to them. They had come to beseech the help of their Amira, only to find her audience tent occupied by the Amir Mahmed and six of his guard, men who were heavily armed and who stared at the supplicants cold-eyed.

'*Saiyid*, we have come to beseech the daughter of Husain to aid us. We are poor men and we depend upon water for our work. We dye cloth in the village of Kubistan. All the villagers dye cloth, *Saiyid*, it is their living, it supports us all, and now our water has gone and we are at our wits' end! *Saiyid*, please let us see the daughter of Husain!'

Mahmed glared, words blocking behind his tongue so that he could not straighten them to get them free. More drought, more whining supplicants! How was he going to sell his bride's land to the French if it was as arid as his own? *Allah*, but he had thought that the waters would return now that he had brought the harlot to heel. In his unsteady mind, where superstition, half-belief and faithlessness all warred for supremacy, he had been so certain of victory. But now...

Sullenly, he surveyed the forlorn little group of people with their blue-red hands and wrists, their feet and ankles multi-coloured from years of dyeing cloth. Their work was not some half-hearted operation. The dyers stood in the vats with their cloth and trod it as they would grapes, or pummelled and banged it with their fists. Undoubtedly, their work wasted volumes of water and so these were some of the ones most to blame for the present shortage.

Glowering, his lower lip jutting forward like that of a petulant child, he got to his feet. Pointing towards the entrance to the tent, he bellowed, 'Out! All of you, *out of my sight!*'

Quailing, the men backed away, stumbling over one another. Then they fled out into the brutal sunshine, breathless, shocked, not knowing which way to turn.

Inside the tent, Mahmed seated himself crosslegged on the cushion where normally Zahra would sit, smiling and alert, her eyes shining with concern for those who came to her with their problems.

If the French heard of this latest development, Mahmed's prospects would be grim. Added to all the other wells and rivers that had dried out, this meant that virtually half the Land of Mirages was stricken by drought. His seer had said that the rains were dropping in another place now, many moons, travel distant, and that they would not be falling here again.

'How do you know?' Mahmed had growled, his fingers flexing, eyes fixed on the seer's scrawny neck.

'I had a dream. I saw the rains falling on a place that was lush and green, where the people lived amongst wealth and plenty.'

'That sounds exactly like this place, you dolt!' Mahmed had snarled, kicking the seer out of his presence. He had long ago lost his faith in seers and sages, as he had lost faith in everything. Going to his daughter's couch had done this to him. When he had taken her, he had unwittingly forfeited his religion though he had concealed it well.

It would not do to let others know that he was now an unbeliever, one of the faithless ones, as thoroughgoing an infidel as the *kaffir* who had dishonoured his bride. No unbeliever could rule the Land of Mirages; that would be unthinkable. Whatever his private beliefs, or lack of them, he must hide his true feelings. When he went to war, men would believe he did so in Allah's name, and when he forgave an erring bride and took her to his couch, men must believe that he did so to placate Him and to bring back the waters to His blessed land.

There was a tradition that in troubled times such as these, sacrifice of some sort must be offered to Allah by the ones who ruled the Land of Mirages. Thirty years before, Husain and Mishaal had journeyed to the pagan temple, on foot, without water, without food, their hearts sustained by faith alone, and their reward had been the Jewels of Destiny and three decades of peace. Such beliefs were deeply ingrained in the land, and the people heeded them. He would let it be known that his sacrifice was the taking of an unchaste bride. No one but he would know that he would have taken forty harlots to wife if it meant that he gained control of the Jewels of Destiny and the promised gold from the French.

Gnawing on his thumb, sinking his teeth into the patch of raw red flesh where previous assaults had fetched blood, he considered his position. What did he care if he were a hypocrite? That would not hinder his ambitions, but drought and poverty would. Who would pay generously for a parched and dusty amirate where the fruit had withered on the trees and the vegetables lay scorched in the soil?

Was it because the *kaffir* was still free?

Tasting fresh blood on his tongue, he bit deeper,

302

finding a masochistic pleasure in attacking his own flesh. The pain made him wince, but in a curious manner he enjoyed it. Somewhere, the remainder of the Jewels of Destiny were hidden, and he must find them; and there was one who must surely know their whereabouts....

Zahra was embroidering, trying to thread her needle with an unsteady hand, growing impatient at the refusal of the kingfisher blue silk to go through the small metal eye. On an intake of breath, she flung them aside, followed by the square of material on which had been embroidered one delicate, high-winged blue bird.

'Blue bird of happiness, Come to me, out of the branch of a silver tree; Blue bird of happiness, bring to me, the love that I long to see.'

Tears filled her eyes as she sang beneath her breath the words that she had written when she was sixteen and avidly romantic, when she had believed that only love and happiness lay ahead of her. Now she knew better. Now she knew that the blue bird was as helpless as she ...

Mahmed's voice made her freeze in trepidation. Freyha, who had been fetching their supper, hurried in ahead of the Amir, a tray wobbling between her shaking hands. Placing it hastily on a nearby chest, she stood at Zahra's side, twisting her wrinkled hands together and swallowing nervously.

'Woman, I must speak to you in private. Send your servant away and be seated.'

Zahra obeyed, the colour draining from her face. What did he want, this hard, angry man who made her skin crawl?

'You must tell me all that you know of the Jewels of Destiny,' he began as soon as Freyha had left. 'I know that some of them are still in your possession.'

'They were sold to enable our people to build a better life.'

303

'All very noble, I know, but some still remain. They were of great value. How many rubies and pearls would be needed to give a Beduin a comfortable life? Very few, I think. His needs are small, and the heavy rains have ensured that crops have been good so you have not needed to buy food.'

'Why do you want to know?' Zahra fixed him with her sharp green eyes.

'I ask the questions here, woman. Tell me where they are, and I shall not hurt your servant.'

'You mean that you would harm Freyha, an old woman whose health is poor, thanks to your villainous behaviour?'

'I am no villain, woman. I am your husband-to-be, and you will honour me and treat me with courtesy as a wife should treat her spouse. Now tell me where they are, and I will leave the old hag alone.'

'There are none left. All of them were sold years ago. If there were some left, would you not have found proof of that when you went through my father's private possessions?' She fixed him with another stare, one that was meant to freeze his blood and almost did.

She made him feel loathsome and dirty, tainted by evil. He had better guard himself in case he let something slip. Her mother had been possessed of the gift; it was said that she could see the truth within people, whatever they chose to say. How did he know that the daughter was not the same? There was something about her that made him wretchedly uneasy, and that in itself made him angry. She had never learned her place, and now she must suffer for it.

'It is unlikely that such evidence would be easily available. I believe that you carry the knowledge in your head. Were you not expecting to wear Zenobia's crown when you married, as your mother did?'

'That was thirty years ago.'

'That does not answer my question, woman. Were you

not expecting to wear it when you married?' Leaning forward, he grasped her wrist cruelly, biting it with his fingers until his nails drew blood.

Zahra fought to free herself, but the fingers tightened mercilessly.

'How could I wear a crown that was sold thirty years ago?' she cried, struggling to rake Mahmed's face with her other hand, only to find that, too, manacled.

'You will not see your servant until you tell me the truth. I am sending her out into the wilderness, without food or water. She will not last a day in the heat. She is too frail.'

'You would not dare.'

'As I was saying, I shall send her out into the wilderness, alone, and not until you tell me where the jewels are hidden shall I give orders that she be brought back to you.'

'There are no jewels. But wait! Let me free!' Stormy-eyed, she told him that there were some jewels he could have, but not the legendary ones. 'They are my own – and here, take thee. The Emperor of the French sent them to me.' Placing the collar, earrings and bracelets of malachite and silver in his arms, she stepped away quickly. 'Would you like your seed pearls back?' she sneered. 'They are of no use to me. They are a gift for a child, not a queen.'

'I knew that.' Mahmed tried to hold her gaze meaningfully, but to his chagrin his eyes fell first.

'So you will take them all?'

'I shall.'

'Who are they for, your favourite?'

'I have no favourites.'

'I can well believe it!' Tenderly, Zahra rubbed the flayed skin of her wrists, bruise dark already, the pain searing down to the bone. 'They say you love only your white camels. Perhaps you will deck them in my jewels and dance with them?'

305

Deeply offended, Mahmed got to his feet, the jewels dangling from his fingertips. She was a harridan as well as a harlot, vile-tongued and rude-mouthed. How glad he was that he had never entertained loving thoughts towards her. Had he done so, then she would have broken his heart by now. Men who displayed their vulnerability to women were fools. He would never do so again.

For a few moments, as he retreated, she thought that she had won; and then, turning to face her, he repeated his threat.

'Your woman will be cast out into the wilderness until you tell me where the rest of the Jewels of Destiny are hidden.'

'No!' she cried, running after him. 'There are none. They were sold, all sold! Bring Freyha to me, bring her here now!' But he had gone and the guards stepped in front of her, their hands on the hilts of the shining curved daggers thrust into their belts.

She had slipped out of the tent unseen on many an occasion before, and she could do it again. Somewhere out there in the unwelcoming wilderness was Freyha, who had cared for her all her life; Freyha who had been abandoned without food or water. When Zahra had found her, and taken her to a safe place, she would go back to Mayne and together they would rally her people and let them know that she was a prisoner and not the willing bride that Mahmed had led them to believe. Within days she could free them of this tyrant, if Allah were on her side.

Of that she was uncertain. He must be angry with her still, or the waters would have flowed again. Freyha had told her of the deputation from Kubistan, the dyers who said that their livings were ruined by the drought in their area. Freyha had talked with the men before they left, had given them milk for the journey home, some ewes' cheese and a blessing, but she had not been allowed to see them alone. Mahmed's guard had superintended the short meeting, ostensibly there to protect her from the strangers – as if she needed such protection from her own countrymen! As she later told her mistress, she had longed to slip them a note telling them the truth about what was happening to their Amira, but the occasion had not arisen.

'Why have the waters not returned, Freyha?' Zahra had asked. 'Where is the rain? I have said I will marry him – the ceremony is only days away. Does God not hear me?'

'He hears, my heart. No is just as much an answer as yes.'

'So his answer is no, the marriage is not enough? *Ya Allah*, what else can I do? I have given up the man I love. Does He want my life, too?'

'I do not know, my heart.' Freyha's voice had trembled. She had lost the vigour that had supported her for years; weight had fallen from her and her hands shook. In just a week or two she had become an old woman. 'I no longer know anything. There is no surety any more. We have no seer; there are no omens.'

'We have had omens! He has forsaken us.'

It had been their darkest hour, but somehow it had expunged the worst of the fears and doubts in Zahra's mind and within moments of her desperate cry, she had begun to feel new energy surging in her. She would escape; she could slip away by night and join Mayne. They would gather reinforcements from her people and defeat Mahmed, for whatever else the Qu'ran said about men being masters over women, it also said, 'O believers, it is not lawful for you to inherit women against their will.'

There was no rain; the drought continued. Zahra was mystified, for she thought that she had carried out God's wishes, but now it appeared she had not. The deputation from Kubistan had proved that to her. Mahmed had let her know of their arrival so that she would stay a humble prisoner and continue obediently with the marriage preparations, but his words had not had that effect. Just the opposite, in fact.

To Zahra the news was a direct message. Marriage to Mahmed was not what God wanted. What did he want from her then? If only she knew the answer to that!

She had hoped that Mahmed would forget his threat about Freyha, but he had not. One day had passed when their life was allowed to continue as normal, or as normally as it could do with a tyrant in their camp, and then Mahmed's guards had come for the old woman. Freyha had been led away, sobbing and screaming, while Zahra had felt her newfound courage ebbing fast.

But she had known then what she should do, and had set about her preparations.

That night she retired to her couch as usual. After turning down the oil lamps herself, a task that was usually Freyha's at bed-time, a humid, shadowy darkness had descended in her tent. Beneath her goatskin, Zahra was fully dressed in a woollen robe and cloak, and by her side was a bag filled with necessities for the journey: water, bread, *laban*, grains that could be eaten raw, and tasty herbs surreptitiously gathered for just this moment.

When the camp was silent, she arose, suppressing her breathing so that not even the smallest sound would alert a guard. Taking hold of the bag of food, she crept towards the rear of the black tent, past sacks of coffee beans and other stores that were concealed by a curtain. Then, taking out her little knife, she gently stuck the point into the goatskin tent. Pushing, she felt the tip delve through the skin, and then, slowly and cautiously, she slit it downwards, inch by inch, until she could smell the odours of night outside: the scent of herbs, the scorched sand and flinty pebbles, a goat nearby. Cautiously, she bent double and edged through the slit, her heart pounding.

When her foot slipped sideways on a shiny pebble, she almost cried out but managed to stifle the sound. Pausing, she looked about her but there was nothing save silence and darkness, and the lucid indigo of the sky above, so vast and clear and breathtaking that she felt she could look right through it to what lay beyond. Her heart beating wildly, she tiptoed on, towards the horses.

There was her darling Ya'bub, whom she had not seen for days, and there was nothing she could do to stifle the mare's joyful whinny of greeting. Zahra rubbed the horse's nose and kissed her repeatedly, caressing her velvet smooth coat and joying in the warmth that emanated from the excited horse.

She could not risk taking a saddle. There would be guards nearby. She had ridden bareback before and she could do it again. Briefly, she thought of the Draisienne and a wistful smile touched her lips. If someone could have made the strangely wheeled machine more mobile, then she could have fled on that. But no, she would rather have her darling, her Ya'bub, descendant of the great Prophet, her father's stallion.

Whispering to the mare to be silent, she led her out of the camp until the blood was flowing freely in her slender, elegant limbs. Then, carefully, she mounted, urging Ya'bub to move as silently as she was able. She had bound the mare's hoofs with bandages to stifle their sound on the flint that embedded the sand thereabouts, and they seemed to be having the required effect. Heading in the direction of the wilderness, the cold night breeze driving against her forehead, she steered Ya'bub to freedom.

If his joints had rusted, Mayne could not have felt older or more incapacitated. Inwardly he cursed his own feebleness. A week at least must have passed and he was ravenous. He had chewed the roots over and over, spitting them out in disgust when they began to taste of parched wood, and then stuffing them back into his mouth when his hunger overtook him again. Dragging his bandaged leg behind him, he crawled along the icy stone floor, feeling debris and grit creasing his palms, and once touching the long, fleshless bone of one of the skeletons. Drawing back his hand in disgust, he shook it as if to free himself of this whole wretched experience.

Where was she now? What was she doing? Was she Mahmed's wife by now? Had they consummated the marriage? Fury and jealousy pounded inside him, driving him on. If he could only get his strength back, then he would continue with his first plan, disguise himself and go to her camp to ensure that she was well and happy. If she was, he would return to his Legion; if not, he would kill Mahmed with his own hands, and to hell with the consequences.

Now he knew why he had learned the subtle skills of the assassin. It was so that he could slaughter the vile and odious Mahmed and free his little queen of her bondage.

Dear God, what was that he had touched? Something cold and slimy and thoroughly repugnant. Gritting his jaw, he moved on, his eyes screwed up at the pain that suddenly shot through his leg. But nothing was going to stop him now, nothing! Eventually, he came to the bottom of the stairs, and then, one by one, dragged himself up the flight, pausing now and again to recover his breath, feeling as winded as if he had run at full pelt. At the bend in the stairs he could look up and see a halo of light high above him. Dear God, but the sun was shining up there, the long forgotten sun, bright and rich and life giving. His heart leapt at the sight and he felt tears prickling behind his eyes, only realising then the depth of despair he had felt during his enforced incarceration. If it killed him, he would get up the last of

310

the steps and into the temple precinct. If it killed him. . . .

He must have lost consciousness, for his eyes jerked open at the sound of some wild creature's cry close by. He found that he was stiff and aching and chilled to the joints, yet his clothes were soaked with sweat again. Through his thoughts drifted a glittering golden hip bath, steaming with hot water and foaming soap, and joyfully he stepped into it, plunging into the steaming water, lathering himself with the soap. Bliss. To his abject regret, the mind image faded and he was back in the abyss again, but there was the streak of light above, a little dimmer now, but still there. He began his ascent once more.

The full blast of light in his face was too much after the abyss, and he shrank from it, screwing up his eyes and turning his head away. The ancient glory before him was dazzling in the late-afternoon sun: the beautiful carved statues and friezes, the stately marble pillars, smooth and pale as milk. Encrusted with the dust and sand of ages, they stared back at him, almost reproachfully, and in his mind's eye, he saw again the women in their snowy pleated robes and strange tall, square headdresses. They were standing, arms outstretched, as if in supplication, before the statue of the pagan goddess.

Then they were gone, and there was nothing but swirling dust motes and a sudden emptiness that chilled him.

There must be food outside even if it was only roots and berries. Having found a solid enough length of wood, he employed it as a walking stick, half-hobbling, half-dragging himself towards the temple entrance where he stood for a while like a man freed from a lifetime in some noxious underground gaol.

The desert had never looked more beautiful to him. Then, blinking again and again, he saw that he was not mistaken. There was a small oasis within walking distance, and beside it was his camel, munching away on

311

camel's thorn contentedly. Overjoyed, he hobbled towards it, crying out at the agony in his leg as he put too
much weight on it. As the afternoon sun slipped in the
sky, he finally reached the little oasis and stood leaning
against a palm tree, sweat streaming from his face and
his heart pounding.

He could not recall having seen this place on the way
here. If he had, they could have got water here. Perhaps
Zahra had found it as she left? He hoped so, for she
would have had desperate need of a supply for her
return journey. Tearing off his sweat-darkened, dusty
clothes, he flung them in the glimmering, satiny smooth
pool, and then jumped in after them, his face splitting
into a broad, delighted grin at the sensation of the water
against his flesh.

For over two hours he swam and floated and swam
again, almost surprised that there was any water left to
bathe in after all he had drunk. When he had finished, he
ate some of the succulent dates that grew on the
overhanging palms, and crunched at the fresh, sweet
herbs flourishing by the water's edge. Never had such
energy flowed through him; never had he felt so
instantly revived.

Climbing out of the water, he looked up at the sky
then at his camel. The beast appeared placid, as if it had
known he was coming, as if it had been waiting especially
for him. Yet it was not hobbled. Everyone knew that
camels strayed if they were not hobbled, and yet, if
Zahra had done that to the beast, it could not have
foraged for food.

But why was he searching for miracles? The beast
must have stayed close because there was plentiful food
and water here, and Zahra had known that while he had
not until now.

Then a thought struck him. When they had arrived at
the temple, they had been waterless and ravenous, yet
all Zahra had given him had been roots. She must have

seen this oasis as she left. Why had she not brought him some of the water in a flask?

Puzzling over this, he drifted off into a dreamy, comfortable sleep, the best and most natural he had enjoyed for days. When he awoke, the late sun had dried the clothes which he had spread over the bushes to dry. He examined the wound in his leg; it seemed well on the way to healing.

Drawing on his clothes again, he considered spending the night in the oasis, but his goatskin was in the temple vault and he would be cold without it. He would fetch it, and make a bed for himself beneath the palms.

The moment that he stepped outside the oasis, he felt the weakness return and knew that he had overtaxed his strength by swimming for too long. In case he could not return that night, he filled the inner pockets of his robe with dates and herbs and then, taking up the walking stick, began to hobble back to the temple, feeling frailer and more vertiginous with every step. Soon that old, warning throb was back in his leg and his head was pounding in sympathy. He wished that he had stayed where he was, despite the cold of night.

Inside the temple, he paused to try and still the whirling in his head, but with little effect. He could only descend the steps by sitting on his buttocks and shuffling downward. Even in the blackness, everything seemed to be circling around him and his stomach lurched alarmingly. But he felt better when he kept still, which he did as soon as he located his goatskin in the blackness. He would have to rest there for the night but he would be back in the oasis at dawn, he vowed, to prepare for his journey to Zahra's camp.

Moonglow lit her path as she scoured the way ahead for any sight of Freyha, but there was none. She had ridden a good way by now and Ya'bub was tiring, but they would not stop for night's cool was more comfortable for a horse than the blaze of day. She would have taken a camel had she been able to steal a saddle, but they were locked away and guarded, and she would have spent more time on the ground had she tried to ride such an unruly beast bareback.

With dawn a white cloud swelling and extending over her like a palanquin, she ate some dates as they galloped along, not daring to stop. They were going in the right direction. She could navigate herself in any direction by the stars. Beduin trackers were renowned for their ability to reach any destination needed, and her father had taught her this invaluable skill during their many rides together.

Venus, night and morning star, huge and sharply bright, shone ahead of her, almost too bright and cleanly outlined to be a simple star. Venus would lead her to the temple and her beloved Mayne.

What if he had gone? What if he were burning up with fever? She shuddered at the thought. And then, a little way ahead of her, saw the one whose tracks she had been following in the sand. She urged Ya'bub onward.

Freyha lay as if reaching out, one arm flung towards the diamond-white star, one leg drawn up beneath her and one outstretched. There was a calm expression on her face, and her eyes, which were open, were peaceful. Astonishingly, there was the trace of a smile upon her mouth.

'Freyha!' Dismounting, Zahra ran towards her servant, flinging herself to her knees by her side and cradling her in her arms. But it was too late. Freyha's body was cold. They must have ridden out this far with her, and then flung her to the earth and left her. Mahmed had kept his word.

Such a mean, vicious, petty thing to do, killing a harmless old woman who had never hurt him, nor ever would. Freyha, who had been with Zahra, close and devoted, since she was a baby. More than eighteen years'

314

loyalty had been repaid with heartless cruelty and a lonely death in the desert.

Zahra knelt for some time, cradling the cold body, but she was conscious that Freyha's spirit had left it. What she held was hardening, empty flesh, the decaying container that was now voided of its soul. In her arms she held mortality, but Freya's soul had escaped this world's boundaries.

When her eyes were free of tears, she looked up to see Venus burning brighter than ever, hurting her eyes with its brilliance. It was an encouraging message. 'Follow where I lead and you will have your revenge,' it seemed to be saying to her.

PART SEVEN

Desert King and Desert Queen

Forget not Memphis and the evening lights
Along the shore, the wind in the papyrus,
The sound of water through the glass-green nights,
The incense curling upward to Osiris.
Forget not Athens and the starry walks
Beside Ilissus under the cool trees,
The Master's garden, and the quiet talks
of Gods and life to come. Forget not these.
And in the after years, forget not this:
How in a withered world allied to death,
When love was mocked and beauty deemed amiss,
We met and pledged again the ancient faith.
For this, of all our lives, the loneliest,
So thwarted and so strong, will seem the best.

Robert Hillyer

Chapter Nineteen

The riders appeared when she was so sure of victory, circling the highest dune to her right and forming a crescent on their camels. Swathed in black, their faces veiled to repel the sand that their camels' hoofs sent flying into the air, they looked formidable indeed and Zahra could not suppress her cry of alarm. Mahmed's men, on his racing camels. No beast could surpass their speed.

All the same she tried, urging Ya'bub on in the baking heat of approaching noon, knowing that her horse was exhausted and that she would die if Zahra continued at this punishing pace. 'Allah, help me, help me,' she prayed, but His face was turned away. When Ya'bub finally came to a halt, gasping and shuddering, head down, legs splayed, Zahra dismounted instantly to relieve her of her weight and stood bravely facing the men who had come to take her captive.

She would not weep in front of them, but neither would they see her face. Drawing her head veil tighter, she swathed it across her nose and mouth, and that was how she kept it fixed during the return journey.

A man had stayed behind to water Ya'bub and wait for her recovery, and then the mare would be led back to camp at a slower pace than the one achieved by the racing camels.

It was the first time that Zahra had ridden one of these

at full tilt and the motion jarred every joint in her body, rattling her teeth and giving her vertigo. The whole world seemed to be throwing itself up and down as she galloped along, Mahmed's men on either side of her.

Knowing that he would be waiting for her, she gritted her teeth, cold shivers scraping down her spine despite the heat. They had lashed her to the camel's saddle so that she could not turn her beast aside, but at this speed she would have needed to be a skilful rider indeed to escape. After a few hours, the blasting sun, her thirst and exhaustion set her head drooping and she would have fallen from the saddle had she not been lashed to it. All she wanted was to close her eyes and sleep. She wanted to forget this wretched journey, Freyha's death, the loss of Mayne, the marriage that was being forced upon her. She wanted to forget life, that was what she most wanted. To forget she had ever lived.

Mahmed was waiting for her, wishing to speak to her the moment she arrived even though she was dead on her feet. She stood before him, still veiled, loathing him and wishing with all her heart that she could kill him. Her eyes were drawn to the gleaming, jewel-studded dagger tucked prominently into his white silk sash. He appeared to guess what she was thinking for, summoning one of his men, he handed the dagger to him then stood before her, unarmed.

There was no humanity in his eyes. If only there had been, they might have been able to build on it, but there was no humour, no sensitivity, no compassion. He was passionless and hard; devoid of feeling. Never had she seen such a disintegration in a man in such a short time. It was as if his soul had been stolen from his body while he slept.

'Woman, you are in grave error and Allah will punish you.'

'Do you not think I have been punished enough? My devoted servant is dead, I have lost my amirate and all

320

those I loved, and all because of you.' Gritting her jaw, she glared at him.

Stepping up to her, he tore away her veil and gripped her face between his palms. He moved so suddenly that she was taken by surprise. When his mouth descended on hers, moist and greedy, she felt her stomach churn. The kiss went on interminably yet she was too proud to step back, to fight or show any hint of a reaction. She stood cold and rigid. He would get no display of passion from her, whatever he did.

'You will be shackled like a slave from this day on. No woman will better me.'

His voice was rasping, thick with desire. To her dismay, she felt a stirring movement against her thigh. He was roused by her humiliation. Realising that, she found the strength to move away, striking out with her fists to knock back his arms. She heard him growl threateningly in response and prepared herself for the blow that must surely come. Not by the slightest flinching movement did she show that she was afraid. When his bunched fist slammed against her ear, she saw a cascade of a trillion stars and behind them the triumphant face of the Amir, his eyes shining with exultation at her agony.

'Devil!' she cried. 'May Allah forgive you, for I never shall!'

'Do you think I care? What are your feelings to me? Nothing, do you hear, nothing!'

'Yet you try to force me into marriage!'

'Those who think that great rulers marry only for love are simple in the head.'

'My father married my mother because he loved her! And did you not love your wife?' Zahra shouted back.

'Never mention her name,' Mahmed rasped, his face darkening.

'I shall mention whom I please, when I please and where I please, and you had best remember that if you

321

wish to consider yourself a great ruler, but ever remember this, Mahmed ibn Beydoun – only you will consider yourself such a one. No one else ever shall! Great rulers earn their titles, they do not steal them by force.'

'I do not listen to the advice of harlots,' Mahmed sneered, but she could tell that he was shaken by her words. 'You will be put in shackles and kept in them until we are man and wife.'

'And what then, great ruler? Will you keep me in shackles for the rest of my life? How will you explain them to my people, to our guests and visitors, and to our children, should we have any?'

He did not answer. As she waited for him to speak, she was aware of a sensation of barren emptiness flowing from him. She knew in that silent yet telling moment that he had no plans for their future life together, but more she could not distinguish. It was not until later, when she was shackled in her tent with guards posted around it, that she realised what had happened.

She had experienced her first premonition. How could she explain it to herself? Not easily. There had been a certainty about it, a total confidence. She had known before that Mahmed wished to make her his bride so that he could control her amirate, but had supposed he would strengthen his claim by giving her sons. She could not understand why this should not be so, yet she had sensed very strongly in that moment after he had hit her that he had no interest in siring children upon her.

'Not without suffering.'

She remembered what the old seer had said to her when she had asked him about the gift. 'It is not easily given. It comes to those who are chosen. The easy livers and the indolent, the pampered ones, they will never have it. It is given, but not without suffering. You cannot ask for it to come. It will find you, my daughter, but not without suffering. Remember that.'

Had he known before he died that her people would have a seer again one day, and that it would be Zahra herself? Her skin prickling at the thought, she shivered.

Perhaps her mother's gift had come to her from the grave, if such a thing were possible?

Curling into a ball, she snuggled beneath the goat-skins on her couch and turned the notion over and over in her mind until exhaustion drove everything but sleep from her.

They had journeyed for nine days from their town but they knew that all would be well once they begged help from their Amira. She would never refuse them or turn them away unheard. Tales of her generosity and noble heart had reached them even in Zudan, and it had been the vision of this compassionate woman before them, their Queen of the Desert, which had enabled them to endure the hardships of the waterless trek. They had bags filled with grain and flour for unleavened bread, and blocks of goats' cheese now high from the beating sun, dried dates and figs in abundance, but no water.

Their wells and their river had run dry for there had been no rain in Zudan for seven months. Many had died, their bodies parched, and their fellow citizens had buried them beneath little mounds of rocks and stones to keep out the hyenas and the carrion. The children had suffered worse than any. Those nursed at the breast died first when their mothers' milk dried up from the effects of the drought.

The leader of the supplicants from Zudan was Mikhail ibn Zalir, a man not entirely Arabic but whose roots were long lost in memory. A tall and imposing figure, he had carried his young son on his shoulders all the way, battling against the beating sun and the harsh, abrasive sand that chafed and infiltrated beneath his protective clothing. Behind him trailed the twenty others who were the sole survivors of Zudan, once a township of two

323

thousand people who had lived in comfort and plenty. Many had migrated to the cities when the drought began, but all too many had died of thirst and fever.

Mikhail ibn Zalir was no ordinary man. He had nursed his wife and three daughters through a killing fever, and watched them die despite all his efforts for how could fever be cured without water? They had drunk all their sherbets and *nabidh*, and eaten all the fruit, shrivelled as it had grown on the trees without the blessing of rain, but bodies drenched with sweat and throats clamped by thirst could not be soothed by sickly sweet sherbet.

Mikhail ibn Zalir had gone without water for three weeks now, surviving on roots dug out of the hard ground and crushed to make a throat-stinging juice. His son was regularly fed the root juice whether he wanted it or not, but now he was too weak to push away the liquid. He sat on his father's shoulders, swaying as if in a dream, eyes glazed, his small body unnaturally shrunken. In his imagination, as did all those trekking with him, he saw a vision of the Amira Zahra, glowing and golden, sweet and benevolent, her arms held out to them to ease their sufferings.

Jolting awake from his dream, the boy saw ahead the black tents of the Amira's camp and a thin smile curved his parched, cracked lips. They had reached her.

Not more! Mahmed felt his belly twist at the sight of the bedraggled, staggering men and women, their faces cracked and blackened by the sun, their limbs little more than bone. Allah, where had they come from this time? Farther than Bakasir, surely, for they had the look of people who had journeyed for many, many miles.

How could he hide them? What if the French heard of this? 'Buy my glorious land, rich with fruits and grain and vegetables and ever-flowing waters,' he heard himself saying to the French General who was even now on his way to treat with him. And in his imagination he

324

saw the man's shocked expression as his eyes fell upon the half-dead people who had trekked here like all the others to whine about the lack of water. Who did they think he was? Clenching his fists, he vanished into his audience tent and awaited the leader of the supplicants from Zudan.

The man was very tall, and still solidly built despite his desert ordeal. His face was square and wide-cheeked, his eyes light brown, his hair streaked with blond and grey in a most un-Arabian fashion, his skin lighter than that of the average desert-dweller. Mahmed could tell that not from the sun-eaten face but from the pale skin at the inside of the man's wrists and the nape of his neck.

'If we might only see our Queen,' the man began, holding out his hands in supplication. 'We have come many miles from Zudan, and we fear death stalks us now. If our Queen would only allow us to see her, then we should be revived and strengthened and not think this journey has been in vain.' His voice faltered painfully as he thought of his wife and daughters, their cold bodies buried beneath protective piles of rocks. How could a man bear to live when all he wanted to do was lie down in death with his beloved ones?

'You cannot see her,' Mahmed almost snarled. 'She prepares for her marriage.'

'*Saiyid*, we beg! In the name of Allah, we beg to see her!' It was the first time in his life that Mikhail ibn Zalir had pleaded on his knees, lowering himself to such a humble degree, but for those who remained, he would do it. What other course was open to him? He had never sought leadership but had suffered it to be thrust upon him. And now he must do the best he could for his people.

'It is not possible,' Mahmed repeated, drawing away in disgust as the ragged man moved nearer, taking the hem of his robe to press it to his mouth in the time-honoured way of the lowborn before the highborn.

325

'But, *Saiyid*, we shall die if we cannot see our Queen! We have been travelling many days. Our women and children are dying of thirst. If we could but see our Queen, she would give us nourishment and we would be revived.'

Mahmed's jaw clenched so tightly that his teeth began to ache. All he ever heard was how marvellous and beloved she was; how her people believed that she could work miracles. Well, he would not listen to any more of it. It was against all that was natural that a woman should be revered and honoured in this manner, and it infuriated him. If they had come direct to him, he might well have given them succour, but this filthy, ragged man had made it more than obvious that no one could aid him save the Amira Zahra. He had said that he would die if he could not see her.

When the man had been dragged bodily from the Amir's tent, and thrust back amongst his people who were even now being shown to tents where they might spend the night, Mahmed took out a tiny silver knife and began to clean his nails. It was something that he did four or five times a day now, however clean they were. In some strange, incomprehensible way, the action made him feel better, temporarily relieving the onslaught of rage and aggression that was growing daily more unmanageable since Zuli's death.

Zahra and Mayne were dreaming, he in his bone-chilling crypt and she in her chains, their minds reaching far beyond their incarceration and flying to meet one another on the plane of the spirit where no bonds could bind them.

In their dream, they were in one another's arms in the Oasis of the Stars, under a silver-limned moon set in the sparkling carcanet of a multitude of stars that watched over that place.

From the sheltering bushes and plants, tiny creatures

326

watched, their furry bodies taut with anticipation, and a lone unicorn stood sentinel, its single horn gleaming pale as milk in the moonlight. It, too, was watching, its heart beating with delight. They were together, the beloved ones, the ones who loved as no others had ever loved, the ones who had been chosen, like Husain and Mishaal before them, to complete the circle and unite gloriously beneath the heart of God.

'I shall always love you, my little queen,' Mayne whispered, between kisses that jewelled Zahra's throat like a collar of rubies flaring with imperishable fires. 'While our spirits live, no one can ever separate us.'

'And I shall always love you, my darling warrior. Whatever happens to us, promise me that you will find me wherever I am, look for me, and take me in your arms again!'

'I promise. Do you think two who have loved as deeply as we could ever be separated? Maybe we have loved before, in other lives, and that was why we loved at first sight in this one. When I saw you, I saw my own soul.'

'And I mine.'

Again they kissed, their arms braiding one another clingingly, immovably, and the unicorn snorted gently through its velvety nostrils, and lightly stamped one hoof in its impatience to see what would happen next. In the dream, its body shimmered like earthed lightning, an eerie, milky silver that threw a phosphorescent light upon the bushes around it while its blue eyes gleamed like Indian sapphires beneath the single slender, twisting horn.

It was a ceremony, ancient and unparalleled, a union between two immortals in a ritual of such profound beauty and spirituality that only a very few are ever allowed to experience it. First, they must love truly and selflessly. Second, they must be willing to pledge their love for one another in this life, and all the lives to come. And here were two who were more than willing, two who·

were eager to confirm what they had already pledged.

Their kisses grew more fierce, and Mayne's hands slipped to Zahra's breasts, marvelling at their firm yet soft roundness. She shuddered, wanting to draw him inside her now, aching to be one with him, but he would not have the moment rushed. Tenderly, he kissed her breasts, nuzzling his mouth in their warmth, conscious of nothing but the closeness of the woman he loved to distraction, the woman who had changed his life and whom he worshipped in return.

Lovingly, he lapped at her taut nipples, gently sucking them to make her squirm, and when she did he held her all the closer, pressing his hips to hers in wonderment at the silky beauty of her flesh, the flat stomach and swelling hips, the strong, shapely thighs. Lowering his head, he kissed a string of pearls around her waist, and then brought rich green emerald kisses down to the ebony triangle that waited, throbbing, for his approach.

Zahra could feel the jewels planted by her lover's mouth. They tingled and burned her flesh deliciously, and she felt as if she were Zenobia, her ancestress, laden with her fabulous gems. In its days of greatness, she had walked among the mighty pillars and colonnades of Palmyra beside her beloved husband, King Odenathus, whose later assassination had almost broken her heart.

'Maybe we loved before in another life and that was why we loved each other at first sight in this life.'

Mayne had said that only seconds ago, never guessing at the truth. Before her now she saw him in the ancient dress of Palmyra, a broad golden collar resting upon his collarbone, his hair thick and black and twisted into narrow ringlets. His eyes were dark and smouldering, almost black as smoke, his nose higher and arched, and a brief white robe half covered his strong brown body, its delicate pleated material edged with gold. On his feet were sandals, their thongs coiling around his ankles and

328

calves Greek-style. And this was Odenathus, her beloved, her husband in the ancient days, the one whom she had lost to ruthless murderers.

So much of her had died with him, but she had endured to defend their country against the Romans, and to conquer Egypt and then Palestine, Babylon, Asia Minor and all Arabia. By the time Zenobia was forty, she would be Queen of the East, and Rome would have lost nearly half of its empire to her.

'Zahra,' her lover whispered, and it was also Odenathus whispering 'Zenobia'. She laughed, throwing back her head and rejoicing to be in his arms again. They were one again, King and Queen of the East as they were meant to be. How many centuries they had waited for this, their resurrection, their rebirth and reunion, so that now they could complete the circle.

She was pliant in his arms as he pressed against her hips, thrusting deep within to the ecstasy that lay in wait for them both. He sank inside, deep, deep within, meeting no barriers, aching to be her, and she him. He thought that he could not hold out, that he must fill her with his loving instantly so much did she affect him, but he forced himself to hold back, controlling himself despite the overpowering sensations that speared through him so rivetingly. Pausing, he drew breath, looking down into her malachite eyes. They were rimmed with kohl more heavily than she would normally apply it, and her hair was twisted into tight ringlets and plaits into which black and white pearls were woven. Around her slender throat was a broad band of gold studded with blood red rubies, and at her waist were ropes of pearls encircling the short white pleated shift that he had torn apart in his eagerness to make love to her.

At first he did not understand, and then she whispered his name 'Odenathus', and he knew everything. That was why he had come here; that was why he had the blood of Arabia in his veins, and why he had loved her at

329

first sight, and why he would continue to love her in this life and the next, into eternity, and why he would die for her if necessary.

When Palmyra had reigned supreme, he had governed in the name of Rome, later rebelling against his overlords to steal into the desert and marshal the Beduin for their great rebellion. And there he had met Zenobia, daughter of the chieftain, Zabbai. He had loved her instantly. She had been eighteen when they married. Very soon, she had been drilling the Beduin beside her husband, helping to train and lead them into battle. On horseback she had been unsurpassed, having learned to live in the saddle like a hardened soldier.

Together they had beaten back the Roman conquerors, taking Persia and Syria, and soon they were joined by those whose lands touched their own, for none wished the Romans to retrieve what they had lost.

And then Odenathus was murdered by assassins.

He could recall the moment with clarity, see the faces of the attackers, the flashing of their knives and the dull impact of their blades thudding into his body. There had been little pain for he was dead almost immediately, Zenobia's name on his lips. But he had vowed that he would return, and find her again if it were possible. And now he had.

Their lovemaking was a timeless ritual, a dizzying ecstasy almost too sublime for mere mortals to endure, yet they must, for in its celebration they were renewing the life force, their love and power. And soon they would be ready to take back what had once been theirs.

Mikhail ibn Zalir woke with a jolt, conscious first of his bruised and aching body then the stinging pain in his sand-cut feet. And then he heard it again, the stifled breathing of someone stealing into the tent. Through sleep-bleared eyes, he saw the coffee-dark shadow looming above him, arm upraised, and the curved

330

outline of the *khanjar* as it descended. It was the last thing he would ever see. His agonies on this earth were over, as were those of the frail son who slept beside him. He died without waking, as did the others who slept in that tent; they who had come to beg help from their Amira and who, instead, found death.

When the slaughter was over, and the twenty-three corpses lay still and bloody, Mahmed came to inspect them. His nostrils flared at the scent of death. They had died with their bellies full, for they had been well fed to allay their suspicions. He could not have let them live, not with the General on his way. If the French heard, they would break the treaty. The Land of Mirages was rapidly becoming as arid and unfriendly as his own amirate.

He prodded the boy's frail corpse with one toe. The child would have died soon anyway; he had never seen a punier one. The father had displayed some courage, and his build had been powerful; had he arrived in any other circumstances, Mahmed could have had him trained for his fighting force. But had he done so, he would have had to find food and shelter for the rest which was out of the question. Life was becoming difficult enough for those already in the camp.

'*Saiyid*, what shall we do with the bodies?'

'Bury them deep, Hawan. Out in the desert some-where, where men do not go. And cover them with rocks to keep away the vultures.'

He was not worrying about the corpses' protection but remembering something that had happened about a year previously. Having ordered the execution of a man who had led a rebellion against him, the man had been buried in a shallow grave without a covering of rocks. A few days later, a bird of prey had flown over his camp with something in its beak, something which proved too burdensome for it to carry further. It had dropped the object which had narrowly missed a woman bearing a

331

pouch of *laban* to her tent. She in turn had dropped the pouch which had burst open, the white curdled milk gushing over her feet as she screamed uncontrollably at the sight of the blackened, blood-stained hand that lay before her on the ground. On its forefinger was a gaudy ring with a cheap imitation jewel... it was the hand of Zebassan, the rebel leader.

He stood as if transfixed as the bodies were silently borne out into the night to be slung unceremoniously over the camels that would bear them into the wilderness for their unhallowed burial. As they journeyed, they would pass the burial place of Husain and Mishaal, but it was a moonless night and no one would look in that direction. Visits to the grave were forbidden now anyway; Mahmed had declared that anyone who went there would be severely punished, and that prayers beside the grave were idolatrous and giving reverence to graven images.

Because no one looked in that direction, for fear of punishment, no one saw the multitude of blooms rioting over the burial ground, glorious scarlets and crimsons, rich buttery yellows and soft jade greens, cornflower blues and pristine whites, flourishing bravely in the waterless, rock hard earth where no rain had fallen for many weeks, and where no faithful had prayed for almost as long. Blooming in arid isolation, a monument to those who lay buried there, nourished on the love that they had held for one another, scented with delicious odours of perfumes and spices, the flowers brightened the darkness and filled the icy, parched air with the promise of renewal and rebirth.

Zahra and Mayne woke to the dawn with smiles on their lips. A blissful dream had helped them to pass the night, a dream of a love that they had shared almost two thousand years before when they had ruled the East together.

332

Zahra pressed her hands to her body, sure that she would find Zenobia's jewels encircling her throat and waist for her dream had been so very vivid, but she was wearing nothing save her light cotton robe. Gone with the dream were Zenobia's faded gems, the Jewels of Destiny that Mahmed would kill for.

Nothing on this earth would make her tell him where they lay. They belonged to her people, and were for their use alone. Mahmed would sell them to buy more camels and weapons, and make war, and that she could not tolerate.

Even the clank of the metal shackles as she moved her feet did not dispel the honeyed bliss of her dream. To have imagined that she was Zenobia, the great warrior queen, the most fearless woman the East had ever known, and that her beloved Mayne was Odenathus... it was quite impossible, of course, and yet her dream had been so utterly convincing. Her body ached deliciously from his lovemaking and she could still feel the fiery imprint of his kisses.

How bitter was reality after such a profound and pleasurable dream. She woke to it slowly, unwillingly, the sounds of the camp gradually impinging on her: the neighing of a horse; the impatient bleating of goats; the calls of the women as they went about their chores. How long had she been incarcerated by Mahmed? She had almost lost count. It must now be weeks, and she was at a loss to know what to do. There was a limit to the action she could take now that she was chained like a slave.

If only she had succeeded in escaping! 'Oh Mayne, Mayne, wherever you are, don't forget me,' she whispered. 'I shall never forget you, whatever happens.'

But in her heart she already felt that their loving was ended, that any chance of future happiness had evaded them. He would have left the temple by now, and gone back to his Legion. Such an attractive and captivating man would not be alone for long. There would always be

333

women eager to flirt with him and welcome him to their beds, and one day he would marry and look back on his sojourn with his Desert Queen as a wonderful illusion – like the dream she had woken from that morning.

Chapter Twenty

Mahmed was relieved to learn that the inhabitants of Zudan were safely buried. It would not have done for a bunch of crazed, ragged nomads to go wailing and weeping and spreading the word that the Land of Mirages had been destroyed by drought.

There had been such a tardy reaction to the marriage invitations he had despatched some time ago, that he wondered if the drought was preventing people from travelling, for who would willingly stay away from their Amira's wedding? He would have held the ceremony by now had he been sure that the union would be unconditionally accepted without witnesses. But if there were none, his bride could claim later that she was forced into the marriage, and then it would become invalid. He did not trust her. Had she not tried to escape him already?

'O believers, it is not lawful for you to inherit women against their will.'

The words came into his mind unbidden. Though he was no longer a believer, the teachings of his childhood could not be forgotten so easily. Yet having faith no longer, how could such tracts affect him? All he need do was appear to believe in them so that others would be convinced of his fidelity.

'Those who devour the property of orphans unjustly,

devour Fire in their bellies, and shall assuredly roast in a Blaze.'

Those were words he had no wish to recall, and he felt himself turning a painful red at their recollection. Curse the Qu'ran. It had a platitude, a threat and a lesson for every action, and he wanted none of it. Where he was going with his payment from the French Emperor, he could put away all pretence at religious fervour and be free, blessedly free.

The painful flush fading, he smirked, thinking of the days of wealth and blessings to come. For a time, he had thought his plans would fail, but all he need do was continue to act decisively, as in the case of the beggars from Zudan. He knew that he could eventually torture his bride into telling him where the Jewels of Destiny were concealed, and his men, who had been scouring the desert for weeks now, would eventually find where the *kaffir* had hidden himself. Tracks could not be covered in such desiccating air, nor had there been any rush of rain to sweep them away. Soon, he would have all he wanted: the *kaffir's* head on a platter, which he would present to his bride as her marriage gift, and the Jewels of Destiny which he would take with him into his new life.

Freyha's grandson, Abdul, unable to sleep, had gone into the desert on foot, tugging his goatskin cloak around him for warmth. The stars were dull tonight, shrouded as if in mourning, and he felt their melancholy as if it were his own. He had been close to his grandmother, for his own mother had died giving birth to his brother, who had also died. The Beduin were close knit, especially where death was concerned. A child would be taken into the bosom of the nearest relative's family and treated as their own, and Freyha herself had raised Abdul with affection, wisdom and only occasional chastisement. He had been taught right from wrong at an early age, a lesson that would remain with him to the grave.

336

'You do not love a child if you fail to teach him right from wrong.' How often his grandmother had said that to him.

The stars had no intention of sloughing off their shrouds and the night air was keen and spiteful against his cheek. There would be a frost tonight, covering the land with its sparkling ivory chill. Such dramatic shifts of climate were what made the desert the challenging and unique place that he loved so dearly, for all its mysteries and dangers.

Freyha had loved it, too. He was thinking of her in the past tense, as if she were dead though he had no confirmation of it. They had been so very close; there had never been a day when she had not seized the chance to speak a word or two to him, however busy she was in the service of their mistress.

'Abdul, when are you going to choose a wife?' she would taunt him, her eyes bright with affection. 'I crave to be a great-grandmother and you deny me this. Have you not found a girl you can woo?'

'I have, but she is married to another,' he would say with a grin. Or 'I have, but she has spurned me'. And then his grandmother would prod him with her forefinger and urge him to make haste in his choice before all the prettiest girls were taken.

The truth was that he was inordinately shy, a rather reserved young man, and unless a girl approached him of her own accord he might well remain single. His grandmother had been losing patience; soon, she would have spoken with one of the men who was nearest to him in blood, instructing him to arrange a union with a suitable girl, and Abdul would have accepted her, whoever she was. If he did not, he knew that he would die a virgin.

Despite the cold blast of air, he blushed. He was twenty-three and all his friends were fathers, yet he had never taken a woman to his couch. He had dreamed of it

337

ceaselessly, aching for sexual union, aching to love and be loved, imagining a girl naked beside him, her soft, honey-scented body pressed to his, her mouth encircling his, rousing him with her voluptuous kisses. There was always a predictable finale to this mind image, but that could not be helped. He was young, and virile and gloriously healthy. Only his shyness incapacitated him.

The mystery of Freyha's disappearance had occupied his thoughts for some time now. He had tried to see the Amira, but was told that she was praying in readiness for her marriage. That was all that they had been told for days now: that she was praying, and would see no one. It was an acceptable excuse, but he had never known their mistress to refuse to see anyone who was in need. Her heart was big, and such warmth and generosity as hers could not vanish overnight.

He felt at one with the wilderness, allowing its silent, ancient ambience to close around him, clasping him as close as his goatskin cloak. From infancy he had been familiar with the desert in all its moods: the savagery of the *simûm*; the bone-chilling nights; the blazing, devouring sun of midday; the shocking deluges of rain that would lash down from the skies and just as swiftly cease, the land drying out within hours.

When he was a child, Freyha had walked with him, telling him of the wild beasts who roamed there, *el-Agab*, the small black eagle; the graceful gazelle, with its delicate limbs and highbred neck, the bustard, *habara*; *hosseny*, the sleek-limbed fox, the *jerboa*, and the *jelamy*, the brown lizard; the *sirruk*, that flew by night. One evening she had crept into the wilderness with him and together they had seen *Ymgebas*, the desert owl, hearing its chillingly melancholy cry and seeing its taut wings unfurled against the white satin orb of the moon.

His grandmother had taught him to love and respect all the creatures of the wild. 'They were here first,' she had told him, 'and you must respect their home.'

338

Where was she now, his grandmother, with her wisdom and her words of comfort? If only he knew that. Matters were awry in the camp, he could sense it. A woman might pray for weeks before her marriage to prepare herself, if it were her wish, but he had a strange feeling that all was not well with Zahra. It was true that the Amira's future husband was a powerful man and that his servants were rougher in their ways than had been expected, but an adaptation would be made for their mistress's sake. Her people had longed for her to marry, and now that she was about to do so, they could hardly grumble.

'Grandmother, where are you?' he asked the shadowy, spiteful cold, yet all was silence.

And then, muffled by distance, he heard the sound of hoofbeats, and knew that men were approaching the camp. Concealing himself behind a clump of rocks, he listened to their conversation as they passed him, their breath gusting like white smoke in the chilly air.

'They died like infants, all unknowing. I prefer a fight, a good, hard fight, and seeing them suffer. Yes, that is the best of it, when they cringe before me and beg for mercy.'

'You are a savage, Jadid. If they must die, they must die, it matters not how. The *Saiyid* said there must be no sound, and we obeyed him, did we not?'

'As we always do.' The first voice sounded bitter.

'Why are you complaining, Amair? *Billah*, but the *Saiyid* has cared for you well.'

'Yes, as long as we kill for him, he pampers us.'

'Would you have it any other way?'

'I thought that love might make his heart more tender, but I was wrong.'

'*Love?*' There was the harsh sound of a throat being cleared and sputum being ejected on to the sand. 'What has love got to do with it? He wants her land. He wants her treasures. If he gets her body, too, then all the better,

339

but he would marry a two-headed hag to gain such wealth.'

'Did she not pursue him?'

'Only because her people wished her to marry. She pleases them and he pleases himself, it is as simple as that. You do not believe in love, do you, Amair? *Allah*, but you are a simpleton! Love dupes a man so he can see neither what he is doing nor where he is going.'

'If the *Saiyid* is not in love, why did he have the Zudans put to death? What purpose was there behind such slaughter? They came to his tent and begged his aid, and he gave them food and shelter and then ordered that they be murdered. Why?'

'Never mind why. We obeyed him, and we shall continue to obey him. One day, if he wishes, we may know why he ordered us to kill them. But if he does not wish it, then we shall not know.'

The voices were receding, and Abdul could no longer hear them. White-cheeked, with sweat swimming down his face and body, he stayed slumped in the comforting shelter of the rock. The people who had come from Zudan, made guests of the Amir and given food and shelter, had been murdered? He could not believe what he had heard. The guest in the black tents was sacred; not one hair of his head must be harmed. It was the unspoken law and no man went against it. Yet Mahmed had. Why? *Why?*

If Mahmed had wanted to close their mouths, why was death the only answer? Could he not have taken them into the camp and found them work, as the Amira had done with others in similar straits? Was it not sensible to show his future wife's people that he could be magnanimous and benevolent? What could he gain by slaughtering the poorest amongst them?

Abdul wished he had not heard the men talking, the men with blood on their hands, for now he must act and in truth he did not know what he should do. He was a shy

340

man, a retiring man, and had never wished for anything other than a quiet, uneventful existence. And even if he went to the Amira's advisers, would they believe him? He did not know if he believed himself. It might have been a mirage. Was the land not famous for them? With all his heart he wished that he was back on his couch asleep, innocent of all this, not knowing, and thus not forced to fret over it. Allah, what should he do? Murdered? Why in the name of Allah had they been *murdered?*

The six Legionnaires rode through the baking, acrid dust of the desert, their eyes narrowed against the blazing sun above the horizon. At their head was their Captain, Paul de Broux, fair-haired, grey-eyed, almost pleasant of face but for the livid scar which marked one cheek. With his face turned to the right, nothing could be seen but smooth, tanned skin that made the grey eyes stand out sharply; with his face turned to the left, there was horror. It need not be said that he had failed to find himself a wife, failed even to find one woman prepared to love him, or attempt to love him. All were fearful of his scar; some thinking that their children would inherit it, some thinking that Paul de Broux would never make his way in life with such a disfigurement.

There had been no tragic accident; the scar had been with him from birth. With time, he had learned to live with it, but no woman had been able to extend her tolerance so far as to accept it. He had visited street women at the darkest hour of night, begging them not to light their lamps, and they had thought him shy when in truth he was petrified they might see him and shrink from him. Finally, at the age of seventeen, unhappy at home from continual arguments with his father, he had run away in search of the great adventure and a woman who would love him despite his ugliness.

He had found adventure of a kind, but also starvation,

and utter misery, so deep and despairing that he had almost returned home, but restrained himself. His father's angry, florid face would come to mind, and he would grit his teeth and vow that he would never seek that insufferable patronage again. He had heard of the Foreign Legion, of the army that asked no questions, sought out no secrets, taking its men beneath its wing for better or for worse. He had gone to them. Where else was there? He had trekked on foot to Marseille and signed away his freedom, believing as he did so that he had sought and found the greatest freedom of all.

The early days had been hard. Life in the Legion was violent, and the softer a man was, the more difficult the adaptation. Many times he had screamed silently for escape, but there was no escape. In his memory, his father's angry face had become a smiling, doting one and he had yearned to see it again. Yet a man fought or he went under, and de Broux had fought, desperately and savagely. Promotion had come fast, a small, steely consolation that did nothing to salve his inner wounds. How was it that he could feel more alone crammed into a hut with thirty men than he had ever done as an only child?

The desert echoed the savagery that had taken root in his heart, the only substitute for love and tenderness. Those bleak, brown dunes, lashed and flurried by the wind, that bald horizon turning to a murky coffee colour in the failing light, mirrored the same tendencies in his own nature, the pretence at gentility stripped away, the void laid bare.

He had volunteered for this sortie. Having fought the Arabs on many occasions before, he knew what he was letting himself in for. There was a small, pale joy in killing those of the infidel faith, although he had never had any faith of his own. The brandished knife, the blade slicing deep, the blood jetting out, the body falling lifeless, the spirit gone; these were his satisfactions now.

342

A Captain was missing, a man of legend and mystery, Mayne Amyan who had been doubly honoured for bravery in the field. He had gone to treat with the Amira of the Land of Mirages and had simply vanished. There had been no word from him now for over two months.

'Find him,' the General had said, 'find him and see what he is about. If he is dead, leave at once and return at full speed. While we await his despatches, we cannot proceed. We must know the truth.'

He had seen Amyan once from a distance. The brief glance had showed him a man with determination and strength etched deep into his features. A man to beware of if one was not on his side; a man who had never known fear. They might have been friends had they ever met.

The desert was more parched than he had expected, the last two oases waterless and deserted. For miles he had passed no one, and there was a sense of desolation to the terrain he had never before encountered, not even in the desert's heart. His men were uneasy, too, and running short of water. They would camp for the night and dig up roots to replace some vital fluid. It was an old campaigner's trick. They should reach the Amira's camp by midday next, and then he would know everything: where Amyan was, and why he had not sent back any despatches.

'Beware the woman. She thinks herself a queen, and she will make you kneel to her and kiss her skirts. But do it if the occasion merits – do anything that will help you discover where Captain Amyan is. If they have imprisoned him, offer terms for his freedom, generous terms. He is valuable to us.'

The General had mentioned a gigantic sum that sounded like a dazzling fortune to Paul de Broux. This was the amount that the Legion would be willing to pay if Mayne Amyan was a hostage of the Amira.

Night was chill and lonely, a waking dream of

343

discomfort and back-breaking stoniness. The roots they had dug had been bitter and unsatisfying. To a man, they dreamt of their favourite foods and craved ice cold water gushing down their throats. Sleep was difficult, and they woke feeling sore and out of sorts. Barely a word was spoken before they set out, knowing that in but a few hours they would meet with success or failure.

The camp looked much like any other Beduin camp, and the men grouped into neat formation before approaching it. Surly guards scanned their faces as closely as if they were lepers and one ran forward to take Paul de Broux's horse by the reins and shout something unintelligible in his face. Having some knowledge of Arabic, he gave the man a brief explanation of their presence.

'We have come to see your Amira, if she is willing to receive us. We have messages for her, and wish to ask for news.'

The Arab glared, wild black brows hunched over his high, hooked nose. He smelt of camels and rancid butter.

Eventually, after a long wait during which they were given nothing to slake their thirsts, the Arab returned and they were ushered into the camp as if they were welcome visitors. Food awaited them, and entertainment. The Amira herself would speak to them, they were told, and they were to be taken straight to her tent. Paul de Broux could not help but grin with relief. This was largesse indeed after their endurance of the desert's blazing heat, their heavy uniforms weighing them down like millstones.

The Amira's tent was decorated with fluttering banners. A guard stood before it, his arms folded before him. He looked relaxed and unconcerned. From inside the tent came the reedy sound of Arabian instruments. The entertainers were awaiting them!

Shoulders back, wishing he had been given the opportunity to wash the sweat and grit from his face and hands, Paul de Broux stepped inside the tent. His men followed slowly, awestruck. None of them had ever seen a desert queen in the flesh before and they had heard that this one was a virago: wilful, rebellious, intent on getting her own way. But it was also believed that she was a beauty. Would she be veiled? They could not wait to find out.

The music was playing gently, hypnotically, and the rich, tempting scent of freshly-brewed coffee pervaded the tent. A group of heavily veiled women, rather large-boned they thought, knelt in readiness to serve them with great platters of food. Their spirits rising, they looked around for the Amira but there was no sight of her. Instead, sitting regally upon a pile of brightly-coloured silk cushions, was a hook-nosed man who gestured them to come closer. Having no reason to disobey, they approached him.

The music grew louder, assaulting their eardrums. Their stomachs gurgled at the scent of the food, the coffee, the thought of any liquid to assuage their thirst. Paul de Broux thought that the man, whoever he was, looked pleasant enough; a little taciturn maybe, but nothing worse.

The interpreter came forward and the Captain, remembering his manners, bowed to him. The man began to speak, his voice high and squeaky, his command of French no command at all but a guessing game of words and phrases. Out of the hotch potch, Paul de Broux managed to decipher the name of the taciturn man. He was the Amir Mahmed ibn Beydoun, future husband of the Amira, and he would speak with the Legionnaires.

'What is it wishing for thee to know?' the interpreter squeaked. As tactfully as he was able, Paul de Broux explained that he wished to know the whereabouts of Captain Mayne Amyan, who had come to the Land of Mirages to discuss a peace treaty with the Amira.

All appeared to be going well until that moment, but upon hearing the name Amyan the Amir Mahmed shifted on his cushions and fresh red blood surged into his cheeks. The glowering expression vanished, to be replaced by savage fury. The dark eyes glinted murderously, the brown hand leapt to the hilt of his sword.

Involuntarily, Paul de Broux took a step backwards, feeling as he did so the boot of one of his men beneath his heel. The fool had come right up behind him! Turning his head, he was about to hiss a command when he registered that the face pushed into his had dark tanned flesh and slitted, venomous eyes. On a gasping inhalation of breath, he saw that his men were being taken prisoner. The large-boned Beduin women swathed in their heavy veils were men!

'Ya Saiyid!' he called out, turning back to beseech the Amir, but the man had leapt from his cushions, all pretence at indolence dismissed. In his broad brown hand was a great curving sword, Turkish in design, and before Paul de Broux could get his hand on his own sword, the shining, sweeping blade sliced through the air and hacked off his arm. Stunned, unbelieving, he felt the pressure, the smashing sensation of metal through bone, but there was no intolerable pain. He would not have known what had been done to him had he not staggered, looked down and seen his bloody arm lying on the ground before him, the fingers still twitching in search of his sword.

The Amir looked delighted; his eyes danced. Up came the curving sword again, and down, and Paul de Broux's other arm thudded to the ground. That was when he fell, his legs turned to tissue beneath him, his life blood draining away. Strange that he could feel no pain, just a warm, wet sensation as he was drenched in his own blood. The Amir was standing over him now, steadying his boot on his victim's windpipe. He was grinning with

346

happiness. Then his face blurred and faded, receding into darkness. Paul de Broux lay still.

The reed-like music had stopped some time ago but no one had noticed. Seeing their Captain hacked to death, the Legionnaires struggled valiantly to escape, but the veiled 'women' who held them were powerfully built, and had no intention of letting them go free. They were holding them in readiness for their master's sword practice.

Mahmed, who had been awaiting the Legionnaires for half a day, ever since his scouts had spotted them far in the distance, dragged his eyes from the Captain's bloody corpse. These men had been doomed from the moment they had ridden into the Land of Mirages. What, let them live and return to their General with tales of drought and famine, and the disappearance of Mayne Amyan? To do that would be to invite invasion, and then all chances of his conciliation efforts with France would be gone. He would kill the fools, the craven infidels, and bury them at dead of night along with all the others he had slaughtered.

The curving sword sang through the air, once, twice, and another Legionnaire's arms were sliced from his body, and then the man was pushed down, forced to kneel, and the sword swept through his neck, a sure, successful movement that ended life on the instant. Blood jetted, eyelids flickered, the mouth opened and closed twice as if attempting speech, and then the head rolled to a stop and lay still.

'Non, non!' the remaining Legionnaires screamed, kicking out, trying to butt with their heads, jerking backwards and forwards in their desperate efforts to escape. They might have been small, weak children fighting giants. One after the other, in ruthless, delighted silence, Mahmed beheaded them. He welcomed this unexpected opportunity for sword practice, his happiness increasing as each man died. By now, his robe was soaked in fresh scarlet blood, and the tent was filled with the strong, metallic odour of it.

When all six were dead, he wiped his sword on the hem of his robe and sheathed it. The treaty was safe; his plans would succeed. It was as if these Legionnaires had never been.

Zahra was still drowsy when the tent flap was thrown back and a gust of frost-laden dawn wind enveloped her. Shivering, she sat up, trying to see in the darkness and wishing that she had left a lamp alight.

'Who is there?' she called, thinking that one of the guards was staring at her for his own pleasure. Mahmed's men were morose and grimly countenanced, one never knew what they were thinking, but she supposed that like all men they had their share of normal human passions. Not that she feared them. Ferocious and brutal they might look, but she would never let them see that they made her flesh crawl when they came near her.

'Who is there?' she called out again, and then the lamp flared into life and by its gathering brightness, the scent of oil strong in her nostrils, she saw Mahmed standing before her.

He was wearing a loose robe, and over it a black woollen cloak with a hood that was pulled close about his head. Once she had thought him so handsome, an attractive and gallant young man, but now she saw what lay beneath that façade and was sickened. It was as if she saw the very bones of his skull decaying before her, the worms creeping in and out of the eyeless sockets, the stench of putrefaction drowning out the powerful odour of the lamp oil.

Shivering again, she pulled her goatskin around her.

'We shall soon be man and wife,' he began, and to her surprise there was a slight tremor in his voice. *Daheelek!* He had not come to rape her! Of all things, that was the last she had expected of him. There had never been an excess of virility about him; rather the opposite, in fact.

'I know that,' she said through clenched teeth. 'Did you wake me just to tell me that?'

He went on as if he had not heard her.

'A wife must always obey her husband. Is that not so?'

'A loving wife may obey a loving husband, if she so chooses.'

'There are no qualifications! A wife must always obey her husband, it is the law by which we live.'

'Hypocrite. You no more care for the law than you care for me!'

Stung that she should thus see through him, he snarled and snatched her wrist, clamping it in ruthless fingers.

'That is a lie, woman. I respect the laws of Allah, as you will, too. If you do not, then I shall *make* you respect them.'

'Is it Allah's laws that are under discussion, or your laws, Mahmed ibn Beydoun? Or are they one and the same in your confused mind?'

She could see so clearly into him, as if he were made of glass, his entire character painted upon the surface in primary colours.

'Now tell me truly why you are here at this hour? If it is to frighten me into submission, then you are wasting your time.'

'Will you run from me, then?' he sneered. 'How far would you get with chains on your ankles?'

Furious, she tried to pull her hand away from his, but there was little chance that she would succeed. There was the bright, steely light of madness in his eyes, and inwardly she shrank. He squeezed harder, not caring that he was crushing her bones together until the intolerable pain made her want to scream out loud, but she would not give him that pleasure. She would be stoic to the end.

'Tell me where they are!' he growled, snatching at her

other wrist and pinioning it mercilessly. 'You think *I* am the fool, but you are! Your servant is dead because you would not tell me where they are hidden, and you will die too if you do not tell me.'

'And then you will never know, will you!' she taunted him, tossing her head so that a waterfall of ebony hair rippled around her shoulders.

'So there *are* some left! You were lying to me, just as I thought!'

'Lying? Pretending that there are some left, or that there are none – which do you mean?'

'You bitch! That there were none – you know full well what I mean. Now tell me where they are, or I will break your wrist.'

'There are none left. I told you that there are none left. Break my wrist if you dare! I shall scream so loudly that –'

His hand clamped violently across her mouth, and she could smell his flesh, rancid from eating buttery *pilaf* with his fingers. One of his rings cut her lip and she tasted blood, but that did not prevent her from biting deep into the crevice between his thumb and forefinger, and then it was he who yelled, and his blood that dripped.

'Mad bitch!' he bellowed, nearly knocking her unconscious with a blow to her face that made her teeth rattle, her neck click. Dazed, she glared back at him, teeth bared, but as she readied herself for his next blow she saw his face change, the snarl turn to lechery, and the next moment he was tearing off his robe and before she fully realised his intent, he had thrown himself on top of her and his fingers were buried deep between her thighs.

Mayne had spent the morning bathing at the oasis, mystified by his returning strength. He had felt as weak and wretched as ever while in the vault, yet as soon as he staggered out into the sun and saw the verdant little oasis awaiting him, he was reborn. The waters were as mellow as before, lapping around him welcomingly, and he swam and dived joyously, his exhaustion forgotten.

Deep in the gentle silken waters were fish of every size and hue, so that when he dipped his head below the surface he saw flashing colours, green and crimson stripes, dazzling silver spotted with blue, deepest rose spangled with silver, and a myriad of tiny, pallid gold fish that darted first one way and then another. Diving deeper, his foot stirred the murky depths and something moved, something not so attractive as the coloured shoals. He saw a fat coiled creature unravelling itself, the smooth broad head rising and two slanting, glittering eyes steadily considering him.

He had never moved so fast, twisting in the water and breaking to the surface to fling himself on to the flower-jewelled sand that surrounded the pool. There he lay, recouping his strength and eventually giving a shout of laughter. When had he been scared of the wild beasts of earth and water? All his life he had loved and venerated them, from the most gentle to the most ferocious. Would the water snake be any more vicious than a wildcat? He doubted it. Next time, he would not flee like a coward.

When he felt restored, he gathered berries and herbs to feed him on his journey to Zahra's camp. When he looked up at one of the palms, he saw that more dates were ready for picking, well before their usual season. He climbed up the tree to reach the first clusters, grinning as he cut them down with the Sword of God. Then, turning his head to view the terrain again, he saw the riders in the distance, seven of them, robed in black and sitting astride white *dhaluls*. He thought instantly of Mahmed and his racing camels, and knew that discovery was frighteningly close.

The riders had stopped where they were and seemed to be surveying the ruined temple doubtfully. Of course, he reminded himself hopefully, it was taboo to them with their anathema to idols and graven images, but

351

they had dismounted and were examining the tracks in the sand. Cursing beneath his breath, Mayne wished that he had gone back to cover them, but he had never thought for one moment that anyone would come so close. Superstition ruled the desert nomads. Even in the most familiar areas, they believed that *jinn* lay in wait to attack and deceive them, but these were riders who must have been travelling for days and they would want to refresh themselves at the oasis.

There was no way that he could retrace his steps without being seen. There was a naked expanse of sand between the oasis and the temple, and the men were gazing directly at it. As he considered his next move, he saw them remounting and turning their beasts in his direction.

She knew that she would have nightmares about this for days to come, yet there was nothing she could do to prevent it. Mahmed was breathing in great, heaving gasps, his face scarlet, his hair tangled over his eyes while she was hampered by the chains that manacled her feet together. If only she could have kicked him away, but she could not. She tried raising her knees together and aiming them at his groin, but he threw himself to one side and hooked his leg around her waist so that she was clamped to the couch.

Beating at him with her fists, she began to scream again for her guards, her own faithful men who had served her all her life, but Mahmed proceeded to tear open her robe, rending it with his bare hands. When he had gathered a suitable piece of material, he thrust it into her mouth, forcing it almost into her throat so that she gagged.

'Your guards will not come. They have been told that their mistress wishes to see no one until her marriage day – she is praying devoutly.'

Zahra tried to scream again, but the moment she

opened her mouth, the clotted material sank deeper into her throat and she retched painfully.

Regardless of her discomfort, Mahmed pushed himself against her, crushing his hips to hers and squeezing her breasts so fiercely that the tears came to her eyes, but the more she squirmed or struggled, the more she roused him and so she forced herself to lie still. As still as if she were dead.

For a time, he continued, pressing at her breasts and sucking them hard until the nipples were raw and red. His fingers delved voraciously between her thighs, probing deep inside her. Then he lay back for a moment, his breath rasping in his throat. When her eyes cleared of tears, she was able to see that he was no longer aroused. A miracle! He was unable to complete the act. He could not rape her. She wanted to laugh out loud, but dared not move nor show that she had seen. If she commented on his impotence, who knew what vengeance he would take?

Yet she was Queen here, and Queen she would remain. This was her land, her heritage, her dominion, and no brutal, avaricious cur was going to deprive her of it.

Pulling the cloth from her mouth, she swallowed to moisten her tongue and gain the strength to speak. Then, looking at Mahmed directly in the eyes, she said: 'Allah watches over me. Dare to rape me and you will pay for it. You forget where you are. This is Allah's land, and He rules here before me or any mortal. Those who wish to put themselves before Him will have the price exacted from them, whether they wish to pay or no.'

Mahmed stared back at her, his mouth hanging open as if his wits had fled. She saw fear and loathing in his eyes, and in that moment she knew what he truly thought of her, and perhaps all women save those who were humble and worshipful of him and who bent their knee to him as if he were a Sultan.

353

He was only half a man. The least sign of spirit or hostility from a woman and he shrank, literally, bested by any who did not sprawl before him and kiss the hem of his robe. And there was the spirit within him of a sad, weeping child. It haunted him, driving reason and tolerance from his mind. The child stood at his shoulder now, the tears streaming down her face. For a few brief, unnerving seconds, Zahra saw her clearly, and then she was gone, but in those seconds, she knew all that there was to know about the man who lay beside her – that he was the most despicable man who had ever lived, and that he was an unbeliever.

'Why do you look at me like that?' he growled, trying to gather the shreds of some pride around himself. 'You are repugnant to me. You cannot rouse a man; you do not know how, and your body is noxious. You are tainted by your sinfulness. Get from me, harlot!'

For answer, Zahra continued to stare at him, saying nothing yet knowing all. Finally he gathered up his robe, pulled his cloak about him, and slipped out into the night.

When he had gone, Zahra tried to collect herself but it was no easy task. Valour in the face of horror faded fast when the horror had gone. Now she began to shake from head to foot, and tears of reaction spurted from her eyes. What if he had succeeded? Dear God, what if he had succeeded? Not until that moment had she realised how much she loathed him, and how impossible it would be for her to adapt to sharing his couch. To think that she would have to lie with him, night after night, for the rest of her life....

'*Allah*, were you truly with me as I felt You were,' she whispered into her pillow. 'Were You watching over me?' She had been sure of it then but now doubt set in. Why should He have protected her after His punishment of her previous temerity? Surely it was luck alone that had saved her? And yet where did fortune come from if not from the most benevolent God of all?

354

Pillowing her head in her arms, she breathed deeply, forcing the tremors to leave her body. After a great effort she slept, and once again her dreams took her back in time.

The Oasis of Stars had never looked more lush and enchanting, and she was in her lover's arms again, his blue-green flecked eyes laughing down at her, his arms braiding her so close she knew nothing could ever harm her again.

'Must we leave here, my warrior?' she was saying, and he was shaking his head.

'We can stay here for as long as we wish. Have we not been together like this for centuries? What will a few more minutes matter? No one is watching.'

'What of the stars?'

'They sleep during daylight, and would you deprive them of their reason for being? They are here to guide us, to bring lovers together and act as their guardians. That is why they are above us, and we are below.'

Dananir had said that to him. In remembering her words and repeating them thus, he was ensuring her immortality. All those who have ever loved are reborn in each new generation of lovers.

'An astrologer drew up my chart when I was born. It is the custom in the East. He told my mother and father that I would rule as Queen one day, that I would be Queen of more than they could ever visualise when I was an infant. They were not too sure what he meant, for my father had no intention of making war on his neighbours and thus adding to his territories. He would always defend but never attack without good reason.'

'And what else did the astrologer have to say? That you would be the most beautiful Queen who had ever ruled the Land of Mirages, and that you would be more deeply loved than any other? That you would be open-hearted and wise and adorable?' Gently, he tilted her chin

355

with his forefinger, their eyes meeting and holding fast.

'You speak like a man bewitched.'

'No, like a man who sees the truth and will not be denied.'

'Mayne, no one has ever loved me as you do, accepted me as I am, without conditions or complaint.' She twisted in his arms, resting her head against his chest where it loved to lie.

'And no one has ever loved me as you do, so generously and with such understanding. Oh, if you could have seen me before we met! Ruthless and raw, racked with torments and longings I thought would never be stilled. Like too many men, I thought that destruction was the answer, that in killing I would find release, but now I know the truth.'

'That love is the answer? I have always known that. How could I have learned anything else with my mother and father loving one another as they did? Love was there before me every day of my life.'

'But sometimes you felt excluded from that charmed circle?'

'Oh, yes. They were always one in their thoughts, their hopes and dreams, and even though my mother spoke her mind and sometimes there were bitter disagreements, in the end they always made it up. It was better for me when they argued because then I could comfort them both, and they would notice me as they never did normally. Most days, they had eyes only for one another.'

'I never had the benefit of loving parents. I was raised in a hovel by a mother whom I never understood. I was harsh to her and blamed all the world's ills on her because she had refused to marry my father. I think I told you that he was a Catholic and she was a Muslim. She put her God first.'

'As we all must, my warrior.' Lifting her head, Zahra met his eyes.

'For many years, I denied Him. How could there be a God when I had suffered so? The Catholic religion could not be more different from ours. They worship the Prophet Christ and His Mother.'

'But they worship the same God! Oh, if only the world could understand, if only all the different religions would come together and stop their wrangling. They are like greedy, spoilt brats who want the best for themselves and hate any who differ.'

'But God made them all, and they must see the truth eventually.'

'Mayne, you have a philosopher's heart, and I love you!'

Why were they talking when the sun was shining just for them, and the oasis lay around them so ravishingly beautiful? As their mouths touched, they heard the answering response of nature, the mellifluous cooing of birds, the plash of silvered fish in the pool, the rustle of the acacia trees as a warm, soothing breeze lulled their branches.

'Say it again, my beloved, tell me that we need never be parted again,' Zahra sighed. 'Tell me over and over, until I can believe it.'

'We shall never be parted again, my honey. We are one, joined together body and soul, and there is no one who can separate us.'

'Body and soul?'

'Body and soul.'

Zahra stirred in her sleep as dawn approached, but the dream lovers kissed and caressed one another, curving their bodies close, eager to give and take all they could, devouring one another with love, and as Mayne slid inside her, exultant at the rightness of it all, his eye was caught by the flashing fire of rubies, the golden collar at her neck and the twisting black ringlets that tumbled onto it, and he knew that there could be no greater or more abiding love than that which had lasted almost two thousand years.

And Zahra, adoring the man who had once been King of the East, raked her fingers through his thick black hair and kissed his kohl-rimmed eyes, his powerful curving cheekbones and proud, arched nose; and then his throat where the symbol of the Venus star hung from its heavy gold chain, the symbol of death and rebirth, for Venus is the brightest star in the east, visible before sunrise in the morning and first to appear at night. Under the name of Athtar it was worshipped by the Palmyrans at the time of Zenobia and Odenathus, together with the Moon Goddess herself.

To please their gods Odenathus wore the symbol of Venus and Zenobia wore, on her forehead where it shone as if her flesh were of polished platinum, the bright, curving crescent of the moon, for those were the days when the Heavens were theirs and the firmament their protector.

They held one another tightly, thrusting hip against hip, eager to be satiated and yet wishing that this ecstasy need never end, coiling their arms around one another's necks and lying entwined like the serpents that were sacred to their Lady Goddess. It seemed that hours passed and yet no time at all as they revelled in their profound intimacy, sharing the same heart, the same breath, the same blood.

Passionate, they arched together, ever closer, ever deeper, he plunging into the dark, moist cave that proclaimed her womanhood, and she drawing him in with glad relish.

'My beloved warrior,' she sighed against his cheek.

'My little Queen, will you take me now?' His voice was urgent, raw with desire.

'Yes, my beloved, yes, yes!' she sighed against his cheek.

And as they gave all they had to one another, they became truly one, joined for all eternity, and the heavens and the firmament were theirs once more.

Chapter Twenty-one

Next morning, at dawn, the torture began again. Zahra woke from her heavenly dreams to see Mahmed standing over her, his arms folded. Gripped in his right hand was a whip with a plaited leather handle.

'How dare you come in here without permission!' she cried, hastily sitting up and pulling her goatskin higher to screen her flimsily-clad body from his gaze. 'Murderer!'

She had been thinking of poor Freyha, but his reaction to her accusation was startling. He turned a wan, sickly greenish colour and his eyes slid away from hers.

'Murderer of poor helpless old women!' she accused, hoping that if she continued in this vein he would be frightened away, but he was not. He seemed to brighten, his shoulders squaring, his fingers grasping the whip more tightly. 'Get out, do you hear me, get out!' she cried.

'Will you say the same to me on our marriage couch, woman?' His voice was a sneer.

'Our marriage is not yet law!'

'But when it is, you will come to me willingly, lovingly, as a wife should?' His eyes flickered.

'In the name of Allah, have we not been through all this before? Why do you come here to goad me, Mahmed? You know full well how things are between us.'

'Do I? I know how you have decided how you think

things should be, but it would seem that you refuse to listen to my viewpoint. I was told that you were a wilful vixen, a scold and a liar, and I have not yet learned anything to change my mind.'

'Then go home, Mahmed ibn Beydoun, go home to your own people and find yourself a bride who is more pleasing to you!' Pulling the goatskin closer, Zahra leaned back as Mahmed took a step towards her.

'I have found her, and she is the one I desire.'

'As you desired her last night?' Zahra could not keep the contempt from her voice as she referred to Mahmed's impotence, but his expression altered as she spoke, changing from gloating to frozen disbelief that she should challenge him in this way. 'You will have to do better than that, Amir of the Wasteland, or our marriage will remain an empty sham!'

'Bitch!' The livid colour throbbed in his face as he lashed the whip down on her, catching her a stinging blow on the shoulder.

'*Bîllah!* You will pay for that, you villain!' Zahra cried, but as the second blow landed, cutting through her thin robe and fetching blood, she knew that she was in serious danger.

'You will pay first, bitch. Tell me where you have hidden the Jewels of Destiny. Tell me, or I shall mark you for life!'

'I told you that they have all been sold to benefit my land. What more can I say? They have gone to other lands, to Persia and India – to England! Victoria, the Sultana of England, now wears one of the diamonds in her crown. They were bought by an Indian Rajah who gave them to her as a gift. If you seek the Jewels of Destiny then you will have to travel far and wide to find them, and pay the asking price.'

'I do not believe you! You are lying to me, and I shall make you tell me the truth if I have to beat you to a bloody pulp!'

'You are wasting your time, Mahmed, there is nothing more to tell.'

'When we are married, the day after tomorrow, the jewels will be mine, all of them.'

'You cannot own what does not exist,' Zahra retorted, but her heart jolted. This was the first that she had heard of their marrying so soon. Had all the guests replied? The last time Mahmed had mentioned them, only three or four days before, he had been railing at their slowness to respond.

'But they do exist, and you are going to tell me where they are!' Raising the whip once more, Mahmed glared at her and she saw the flickering, dilated eyes of a man on the verge of total disintegration.

'I tell you that they have killed the people from Zudan! If they are still alive, where are they? They were weak from thirst and their long trek; they could not have survived the return journey to their home!'

'Maybe that is what he ordered. Maybe he knew that they would die so he ordered them out into the desert while we all slept.'

Freyha's grandson, Abdul, and old Abidul, Zahra's scribe, after whom the boy had been named in the hopes that the old man's skills would be reborn in him, were sitting by the camp fire waiting for water to boil so that Abidul's great-granddaughter Amaliya could make their coffee. The day was harsh with the taint of approaching winter; they could taste it in their mouths and scent it in their nostrils, but as yet there had been no rains. Zudan, Bakasir, Kubistan and the Oasis of Rajab were amongst the worst hit where the drought was concerned, but so far their camp had continued to find water when necessary, and for such everyday tasks of hair washing there was always camels' urine, sweetly scented with herbs as it was from the animals' diet.

'Either way, why should he do it? They say that our

Queen is praying in readiness for her marriage, and that is good, yet have you not noticed how things have changed here, Abidul?'

The old man sighed. His sight was failing, although pride dictated that he should tell no one of it. How could a scribe write for his Queen when he could not see? He would be retired, and have to spend the rest of his days sucking on his teeth and remembering the past while Amaliya waited on him as if he were an invalid.

'I have been occupied these past days and I have noticed nothing.'

'Did you not wonder where Freyha has gone? Did she not come to your tent twice weekly with messages from our Queen?'

'Yes, she used to do that, it is true, but our Queen would not send messages if she is praying, would she, ignorant boy? She shuts herself away to purify her soul in readiness, as her mother did before her thirty years ago. It is a great step to marry a man from another tribe.'

'I know all that, but would Freyha not come anyway? She never missed speaking a word or two to me, not by one day, and yet I have not seen her now for almost a week. When I have asked after her, everyone says the same – that they have not seen her.'

'Then she is praying with her mistress.'

'With respect, my grandmother would not abandon the tasks that she has undertaken for the Amira for over two years now. Every day she would choose her food and prepare it, mix her sherbets, fetch oil for her lamps, take messages, and collect them, yet this has not been done for nearly a week.'

'The Amira is without food?' Abidul's eyes opened wide in disbelief.

'No, she is not without food, yet no one from our camp takes it to her. Ask Amaliya if she knows of anyone who takes food to the Amira. I have asked her, and she says she knows of no one. All the Amira's food is taken to her by one of Mahmed's guards!' Abdul lowered his voice, leaning forward conspiratorially so that the bubbling water and the hissing steam would drown out what he said.

'Why should that be alarming?' Abidul looked puzzled.

'Do you not find it odd that our mistress has apparently abandoned her own servants in favour of her future husband's?'

'She is practising diplomacy, my boy. It is an art much favoured in a wife. Mahmed is an ill-tempered man, I have seen him scowling and glowering about the camp. The Amira wishes to sweeten his mood by showing that she accepts his people without condition.'

'*Shaikh*, you have known our mistress many years, and spoken to her frequently. Would you say that she would behave in this peremptory fashion without telling us of her plans? Does she not usually announce her intentions? How did her women learn that their services were no longer required? Did the Amira tell them herself?'

'I believe that she did, but Amaliya will tell us. She and the women have been discussing it, I know.'

When Abidul's great-granddaughter sat between them, the coffee in readiness on a tray, the scribe asked her what the women had been saying.

'Were they offended when their mistress told them that she did not want them to wait on her ever again, or was it just for the few days before the marriage?'

'Oh, but she did not tell them, Grandfather. They went to her tent as usual, and so did the musicians, but they were turned away.'

'By whom?' The old man looked startled.

'By two of the Amir's guards, but it was on the Amira's orders, they said. They were quite amiable and I believe that they flirted with Fatima and her sister and a romance is growing between them, but I should not have told you that, Grandfather, for Fatima's father does not yet know.'

363

'There, you see, Abdul, your fears are groundless. The guards acted on the orders of the Amira, and they are normal healthy men from the sounds of it.'

'Has anyone ever said that assassins are sexless, *shaikh*?' Abdul was flushed now, quite convinced that he was right yet seeing that he was getting nowhere with the old man. 'Because a guard flirts with a girl it does not mean that he is a good man, and plans nothing more serious than marriage to one of our people! I tell you, I heard them talking of the people of Zudan, and of their murder, deliberate murder by order of Mahmed!'

Abidul sighed, his coffee cooling in his pouched and wrinkled hands.

'All this talk of murder is upsetting to me at my age.'

'But even more upsetting to the ones who have been brutally slain!'

'Are you quite positive you heard what you did, Abdul? You were not half asleep or drunk on fermented date juice?' Amaliya asked the question, taking both old man and youth by surprise, but before Abidul could order her into silence and tell her that the matter was men's concern and not hers, Abdul replied fervently: 'Yes, quite sure. They murdered the Zudans while they slept and then took their bodies away for burial.'

'Then there will be some signs left in the tents where they slept, will there not? A blood stain or two, or the signs of struggle perhaps?' Amaliya looked from the face of the old man to the face of the young one whom she had secretly adored for almost a year now but from whom, being too shy to speak out first to him – although a Beduin girl may always do that – she had concealed her feelings.

'Yes, that could well be so!' Abdul's expression had brightened and he seemed to be looking at Amaliya with new eyes. She was small and plump and her long carob-brown hair was neatly plaited, one fat braid on either side of her heart-shaped face. Her eyes were slanting, and a rich luminous brown, her nose was slightly tiptilted, her mouth broad and generous. He knew that she cared devotedly for her great-grandfather, that her mother had died when she was born, and that her father had died soon after in a fall from a horse so she was an orphan like him, but he had never truly looked at her with the seeing eye.

How many times had she made him coffee when he called to chat with the old man, and how many times had he taken it from her hands and never looked into her face or smiled at her because of his own acute shyness? And now she was proving that she had a good mind, too, a sharp and logical mind. He was almost breathless at the revelation, not knowing where to look as her bright brown eyes sought his, yet wanting to look only at her. His heart thumping painfully, he lowered his head to sip his drink, but some went down the wrong way and he ended up choking, with Amaliya slapping him on the back and showing a great deal of concern for his discomfort.

Eventually they decided on a plan of investigation. Amaliya, as a woman, could go to the tents where the Zudans had slept and pretend to be trimming the oil lamps or clearing out rubbish. There, under the pretext of polishing and cleaning, she could search for bloodstains or anything else suspicious, and report back to the two men.

'Be careful, my dearest.' The old man kissed her smooth cheek, and in his heart Abdul was doing the same, not knowing that she too longed for his kiss.

The whip had cut her arm and breast and the pain was unbearable, making her see flashing stars before her, but she would not show her fear. Zahra knew now that nothing would force her into marriage with this appalling man; there was no place in her land for one who sought to have by brutal force what could quite easily

365

have been gained by tenderness and understanding.

Her loathing was shimmering in her eyes as she saw the whip descend for a fifth time, only the goatskin protecting her from its lash. She could not run for her ankles were chained and even the slowest movement was fraught with problems, but hidden beneath her pillow was a small yet deadly knife that she had concealed from the guards. If Mahmed came near enough, she would drive that knife, small as it was, directly into his heart.

With polishing rags and a flask of lamp oil, Amaliya began her work, first attending to two tents where the Zudans had not slept, for she did not wish to draw attention to what she was doing. By mid-morning, she was in the second tent where the Zudans had spent the night, the first having revealed nothing for it was clean and neat as if someone had already swept it out and put it to rights. The second tent had a strange scent which she soon identified as that of clove oil. She remembered the man, Mikhail ibn Zalir, whose height had caught her attention. His had been a noble face, despite his haggard appearance after his ordeal.

Her great-grandfather had instructed her to ask the Zudans if there was anything they required apart from the food and drink that was being taken to them before they rested. Mikhail ibn Zalir had said that he was suffering from raging toothache, and so her great-grandfather had sent him a vial of clove oil. She had taken it to him personally, and he had thanked her with a warmth that belied the exhaustion he must have been feeling. Somehow, the clove oil had been spilled, and in this tent. Had Mikhail ibn Zalir been holding it to his throbbing tooth when the assassins burst in to finish him?

The hair on the nape of her neck lifted involuntarily, and she could not prevent herself from looking over her shoulder, imagining some shadowy figure waiting to leap out on her. But there was nothing, just the powerful, cloying odour of cloves.

Going about her work, she checked the oil in the two lamps suspended on chains and began to polish their surfaces, humming beneath her breath to try and allay her sensation of uneasiness.

Mikhail ibn Zalir had been a good man, an honest man, she had seen that despite the brevity of their meeting. He had brought his people here in appalling circumstances, expecting to find succour, and instead he had found what? Perhaps she was growing accustomed to the scent of cloves for it seemed to have faded. Now she could smell something else, equally strong yet nowhere near as innocuous. All women are familiar with the scent of blood; to them it is associated with new life, their woman's time each month – and death. Was that strange rusty, sickly smell in the tent caused by blood that had been shed here?

Amaliya wanted to run. Her heart was banging and there was a choking, stifling sensation gathering in her breast. Sweeping up her cloths with shaking fingers, she prepared to leave. Then she realised that she could not return to her great-grandfather with nothing more than talk of a strange scent in the air. She wanted to have concrete proof for Abdul, something that would make him look at her again in that awe-filled, admiring way. A year she had waited for him to speak, hoping that he would notice her, but all that time she had been nothing more to him than the young girl who handed him his coffee and his bread when he came to speak to her great-grandfather. Now she had the opportunity to make him remember her for the rest of their lives.

Turning back into the tent, she began to search, lifting up rugs and examining the hangings that concealed the storage area at the back. There was nothing. Then she realised something. The sandy floor of this tent had once been covered by a wide coffee brown carpet, on which rugs had been strewn for extra comfort. Now the carpet was a different colour.

Amaliya lifted the edge of the new carpet and rolled it back a few feet, her arms aching. Beneath was only the protective mat that kept out damp, and she could see no stains on it. Trying again, from another side of the carpet, she had the same result. She was wasting her time – and what if one of the Amir's guards came in and caught her? Just one more try, and then she must get out of this ill-omened tent.

Beneath the third area of carpet there was so much blood that Amaliya caught her breath as if it were she who had been bleeding, unknown to herself. Someone had attempted to wipe it clean, but the stain was there, a deep red brown, clotted in places to the new carpet so that she had to pull hard to raise it. This was the area where they had been sleeping, this very spot where she now knelt in horror.

'Allah, save us all!' she gasped beneath her breath, and then a shadow darkened the entrance to the tent. Eyes dilated with fear, she crouched where she was, not daring to look up.

'A woman who thinks she can best a man is the unhappiest in the world. It is woman's place to obey man, to listen to his wisdom and heed his advice. That is why you are marrying me.' Mahmed stood over a white-faced Zahra, talking quite reasonably, the whip still in his hand.

'Never!' she gasped, her voice faint.

'If you do not marry me, you will be dishonoured in the eyes of your people.'

'According to you, I already am!'

'You will have gone back on your word and broken your betrothal vow, and no man will have you after that.'

'Just as well, because I want no man,' she retaliated.

368

'Save you, my darling Mayne, save you!' she silently added.

'The time has passed for words. What are words beside actions? You have strung me along all these months but now I am master here.'

She wanted to hiss, 'Then prove it if you can, you cur!' but his hand was over her mouth, his eyes riveted to the trickle of blood that was spilling from the cut on her breast. He seemed mesmerised by the sight, kneeling to press his mouth to the cut, his tongue digging and probing at her bleeding flesh. That was when the chills began, scraping over her flesh like dragging fingernails. He seemed to have lost his senses completely and she was in terrible danger of her life, she sensed it.

Where was the knife? Carefully, so as not to distract him, she felt for it beneath the pillow with her left hand, her heart leaping as her fingers closed around its slender hilt. Slowly, she brought her hand round, positioning it above his back as he leant over her. Then, with all her might, she brought the knife flashing downwards – only to hear the clatter of metal on metal as it met the steel corselet that Mahmed was wearing beneath his robe.

Furious that she had failed, she tried to drive the dagger into him from another point but he caught her hands, squeezing them so brutally that the knife fell from her nerveless fingers. He fell on top of her, crushing her to her couch, and she thought from the murderous look in his eyes that he intended to kill her there and then. She knew his secret now: he lived in fear of being assassinated.

Crying out, she brought up her knees to drive them deep into his lower belly while twisting her head from side to side to try and avoid his blows. One after another they rained down on her, fuelled by an outpouring of suppressed venom, and yet he seemed to be aroused by her determination to fight back. His eyes had the glazed look of lust and it was no surprise to her when she felt

369

what pressed against her thigh, thin and hard and seeking.

Scrabbling for the fallen dagger, she found it and Mahmed lunged away, thinking she would try again to kill him. Instead, she pressed it to her own throat and said, 'Move one inch closer and I take my own life. Then you will have nothing, Mahmed. You will be hunted down for the rest of your life. My people will not rest until you are executed in avengement for my death!'

Mahmed wavered uncertainly, not daring to move in case she carried out her threat, seeing the destruction of all his plans if she died now, while Zahra waited to see what he would do next, sharp pains spearing through her face and shoulder from his whip lashes and blows, and the lights from the oil lamps seeming to shimmer and dance tauntingly before her gaze.

'Abdul! You nearly scared the life out of me!' White with relief, Amaliya staggered shakily to her feet and almost fell into his arms.

'I am sorry, Amaliya, so sorry!' But he was not being entirely truthful because Amaliya was sheltering in his arms as if he were the strongest protector in the entire world, and her eyes were shining up at him. 'I had to make sure that you were safe.'

'It was as you thought, Abdul. See, there beneath the carpet there is blood. Look, they tried to clean it but they were in such haste that they left the drying stain. Abdul, there was murder here. Those poor Zudans were murdered in this tent!'

In her fear and shock her voice had risen, and Abdul gently put his hand over her mouth to quieten her. Then, his own heart thumping, he knelt down to examine the stains. When he had done so to his satisfaction, he tossed back the carpet and led Amaliya out of the tent. Grasping her hand tightly and with his arm around her shoulders, he gazed down on her with
370

love-filled eyes so that if they should be seen it would be thought they had slipped inside the tent for a few moments of stolen loving.

Amaliya, who guessed the reason for his actions, at first thought he was play acting entirely. And then, to her astonished delight, she realised that there was affection in his eyes, and that the hand that held hers was shaking with genuine emotion.

Mayne could not understand it. The riders proceeded to gallop towards the ruined temple without pausing to refresh themselves at the oasis where he was hiding. He had never known such a thing. Anyone in the desert, especially out here in this wilderness, usually could not wait to drink from even the muddiest of puddles. And yet Mahmed's men had ridden past the shining pool, the fertile trees begemmed with luscious dates, the tender, succulent herbs and berries that grew by the water's edge. Were they blind?

He was relieved they had not stopped but remained hidden in the branches of the palm tree, positive that they would stop for water on their return.

He watched them, knowing that this place was considered taboo by the local people who never approached the pagan temple for fear of the wrath of Allah. He expected them to turn back at the door but they did not. And then he felt the cold clutch of horror as he remembered what he had left down in the vault, the proof that he was hiding there: the goatskin and his Legionnaire's uniform. Thank God he had kept the Sword of God with him! Already he felt as if he had wielded it all his life; as if it had been forged specially for him and him alone.

He waited in anguish until the men came out of the temple with his goatskin and saddle roll. Then, as they stood jabbering together excitedly, his camel was spotted grazing in the distance. Two of the men ran towards it, and within moments it was in their charge. Mayne's heart sank. How would he escape now? Why had he not gone earlier?

He could not help the tide of bitterness that surged through him. In the past few days he had felt closer to God than ever before in his life, confident of His care and protection, assured of a better future in some strange, uncanny way even though he knew that he would never be truly happy again without his little Queen, and now this. Now his enemies knew where he was. They had found his hiding place, and entered the taboo temple without fear of Allah's reprisals. Were they non-believers, or simply impious?

Watching them as they rode away, Mayne did not try to guess. If there was a God it had been His will that Mayne should lose the woman he loved more than life itself, His will that his hiding place was found, His will that his only means of escape be taken.

The lush haven that surrounded him faded into dim shadowy greyness. He forgot that he should rejoice because they had ignored the oasis for a second time as they rode off. He forgot everything except the conviction that he would die in the desert before very long. Captain Mayne Amyan of the Dark Legion, going to his even darker demise.

Chapter Twenty-two

The moment seemed to stretch into an eternity with Mahmed looming over her, and her hand pressing the dagger to her own throat until her sinews screamed with pain and her palm was slippery with sweat.

The blurred light of the lamps was dancing, heaving up and down crazily until she felt nausea beginning deep in her stomach.

'What are you waiting for, Mahmed? Are you so eager to see me die?' she taunted him, but her voice was a feeble croak. 'Stay another minute and you will see it . . . but it will be the end of all your schemes if you do.'

Mahmed stood irresolute, hands hanging limply by his sides. Where was he now, the great battle hero who charged so readily into assaults and skirmishes, hacking down anyone who crossed his path? Slowly, he stepped back from her, obviously believing her threat and unwilling to push her further.

Not daring to lower her hand, Zahra watched him retreating. Not until he had gone from the tent did she breathe easily again, lowering the hand that held the dagger so rigidly she doubted she could relax her fingers. Pain racked her arm and paralysed fingers, and she forced herself to breathe deeply for some time, calming herself in the way that Freyha had taught her. Her tortured grip relaxed, allowing the knife to fall into her lap. She was drenched in sweat, her robe clinging to her as if newly washed, her back aching, throat taut and dry – yet she had triumphed over Mahmed, for the time being. He would be bound to try again. All she had done was win herself a little more time.

Reaching for the jug of water at her couchside, she drank from it in great gulping draughts, feeling its chill throughout her body. Then, flinging off her damp robe, she washed herself as best she could with the remaining water and drew on a fresh robe. Once, Freyha had seen that she had all she needed. How Zahra missed her ministrations, her kindly heart and solid wisdom. Poor, faithful Freyha.

The chains were chafing her ankles, dark bruises appearing where they had pressed against her skin, but nothing could be done about that. Everything had been taken from her save for the barest essentials, or she would have attempted to break off the manacles long before this. She could not run while they were hampering her, nor could she walk. It was an effort to stumble a few feet to the leathern bucket behind the curtain which now served as her toilet. At regular intervals, an unknown woman would come to empty and replace it. Heavily veiled, and refusing to speak, she was obviously one of Mahmed's people.

Another day of inactivity yawned endlessly before her. She did not know if she could bear it. Even Mahmed's whirlwind visits, shocking and disruptive as they were, helped to alleviate the dullness and frustration of being incarcerated day after day since her attempt to escape. If only she could get away...

One more day before marriage was forced upon her, but she would not give in without a fight. He would have to bind and gag her before she would submit. And the moment that she could escape, she would make it public knowledge that she had been forced into marrying him. Did he think that he could gag her for the rest of her life?

374

She was Zahra, Queen of the Desert like her famed ancestress Zenobia before her. She, and only she, would decide whom she made her husband.

'*Saiyid*, we have found his hiding place. Here is his goatskin and his water flask, and wrapped in this bed roll is his infidel uniform. We searched the temple and we could not find him, but the roots that he had been depending upon for water were still moist so he could not have been gone long. He might only have been out hunting for food. Mindful of your command that you wished to execute him yourself, *Saiyid*, we fled back to you with all speed, leaving two men to overcome the *kaffir* when he returns.'

Mahmed threw back his head, his eyes half closed in relief. Just when he had thought that all was lost, here was this sign, this marvellous sign, that the *kaffir* was close at hand. And then his servant's words sunk in properly.

'Temple? What temple is this?'

'The pagan temple, the one of idols and images, *Saiyid*. The place where the people of this land will not go for they say it is taboo and Allah will punish them for entering its door.'

Mahmed experienced a queasy sensation of excitement while at the same time a tight, rasping pain grew and expanded in his chest, as if a hard, constricting ball were forming there. The temple – the taboo place – why had he not thought of that? What a fool he had been! Of course that was where the Legionnaire would go, and probably where the bitch had hidden the jewels, too. After all, was that not where they had been found originally by her mother?

'Describe this temple,' he said, the pain in his chest growing by the minute.

'It is the ancient one, the one of ruins, *Saiyid*, with the graven images within of the female god who was once worshipped there many centuries ago. It is lying in

375

wasteland now, and long forgotten. No one goes there. I cannot say more, *Saiyid*.'

'A graven image! An idol!' Mahmed shuddered as if such a thing were anathema to him. And then quoting from the Qu'ran as if he were the most pious Muslim ever born, he cried, '"It is not for the idolators to inhabit God's place of worship, witnessing against themselves unbelief; those – whose works have failed them – in the Fire they shall dwell forever. Only he shall inhabit God's places of worship who believes in God and the Last Day, and performs the prayer, and pays the alms, and fears none but God alone!" This temple must be destroyed, along with the non-believer who dared to lay a hand upon my bride!'

'Ride with us, *Saiyid*, and we shall show you where we found the goatskin and the infidel uniform.'

'Make yourselves ready,' Mahmed ordered. 'We ride within the hour.'

'We have found your lover,' Mahmed sneered. He was standing before Zahra, wearing desert riding clothes and smacking his riding crop into the palm of his left hand. He looked every inch a man in total control of his own destiny – and of hers.

'I do not believe you!' Zahra retaliated. 'You are lying, as you always lie!'

'So, I am lying,' Mahmed said silkily. 'We have found him in the temple, the place that your people say is taboo.' Silently, he waited for her reaction, saw the colour ebb from her face and the pupils of her eyes dilate, and knew that he had struck home.

'He-he is not – you have not harmed him!' Zahra could barely speak. There was a drumming in her head, a splitting pain at the base of her neck.

'He is my prisoner and now I go to execute him. Remember my promise? I said that his head would be the central dish at your marriage feast, and I intend to keep

that promise. When I return, you will become my bride –
a few days later than planned, but my bride all the same.
Until I return, you will be more closely guarded than
before. There will be no chance of your escaping.'

He ushered forward a servant who knelt before
Zahra, but not because of her high rank. In his arms he
bore more chains of a heavier gauge which he proceeded
to add to her ankles, and then her wrists were chained
together so that she could only just raise them to her
mouth to eat.

'I will not be here when you return!' Zahra screamed
after Mahmed as he strode out, but he did not even
pause to look back at her. He knew that she would be
there, and she knew it, too. Hanging her head, she wept
bitterly. Mayne had not escaped after all, and now he
would be killed. Oh, she could not bear this pain!

Before Mahmed returned with her lover's head, she
would take the only method of escape left to her. She
would kill herself, so that she could be with her brave
warrior again, united in death.

When Abdul learned that Mahmed was leaving the
camp, he considered it a miracle sent by Allah. Now they
would not have to overpower him and his bodyguard as
well as the skeleton force he was leaving at the camp.
When he returned, the Amira's men would be in control,
waiting to take him prisoner.

Amaliya had watched Abdul blossoming from a shy
and reserved young man into a dashing and sagacious
desert warrior. He had spoken with Zahra's ministers,
telling them what he had learned and of the blood he had
seen in the tent where the Zudans had slept. He had not
rested until they agreed to investigate for themselves.
Three of them had crept into the Zudans' tent at dead of
night, and seen by torchlight the fresh bloodstains
beneath the new carpet, and then they were willing to do
anything that Abdul suggested, but they must step

377

carefully for Mahmed's men were trained killers. And then came the news that Mahmed was leaving.

The moment that he and his men rode out of sight, Abdul and his followers would strike. They planned to overpower those who cared for the white racing camels, and the guards both on and off duty. Having done this, they would free their mistress and prepare themselves for Mahmed's return.

The attack would be by night, and only the strongest and fittest would participate.

Amaliya hugged Abdul so fervently that he could barely breathe, not that he was complaining.

'Take care, my heart, take care! I shall be praying for you every moment.'

'I intend to return to you with all my vital parts intact.' Abdul grinned at her, revelling in her attention.

'Oh, Abdul, if only we had realised sooner we could have kissed a thousand times before this and I would have the memory now to sustain me through the darkness.'

'My beloved, I am not dead yet!' Abdul replied, holding her at arm's length, 'nor do I plan to be. Believe me, I shall return to you in one piece, and you shall be my bride as soon as it is possible. How could it be otherwise now that we love one another?'

'Do you love me, Abdul?' It was the first time that he had actually put it into words.

'Of course. Would I not be a fool to do anything else? I have the fairest sweetheart in the Land of Mirages, and soon she will be sharing my couch.'

Blushing hotly, Amaliya pulled him close again and they kissed as if the very stars were passing judgement on their prowess. Then, hearts beating as one, they renewed their vows of love and fidelity to one another. In those heady moments the darkness and dangers of the night to come seemed very far away.

*

Mahmed had taken Zahra's small dagger away, which was only to be expected, but she was sure that she could find some other suitable sharp instrument if she searched hard enough. Somewhere at the bottom of one of the chests of clothes and accessories, there must be a pin or a brooch with a pointed fastener.

It was not easy, stumbling from chest to chest with her burden of chains at ankles and wrists, but she persevered. Once the guards entered her tent to see what she was doing, but she stared them down. All she had been doing, as far as they could see, was looking for some article of clothing.

Somewhere there was a robe with a brooch pinned to it, one that had belonged to her mother, of heavy gold with a long, sharp pin. Zahra shivered as she visualised driving the pin deep into her heart, but she would do it. Anything rather than be forced to see her beloved Mayne's head dangled before her eyes.

But she could not find it. Coming to the end of her search, she sank to her knees with the sobs catching in her throat. Then she remembered. The hinge had snapped, and it had gone to a goldsmith's in the city to be mended. That had been months ago; perhaps Mahmed had intercepted the messenger who was returning it? Anything might have happened to it. They might all be dead of thirst in Abeesha.

As for the rest of her jewellery, Mahmed had misappropriated all of it to finance his nefarious schemes.

More tears came, rending her. Her people were dying, she was a prisoner, and she had brought all of it upon them. She was the woman whose name would go down in history as the one who had caused the destruction of the Land of Mirages.

'Allah, help me! I meant none of it, none of it,' she wept. And then she slept, exhausted by the weight of the chains and longing for her dreams to reunite her with the man she loved.

The scrunch of leather on sand woke her in alarm. Was Mahmed back already? Dear God, let it not be so! Trying to peer through the darkness, she distinguished shadowy figures surrounding her, three or four of them, and knew she was about to be murdered on her couch. Mahmed had tricked her; he had ordered that she be killed while he was away. Her heart thudding, she waited for the knife to strike, believing it to be Allah's will, the release that she was yearning for.

'Highness, is that you? It is Abdul, and here is Amaliya to wait upon you. Do not fear us. We come to rescue you.'

Someone lit the lamps and the tent was flooded with orange-gold light. Zahra saw the little deputation before her, and as they sank to their knees in reverence she felt the tears welling up inside her. Then they were rolling down her cheeks and she was sobbing out loud. Amaliya hastened to hold her close, her own tears flowing in sympathy. After a while, Zahra smiled tremulously at her rescuers then, while two men hacked away at her chains with chisels and hammers, listened to Abdul's account of the surprise attack that had overwhelmed Mahmed's men-at-arms. Those who were not dead already were lying tightly bound and gagged, to be dealt with later.

'Highness,' Abdul pleaded, 'will you forgive us for thinking that you wished this incarceration? We were led to believe that you were praying in readiness for your marriage, and that you wished to be alone. Because we knew that you were not fully reconciled to becoming a bride, we truly thought it was what you wanted.'

'If I were left alone to pray for a thousand years, I would not be ready to marry Mahmed ibn Beydoun,' Zahra said wryly.

'Forgive us, Highness, we never guessed. We have been fools and idiots. Can you forgive us?'

'You are all forgiven, my dear, dear, ones. And now I must make ready for the journey.'

'What journey, Highness?' Abdul and the others looked at her in astonishment. There she sat, thin and pale, her wrists and ankles chafed raw and bruised by chains, face flushed from her tears, and yet she was talking of travelling!

'I must go to the temple of the Mother Goddess. Mahmed is heading there. If we ride his racing camels, we may be able to catch up with him. We cannot wait for him to return.'

'But, Highness, why should we not wait?'

'You will see when we get there, Abdul.'

The very first well to run dry had been the one in Abeesha, in the court of the house where Mishaal's foster mother, Rhikia, had lived over thirty years before. There, on that fateful night more than three decades ago, the boy Yusuf had gone to the well to fetch water for his sick mother. Staring into its depths, he had seen nothing save brown sludge and sticky stones. The water had gone from the revered well where, it was said, the Prophet Mohammed had drunk many centuries before, and had blessed it for its refreshing waters. As the old legend had played itself out, no one was surprised that such a well had been the first to dry.

'No unbeliever's hand shall touch the Jewels of Destiny, or all the wells and rivers of the Land of Mirages shall run dry unto the Day of Judgement.'

So ran the old legend, and when those very Jewels had been in danger of being discovered and stolen by the American *kaffir*, Lord Drew Huntington, the wells and rivers had begun to evaporate, some almost overnight, so that the people were left gaping at the speed of the destruction.

Not until the final moment, when Huntington and their beloved Amir Husain had fought over the Jewels, had the true meaning of the legend revealed itself. It was not enough that one of the faithful be first to touch the gems that had lain hidden in the temple vault for centuries; no, it must be a woman, and not just any woman.

'One day, Mishaal shall be the torch that shall light the way for the people of the Land of Mirages.' Those had been the dying words of Mishaal's mother, and how often Rhikia had pondered their true meaning, until it had come to pass, the fulfilment of the old legend. The American Lord had been revealed in his true light, and Husain had chosen his beloved Mishaal before the Jewels of Destiny, for the true treasure of life lies not in material objects. And Mishaal's hand had been the first to lift the gems from their ancient cache....

Suddenly, swiftly, as if removed from an enchanter's spell, the wells and rivers had begun to flow and gush again, and first to refill had been the well outside the house where Rhikia lived.

The boy Yusuf was past forty now, but he had never forgotten that sight, the waters bubbling back as if from God's storehouse deep in the earth. They had returned during the night, making such a swishing, seething sound that everyone who lived there had been roused from sleep. They had hastened down the stairs and out into the courtyard, to look and listen, their faces wrapt in smiles when they realised what was causing the sound.

Those who had deserted the waterless place had soon returned and life had continued as before, but Yusuf would never forget his small part in the old legend.

He had a wife now and four sons, but life had been miserable and without hope since early that year when the well had failed them again. This time, as before, his family had not left their little house even though it had meant a long journey each day to fetch the water they needed, and all the family had been enlisted to help with a task that was beyond the efforts of Yusuf's wife alone.

382

Today, he stood staring into the well, remembering. In his heart, he knew that it was finished for them. It would never happen again, the miraculous reprieve as the ancient legend was re-enacted. Allah had forsaken them, yet none of them knew why. Some had babbled about the Amira, saying that she had offended Allah and He was punishing them all because of it. What of that infirmary that she had built to care for the Beduin children? Had it not been a foolish plan, an attempt to divide families by stealing away their sons and putting them beneath a roof that would sap their lifeblood and weaken them? But others had shouted down the babblers, calling them fools and ignoramuses.

Did they not know the true reason why the Amira's hospital had been forsaken? Although they loved their mistress and would follow her to the ends of Islam, nothing would induce them to leave their children in a place that had been built on a *nasrani* burial ground. It was true that the burials had been centuries before, when Christian slaves had died *en masse* of a fever, but nonetheless the taint remained, and none of them wished to be infected by it. Not the taint of fever but something far more insidious and dangerous: the taint of an infidel religion.

'*Daheelek!*' Yusuf groaned beneath his breath. What had any of them done to deserve this? His livelihood had been ruined. He was a sherbet maker, and how could he make sherbet without water or the fruit that was needed for it? The oranges had failed; so had the lemons and the other succulent fruits that gave their juices and flavour to the different varieties of one of Islam's favourite drinks. He had been living off his savings for seven months now. Soon they would be finished, and so would he.

Yusuf ibn Ali gazed down into the dank, parched well. It was like gazing deep into his own throat which grew ever tighter and more painful for lack of fluid.

His wife's gums were bleeding, her teeth loosening; his two youngest sons were plagued by aching joints. He had lost so much flesh that his robes hung on him like sacks and he could bind his cord belt round his waist four times over. Resting his elbow against the well's edge, he sank his head into his palm and tried to block out the anguish of the last few months: the wailing of his small sons, and the tears and rebukes of his wife who found it less painful to blame him for their plight than face the fact that they were Godforsaken.

It was bliss for her to be free again, to be riding on the back of a racing camel not caring that she was speeding along at a breakneck pace, and that when the beast put his foot into a slope or dip, she lunged forward as if she would be cast over its neck. She was going to save her beloved, her darling warrior, and Allah was with her, she could sense it.

How radiant was the desert dawn after the stifling tent where she had been imprisoned. The sky was hazy and gloriously bright, a delicate harebell blue. The hoarfrost was melting, its thick, encrusting silvered chill forgotten. Soon, autumn would be fully unwrapped and there must be rain. Surely there must be rain?

'*Inshallah*,' she whispered beneath her breath. 'Please let there be rain!'

Behind her rode her people, led by Abdul and the other young men who had bested Mahmed's supposedly seasoned warriors. Lazy from weeks of over-indulgence and too little exercise, and taken by surprise, the latter had been overcome rapidly. Zahra kept well ahead of her troops, determined that she herself would catch up with Mahmed and save her lover from death if it was her last act on earth. Yes, she would willingly die for him. Was that not the deepest meaning of love?

She did not want to stop to rest or eat, but her body craved sleep. After nearly plummeting from the saddle

384

twice, she halted the *dhalul*. Hobbling him, she curled up into a ball beneath her goatskin and shut her eyes, meaning to sleep for a few moments only.

When she woke, the heat of noon had dissipated and she cried out in alarm. There was Abdul, sitting gazing into space, and she berated him for not having woken her earlier. He looked shamefaced but said that he had no reason to disturb her. White-faced, she mounted her camel again and ordered the men to make haste.

They received no challenge: no beast or interloper, no stray enemy or alien crossed their path. Onward they rode, not knowing why their mistress wished to make such haste but following her loyally for she was their Queen.

The first day and night passed uneventfully and still they rode, following blindly. The scenery became more barren, the rocks more blanched, the bushes stunted from the tyranny of decades of battering sun. It was so breath-snatchingly hot that no flies taunted them or their *dhaluls*, and the little plants that had brightened their way so far vanished, baked into dust and ashes.

Zahra knew the route as if it was engraven in her mind, and it seemed that Mahmed did, too, for there were his tracks ahead of them. Then she remembered. He had searched through her father's belongings, the carved chest of papers and scrolls, finding the maps that clearly showed the desert highway that would lead to the taboo place.

They stopped to rest only twice. On the afternoon of the second day, stiff, aching and bruised, with her hands raw from grasping the reins of the *dhalul* and her eyes bleary from too much sun, Zahra saw it in the distance, the ancient temple. It shimmered like mother-of-pearl against the harsher ochres, rusts and tans of the wilderness. Instantly Zahra was fully alert, her eyes scouring the harsh terrain for a sight of Mahmed and his men, her body braced for action.

'Allah, let him be safe!' she prayed beneath her breath

as her camel galloped towards the temple. 'Let him be safe and I will give You anything You ask, *anything!*'

The ancient stones seemed to glow in the dusk as Zahra approached them, but she did not have the time or patience to wonder why. If Mayne was still in the temple vault, she must reach him and warn him. And then she would bargain with Mahmed. If he let Mayne go free, she would marry him willingly and tell him all that he wanted to know, including the hiding place of the Jewels of Destiny.

She was mentally rehearsing what she would say when she heard the snort of a camel close by. Was it Mayne's? Looking round, she saw a hobbled *dhalul*, and then another, and on its back was a black-robed rider. Three more riders idled beside him, their faces averted. She could not understand how they had not seen her. It must be the angle of the building that screened her approach from their view.

Dear God, so Mahmed was here already!

Legs quivering, she dismounted from her camel and ran through the temple entrance. It was dark inside after the leeching desert sun, but she would have known the way blindfold. Her eyes would soon accustom themselves to the gloom.

Without pausing to think, she raced through the temple towards the stairway that led down into the vault, hurling herself down the steps without considering what she might find there.

Abdul could not understand it. His *dhalul* had come to an abrupt halt and would go no further. He had coaxed and cajoled the beast, dug up some tinder dry camel's thorn for it to eat, but been refused. What was more, seeing the reluctance of their leader, the other camels were behaving similarly, standing with their heads lowered as if they were sick.

386

Time was passing and their Amira was out of sight. They would have to follow her on foot. Allah protect and preserve her from danger!

Gathering their weapons together, and tucking water flasks into their belts, Abdul and his men headed after their mistress, leaving the stubborn camels where they stood, legs hobbled just in case they decided to gallop away. If the beasts were sick, then they would have to return to camp on foot, and that would take them many days. Abdul had never seen the beasts behave so strangely. They could be difficult and temperamental, as everyone knew, but this paralysis was unfathomable.

The sun was dipping, its dying rays smearing the sky with rich rose gold, a wide, breath-snatching vision that made Abdul think of Amaliya, and he wished this journey over so that he could take her in his arms once again and teach her to kiss without letting her know that he was learning too.

The rose-gold light seemed to be affecting him strangely. His mind a sudden blank, he could not imagine why he was half-running, half-stumbling in this tinder-box heat. Bemused, he came to a sudden halt, his tortured breath twisting in his lungs so that the pain drove everything else from his mind. Behind him, his men looked at one another in puzzlement. What were they doing out here in this wilderness? Had they been bewitched by the *jinn*?

Zahra flew down the crumbling stairs, anticipating the mud-dark blackness of the vault that she remembered but seeing instead the flare of a torch and another strange luminous light, as if the vault had been prepared for just this moment.

Gasping out loud, she saw her darling Mayne, the Sword of God in his hand. Gaunt-faced, and far thinner than she remembered him, he was standing awkwardly as if his wounded leg had not healed and he could not

387

bear to put his weight upon it. Then she saw Mahmed, his features twisted in a grimace as he faced her beloved, a curving scimitar in one hand, a dagger in the other.

'No! Let him go safely and I will marry you willingly!' Zahra screamed, but in his homicidal fury Mahmed heard nothing. There before him was the *kaffir* who had enjoyed his bride's favours. He had taken her virginity, turned her against her rightful husband and endangered all Mahmed's plans to steal the riches of the Land of Mirages.

Mahmed gripped his weapons so fiercely that his knuckles stood out whitely against his tanned hands, and then, letting out a venomous roar, he lunged at the man who had caused him so much grief and anguish.

Chapter Twenty-three

'*No!*' Zahra screamed again, but Mahmed behaved as if he had heard nothing. There, before her, the two men began to fight while she could do nothing save watch, the breath twisting in her lungs.

It was as if history were repeating itself, as if her father and the American of thirty years before were duelling there again.

It was destiny, the will of Allah and of the ancient temple still haunted by the power of the great Mother Goddess worshipped there centuries ago, yet surely it could not be her destiny to see the man she loved hacked to death before her eyes? Yet nothing could alter the fact that her darling Mayne was a non-believer, that he should not be here in this place. She should never have brought him. It was her doing that the peace of the sanctuary had been disturbed and Allah offended; she had brought a non-believer here, into the very vault, the very heart of the temple where worshippers had once stacked their treasures as offerings to Inanna, a rich, glittering storehouse, a pulsing heart of fiery rubies and flashing emeralds, gleaming pearls and purest, richest gold. . . .

'*Thy will be done.*'

It was her mother's voice, a susurrescence of a

whisper, yet louder than if Mishaal stood close beside her.

'*Thy will be done. So has it been and so shall it always be, my daughter. Be strong in thy faith. Be strong!*'

Now Zahra knew the truth. She had betrayed her people, and her mother's shade had brought all this into being, this terrible, hideous duel, to impress on her the error of her ways. Mishaal had been no ordinary woman – even after death flowers rioted on her grave in the middle of appalling drought – if she wanted to show her foolish daughter how great was her error, then she could do it in any way she chose.

Her punishment was to see the man she loved, the unbeliever who had tainted this sacred place, killed by her future husband.

Zahra began to pray aloud as the first ear-smacking crash of metal on metal reverberated around the vault.

Was she imagining it, or was the vault growing brighter by the second? Narrowing her eyes against the glare, she tried to comprehend what was happening but could not. The harder she tried to see beyond the light, the more dazzling it became until she had to crush her eyes against it.

Metal clashed on metal again and Zahra forced open her eyes to see Mayne staggering, as if he had been struck. She screamed, and covered her face with her hands. How could she watch this insane slaughter, this hideous, wretched killing that she had caused? Dear God, she would never forgive herself, never! This was the punishment for her wilfulness, for wanting to go her own way when she knew that the needs of her people should be paramount. Instead, like a greedy, selfish child, she had put her own desires first, her need for love and passion and reassurance, and now the man who had given her these was to die, a sacrifice to placate the Mother Goddess of old, the One whose ways had lived on in Mishaal's heart and in her own.

While Mayne battled to regain his balance, Mahmed's dagger cut deep into his left arm, slicing swiftly through the flesh and fetching a gout of blood. Dimly, Mayne heard Zahra's screams and was wretched that he could do nothing to comfort her, even in the last few moments of his life. He ached to tell her how much he adored her, how much she had come to mean to him. He would have loved and worshipped her unto death and beyond if fate had only allowed it. There was so much that he wanted to tell her.

He had not been able to trick a woman who trusted and adored him. He would never have cheated her of her patrimony, her ancient inheritance. She was not arrogant and cold-hearted as he had been led to believe but a young woman who had needed him more than any other, a tender-hearted girl lacking in confidence, certain she would fail in the enormous task she had been given. When they had fallen in love, it had changed them both. He had learned to respect the ways of her people as he learned to love her, and in doing so he had accepted her religion, the faith of Islam, the faith of his childhood.

She had led him back to the fold, her tenderness and vulnerability bringing out qualities in him which he had never known he possessed.

While he was forced to languish in the temple vault, there had been time then to reflect, to perceive and comprehend the truth. But it was too late now to tell her. Far too late....

The blood was gushing from his arm, fashioning a wine-dark pool on his robe and down to his feet, but he fought on, wielding the Sword of God as if it were light as rose petals while Mahmed breathed stertorously from the effort of hefting his huge Turkish scimitar. It was strange that he, the merciless warrior of so many brutal battles, should tire like a raw beginner while Mayne, who had languished wounded in this sunless place, should feel a surge of renewed energy. It was as if he knew in advance every move that his vicious opponent would make.

How could any true believer betray his people as Mahmed had done, murdering those who endangered his schemes in his lust to make himself rich? Guests in the black tents were sacred; no true believer would harm a square of their flesh, yet Mahmed had ordered the slaughter of all the Zudans, and would have gone on to murder anyone else who stood in his way, even the daughter of Husain and Mishaal.

It was as if the temple were judging them, finding Mayne the true believer and Mahmed the hypocrite, the betrayer. Zahra, who had thought her desires the sign of wilfulness and cupidity, was slowly realising that she had been walking the very path ordained by Allah. And hand in hand with her on that path was Mayne.

The ancient temple, the source of all destiny and enchantment, would act as judge as it had with Zahra's own father and the perfidious American thirty years before. Nothing could withstand the hand of Fate.

Zahra understood it all as the two men fought, sword to sword, dagger to dagger, weaving first one way and then the other. First Mahmed was pushed to the wall, and then Mayne, while the vault grew ever brighter.

The battle seemed to wage for hours, days, on and on, the forces of good and evil locked in combat as they have been from the beginning of time, but the Sword of God was glowing now, flashing its platinum fire to left and right, deftly parrying Mahmed's thrusts. Mayne could feel new life stirring within him, divine reinforcement, and he, too, understood that this was the moment of destiny. Everything that had happened in his life so far had been leading him to this final battle: all the anguish and terror, the doubts and uncertainties – and the love, yes, most of all, the love.

Zahra could bear it no longer. The surest belief was not enough to support her as her beloved staggered and almost lost his footing, the dull clatter of ossified bones telling her that he was standing where the American had been killed all those years before.

What if she were wrong? What if, after all, she was forced to watch Mayne hacked to pieces and his head sliced from his body by the maniacal Mahmed? Trickles of ice danced along her spine and encircled her flesh; she was clasped in ice, paralysed, enfeebled by it, seeing only long, desperately lonely years ahead of her without the man she adored. She would be as she had been when he had found her, but this time she would not recover; she would languish and fade. One who has been so blissfully two cannot be one again.

The smack of steel on steel was such an assault on her ears that she wanted to cover them, but she could not take her hands from her eyes. She stood transfixed, her breath coming in panic-stricken gulps, her heart fiery with pain. He would die. She would be left with nothing again, and they had waited so long, so very long, to be together, century upon century.

Yet had that not been the stuff of dreams, beautiful and reassuring, but nonetheless dreams. It was only to be expected that she should think of her ancestress Zenobia even in her sleep when the Queen of the Desert's jewels had played such a vital part in the well-being of the Land of Mirages, though it was strange that she had never thought of Odenathus before in her dreams.

Zahra forced herself to raise her head and open her eyes. The vault was now bright as day; she could see everything clearly, every detail of the centuries that had passed. The pile of rocks with the half-protruding skeleton of Drew Huntington beneath, his skull a rictus of disappointed agony and one arm outstretched, skeletal fingers clutching after the jewels that had eluded him. Nearby the bones of the men who had been killed by her father in that last desperate battle lay scattered where they had fallen, slaughtered by the Sword of God.

There was dust, too, the sandy, gritty dust of ages, and on one wall a mural. At first she could not make the figures out and stared fiercely at them to try and take her mind off the desperate duel being waged only feet away from her.

With a gasp of astonishment, Zahra realised that the man of the mural, tall and dark-haired and clasping a ghostly gleaming sword, was none other than Husain, her father. And beside him, long ebony hair streaming free around her shoulders and wearing her multi-hued peacock robe, was Mishaal, her mother. There they stood, captured by some unknown artist's hand for all time. At their feet lay the remains of the ones who had tried to trick and defeat them, the American and his mercenaries.

Mesmerised, Zahra's eyes swept on, seeing the glittering mound of Zenobia's treasure hoard painted in crimsons and scarlets, emerald, rich yellow, cerulean blue and gentle amethyst. And then there was another mural, of Mishaal kneeling, head bent, as Husain placed on her head the Crown of Zenobia, studded with flashing rubies.

Her heart was banging now, for if these murals of the past had been completed, could there not be others of the future? Sure enough, as her eyes moved on, she saw the outline of an Arab, his face contorted with venom. His robe was swirling around him as he plunged his sword into the huddled body of a helpless figure wearing the uniform of the Legionnaires. And then she wanted to scream out loud, over and over, for she had seen how it would end and all hope sped from her.

Chapter Twenty-four

Mayne had thought that he was growing stronger, yet now he felt his head spinning, his body weakening beneath Mahmed's impassioned onslaught. He knew that he could not endure much longer. His leg was a searing agony and its muscles trembled crazily as if his coordination had gone. He could not catch his breath. The act of standing upright had become an almost intolerable strain.

Mahmed's shriek of victory echoed round the vault, shaking Zahra to the soul. Leaping like a tiger upon its prey, he crouched over the fallen Mayne, angling his sword for the killing thrust. From her vantage point, Zahra saw his arm move backwards and forwards, two, three, four times as he drove the blade into his opponent's body. His expression one of exultation at the glorious sensation of being splashed by an enemy's life blood.

Zahra, numbed with horror, saw him stand back, a mirthless grimace distorting his features, a glow of insane triumph irradiating his face. She saw him sweep a hand gloatingly through the blotches of blood that dappled his robe, and could not hold back her screams no longer. Ringing, piercing, they seemed to fill the vault. This time Mahmed heard her. When he looked in her direction, she saw his eyes filled with blood lust.

She was ready to kill him herself, taking the small curved dagger from her belt preparatory to lunging at him when he stepped at an angle to steer around the bloody corpse and trod on one of the stones that had fallen thirty years before to protect the Jewels of Destiny. His foot slipped sideways, his ankle gave way and he let out a shout of surprise. It was in that moment, as he flung up his arms to try and balance himself, that the miracle happened.

Zahra was already halfway towards him, dagger out-thrust, when she saw the Sword of God rising up out of a dark corner as if borne by a spirit hand. Her heart jolted and her breath caught in her throat in a strangled gasp. Then she realised that no spirit hand supported the sword as she had first thought. It was being held by Mayne! He was not dead! Somehow, Mahmed's furious, vituperative sword thrusts had failed to strike deep enough to kill him, or perhaps they had not been thrust into him at all but into some figment of Mahmed's crazed imagination?

He had wanted to hack Mayne to death, had wanted him in pieces at his feet. In his mind's eye so it had been, but imagination had not been enough to fashion the fatal blow. Instead, it had misled the Amir so that he had believed his sword was plunging into the *kaffir's* body when in fact it was plunging into the rag-covered skeleton of the American who died there three decades before.

As Mahmed yelped in pain, his balance lost, Mayne thrust the Sword of God directly upwards, holding it like a medieval pike so that its sharp, steely blade was in readiness for the *coup de grâce*. Mahmed fell, his yelp of surprise transmuted into an unearthly shriek as he flopped like a stringless puppet, his body speared by the glowing blade.

Zahra stood momentarily transfixed, barely believing the miracle she was seeing. Mayne come back from the dead, to deliver her from evil, the Sword of God dispatching Mahmed.... Sweat was pouring from her and her head was pounding but she flung herself across the few yards separating her from her love. She almost knocked him over again just as he had got to his feet. They clung to one another, laughing, crying, and babbling joyous greetings.

'My little Queen, oh, my darling little Queen, it's finished, finished!' Mayne cried over and over, while Zahra could barely find her tongue. It seemed to have turned to paper in her mouth, but later she would make up for her temporary silence.

'If it hadn't been for that rock,' he continued, and their eyes turned automatically to the spot where the stone had thrown Mahmed off balance, there was nothing there: no rock, no stone, not so much as a minute pebble. Nor had his fall rolled the stone elsewhere, for there was nothing but smooth stone floor all around them.

They clung together more tightly as the spirit of the ancient place overwhelmed them.

'I saw him kill you,' Zahra whispered. 'I saw him kill you, and your blood splashing on to his robe! I saw it, yet there is only that small wound in your arm. I thought he had pierced to your heart!'

'And you were going to kill him to avenge me.' His voice softened. 'My darling, I don't know how it happened. When he was plunging that sword with such fury he obviously believed he was murdering me, but see the skeleton lying there, that poor dead thing? That took the brunt of his attack. He thought that it was me. I know I've lost weight while I've been here, but not that much!' His flecked topaz eyes glittered.

'But I saw the blood spurting. I saw blood!' Zahra cried, clinging to Mayne. 'Are you sure you have no other deeper wounds?'

'None at all.' Tenderly, he bent his head to kiss her, their lips meeting like a benediction. How they had yearned for this reunion; nothing else was of any importance, only their being together. 'Remember what I said to you? "The circle of Solomon, son of David, is between the world and us, and if anything should break it, then Allah shall break the world, but not us, never us, my beloved." Did you not believe that I spoke true?'

Mahmed had ordered his men to wait outside, for he wished to kill the *kaffir* with his own hands, but when their master did not emerge from the temple after a suitable time, they grew restive and began arguing over whether or not they should go in search of him. His venomous temper was to be feared, but if they left him injured and untended he would punish them. Doubt and fear kept them squabbling at the temple door for some time. Eventually, when their master had still not emerged, they stepped warily inside, glancing about them with dilated eyes and gaping mouths. An infidel place, a pagan mosque! Who knew what devils might not leap out from the shadows?

A bird suddenly taking flight into the eaves shocked them all, and one cried out: 'Allah be merciful!' It was this cry that alerted Zahra and Mayne as they mounted the steps from the crypt.

'Back,' hissed Mayne, thrusting her behind him. 'Stay here until I come for you!'

'I will fight beside you,' she retorted. 'You cannot stop me! If we die, then we die together. I have vowed it.'

Angrily, he picked her up and carried her bodily back into the crypt. 'You are too precious to risk. Think of your people: with you dead, where would they be? Stay here, and do not make a sound.'

She watched him mount the steps stealthily, the Sword of God at the ready. She set her jaw in annoyance. How long had she been a prisoner, shackled and bound and unable to do as she pleased? It had been unendurable, and she would not suffer it again.

Looking about her in the half-darkness, she searched for a weapon. She shuddered as her eyes alighted on the corpse of Mahmed ibn Beydoun, but he was dead and could threaten her no more. There beside his hand lay his sword, the one of Turkish design that had been responsible for so many deaths. A few more would not hurt it. Snatching up the weapon, she crept up the steps and into the blazing light of the temple precinct.

Mayne was in fierce hand to hand combat with six or seven of Mahmed's men. They were attacking him savagely, but he was keeping them at a safe distance, spinning lightly on his feet, sweeping his blade through the air with such agility that they could only dart backwards out of its way. No one would have guessed that he had been on his feet fighting for almost an hour before this. His full vigour had returned to him and he was exultant at being able to defend himself properly again.

Zahra watched for a few moments, thinking that she might not be needed after all, and then she saw the last man sliding along the temple wall, keeping to the shadows where he could. He balanced a dagger in his hand in readiness, aiming it at Mayne's back.

Swiftly, on soundless feet, Zahra flew at him. His eyes were fixed upon Mayne and he did not see her. She had never succeeded in killing a man before, but to save her darling's life she would, at any cost to herself. The blade she wielded was heavy and unfamiliar in her grasp, but she clutched it tightly in both of her small hands and brought it down with all her might against his shoulder. Wincing, she felt the impact along her arms as the steel cut through flesh and sinew and a little way into the bone. Groaning, the man collapsed at her feet. Heart pounding, she stared down at him until she was quite sure that he would never get up again. Blood was pouring from his wound and his face was a sickly grey colour. Allah, was it so easy to kill?

Three men were still alive when she looked up, alerted by the clash of steel as Mayne disarmed one of the villains, sending his sword spinning away across the temple floor. The man fell back, begging for mercy on his knees, but as Mayne approached him Zahra saw the secret glint of metal in the man's hand and knew that his capitulation was only a pose. Not stopping to think, she flung herself at him and the great curving blade descended again, slicing into his neck. Her aim was surer this time; she was growing accustomed to the sword.

Mayne glanced at her with a mixture of fury and gratitude as the man keeled over on his side, the concealed dagger slipping from his grasp.

'Mayne, look out!' Zahra screamed, as the two remaining villains leapt on him, knocking him face down on the ground.

She flew at them, stabbing, slicing, cutting. Nothing in their culture had prepared them for the sight of a woman fighting like a man with a man's sword in her hands, and their reactions were slow. They half believed she was some pagan devil, a Satanic figment of their imaginations. How could she be real? However, her blade was real enough and the blood that oozed as a result was far from imagined. Within seconds one man had lost three fingers, and the other was wounded in his side. By that time, Mayne was on his feet again. He dispatched them quickly while Zahra looked away, sickened by the sight of so much blood.

Later, when Mayne had cleared away the bodies, piling them outside for the carrion, they rested in one another's arms. They had eaten the figs that Zahra had brought with her in a pouch at her belt, and emptied a flask of water, welcoming the refreshing sweetness. After such a battle it tasted like nectar.

Outside, Abdul and his men were resting, too, waiting for their mistress to emerge from the temple. Their *dhaluls* seemed fully recovered from the mysterious

400

ailment that had kept them stubbornly rooted to the spot so that the final glorious victory would be Zahra's and Mayne's alone.

Zahra told her lover all that had happened while they were apart. Giving thanks to God for her safe delivery, he kissed her wrists and ankles where the bruises from the manacles were livid in her flesh. Then he told her how he had spent his time in the vault, sometimes strong and full of health, and others so weak he could scarcely move.

'I was going to disguise myself and return to the camp to watch over you,' he confessed, 'but every time I prepared for that, I felt the strength flowing from me.'

'It was not meant that you should come. You had to stay here and fight him, like my father fought the American all those years ago. When the Sword of God decides, nothing can be done to alter it. This was the place where the battle had to be, beneath Her gaze.'

Zahra looked up at the effigy of the Mother Goddess, at the sweetly tolerant face, the understanding eyes, and with a sudden pang she felt some of the loneliness that the Goddess had endured, shut away in this taboo place for so many centuries, forgotten and rejected by Her people.

'Mayne, my mother was crowned here, in this very place. My father placed Zenobia's ruby coronal on her head himself. He said that the temple was filled with brilliant sunlight then, so bright that it almost dazzled him. And as he lowered the crown on to my mother's hair, he swore that the effigy of the Mother Goddess was smiling. I never believed him, of course. Effigies do not smile, or so I thought. Now, I am willing to believe anything.'

She leant back against him, revelling in the closeness of his body to hers, the beloved face that was far too haggard after his strange illness. 'Mayne, in that old bundle of rags that you guarded with your life, you will find one or two rather unexpected things,' she told him softly.

'This bundle?' He looked surprised. It was the one that had served as a pillow when he slept. Padded with straw and crumpled material, it had been reasonably comfortable.

'Yes, that is the one. Would you pass it to me, please?'

Barely able to keep the smile from her mouth, Zahra tore open the loose stitching that had kept the bundle from spilling open, pulling out some straw and rumpled cloth. After it, in an ivory stream, flowed the opals that all the women of her father's line wore on their marriage day; the earrings, rings, bangles, and a wide, beautiful collar of deep orange-red gold.

'And that's not all,' she grinned, delving deeper. Next came what remained of the Jewels of Destiny: the ropes of emeralds from the mines of Queen Cleopatra; the sapphires and black pearls; the rubies that bejewelled the solid gold, three-tiered coronal that had graced Zenobia's head and that of Mishaal. Last was a slender circlet of gold at the centre of which was one blazing star-shaped diamond, its rays picked out in smaller stones so that it flashed blindingly as Zahra raised it in her hand. 'I thought this was Zenobia's also, we all did, but now I know better. It belonged to Odenathus. See that star? The Palmyrans worshipped Venus, the dawn star, and this crown is their representation of it. Kneel, my beloved warrior.'

Zahra could not keep the broad smile of happiness from her face as she placed the slender gold coronal on Mayne's head, ensuring that it was safely in place before she tilted his head upward with her forefinger and looked deep into his eyes.

'In this temple I crown you as my husband and Amir, my guardian warrior and my dearest love. If the Gods

402

are kind, may we never be parted again, and may we live all the days of our life in joy and contentment together.'

'Amen,' Mayne said beneath his breath, and it was then that he caught the eyes of the Mother Goddess towering above them in her ageless grace. It might have been a trick of the light, but he could have sworn that she was smiling broadly.

Strange magic had been at work for them. Even as they kissed in the temple, where their lives had been decided for them a second time, the wells were beginning to gush water, the rains were starting, and the oasis by the temple, that had served its purpose, was vanishing into the dust.

Yusuf was weeping in his mournful vigil as he felt the first fat droplets of rain bouncing from his head and shoulders. Glancing up into the skies, he saw the black and burdened clouds ready to drench his land. Below he heard the hiss and gurgle of the well water as it surged back.

Now the legend would begin anew: of Zahra, Queen of the Desert, and the husband whom Allah had chosen especially to rule beside her, the one whom they would call *Il 'Atiyi*, the Gift, for he had been given to their Queen by Allah Himself. *Il 'Atiyi* had been sent to help destroy them, but by a miracle had been converted back to the religion of his childhood.

The French would reconsider their invasion now that they had lost the support of Mahmed, and believed that their hero, Captain Mayne Amyan, was dead – as indeed he was, the Mayne Amyan of old who had dealt in falsehood and deception.

From that day forward, Zahra and her beloved would rule in wisdom and concord, as once they had ruled in ancient days. They would build again, this time on solid ground, the immovable, unchanging fabric of their love.

*

They shall not hunger nor thirst; neither shall the heat nor sun smite them: for He that hath mercy on them shall lead them, even by the springs of water shall He guide them.

Isaiah, 49: 10